Praise for

Lisa Gardner and Her Novels

"Lisa Gardner's work has the chills and thrills to excite and the heart to draw you in."

—Sandra Brown

"No one owns this corner of the genre the way Lisa Gardner does."

—Lee Child

"Lisa Gardner is one of the best thriller writers working today."

—Steve Berry

"Lisa Gardner is one of my favorite authors. Her fast-paced and exciting novels twist when you expect a turn and turn when you expect a twist. I cannot recommend her more."

—Karin Slaughter

One Step Too Far

"An authentic Wyoming setting, a tantalizing mystery, and a Labrador named Daisy. What's not to like?"

—C. J. Box, #1 *New York Times* bestselling author of *Dark Sky*

"Master storyteller and avid hiker Lisa Gardner has written the book she was meant to write, an immersive, propulsive, utterly chilling, and yet deeply moving wilderness thriller in which her intimate knowledge of and love for the rugged Wyoming backcountry shine through on every terrifying page. Without a doubt, the best book I've read all year."

—Karen Dionne, author of *The Marsh King's Daughter*

"Visceral, unpredictable, and terrifying. You'll never hike into the woods again without thinking of Lisa Gardner's *One Step Too Far*."

—Robert Dugoni, #1 Amazon bestselling author of the Tracy Crosswhite series

"Propulsive, adrenaline-fueled, terrifyingly real."

—Clare Mackintosh, bestselling author of *Hostage*

"[An] outstanding crime novel . . . Gardner pulls no punches in this so-cially conscious standalone."

—*Publishers Weekly* (starred review)

When You See Me

"Lisa Gardner is a master of the psychological thriller that dives deep into the minds of characters that experience trauma and come out stronger from the experience."

—Associated Press

"A stunner of a tale that finds [Gardner] at the top of her game . . . [A] relentlessly riveting psychological thriller that never lets up and never lets us down."

—*Providence Journal*

"An emotionally powerful page-turner. Fans of kick-ass female investigators will be well satisfied."

—*Publishers Weekly*

"Another edgy thriller from one of my favorite authors. A string of murders, a crack FBI team, and a voiceless girl desperate for revenge, *When You See Me* has it all."

—Karin Slaughter

"This is top-notch suspense by a bestselling master of the genre."

—*Booklist* (starred review)

Never Tell

"Gardner knows how to weave a deeply moving and psychological thriller that pulls no punches in its authenticity. She is one of the masters when it comes to crime fiction. Fans of her novels will consider this one of her best, and newcomers will be in awe of the compelling story and unpredictability of the proceedings."

—Associated Press

"This is easily Gardner's most ambitious, complex tale ever, a shattering emotional journey that's utterly relentless in pacing and suspense. Tell everyone that *Never Tell* is an early candidate for the best thriller of 2019."

—*Providence Journal*

"Nail-biting . . . Gardner's commendable storytelling will keep fans eagerly waiting for the next outing for D.D. and Flora."

—*Publishers Weekly*

"If you're into secrets, lies, Gardner's amazing words, or simply an action-packed mystery that does leave you breathless, this is the one for you! It is so good, it almost feels like the author sat down and created a holiday gift for her fans around the globe."

—*Suspense Magazine*

"*Never Tell* is another nail-biting page-turner from Lisa Gardner, the undisputed queen of suspense, and the kind of thriller that'll stay with readers weeks after turning the final page."

—*The Real Book Spy*

Look for Me

"An utterly absorbing story about troubled families and twisted fates. You won't be able to put it down—and it will haunt you long after you turn the final page."

—Shari Lapena

"Family, friendships, and foster relationships are explored in this emotional, page-turning thriller."

—*USA Today*

"A splendidly dark foray into the blood-soaked reality of family secrets and squabbles, and a relentless page-turner of a tale chock-full of Gardner's trademark twists and turns."

—*Providence Journal*

"Suspenseful and wholly believable, this ninth entry will win new fans for the series, especially among those who favor Karin Slaughter's gritty procedurals."

—*Booklist* (starred review)

Right Behind You

"Gardner knows how to get the reader emotionally hooked into the story, and the police procedure elements of the novel shine. . . . Gardner still knows how to surprise and tantalize. She's a master of the psychological thriller, so don't leave this one behind."

—Associated Press

"*Right Behind You* . . . solidifies [Lisa Gardner's] claim as the queen of psychological suspense."

—*Providence Journal*

"Devilishly clever twists propel Gardener's tale."
—*Publishers Weekly* (starred review)

"A long-awaited delight . . . and a thrilling escape."

—*Booklist*

Find Her

"For years Lisa Gardner has been one of the best in the thriller business, but *Find Her* is something new: taut psychological suspense, an intricate mystery, emotionally devastating, ultimately empowering—a novel that should not be missed."

—Harlan Coben

"Lisa Gardner is the master of the psychological thriller. . . . The world of the FBI, the terror of abduction, and victim advocates blend into this tense . . . thriller."

—Associated Press

"A psychological thriller both chilling and emotional. Her narrative thrums with heart-pounding scenes and unexpected twists that have you furiously flipping pages."

—*USA Today*'s *Happy Ever After*

"Gardner doesn't disappoint. . . . Longtime fans as well as those new to the series . . . will delight in this suspenseful offering."

—*Library Journal* (starred review)

"Superb . . . Always a great storyteller, Gardner here proves herself a novelist par excellence, fashioning a masterpiece of form as well as function that provides no easy outs for characters struggling to wade through their own moral morass. The first can't-miss thriller of 2016."

—*Providence Journal*

Fear Nothing

"An intelligent, sophisticated psychological thriller . . . Gardner continues to show us why she is on the short-list of top thriller writers today."

—*Suspense Magazine*

"Absorbing . . . Gardner repeatedly ratchets up the tension."

—*Publishers Weekly*

"Gardner retains her place on thrillerdom's top tier . . . Gardner has a reserved seat on most bestseller lists, and she'll be claiming her spot once again."

—*Booklist*

Crash & Burn

"With labyrinthine twists and surprises on just about every turn of the page, Gardner has crafted a delight of a suspense novel."

—*New York Journal of Books*

"This page-turner, with its contemporary, hard-edged flavor, is sure to satisfy Gardner's ardent fan base."

—*Booklist*

"Lisa Gardner delivers another gut-wrenching emotional thriller with her latest psychological tale, *Crash & Burn*. . . . [Her] most unpredictable novel to date."

—Associated Press

"Lisa Gardner never disappoints." —*Suspense Magazine*

LISA GARDNER

FEAR NOTHING

A NOVEL

DUTTON

DUTTON

An imprint of Penguin Random House LLC
penguinrandomhouse.com

Previously published as a Dutton hardcover in January 2014 and
a mass market edition in January 2018

First Dutton trade paperback printing: October 2023

THE LIBRARY OF CONGRESS HAS CATALOGED THE HARDCOVER EDITION OF THIS BOOK AS FOLLOWS:
Fear nothing : a detective D. D. Warren novel / Lisa Gardner.
pages cm
ISBN 978-0-525-95308-1 (hardback)
1. Warren, D. D. (Fictitious character)—Fiction. 2. Police—Massachusetts—Boston—Fiction.
3. Serial murderer—Boston—Fiction. 4. Boston (Mass.)—Fiction. 7. Psychological fiction. I. Title.
PS3557.A7132F43 2014
813'.54—dc23   2013037180

ISBN 9780593473351 (trade paperback)

Printed in the United States of America
1st Printing

Book design by Leonard Telesca

FEAR NOTHING

Prologue

Rockabye, baby, on the treetop . . .

The body was gone, but not the smell. As Boston homicide detective D. D. Warren knew from experience, this kind of scene could hold the stench of blood for weeks, even months to come. The crime scene techs had removed the bedding, but still, blood had a life of its own. Seeping into drywall. Slipping behind wooden trim. Pooling between floorboards. Twenty-eight-year-old Christine Ryan used to have approximately 4.7 liters of blood pumping through her veins. Now most of it saturated the bare mattress occupying center stage of this grim, gray space.

When the wind blows, the cradle will rock . . .

The call had come in shortly after 9:00 A.M. Good friend Midge Roberts had grown concerned when Christine hadn't answered the knocks on her front door or the texts to her cell phone. Christine was the responsible kind. Didn't oversleep, didn't run off with a cute bartender, didn't come down with the flu without providing a heads-up to her best bud, who picked her up promptly at seven thirty each weekday morning for their joint commute to a local accounting firm.

Midge had contacted a few more friends. All agreed no one had heard from Christine since dinner the night before. Midge gave in to instinct and summoned the landlord, who finally agreed to open the door.

Then vomited all over the upstairs hall upon making the find.

Midge hadn't come up the stairs. Midge had stood in the foyer of the narrow duplex, and, as she'd reported to D.D.'s squad mate Phil, she'd known. Just known. Probably, even from that distance, she'd caught the first unmistakable whiff of drying blood.

Rockabye, baby . . .

Upon her arrival, the scene had immediately struck D.D. with its marked contrasts. The young female victim, sprawled spread-eagle on her own bed, staring up at the ceiling with sightless blue eyes. Pretty features appearing nearly peaceful as her shoulder-length brown hair pooled softly upon a stark white pillow.

Except then, from the neck down . . .

Skin, peeled off in thin, curling ribbons. D.D. had heard of such things. At eleven this morning, she got to see them firsthand. A young woman, flayed in her own bed. With a bottle of champagne on her nightstand and a single red rose placed across her bloody abdomen.

Next to the bottle of champagne, Phil had discovered a pair of handcuffs. The kind purchased in high-end sex shops and fur lined for comfort. Taking in the cuffs, the sparkling wine, the red rose . . .

Lovers' tryst gone awry, Phil had theorized. Or, given the level of violence, a jilted boyfriend's final act of vengeance. Christine had broken up with some sorry sucker, and last night, the sorry sucker had returned to prove once and for all who was in charge.

But D.D. wasn't on board. Yes, there were handcuffs, but not on the victim's wrists. Yes, there was uncorked champagne, but none poured into waiting flutes for drinking. Finally, sure, there was the rose, but not in a florist's wrap for gifting.

The scene felt too . . . deliberate to her. Not a crime of passion or a falling-out between consenting adults. But a carefully staged production that involved months, years, perhaps even a lifetime of careful planning and consideration.

In D.D.'s opinion, they weren't looking at just a crime scene. They were looking at a killer's deepest, darkest fantasy.

And while this might be the first scene they were investigating, a homicide this heavily ritualized was probably not the last.

When the wind blows . . .

D.D.'s squad, the crime scene techs, the ME's office, not to mention a plethora of other investigators, had spent six hours working the space. They'd documented, dusted, diagramed and discussed until the sun had set, the dinner commute was on and tempers were flaring. As lead detective, D.D. had finally sent everyone home with orders to refresh, then regroup. Tomorrow was another day, when they could search federal databases for other murders matching this description, while building the profiles of their victim and killer. Plenty to do, many angles to investigate. Now get some rest.

Everyone had listened. Except, of course, D.D.

It was nearly 10:00 P.M. She should be returning home. Kissing her husband hello. Checking in on her three-year-old son, already tucked into bed at this late hour. Working on her own good night's sleep, versus hanging out at a darkened crime scene with her toddler's current favorite nursery rhyme running through her head.

But she couldn't do it. Some instinct—insight?—had driven her back to this too-quiet town house. For most of the day, she and her fellow detectives had stood here and debated what they saw. Now she stood with the lights out, in the middle of a blood-scented room, and waited for what she could feel.

Rockabye, baby . . .

Christine Ryan had already been dead before the killer had made his first cut. That much they could tell from the lack of anguish stamped into her pale face. The victim had died relatively easily. Then, most likely as her heart emitted a final few pumps, the killer had delivered his first downward slash across her right flank.

Meaning the murder hadn't been about the victim's pain, but about . . .

Presentation? Staging? The ritual itself? A killer with a compulsion to skin. Maybe as a kid, he'd started with small animals or family pets, then, when the fantasy had refused to abate . . .

The ME would check for hesitation marks, if determining jagged edges was even possible given the mounds of thin, curling skin, as well as test for evidence of sexual assault.

But once again, D.D. suffered a nagging sense of discomfort. Those elements were the things a criminal investigator could see. And deep inside, D.D. already suspected that was the wrong track. Indulging, in fact, in exactly what the killer wanted them to focus on.

Why stage things just so, if not to manipulate your audience into seeing exactly what you wanted them to see?

Then it came to her. The thought she'd had in the back of her head. The first and foremost question worth pursuing and the reason she now stood in the dark, her vision deliberately obscured: Why set a scene?

A sound. In the distance. The town house's front door, easing carefully open? A creak of the stair riser as a heavy foot found the first step? The groan of a floorboard just down the hall?

A sound. Once distant, now closer, and that quickly, Sergeant Detective D. D. Warren realized something she should've figured out fifteen minutes ago. Jack's favorite lullaby, the children's song she'd been humming under her breath . . . That tune wasn't coming from solely inside her head.

Someone else was singing it, too. Softly. Outside the bedroom. From elsewhere in the dead woman's apartment.

Rockabye, baby, on the treetop . . .

D.D.'s hand shot to her sidearm, unsnapping the shoulder holster, drawing her Sig Sauer. She whirled, dropping into a crouch as her gaze scanned the corners for signs of an intruder. No shifts in the blackness, no shadows settling into the shape of a human form.

But then she heard it. A creaking floorboard elsewhere in the apartment.

When the wind blows, the cradle will rock . . .

Quickly, she crept from the bedroom into the darkened hall, leading with her weapon. The narrow corridor didn't offer any overhead lights. Just more shadows from the glow of neighbors' apartments casting through the uncovered windows. A wash of lighter and darker shades of gray dancing across the hardwood floor.

But she knew this house, D.D. reminded herself. She'd already trod this hall, judiciously avoiding the pools of vomit, while noticing every pertinent detail.

She reached the top of the stairs, still looking from side to side, then peering down into the inky pool that marked the landing below. The humming had disappeared. Worse than the singing was the total silence.

Then, from out of the darkness, low and lilting: "*Rockabye, baby, on the treetop . . .*"

D.D. halted. Her gaze ping-ponged reflexively, trying to determine the location of the intruder as the singing continued, slow and mocking: "*When the wind blows, the cradle will rock . . .*"

She got it then. Felt her own blood turn to ice as the full implication sank in. Why do you stage a scene? Because you're looking for an audience. Or maybe one audience member in particular. Say, a hardworking detective stupid enough to be found after dark at a crime scene all alone.

She reached belatedly for her cell.

Just as a fresh noise registered directly behind her.

She spun. Eyes widening.

As a figure darted out of the shadows, heading straight for her.

"*And when the bough breaks, the cradle will fall . . .*"

Instinctively, D.D. stepped back. Except she'd forgotten about the top of the staircase. Her left foot, searching for traction, found only open space.

No! Her phone, clattering down. Her Sig Sauer, coming up. Trying belatedly to lean forward, regain her balance.

Then . . . the shadow reaching out. Herself falling back.

Down, down, down.

At the last second, D.D. squeezed the trigger. An instinctive act of self-preservation. *Boom, boom, boom.* Though she knew it was too little, too late.

Her head connected with the hardwood landing. A crack. A shooting pain. The final lyric, whispering through the dark:

"*And down will come baby, cradle and all . . .*"

Chapter 1

MY OLDER SISTER discovered my condition when I was three years old. Our foster mother walked in on her wielding the scissors, while I stood there, bare arms obediently held out, blood dripping from my wrists onto the olive-green shag carpet.

My six-year-old sister said, "Check it out, she doesn't even care." And slashed the scissors across my forearm. Fresh blood welled.

The woman screamed, then fainted.

I peered down at her, wondering what had happened.

After that, my sister went away. And I was taken to the hospital. There, doctors spent weeks running various tests that should've hurt more than my sister's sharp-edged ministrations, except that turned out to be the point: Due to an extremely rare mutation of my SCN9A gene, I don't feel pain. I can feel pressure. The scissors, pressing down against my skin. I can feel texture. The smoothness of the freshly sharpened blades.

But the actual sensation of my skin splitting, blood beading . . .

I don't feel what you feel. I never have. And I never will.

AFTER SHANA CARVED UP MY ARMS with sewing shears, I didn't see her for another twenty years. My sister spent most of that time in various institutions, gaining the distinction of being one of Massachusetts's youngest kids ever placed on antipsychotic meds. She attempted her first murder at eleven, then succeeded at fourteen. Our own peculiar family legacy.

If she became another casualty of the system, however, then I became the state's poster child for success.

Given my diagnosis, the doctors were not convinced foster care could adequately meet my needs. After all, babies born with the same genetic mutation had been known to chew off their tongues while teething. Then there were the toddlers who suffered third-degree burns by placing their hands on red-hot burners and leaving them there; not to mention the seven-, eight-, nine-year-olds who ran for days on shattered ankles or keeled over from burst appendixes they never knew were inflamed.

Pain is very useful. It warns you of danger, teaches you of hazards and provides consequences for your actions. Without it, jumping off the roof can sound like a great idea. Same with plunging your hand into a vat of boiling oil to grab the first fry. Or taking a pair of pliers and ripping out your own fingernails. Most kids with congenital insensitivity to pain report that they're acting on impulse. It's not a matter of why, but of why not?

Others, however, will tell you, a note of longing in their voices, that they did it to see if it would hurt. Because to *not* feel something known by so many can turn it into the Holy Grail of your entire life. A singular driving force. A relentless obsession. The pleasure of finally feeling pain.

Children who suffer from pain sensory disorders have a high mortality rate; few of us live to adulthood. Most require round-the-clock care. In my case, one of the geneticists, an older man with no wife and kids, pulled some strings and brought me home, where I became his beloved adopted daughter as well as his favorite case study.

My father was a good man. He hired only the best caretakers to monitor me 24/7, while dedicating his weekends to helping me manage my condition.

For example, if you cannot *feel* pain, then you must find other ways to register potential threats to your physical well-being. As a small child, I learned boiling water equaled danger. Same with red-hot burners on stoves. I would feel an item first for texture. Anything that registered as sharp, I was to leave alone. No scissors for me. Or hard-edged furniture. Or kittens or puppies or any life-form with sharp claws. Walking only. No jumping, no sliding, no skipping, no dancing.

If I went outside, I wore a helmet and appropriate padding at all times. Then, upon my reentry, my armor would be removed and my body inspected for signs of damage. Including the time my caretaker went to remove my shoe and my foot twisted around a full one-eighty. Apparently, I had ripped out all the tendons walking down to the gardens. Or another time when I arrived covered in bee stings. I had stumbled upon a hornet's nest and, with a five-year-old's naïveté, assumed they were dancing with me.

With age, I learned to conduct my own physicals. Daily tempera-ture checks, so I can judge if I have a fever, which might indicate my body is suffering from some kind of infection. Nightly inspections, standing naked before a full-length mirror, where I study every inch of my skin for bruises and lacerations, then inspect my joints for signs of swelling or stress. Next, on to my eyes: A red eyeball is an angry eyeball. Checking my ears: Blood in the ear cavity could indi-cate a ruptured eardrum and/or possible head injury. Then my nasal passageways, the inside of my mouth, teeth, tongue and gums.

My body is a vessel, a useful item, to be inspected, managed and tended. I have to take extra care of it because the lack of molecular channels to direct electrical impulses from pain-sensing nerves to my brain means my body can't take care of itself. Someone with my con-dition can't afford to trust what I feel. Instead, I need to go by what I can see, hear, taste and smell.

Mind over matter, my geneticist father would tell me time and time again. Just a simple exercise of mind over matter.

When I made it to thirteen without succumbing to heatstroke, internal infection or basic carelessness, my father took his research one step further. If there were a couple hundred kids in the world born with this condition, then there were about forty still alive to contemplate adulthood. Studying these cases revealed further weaknesses of a life spent never experiencing physical discomfort. For example, many subjects reported difficulty empathizing with others, stunted emotional growth and limited social skills.

My adoptive father immediately ordered up a full psychological assessment. Could I sense pain in others? Recognize signs of distress on a stranger's face? Respond appropriately to the suffering of my fellow human beings?

After all, if you never cry over a paper cut, will you weep when your sixteen-year-old best friend suddenly severs all ties, calling you a freak? If you can walk miles on a shattered knee, will your heart constrict when at twenty-three your birth sister finds you again, and the letter is postmarked from the Department of Corrections?

If you've never experienced one second of genuine agony, can you honestly comprehend your adoptive father's last dying breath, as he clutches your hand and gasps:

"Adeline. This. Is. *Pain.*"

Standing alone at his funeral, I thought I understood.

But being my father's daughter, I also realized I could never truly be certain. So I did as he trained me to do. I enrolled in a top-notch doctorate program where I studied, I tested, I researched.

I made pain my business.

A useful specialty for more reasons than one.

BY THE TIME I ARRIVED at the Massachusetts Correctional Institute, my sister was waiting. I signed in, stuffed my purse in an available locker, then waited my turn to pass through security. Chris and Bob, two of the longtime corrections officers, greeted me by name. Bob passed his wand over my medical bracelet, same test he did the first

Monday of each month. Then Maria, a third corrections officer, escorted me to the enclosed privacy room, where my sister sat with her cuffed hands on her lap.

Officer Maria nodded her consent and I entered the room. The eight-by-eight space contained two orange plastic chairs and one Formica wood table. Shana already sat on the far side of the table, back protected by the cinder-block wall, front taking in the view of the corridor through the single window. The gunslinger's seat.

I claimed the chair opposite her, my own back exposed through the window to the passing masses. I took my time, pulling out the plastic chair, positioning my body just so. A minute passed. Then two.

My sister spoke first: "Take off the jacket." Her tone was already agitated. Something had set her off, probably well before my visit, but that didn't mean I wouldn't be the one to pay the price.

"Why?" In contrast to her edgy command, I kept my own voice deliberately calm.

"You shouldn't wear black. How many times do I have to tell you that? Black washes you out."

This from a woman clad in drab blue scrubs, her shoulder-length brown hair hanging down in greasy hanks. My sister might have been pretty once, but years of harsh living conditions and fluorescent lighting had taken their toll. Not to mention the hard look in her eyes.

Now I removed my fitted Ann Taylor blazer and hung it over the back of my chair. Beneath it, I wore a long-sleeved gray knit top. My sister glared at my covered arms. Brown eyes boring into mine, she took a few experimental sniffs.

"Don't smell any blood," she said at last.

"You don't have to sound disappointed."

"Please. I spend twenty-three hours a day staring at the same ass-white cinder-block walls. Least you could do is bring me a paper cut."

My sister claimed she could smell the pain I couldn't feel. There was no scientific basis for this, just sisterly superiority. And yet on three separate occasions, within hours of leaving her, I'd discovered injuries she'd already warned me about.

"You should wear fuchsia," Shana continued. "You're the one living on the outside. So live a little, Adeline. Then maybe you can bring me some real stories. No more job, patients, pain practice, blah, blah, blah. Tell me about some hard-bodied guy ripping a fuchsia bra from your bony chest. Then I might actually enjoy these monthly meetings. Can you even have sex?"

I didn't answer. She'd asked this question many times before.

"That's right; you can feel the good stuff, just not the bad. Guess that means no S and M for my little sister. Bummer, dude."

Shana delivered the words tonelessly. Nothing personal. She attacked because it was what she did. And no amount of imprisonment, medication or even sisterly attention had ever been able to change that. Shana was a born predator, our father's daughter. Murdering a young boy when she was only fourteen had landed her behind bars. Killing a fellow inmate as well as two corrections officers now kept her here.

Could you love a person such as my sister? Professionally speaking, she was a fascinating study of antisocial personality disorder. Completely narcissistic, totally devoid of empathy and highly manipulative. Personally speaking, she was the only family I had left.

"I heard you signed up for a new program," I offered. "Superintendent McKinnon says your first few paintings show a good eye for detail."

Shana shrugged, not one for compliments.

She sniffed the air again. "No perfume, but your outfit looks professional. Means you're working today. Going from here to your office. Will you mist yourself in the car? Hope it's strong enough to cover Eau d'Institution."

"I thought you didn't want to talk about my job."

"I know there's nothing else to talk about."

"The weather."

"Ah fuck it. Just because it's Monday shouldn't mean I have to waste an hour serving as your pity project."

I didn't say anything.

"I'm tired of it, Adeline. You. Me. These monthly meetings where you show off your bad taste in clothes and I have no choice but to sit here and take it. You have enough patients you should be able to leave me alone. So get out. Toodle right along. I mean it!"

A knock on the door. Officer Maria, who could see everything through the shatterproof window, checking on us. I ignored her, keeping my gaze upon my sister instead.

Her outburst didn't bother me; I was well accustomed to such displays by now. Rage was Shana's preferred emotion, serving for both offense and defense. Plus, my sister had reason enough to hate me. And not just because of my rare genetic condition, or because I'd found my very own Daddy Warbucks. But because after I was born, my mother chose to hide me in the closet, and there hadn't been room enough for two.

Shana cursed me, her eyes a flat display of dull anger and deeper depression, and mostly, I wondered once again what had happened this morning to put my battle-hardened sister in such a mood.

"Why do you care?" I asked her suddenly.

"What?"

"The color fuchsia. Why do you care? About my clothes, what color I wear, whether or not it makes others find me attractive? Why do you care?"

Shana frowned at me, clearly perplexed by such a question. "You," she said at last, "are a fucking retard."

"And that," I observed, "is the most sisterly thing you've ever said to me."

A winning barb. Shana rolled her eyes but finally, grudgingly smiled. The tension in the room eased at last, and both of us could breathe again.

Shana might talk a good game, but according to the prison superintendent, my sister seemed to genuinely look forward to these monthly meetings. Enough so that during extreme episodes of disorderly conduct, the threat of losing my upcoming visit was often the only punishment severe enough to bring her round. Hence, we continued our monthly dance, which had been going on now for nearly a decade.

Perhaps as close to a true relationship as one got with a born psychopath.

"How are you sleeping?" I asked.

"Like a baby."

"Read anything good?"

"Oh yeah. Complete works of Shakespeare. Never know when iambic pentameter might come in handy."

"*Et tu, Brute?*"

Another faint smile. Shana relaxing further into her chair. And so we went, another thirty minutes of conversation both pointed and pointless, as we did the first Monday of each month. Until Officer Maria rapped on the window, and just like that, our time was up. I rose to standing. My sister, who wasn't going anywhere, chose to remain in her seat.

"Fuchsia," she recommended again, as I undraped my black jacket.

"Maybe you should follow your own advice," I said, "and introduce some color into your artwork."

"And give the shrinks more to study?" She smirked. "I think not."

"Do you dream in black and white?"

"Do you?"

"I'm not sure I dream."

"Maybe that's a perk of your condition. I dream plenty. Mostly bloodred. Only difference is sometimes I'm the one with the knife and sometimes it's dear old Dad."

She stared at me, eyes suddenly flat, like a shark's, but I knew better than to take the bait.

"You should keep a journal of your dreams," I advised.

"What the fuck do you think my artwork is?"

"A disturbing explosion of deep-seated violence."

She laughed, and on that note, I headed out the door, leaving her behind.

"She okay?" I asked a minute later, following Officer Maria down the corridor. There were no visiting hours for the general population on Monday, so the halls were relatively quiet.

"Not sure. You know it's nearly the thirtieth anniversary."

I gazed at the CO blankly.

"Shana's first victim," Officer Maria filled in. "The twelve-year-old neighbor, Donnie Johnson? Shana killed him thirty years ago next week. Some local reporter has been calling for an interview."

I blinked. Somehow, I'd managed not to connect those dots. As both a therapist and a woman dedicated to self-management, later I'd have to ask myself why. What pain was I trying to avoid? A moment of ironic self-reflection.

"She won't answer any questions, though," Maria was saying. "Good, if you ask me. I mean, that boy can't very well talk now. Why should his killer?"

"Keep me posted."

"No problem."

At the front, I collected my purse, signed out and headed for my car, parked in the vast lot hundreds of yards from the sprawling brick-and-barbed-wire compound that served as my sister's permanent home.

In the passenger's seat lay the rich purply-pink cardigan I'd been wearing when I arrived. Except I'd changed tops while still sitting in my car, removing my jewelry, per visitation rules, and opting for a more subdued look given the environment.

I'd set aside my new sweater, purchased just two weeks ago, and I swear, the only fuchsia-colored item that I owned.

Now I looked up at the brick corrections facility. There were windows everywhere, of course. Even a narrow slit in my sister's segregation cell. But from this distance, myself hunched awkwardly behind the steering wheel, further obscured by my SUV's tinted windows . . .

I could never explain everything about my sister. But then, I suspected she often thought the same about me.

Putting my Acura into gear, I drove toward downtown Boston, where I had a busy afternoon ahead of me, filled with patients seeking relief from their various afflictions, including a new patient, a Boston detective recently injured on the job.

I loved my job. I looked forward to the challenge, as I greeted each patient, then said, as befitting a woman with my condition, "Please, tell me about your pain."

Chapter 2

IN HER HEART, D.D. knew she was a lucky person. Her head just couldn't seem to accept that fact yet.

She woke late. After ten, which confused her. If someone had ever told her she was capable of sleeping till ten on a Monday morning, she would've called him a liar. Mornings were for getting up and heading out. Guzzling black coffee, catching up with her squad and possibly attending a fresh homicide.

She liked black coffee, her fellow detectives and interesting homicides.

She didn't like yet another restless night of fitful sleep interspersed with even more disquieting dreams. Where shadows sang and sometimes grew arms and legs before giving chase.

And she fell down. Each and every time. In her nightmares, the great Sergeant Detective D. D. Warren plunged to her doom. Because her heart knew she was a lucky person. But her brain just couldn't accept it yet.

The child monitor remained on the nightstand next to her. On, but quiet. Alex had most likely delivered Jack to day care. Then Alex could head to work at the police academy while D.D. . . .

D.D. dedicated her day to getting out of bed.

She moved gingerly. Any movement of her left arm and shoulder still led to instantaneous shooting pains, so during the past few weeks, she'd perfected the art of rolling onto her right side. From there, she could swing her feet down to the floor, which helped heave her torso into the vertical position. Having achieved sitting up, she would then spend the next couple of minutes regaining her labored breath.

Because what happened next really, truly *hurt,* and heaven help her, but six weeks later she was growing more averse to the pain, instead of simply resigned to it.

Strained muscles. Inflamed tendons. Overstretched nerves. And the winning injury, an avulsion fracture. The ripping away of a piece of bone in her left humerus. In a matter of seconds, D.D. had sustained enough damage to her forty-four-year-old body that she now moved like the Tin Man, unable to turn her head, lift her left arm or rotate her torso. No surgical options, she'd been told. Just time, fortitude and physical therapy. Which she did. Twice-weekly appointments followed by daily homework assignments that made her scream in agony.

Because forget ever holding a gun again. Right now, D.D. couldn't even pick up her own child.

Deep breath. Counting to three. Then she stood. The movement was abrupt, nearly impossible to perfectly balance. Meaning she instinctively countered with a shoulder shrug here and a neck rotation there, as her teeth gritted and her right hand clenched and she used the worst, most vile words she could think of, which after twenty years as a Boston cop included curses that would make a long-haul trucker with a kidney stone blush, and even then, she nearly vomited from the pain.

But she was standing. Sweating. Swaying slightly. But fully vertical.

And she thought, not for the first time, what the hell had she been doing at that crime scene at that hour of the night? Because six weeks later, she still couldn't remember a thing. She'd suffered the worst injury of her life, put her career in jeopardy and her family in crisis and she still didn't have a clue.

One day, six weeks ago, she'd shown up for work. And life had been a mystery ever since.

Another thirty minutes while she managed to brush her teeth, comb her hair. Showering required Alex's help. He'd been gracious about it. Saying he'd do anything as long as she was naked. But his deep blue eyes maintained a watchful look. As if she were suddenly spun from glass and needed to be handled delicately at all times.

The first day home, she'd caught him staring at the dark bruises welting her back, and the look on his face . . .

Stricken. Horrified. Appalled.

She hadn't said a word. After a moment, he'd resumed rinsing the shampoo from her short blond curls. Later that night, he'd reached for her, very carefully, but she'd hissed reflexively in pain and he'd snatched his hand back as if slapped, and that was the way it had been ever since.

He helped her with the day-to-day tasks of life. And in return, she felt herself slowly but surely turn into a shadow of herself, a second child for her incredibly patient spouse to tend.

In her heart, she knew she was lucky. But her brain just couldn't accept that fact yet.

Time for clothes. She couldn't move her left arm enough to pull on a shirt. Instead, she stole one of Alex's oversize flannel shirts, slipping her right arm into the sleeve but leaving her left arm tucked against her ribs. She couldn't manage all the snaps but enough to get her through breakfast.

Walking wasn't so bad. Once she'd achieved vertical, as long as she kept her shoulders square and her torso straight, her neck and shoulder didn't mind so much. She took the stairs carefully, right hand glued to the railing. Last time she'd dealt with stairs, they'd clearly won, and she couldn't bring herself to trust them again.

Rockabye, baby, on the treetop . . .

Excellent. Another morning, same old creepy lullaby still stuck in her head.

Upon arriving in the living room, D.D. became aware of voices coming from her kitchen. Two men, hushed tones. Maybe her father-in-law, over for a cup of coffee? Alex's parents had moved to Boston six months ago in order to spend more time with their only grandson. D.D. had been nervous at first, preferring her own parents' living arrangements in Florida. But Alex's parents, Bob and Edith, had quickly proved to be as easygoing as their son. Not to mention that little Jack clearly adored them, and given her and Alex's work schedules, a couple of grandparents on speed dial was never a bad thing. Of course, she'd liked it better when they'd been helping out with Jack because of her job, not because she was a complete and total invalid who couldn't even dress herself anymore. Details, details.

Both men were clearly making an effort not to wake her. She took that as an invitation to enter.

"Morning."

Alex immediately looked up from his seat at the round kitchen table. Not his father, but her squad mate Phil, was slower to follow. Alex's features were already politely composed. Clearly he'd been up for hours, having showered, shaved and taken care of their three-year-old. Now he was dressed for work, a navy blue academy shirt tucked into his dress khakis. The shirt emphasized his dark eyes, salt-and-pepper hair. A good-looking man, she thought, not for the first time. Handsome, intelligent, dedicated to their son, sensitive to her needs.

Across from Alex sat D.D.'s oldest partner, Phil, thinning brown hair, married forever to his high school sweetheart, Betsy, father of four kids, who once claimed he'd joined Boston homicide to escape the gore.

Already she was suspicious.

"Cuppa joe?" Phil asked brightly. He wouldn't meet her gaze, pushing back his chair, heading straight for the coffeepot.

"You don't golf," D.D. said.

A small smile lifted the corners of Alex's mouth.

"What?" Phil, still diligently focused on how to best pour coffee into an oversize mug.

"Neither of you gamble. Nor do you have best buds in common for a bachelor party. In fact, your only connection is me."

Phil finished pouring the coffee. Carefully eased the carafe back in place. Slowly picked up the steaming mug. Deliberately turned toward her.

D.D. pulled out a chair and sat abruptly, wincing as she did so. Suddenly she wasn't sure she wanted to know.

Alex wasn't smiling anymore. Instead, he reached across the table and gently touched the back of her right hand.

"Get any sleep?" he asked.

"Sure. All sorts. Never been so rested. Just wish I could fall down the stairs again so I could lie around in bed even more."

D.D. kept her attention on Phil. He was the weak link. Whatever was going on here, he'd be the one who'd cave.

"FDIT?" she guessed softly, when Phil remained standing before her, still holding the coffee mug between his cupped hands.

In copspeak, *FDIT* stood for *Firearms Discharge Investigation Team*. Anytime an officer discharged her weapon, including in a darkened crime scene at no identifiable target, FDIT had the responsibility to investigate the event and determine if the officer acted appropriately or with negligence.

By the time D.D. had regained consciousness at the hospital, the FDIT team had already taken possession of her firearm, and the future of her policing career rested on the report they would eventually deliver to the Bureau of Professional Standards.

Her fellow detectives had told her not to worry. Most likely, her weapon had discharged during her tumble down the stairs. Except Sig Sauers didn't simply fall out of snapped shoulder holsters. Nor did an officer's right index finger generally land on the trigger while cascading backward through open space, then fire off three consecutive shots.

D.D. had deliberately pulled the trigger of her department-issued weapon. At something, or someone.

Even she could figure out that much.

But at what or whom and with or without probable cause? Because her fellow cops never found anyone else at the scene. Just her unconscious form in the foyer of Christine Ryan's apartment and three bullet holes in the wall. One of the slugs had passed through into the adjacent unit. Thank God it hadn't hit anyone. But the neighbor hadn't taken it well, and why was some cop shooting up the place next door, and . . .

Reports to the Bureau of Professional Standards inevitably included not just what an officer did, but how those actions made the entire department look.

D.D. was vulnerable, and she knew it. Only reason things hadn't come to a head sooner was that the extent of her injuries had earned her immediate medical leave. No need for the department to rule too quickly about her return to work. Her doctor already said it wouldn't be happening anytime soon.

"No word," Phil said.

"Oh."

"Which is probably good news," he continued briskly. "If there was obvious proof of misconduct, the administration wouldn't hesitate to strike. No news is good news, and all that."

D.D. eyed her longtime partner, thinking if only his words matched the expression on his face.

"Shoulder?" Phil asked.

"Ask me in another three months."

"That long?"

"More like I'm that old. But I'm doing my PT. And practicing patience."

Phil gave her a dubious look; he'd worked with D.D. long enough to know the extent of her patience.

"Exactly," she agreed with him.

"Pain?"

"Only most of the time."

"They didn't give you anything for it?"

"Hell, they gave me all sorts of meds for it. But you know me, Phil. Why ease my pain, when I can share it with everyone else instead?"

Phil nodded in agreement. Alex stroked the back of her right hand.

"I see a new doc today," she continued with an awkward, one-shouldered shrug. "Some therapist who specializes in mental techniques for pain management. Mind over matter, that kind of crap. Who knows, maybe I'll learn something."

"Good." Phil finally handed over the mug of coffee, placing it carefully on the table where she could reach it with her one good hand. Mission accomplished, he didn't seem to know what to do with himself.

"If you weren't here to talk about the discharge investigation report," D.D. asked quietly, "why'd you come?"

Then, when Phil still wouldn't look up, and Alex once more rubbed the back of her hand, she closed her eyes and let herself know what she'd been suspecting all along.

"There's been another murder."

"Yeah."

"Same flayed skin, rose across her abdomen, bottle of champagne on the nightstand."

"Yeah."

"You need me to remember." Then, on the heels of that thought: "You're not here as my partner, are you, Phil? This isn't cop to cop. You need to know what I saw that night, detective to witness."

He didn't say a word. Alex continued to run the ball of his thumb across the ridge of her knuckles.

She stared at her coffee mug.

"It's okay," she whispered. "I totally understand. And of course I'll help. I'd do anything to help."

Former detective D. D. Warren, she thought. And tried to remind herself that in her heart, she knew she was lucky, even if her brain couldn't accept it yet.

Chapter 3

ONE P.M. MONDAY, I confronted my newest patient and knew immediately that Sergeant Detective D. D. Warren was a born skeptic.

It didn't surprise me. I'd been in the pain management business long enough to have assisted numerous first responders—police officers, EMTs, firefighters. People drawn to jobs that demanded the most of them, physically as well as mentally. People who thrived on being in the thick of things, calling the shots, running the action, controlling the plays.

In other words, people who didn't do well sitting on the sidelines, while a therapist in a thousand-dollar suit explained how the first step to managing her pain was to get in touch with it. Give it a name. Develop an ongoing relationship.

"Seriously?" Detective D. D. Warren asked me now. She sat rigidly, perched in a simple wooden chair versus the low-slung sofa that was also available. Without even examining her medical charts, I could tell she suffered from acute neck and shoulder pain. It was written in her stiff posture, how she rotated her entire body to take in the room, versus simply turning her head. Not to mention the tight way she held her left arm tucked against her side, as if still protecting herself from an incoming blow.

I suspected the blond detective was rarely described as a soft-looking woman. But now, with her dark-rimmed eyes, grim-set mouth and thinly drawn cheeks, she appeared harsh, a woman well beyond her forty-four years.

"The basis of my practice is the Internal Family Systems model," I explained patiently.

She arched a brow, didn't say a word.

"One of the basic assumptions of IFS is that the mind can be sub-divided into a number of distinct parts. First and foremost of those parts is the Self, which should serve as leader of all the parts. When your Self is clearly differentiated and elevated from the other members of the system, then you are in the best position to understand, manage and control your own pain."

"I fell down the stairs," D.D. said flatly. "If my *self* was supposed to manage that, it's a little late now."

"Let me ask you a different question: Are you in pain?"

"You mean, like, right now?"

"Like, right now."

"Well, yeah. According to the docs, my own tendons ripped away a chunk of bone in my left arm. It hurts."

"On a scale of one to ten, one being slight discomfort, ten being the worst agony you can imagine . . ."

The detective pursed her lips. "Six."

"So slightly above average."

"Sure. I want to build in some room. Tonight is shower night, which will bring me to a seven, followed by attempting to sleep, which I'd place at an eight, because I can't seem to stop rolling onto my left side; then, of course, there's getting out of bed tomorrow morning, which is an easy nine."

"What would you consider a ten?"

"I don't know yet," she said tersely. "I'm still new at this walking-wounded business, but from what I can tell, that's what physical therapists were put on earth to find out."

I smiled. "Many of my patients would agree with you."

"I know about the scale," D.D. said. "Russ Ilg, my personal torturer, already walked me through it. Don't think of pain as a single point, but as an entire spectrum. Where are you on the spectrum right now, this afternoon, for the whole day, for the week? Then, instead of just being in pain, you can experience the full rainbow of physical agony. Or something like that."

"He has you rate your level of discomfort when he is working with you?"

"Yeah. He raises my left arm. I yelp. He tells me to breathe through my mouth. I yelp some more. He asks me if I'm at an eight yet. I say no, he raises my arm an inch higher." D.D. wasn't looking at me anymore. Her gaze had gone beyond my right shoulder, to a spot on the wall, while her right leg began to bounce restlessly.

I had scanned her medical reports. The avulsion fracture she'd suffered in her left shoulder was a particularly rare and painful injury that called for an even more agonizing remedy—physical therapy. Lots of extremely excruciating exercises designed to keep her left shoulder from locking up, while minimizing scar tissue during the healing process.

According to the detective's charts, she worked with a physical therapist twice a week. Most likely, she ended those sessions with tears running down her cheeks.

I wondered, already, how that must feel to a woman accustomed to operating under complete control.

"So you take the time to consider and rate your pain?" I asked now.

She made a motion that may or may not have been a nod.

"How often?" I pressed.

"Well, you know, when Russ asks me."

"So during physical therapy?"

"Yes."

"What about at home? Say you wake up in the middle of the night and you're uncomfortable. What do you do then?"

She didn't answer right away.

I took my time, waiting quietly.

"I tell myself to go back to sleep," she said at last.

"Does that work?"

That motion again, the nod that was not a nod.

"Do you want to be here?" I asked abruptly.

She seemed startled. "What do you mean?"

"Today. Right now. Do you want to be in my office, talking to me?"

The detective stopped staring at my wall, met my eyes instead. Her gaze was mutinous. It didn't surprise me. Some people internalized their pain. Others externalized it, lashing out. Not too hard to judge which camp D. D. Warren fell into.

"No," she said bluntly.

"Then why did you come?"

"I want to return to work. I like my job." Her tone turned less hostile, more defensive.

"You're a homicide detective, yes?"

"Yes."

"And you enjoy your job?"

"I love my job."

"I see. So your injury, not being able to work right now, that must be difficult."

"I'm on medical leave," the detective stated briskly. "Might sound clear enough: You're hurt, you stay home. You get fixed, you return to work. But like any good bureaucracy, the department likes to make it complicated. Because maybe my shoulder gets better, but what about my head? Am I still the cool, calm detective I was before? Maybe I regain my physical ability to charge into a crisis situation. But will I? Or will I hang back, unnerved by the thought of jostling my left side, straining my shoulder? The department doesn't want my body to return to work but my head to stay at home. I understand their point, but still . . ."

"You're here to humor your bosses."

"Let's put it this way: The deputy superintendent of homicide personally handed me your business card. I took the hint."

"So what's your plan?" I asked, leaning forward, genuinely interested now. "You'll have to attend more than a single session with me—no one will believe you took pain therapy seriously with only one visit. Six is maybe a bit much. I'm pegging you at three. You'll see me three times; then the 'rescheduling' will begin."

For the first time, the detective appeared impressed. "I was thinking three would be a good number."

"Fair enough. Three sessions it is. But you have to take your visits with me seriously; that's my condition. You don't have to believe in everything I say. But as long as we have three appointments together, you might as well listen. And do your homework."

"Homework?"

"Absolutely. Your first assignment is to name your pain."

"What?" I had the good detective's full attention again, most likely because she thought I was nuts.

"Give your pain a name. And next time you wake up in the middle of the night, instead of telling yourself to go back to sleep, I want you to address your pain by name. Talk to it. Then listen for what it might have to say."

"You mean, like, 'Give me Percocet'?" D.D. muttered.

I smiled. "Speaking of which, are you taking anything?"

"No."

"Why not?"

That seminod, or maybe it was a half shrug. "Just say no to drugs, yada, yada, yada. Prescription, nonprescription, it's a fine line out there with narcotics, and I'd prefer not to cross it."

"Are you afraid of drugs?"

"Say what?"

"Some people are. They're afraid of how the drugs may make them feel; they're afraid of becoming addicted. I'm not saying there's anything wrong with that. I'm just asking."

"I don't like meds. Plain and simple. They're not for me."

"You consider yourself tougher than that?"

"You're stereotyping me."

"And you're avoiding my question."

"Is it true you can't feel pain?"

I smiled, sat back fully and glanced at the clock. "Twenty-two minutes," I said.

The detective wasn't dumb. She glanced at the wall clock hanging beside my desk, then scowled.

"You're a detective," I continued. "Of course you ran a background on me. And since the *Boston Herald*, not to mention numerous science publications, have found my condition fascinating, you learned quite a bit. Then it was simply a matter of waiting until you needed to distract, evade. The best defense is a good offense, yes?" I kept my voice even. "For the record, Detective, I can't feel any physical pain. Which means I have nothing better to do than focus on yours. And you *still* haven't answered my question. Do you consider yourself tough?"

"Yes," she bit out.

"So tough, your back, your shoulder, shouldn't be slowing you down like this?"

"I can't wash my hair!"

I waited.

"I can't lift my son. My three-year-old son. And last night, he went to hug me and I stepped away because I knew it would hurt. I couldn't take the pain!"

I waited.

"And the docs all say it'll get better. Do this, take that, but in the meantime, I can't sleep, I can't move and I can't even enjoy lounging around in bed, because I fucking hate my bed. It hurts too much to get in and out of it. I'm old, I'm broken and I'm basically unemployed. Shit!"

Then: "Goddamn, shit on a stick, bite me, fuckety fuck fuck. Shit!"

"Melvin," I said.

"What?" D.D. looked up, a semiferal gleam in her eye. A look I'd seen many times in my practice; the gaze of an animal in pain.

"Melvin," I repeated calmly. "I think you should name your pain Melvin. Shit on a stick, fuckety fuck fuck Melvin. And every time he bothers you, yell at him. Curse him out. Why not? You might actually feel better. Discover that putting your Self in charge of Melvin makes him smaller and your Self more powerful. And isn't that really what you miss? Feeling powerful?"

"Melvin," D.D. said.

"Just a suggestion. Obviously, you want a name that resonates for you."

"How much do you charge an hour again?"

"Well, I am a doctor. Have initials after my name and everything."

"Melvin. Good God, my pain is called Melvin."

"The Internal Family Systems model subdivides the mind into four main parts. At the core is your Self, the natural leader of the system. Then there is the section called the Exiles, which include pain and trauma you're not ready to process yet so you have cast aside. Unfortunately, the Exiles need to share their stories. They will continue to act out, in the form of rage, terror, grief and shame, until they are heard.

"When the Exiles act up, the next group, the Firefighters, kick into gear. Classic firefighting techniques include drug or alcohol abuse, binge eating, other short-term cover-ups for long-term pain. Finally there are the Managers. This section also tries to keep the Exiles at bay through hypercontrolling every situation. Striving, judging, self-criticizing, all come from the Managers. Basically your exiled pain/trauma causes emotional distress, which in turn goads the Firefighters into various self-destructive acts and the Managers into various repressive acts. And around and around you go, whirling through the dysfunctional cycles of life, caused by the core Self not being the one in charge."

"I fell down the stairs," D.D. said.

"Yes."

"I don't get what that has to do with Exiles and Firefighters and Managers. Oh, and my true Self."

"The fall is trauma. It caused pain but also created fear, powerlessness and impotence."

The detective hunched her shoulders slightly, wincing.

"Those emotions are your Exiles," I supplied gently. "They're screaming to be heard. The Firefighters in the system might respond with a compulsion to drink or abuse of prescription medication—"

"I'm not taking anything!"

"Or the Managers might rise to the forefront," I continued, "micromanaging the entire system by controlling and judging your response to the pain. Demanding, in fact, that you be tough enough."

D.D.'s eyes widened slightly. She stared at me a full minute. Then her gaze narrowed.

"The Exiles must be heard," she murmured. "That's why you want me to talk to my pain."

"Melvin. Generally speaking, it's easier to carry on a conversation when the other party has a name."

"And Melvin will say what? Hey, I'm hurt. I'm powerless. I hate stairs. And I'll say, okay, and then my pain will go away?"

"And then your pain might feel more manageable. The rest of the system can ease while your core Self rises to the front. For the record, there have been numerous studies on physical pain. One of the most interesting findings: Everyone has pain, but only some people are bothered by it. Meaning, colloquially speaking, attitude is everything."

"I think," the detective said slowly, "that's the biggest bunch of BS I've ever heard."

"And yet, here we are. One session down, two more to go."

D.D. gave her awkward half shrug, rose slowly to standing. "Fucking Melvin," she murmured under her breath. Then, "I kinda like cursing him."

"Detective," I asked as she started for the door, "given that we have only two more appointments, what goal would be most valuable to you? What do you want most right now so that we can pursue it?"

"I want to remember," she said immediately.

"Remember . . . ?"

"The fall." She looked at me quizzically. "I have physician-patient privilege, right?"

"Of course."

"My injury—I fell down the stairs at a crime scene. Discharged my weapon. Except I don't remember why I was there, or who I was firing at."

"Interesting. Concussion from the fall?"

"Possibly. Which according to the docs can cause memory loss."

"What's the last thing you do remember?"

She fell silent for so long, I thought she hadn't heard my question. Then, "The scent of blood," she whispered. "The sensation of falling. Down will come baby, cradle and all."

"Detective Warren?"

"Yes."

"In the middle of the night, when you're done cursing out Melvin, I want you to ask him a question. I want you to ask him why he doesn't want to remember."

"Seriously?"

"Seriously. Then I want you to tell him it's okay. You're safe, and you can handle it now."

"The memory of what happened?"

"Yes. Then prepare yourself, Detective Warren. Melvin may have a very good reason for wanting you to forget."

Chapter 4

M Y PAIN IS NAMED MELVIN."

"Better than Wilson," D.D.'s husband, Alex Wilson, observed. "Or, say, Horgan." Deputy Superintendent of Homicide Cal Horgan was D.D.'s boss.

"Please, you two are minor pains in the ass, while Melvin is a major pain in the neck."

D.D. continued walking toward her husband, who already stood on the front porch of the modest redbrick town house. It was dusk. Sun sinking, evening air sharp with early winter bite. She'd parked three blocks back. Maybe a local, arriving home from a day's work. Or an injured detective, who just happened to be in the neighborhood of a recent homicide, out for an evening stroll.

She shouldn't be here. Had no right to be here, in fact.

And yet, leaving her new doctor's office, she'd known the most recent murder scene was exactly where she'd go. As she'd eased herself into the driver's seat, carefully reached across her body for the strap Alex had jury-rigged to the inside of the driver's door, then used the strap to awkwardly pull the door shut without overjostling her left arm. The process was slow, uncomfortable, laborious.

Meaning she'd had plenty of time to change her mind.

Putting the key in the ignition. Shifting the vehicle from park into reverse.

Suddenly experiencing a strong sense of déjà vu. That she'd done this before. Told herself to go home, while heading toward a crime scene instead.

Of course. She'd repeated this pattern most of her adult life.

The only difference was that this time, her husband was already standing before the murdered woman's home, and he didn't appear surprised to see his wife approach.

"Doctor's appointment okay?" Alex asked, lifting the bright-yellow tape so she could pass beneath it, onto the covered porch.

"I'm supposed to talk to my pain. What the hell do you think?"

"Does your pain speak back?"

"Apparently, that's the nature of pain."

"Interesting," he said.

"Bullshit," she declared.

She came to a halt beside him. Alex's gaze was as calm as always, his face inscrutable. She felt her own heart race unsteadily, her breathing shallow. The pain, she told herself. Her own physical healing that depleted so much energy, even climbing up three damn steps required massive effort.

"They call you out?" she asked finally. "Require your expertise?" Alex spent most of his time teaching crime scene analysis at the police academy. He also served as a private consultant. And on occasion, to keep his skills current, he liked to work in the field, which was how they had met, so many years ago. At another townhome, not unlike this one, except there, it had appeared that a man had killed his entire family before turning the gun on himself.

D.D. still remembered walking that scene, following the trails of blood as Alex recited the story he saw written in each pool and spatter, of a wife, spinal column brutally severed from behind, an athletic teenage son, ambushed with a single thrust of a blade between the ribs, then the two younger kids, making their last stand in a back bedroom. The one who never made it out of that room. And the unluckier one who did.

"I knew you would come," Alex said simply.

"Gonna wave me off? Put me back in my car where I belong?"

Her husband merely smiled. He reached out and tucked an errant blond curl behind her ear. "Might as well tell the wind not to blow. Come on, D.D. As it turns out, Boston PD would like some help on this one. As long as I'm here, why don't we both take a tour?"

"This is why I didn't name my pain Wilson," she told him honestly.

Alex's expression, however, had already turned somber. "Oh, I wouldn't thank me just yet."

Stepping into the shadowed foyer, D.D. was struck first by the smell. Which set off another bout of déjà vu. She could picture herself entering Christine Ryan's apartment, inhaling this same pungent scent, and knowing, before ever laying eyes on the body, that this would be a bad one. Then, that first, shuddering moment when she realized she was staring down at the remains of a young woman, skin peeled in long, curling ribbons and mounded next to her body.

Alex was studying her. Not the floor, the walls or the rising staircase, all valid elements for a criminalist's analysis. He stared at her, and that, as much as anything, forced her to pull it together.

She took a deep breath, through her mouth this time, and got her game face on.

Alex pointed to a bin next to the wall. It contained shoe booties and hairnets for all attending investigators, an extra precaution generally taken when a crime scene was deemed especially involved, or the evidence particularly vulnerable.

Different protocol from the first murder victim, then. That scene had been horrific but mostly contained to the victim's blood-soaked mattress. This one . . .

D.D. pulled the blue booties over her low-heeled boots. The booties were large and elastic, not too hard to manage with one hand. The hair covering proved more challenging. She couldn't figure out how to pull it into place, while simultaneously gathering up her wayward curls. Alex had to help, his fingers skimming along her hairline, corralling her blond ringlets and tucking them in. She held still, letting him work his magic, as his breath whispered across her cheek. Outside of him assisting her in the shower, it was the most they'd touched each other in weeks.

"Look," Alex murmured, and pointed to the wall adjacent to the staircase.

She followed his finger and immediately spotted it, just above the lowest riser, a dark smudge against the lighter paint. The first smear of blood.

"And again." He indicated a spot on the floor now, six inches from her left foot. In the dimming light, it was hard to see, but this mark was larger, more distinct.

D.D. dropped down for closer examination, while Alex snapped on his high-intensity light. He illuminated the mark, and D.D. couldn't help the small gasp that escaped.

"Paw print."

"Victim owned a small dog named Lily. A fluffy small dog, by the look of the stair riser."

Upon closer inspection, D.D. saw what he meant. The bloodstain there had formed a distinct smear pattern, featuring dozens of thin red lines, such as what happened when blood-soaked hair brushed along a floor or slid down a wall.

"Straight hair, not curly," D.D. murmured. "But yes, Lily is one fluffy dog."

The reason behind the booties, D.D. realized now. Because the dog, however innocently, had already contaminated the scene, and the detectives couldn't afford any more distractions.

Alex headed straight for the staircase, but D.D. stopped him. She wanted another minute to get her bearings, form an initial impression of this house and the woman who'd lived here.

A modest foyer, she noted now, with a floral cushion–topped bench surrounded above and below with a clutter of shoes. She saw boots, clogs and several pairs of heels. Practical shoes, in neutral tones of brown and black with modest heels. All women's, size eight.

From the foyer, the space opened up to a small sitting room, with a slightly threadbare, overstuffed sage green sofa and matching ottoman. A fleecy throw blanket was piled on one corner of the love seat, while a dog blanket covered the ottoman. Piles of clothes decorated what was probably the extra chair—the to-be-folded pile?—while the sofa faced a medium-size flat-screen TV.

From the family room, D.D. passed into a vintage-1970s kitchen, complete with aging gold linoleum and an ancient olive-green oven. In contrast to the well-used sitting room and foyer, this space was nearly sterile. One Keurig coffeemaker, one tiny microwave on the counter. A single plate, fork, knife and glass in the sink. Definitely the kind of kitchen used by people partial to takeout. D.D. knew because before she'd married Alex, her kitchen had appeared almost exactly like this.

She and Alex returned to the foyer. "I'm going to guess nurse," she mused out loud. "Makes a decent living, enough to purchase the condo, but not enough to update the cabinets or splurge on Pottery Barn. Spends most of her job on her feet, hence the sensible shoes. Single, or just beginning a relationship. But if so, they go to his place, as this is her domain and she's not ready to share it yet."

Alex arched a brow. "Close. Regina Barnes. Forty-two years old, recently divorced occupational therapist who worked at a nearby senior-care facility. Don't know about any new boyfriends, but no witnesses and no sign of forced entry."

"Maybe she met someone recently. Or an online relationship. She let him in."

Alex didn't say anything. The tech geeks would mine the victim's computer and other devices for records of online activities. Alex's domain was the bloody paw prints and the intermittent pattern of smears leading up the stairs.

"No sign of forced entry at Christine Ryan's house," D.D. considered. "And her friends swore they would've known if there was a new guy, virtual or otherwise. Neighbors hear anything?"

"No."

She reached over, knocked on the internal wall experimentally. Generally speaking, town houses in this kind of neighborhood weren't known for their solid soundproofing. A life-or-death struggle, screaming, shouldn't have gone completely unnoticed.

"Neighborhood cameras, home security system?"

"Nada."

"Time of death?"

"Between midnight and two."

"Maybe he ambushes his victims while they're asleep. That's why there's no sign of a struggle."

"But how does he get in?"

"Picks the lock?" D.D. turned around, inspected the front door's locking mechanism. As befitting a single woman living in a city, Regina had taken home security seriously. D.D. noted a steel bolt lock in relatively new condition. Christine Ryan, the first victim, had been equally diligent.

Alex waited quietly as she arrived at the answer he already knew.

"Could be done," D.D. murmured. "But not easily."

"Probably not."

"But if she let him in . . . one plate, one cup in the kitchen sink. It wasn't social. Say, inviting a special friend over for a nightcap. Any evidence recovered from the family room or kitchen? Footprint, hair and fiber?"

"No footprints. Still processing hair and fiber."

She nodded, looking down at the paw print on the floor, as Alex leaned once more toward the stairs.

She was stalling. Her feet remaining in place versus taking that overdue step forward, up the stairs, into the master bedroom, arriving at the heart of the matter. Was she dreading the scene she would find in the bedroom so much? Or was it worse than that? Was she dreading the stairs?

Alex finally did the honors. He climbed the first few risers. D.D. had no choice but to follow.

With his high-intensity beam, Alex illuminated more blood evidence along the way. Paw prints, some full, some partial, as the small dog had gone up and down the stairs. Then, at the top of the stairs, a significantly larger streak, as if someone had found a large pool of blood and tried to mop it up.

"We'll have to conduct some experiments to see if we can reproduce the pattern," Alex was saying, "but I believe this smear pattern is from the dog as well. She was agitated, spending time next to the body, then running back and forth in the hallway. Here, at the top of the stairs, I think she lay down for a while. Maybe waiting for help to arrive."

D.D. was having a hard time breathing again. The climb up the stairs, she told herself. But she had a death grip on the right handrail and her chest felt unnaturally tight. As if a giant had reached inside her body and was now squeezing her lungs with his meaty fist.

She bent over slightly. Found herself panting.

Then, as white dots began appearing in front of her eyes . . .

Rockabye, baby, on the treetop . . .

"Hold my hand. Steady. Now breathe. Inhale through your mouth, one, two, three, four, five. Exhale through your nose. One . . . two . . . three . . . four . . . five.

"Easy, sweetheart. Easy."

Another minute. Maybe two, three, ten. She was embarrassed to realize her whole body was shaking uncontrollably. And she was sweating. She could feel the beads of perspiration dotting her brow, rolling down her cheeks. For an instant, she was seized by the overwhelming compulsion to bolt back down the stairs and race out the door. She'd flee the scene. Run away and never look back.

Alex's fingers, enmeshed in her own.

"You don't have to do this," he said quietly. "Anytime you want, D.D., we can walk away. I'll drive you home."

That did it. His voice was so patient, so understanding, she had no choice but to grit her teeth and steel her spine. She did not want to be this person. This weak, trembling woman who required her husband's support just to climb the damn stairs.

She inhaled, counting to five. Then exhaled. Then got her head up.

"I'm sorry," she said shortly, looking at anything but Alex's face. "Clearly, time to boost the cardio."

"D.D."

"All this lying around. Doesn't do a body good."

"D.D."

"Maybe instead of naming my pain, I should force it to run laps instead. That'd teach it."

"Stop."

"What?"

"Don't lie to me. If you need to lie to yourself, fair enough. But don't lie to me. This is the first time back at a crime scene since your accident. That you're suffering some kind of panic attack—"

"I don't panic!"

"Some kind of emotional response isn't unwarranted. You're not carved out of stone, sweetheart." Alex's voice grew gentle. "You're a real person. And real people feel fear and pain and uncertainty. It doesn't make you weak. It just means you're human."

"I don't panic," she muttered, still looking away. Then, because she simply had to know: "Is the dog okay?"

"Staying at the neighbor's, which I gather was already like a second home to her."

"She was covered in blood. The dog, right? Only way a smear this big . . . The dog's legs, stomach, would have to be covered in blood. From the mattress. From lying down next to her owner and the mounds and mounds of flayed skin . . ."

"We can go home, D.D., anytime you'd like."

"When the wind blows," she murmured.

"What's that?"

She merely smiled, then got her head up and her shoulders back. "And down will come baby, cradle and all."

She continued down the hall.

THEY HAD LEFT THE SCENE relatively intact. The body was gone, of course. But the blood-soaked mattress, bottle of champagne, fur-lined handcuffs, remained. And the bloody sheet, now tacked up on a bare wall. D.D. had witnessed the technique before, bedding, clothes, even entire sections of flooring, suspended at the original crime scene to enable better spatter analysis. Even then, she had to steel herself as Alex flipped on the overhead light, chasing away the thickening shadows and revealing the full bloody glory.

"I asked them to leave as much of the initial scene as possible," Alex said quietly. "Allow me the opportunity to study it in situ."

D.D. nodded. Her left shoulder had started a deep, throbbing ache.

"Same bottle of champagne," she observed, looking at anything but the suspended sheet.

"Phil believes the killer brings everything with him—the champagne, handcuffs, rose."

"Props for his play."

"He wants it to be just so," Alex said. "Not just any bottle of wine, or any kind of flower. But these specific items."

"Ritualized." She'd thought this before. They were looking at a killer's highly developed fantasy. Now other thoughts returned to her, like shadows of a dream. "ViCAP?" she asked, referring to the Violent Criminal Apprehension Program, which included a searchable database filled with pertinent details from criminal cases all around the country. Investigators could use it to match a crime in their jurisdiction with similar deeds from other localities.

"I'm sure they're checking it."

"He makes it appear romantic," she murmured. "Flowers, champagne, lovers' toys. But it's about control. Him, in control of everything."

Alex didn't say anything. He twisted behind them and pointed the tight beam of his high-intensity light back toward the hallway. The bright white beam immediately illuminated dozens of stains, mostly bloody paw prints from the dog pacing back and forth. Then he turned his beam onto the floor in the master bedroom and D.D. was immediately captivated by the contrast. A series of paw prints led from the queen-size bed to the door; then a thinner smear appeared on the floor near the right-side nightstand, where there had been blood, but the killer had made an attempt to wipe it up.

Otherwise . . . nothing.

Here, in the room that had served as center stage for one of the most gruesome homicides D.D. had ever seen, there was almost no blood evidence. Not on the floors. Not on the walls.

"But . . . but . . . ," D.D. found herself sputtering. Then, more firmly: "Not possible. No way you can fillet a human being without being positively coated in blood yourself. And no way the killer could then move around this room, let alone exit the house, without leaving an obvious trail. Even if he cleaned up after himself with a bleach-soaked mop, you can't get it all. It's the whole magic of your job. Even when you can no longer see blood with the human eye, it lingers, just waiting for the right high-intensity beams or proper chemical solution to tell its tale. This"—she waved her hand toward the relatively blood-free expanse of hardwood floor—"I'm seeing it, but I'm not believing it."

"As I mentioned, the Boston PD wouldn't mind some help with this one." Alex walked deeper into the room, his beam sweeping methodically right, left, right. "Shall we start with the bedsheet? I believe it serves as the beginning of the story."

She nodded once. Responding to his hand signal, she obediently killed the overhead lights. In the near gloom, it was easier to focus on Alex's high-intensity light and the way it cast a single fitted sheet into a terrible inkblot of dark, deadly stains.

Blood patterns, D.D. had learned by now, varied depending on the velocity of the blow and the porosity of the surface area. Bedding, such as blankets and mattresses, was obviously very soft and porous, meaning the blood spatter soaked straight in versus ricocheting or forming a starburst pattern on impact. In fact, the white sheet now bore a single, very long, almost cylinder-shaped bloody print, broken in two places by bars of white. She and Alex both stepped closer, inspecting the outer edges of the print.

"I don't see any signs of fine mist," D.D. murmured, "such as blowback from high-velocity gunfire."

"Victim wasn't shot. Blood patterns indicate a low-velocity impact."

Which was consistent with most stabbings, D.D. knew. She still frowned. "But there's no spatter at all, not even random drippings from the handle of the knife or edge of the blade. How do you explain that?"

"Killer's not stabbing. Cause of death is unknown. But given the lack of defensive wounds, arterial spray and spatter, the victim was dead before the killer began removing her skin. I'm just a criminalist, not a behavioralist, but it would appear the crime is about control, not about pain and suffering. What we're seeing here is purely the result of postmortem work."

It should've been a reassuring thought. That the victim was already dead before the first slip of the cold blade beneath the surface of her skin . . . And yet, D.D. found herself almost slightly more horrified. A sexual-sadist predator with an overwhelming compulsion to inflict pain and suffering was something she could almost understand. But this . . . a killer who skinned his victims for sport?

"The voids?" she whispered now, pointing to twin patterns of clean white sheet amid the large cylinder of blood.

Alex got out a pencil. With his left hand, he started pointing and explaining. "Remember, the postmortem mutilation is mostly to the torso and the upper thighs. If you look at the bloodstain, you can see feathering at the top, and imprints here, which I believe are from the victim's shoulder blades pressing into the sheet and limiting the absorption of blood. Orienting ourselves, then, here is the head, the shoulders, the torso, the legs. Given that . . ."

"The voids are on either side of the victim's thighs."

"From the lower part of the killer's legs, I presume. Essentially, he was straddling her body, the front part of his shins pressing against the mattress on either side of her thighs, which shielded that part of the sheet from blood."

"He incapacitates his victim," D.D. murmured, trying to form a sequence of events in her mind. "Then, most likely, he sets the scene. The champagne, handcuffs, single rose. He'd want to get everything out before things get too . . . messy."

Alex turned, sweeping his high-intensity beam across the night-stand where the champagne bottle and other props awaited. The light didn't expose a single drop of blood.

"Fair assumption," he said.

"Next . . . he would have to strip the victim. Expose her skin."

Light beam to the left-hand side of the bed, where D.D. now saw a puddle of dark clothes.

"Black sweats, oversize Red Sox T-shirt, underwear," Alex reported.

"Sounds like suitable PJs for a single woman. He cast them aside." Another nod.

"Then"—she turned toward the bed—"he climbs aboard, positions himself astride the victim's naked body, and begins to . . . skin her. Why?"

Alex shrugged. "Part of the ritual? Maybe the killer is really some kind of necrophiliac, and it's these moments with the body that are most fulfilling for him. The strips of skin are thin, and based on the ME's study of the first victim, they're precise, methodical. In his estimation, the killer spent at least an hour on the filleting process, if not two or three."

"Semen?" D.D. asked. "Signs of sexual assault?"

"First victim, no. Second victim, results still pending."

"I don't get it. He gains access, incapacitates his victims. Drugs them?"

"Tox screen also pending."

"Then . . . starts in with the knife. For at least an hour?"

"With some skill," Alex provided. "ME suggests either a hunter or maybe even a butcher. But based on the smooth, even strokes, our killer has some experience."

"Kind of blade?"

"Most likely something small and razor-sharp, perhaps even designed especially for the job. Here's the other point of consideration. Often in these kinds of crimes, the killer will eventually set down his weapon. You know, resting for a moment, readjusting his grip, or even laying down the knife while getting on and off the bed. A reflexive movement, not even thought about, but an act that leaves a bloody imprint of the blade behind as further evidence. In a case where a killer spends this much time with a body at a scene this bloody, it's the kind of evidence you'd almost expect. Except . . ."

"He didn't do it."

"Or he was aware enough, controlled enough, to rest it in the middle of another bloodstain, the kind of place where he thought it wouldn't leave a pattern."

D.D. glanced at her husband. "You just said he *thought* it wouldn't leave a pattern . . . ?"

Alex smiled faintly. He had returned to the bloody sheet hanging on the wall and was hitting it up close and personal with the beam from his flashlight. "In this kind of attack, where the victim is bleeding out from multiple wounds over an extended period of time—"

"That's one way of putting it."

"You get blood-on-blood patterns. Blood, as it starts to dry, thickens, the edges turning yellow as the plasma separates. The old blood starts to form a surface for the new blood to drip upon."

She could almost picture this. "Meaning if the killer set down a knife covered in fresh blood upon an area of drying blood, it could leave an imprint on the surface of the old blood."

"Precisely."

"And in this case . . ."

Alex, his face a mere two inches from the stiff, red-encrusted surface: "I think . . . I can see an outline. Faint, but there. I would guess a filleting knife, but to be fair, it's hard to know sometimes if you're seeing what you *want* to see or what's really there. We can fine-tune this, however, enhance the contrast using some chemicals back at the lab. Certainly it's worth pursuing."

"Certainly," she agreed.

He frowned one more time, peering intently. For the sake of argument, D.D. did the same, but the nuance of a stain within a stain was lost on her. Mostly, she was aware of the overwhelming stench of blood. So much. This sheet. This mattress.

And yet, as she turned around, not in the rest of the room.

Alex followed her lead, once more sweeping the walls and floors with the high-intensity beam, as they considered the final step of the murderer's process.

"Cleanup," D.D. muttered.

"Definitely," Alex concurred. "He cleaned up."

He worked the beam in slow, rhythmic patterns around the perimeter of the queen-size bed, illuminating paw prints, another larger smear stain near the bedroom door that matched the one down the hall. Lily the dog, once more lying down.

"The dog didn't bark?" D.D. asked.

"Not that anyone heard."

"And yet, clearly the dog was distressed." She indicated all the paw prints, back and forth and back.

"Distressed, but maybe more confused? Remember, as strange as it sounds, this wasn't a violent attack. At least we have no evidence of a killer breaking into the home and overpowering the victim. Whatever happened, it was . . . subdued. Even the postmortem mutilation. He would've sat upon the body. No screaming, no struggling, no outward signs of the victim's distress."

D.D. shuddered. She couldn't help herself. "He had a plan," she stated out loud, refocusing. "He enacted the plan. And then . . ."

"And then he tidied up after himself," Alex said, then frowned. "Which is the part I don't understand. Even if it's not a chaotic scene—no running, no chasing, no restraining—the amount of blood, seeping from the victim's body, soaking into the mattress . . . The killer's hands, forearms, would be covered in it. Not to mention his legs from sitting astride the body, his feet . . . This floor should be a case study of blood evidence. If not covered in bloody footprints, spatter, etcetera, then, at the very least, covered in smear patterns from him attempting to wipe up all of the above. So why isn't it?"

D.D. saw Alex's point. She could count more than a dozen paw prints from the dog tracking back and forth across the floor. And that was it.

"He cleans up in the bathroom afterward?" D.D. considered. "Maybe showers? I'm sure Phil had the team swab the shower and sink drains for bodily fluids."

"I'm sure Phil did. But how did the killer get there? Levitation?" Alex swept his beam from the bed to the doorway of the master bath. The floorboards didn't offer up one glimpse of stain. He lit up the brass doorknob as well. Equally clean of bodily fluids. Then, just to be thorough, he swept the high-intensity light beam across the cracked linoleum floor, tired white bathtub, pedestal sink, toilet. Nothing, nothing, nothing.

"Some kind of special cleaner?" D.D. thought next. "He scoured the space with a toothbrush and bleach, got every square inch. . . ."

"Possible, but probable?" Alex's expression remained dubious. As he had stated, blood was nearly impossible to remove 100 percent. Hence, criminalists could build entire careers using blood evidence to catch savvy killers who'd bleached walls but forgotten the window latch, or loofahed off a layer of their own skin but forgot about the wind-up dial of their watch. Killers could clean only what they could see. While thanks to tools such as high-intensity lights and chemicals such as luminol, a savvy investigator essentially approached every scene with X-ray vision.

D.D. was struck by a fresh thought. "Let's consider this from another angle. We have a killer who not only entered undetected but also left that way. Except on the way out, he should've appeared disheveled, even bloody from all the knife work. So how did he disguise all that?"

Alex shrugged. "Most obvious solution would be for him to shower after the killing, as you suggested. He washed off all traces of blood, changed into fresh clothes, then walked out the front door, just another guy in the neighborhood."

"Except, as you said, we'd see traces of blood leading from the bed to the bathroom, not to mention on the bathroom floor, shower, sink. Meaning . . . What if he was naked? What if, after subduing his victim . . . before getting started with the main event, the killer removed his own clothes?"

"Prudent," Alex said. "Blood is easier to remove from skin than clothes."

"Other thing I'm noticing is that there don't seem to be any towels missing from the victim's bathroom. There's a hand towel in the hand towel ring, and two bath towels on the rack. So if he showered here, what did he use to dry off?"

Alex nodded shortly, considering.

"Maybe," D.D. continued, "as long as the killer is bringing in props for the murder, he's also providing his own cleanup kit. Packed a couple of towels, maybe even his own bath mat, for the floor next to the bed. See this mark here?" She gestured to the lone smear pattern, near the right-side nightstand. "He lays down the bath mat, strips off his clothes, then climbs on the bed to do what he's going to do. Afterward, he steps from the bed back onto the bath mat, wipes himself down with his towel, replaces his clean clothes, socks, shoes. Then it's a simple matter of rolling up the mat, bloody towel, knife, etcetera, tucked safely inside. Sticks everything back in his duffel bag and he's good to go. Certainly that would explain the lack of blood evidence in the rest of the house, including the bathroom."

"Not just prudent," Alex amended. "Clever."

"Experienced," D.D. emphasized. "Isn't that what the ME said? This guy knows what he's doing. And he's controlled. From the beginning through the middle to the end. We're not going to find any magic answers here."

Alex turned on a bedside lamp, snapped off his flashlight. "I wouldn't be so sure about that. Removing his clothes may limit his risk of blood-transfer evidence, but it increased the killer's chances of leaving behind hair, fiber, DNA."

"Fair enough."

"And there's still the small matter of he has to incapacitate his victims somehow. Once the ME figures that out, we'll have something more to pursue."

They turned away from the bed, toward the hallway, the descending flight of stairs.

"I don't want to be injured anymore," D.D. heard herself say, gazing toward the staircase.

"I know."

"I don't want to feel this weak and useless. I want to be on the job. I want to be tracking this killer."

"Do you remember anything more?"

"You mean like why I tried to fly down a staircase? Or fired my gun three times into drywall?" She shook her head.

"You've helped tonight."

"Not officially. Officially, I'm a detective who returned to a crime scene all alone and may or may not have discharged my weapon without probable cause. As things stand right now, I'm a liability for the department, and we both know even if my left arm miraculously heals overnight, they're not going to simply return my badge. I'm an unanswered question, and cops hate that."

"You are an unanswered question," Alex agreed, walking over to her.

"Gee, thanks."

He regarded her thoughtfully. "But you know what? You're something more."

"A brilliant detective? Perfect wife? Loving mother? It's okay; you can lay it on thick. Melvin's starting to really piss me off, and I could use some sickeningly sweet platitudes right now."

"Actually, I was thinking more along the lines of how detectives answer questions. Or really, how I answer questions."

She stared at him. "You're a criminalist."

"Exactly. I study crime scenes. And you, D.D., your shoulder, your arm, your injuries, you are a crime scene. Better yet, you're the one scene our killer didn't control."

Chapter 5

PAIN IS . . .

A conversation. My adoptive father started it when I was twelve, seeking to help me understand all the various forms and functions of both physical and emotional discomfort. Pain is . . . watching our housekeeper break a glass, then use tweezers to remove a shard from the meat of her thumb, her breath hissing sharply.

Pain is . . . forgetting how to spell *vertebrae* on a test, though I had studied it just the night before. Thus, I scored ninety, which my father said was okay, but which we both knew wasn't excellent.

Pain is . . . my father not making it to the state science fair. Another case, a pressing paper, work forever demanding. But assuring me that he loved me and was sorry, while I studied him closely and attempted to understand those sentiments as well. Regret. Remorse. Repentance. Emotions that were by definition corollaries of the pain process.

Pain is . . . my best friend reciting every detail of her first kiss. Watching her face glow and hearing her voice giggle and wondering if I would ever feel the same. My father had found two case studies of sisters with congenital insensitivity to pain who'd married and had children. In theory, the inability to feel pain did not preclude the possibility of falling in love, of being loved back. It didn't stop the genetically abnormal from hoping to grow into normalcy.

It didn't keep you from wanting a family.

My adoptive father loved me. Not right away. He wasn't the type. His was a measured, controlled approach to life. Understanding the hard realities facing a foster child, he made the necessary investment in my future care by opening his large home and considerable financial resources. Most likely, he assumed proper staffing would meet my everyday needs, while he continued to study my condition and write up stunningly dry academic reports.

He hadn't anticipated my nightmares, however, or foreseen that a little girl who couldn't feel pain was still perfectly capable of dreaming of it, night after night. In the beginning, he puzzled over this phenomenon, asking me endless questions. What did I see? What did I hear? What did I feel?

I couldn't answer. Only that I did fear. The night. The dark. The sound of canned laugh tracks. Dolls. Scissors. Nylons. Pencils. Once, I spotted a shovel leaning against the gardening shed; I ran screaming for my closet and wouldn't come out for hours.

Thunder, lightning, hard rain. Black cats. Blue quilts. Some of my fears were ordinary enough in the lexicon of childhood. Others were completely bewildering.

My adoptive father consulted with a child therapist. Under her advice, he asked me to draw pictures of my nightmares. But I couldn't. My artistic vision was limited to a black pool, bisected by a faint line of yellow.

Later, I overheard the therapist saying to my father, "Probably all she could see, shut up in the closet like that. But understand even an infant is capable of recognizing and responding to terror. And given what was going on in that house, the things her father was doing . . ."

"But how would she *know*?" my father pressed. "And I don't mean because she was just an infant at the time. But if you can't feel pain, then how do you know what to fear? Isn't the root of most of our fears pain itself?"

The therapist had no answers, and neither did I.

When I was fourteen, I stopped waiting for my nightmares to

magically reveal themselves and started researching my family instead. I read about the various exploits of my birth father, Harry Day, under headings such as "Beverly House of Horrors," and "Crazed Carpenter's Killing Rampage." Turns out, not only did my birth father murder eight prostitutes, but he buried them beneath his private workshop as well as our family room floor. The police theorized some of the women had been kept alive for days, maybe even weeks, while he tortured them.

For a while, I was obsessed with uncovering every piece of information I could find about Harry Day. And not just because my past was horrifying and shocking, but also because it was so . . . alien. I would gaze at pictures of the house, a rusted-out bike propped against the front porch, and I would feel . . . nothing.

Even staring at the photo of my own father, I couldn't summon the tiniest flicker of recognition. I didn't see my eyes or my sister's nose. I didn't picture large calloused hands or hear a faint, deep chuckle. Harry Day, 338 Bloomfield Street. It was like staring at scenes from a movie set. All real, but all make-believe.

Of course, I was only eleven months old when the police discovered Harry's homicidal hobby and rushed our house. Harry was found dead in the bathtub, wrists slit, while my mother was taken away to a mental hospital. She died, alone and still restrained for her own safety, while my sister and I became official wards of the state.

Some days, when not staring at Harry's grinning face, I would study my mother instead. Not many photos of her existed. High school dropout, I learned. Ran away from her own family, who lived somewhere in the Midwest. She made her way to Boston, where she worked as a waitress in a diner. Then she hooked up with Harry, and her fate was sealed.

The only pictures I could find were police photos of her standing in the background while detectives ripped up the floorboards of her home. A gaunt-looking woman with washed-out features, unkempt long brown hair and an already broken posture.

I didn't see my eyes or my sister's nose when I looked at her, either. I saw merely a ghost, a woman who was lost way before outside help arrived.

Eventually, my nightmares faded. I worried less about the family that had gifted me with faulty DNA and worked harder to gain my adoptive father's praise. And in turn, my father began excusing the weekend staff, helping me himself with school projects and, in time, even sitting up with me the nights I couldn't sleep, offering the quiet reassurance of his solid, contemplative company.

He loved me. Despite his academic's heart, despite my flawed wiring, we became a family.

Then he died, and my nightmares returned with a vengeance.

First night, all alone after my father's funeral. Having consumed too much port. Finally closing my eyes . . .

And seeing the closet door suddenly swing open. Recalling the thin glow cast by a bare bulb across the tiny, cluttered bedroom. Seeing my toddler sister in the center of the room, clutching a threadbare brown teddy, as my father's gaze cast from her to me to her.

Hearing my mother say, "Please, Harry, not the baby," before I was plunged once more into the gloom.

Pain is not what you see and not what you feel. Pain is what you can only hear, alone in the dark.

I WOKE FOR THE FIRST TIME shortly after eleven. I'd been asleep for approximately ten minutes, and yet my heart was pounding uncontrollably, my face covered in sweat. I stared at the tray ceiling of my bedroom. Practiced the deep-breathing exercises I'd been taught so many years ago.

The noise machine in the corner of my bedroom. I'd forgotten to turn it on. Of course.

I got out of bed, hit the large button of the Brookstone unit and was rewarded with the soothing sound of crashing ocean waves and crying seagulls. Back to bed. I assumed the position, on my back, lying coffin straight, arms by my sides. I closed my eyes, focused on the sound of some exotic, salty shore.

Eight minutes, to judge by the glowing red numbers of my bedside clock. Then I bolted upright, fisting the sheets while swallowing the scream and staring intently into the shadows of my expansive bedroom. Three night-lights. Oval LED plug-ins that offered pools of soft, green glow. I counted the lights five times, waiting for my heart to decelerate, my breathing to slow. Then I gave up and snapped on my bedside light.

I have a beautiful master bedroom. Expensive. Carpeted in the softest wool. Designed using only the richest silks, including custom bedding and hand-stitched window dressings, all fashioned in shades of soft blue, rich cream and sage green.

A soothing oasis of look and feel. A reminder of my adoptive father's generosity and my own continued success.

But tonight, it wouldn't work for me. And I knew by eleven thirty what I would do next.

Because even though I was the product of some of the finest intellectual upbringing, both a person and a case study, a doctor and a patient, I was still a member of the human race. And humanity is a messy business, where knowing what is right doesn't necessarily preclude you from doing what is wrong.

I showered. Donned a tight black pencil skirt, knee-high black leather boots and, without even thinking about it, my sister's preferred fuchsia top. I made my face up, left my brown hair down and added a simple gold band to my left ring finger. I'd learned years ago that was the key to success; to appear as married as they were. It reduced their fear of future entanglements while adding to their sense of mutual culpability. You were no better than them, hence a desirable target.

Ten minutes till midnight. I grabbed the plastic kit I kept hidden away in the back of the lower bathroom drawer. Tucked it in my gray bag. Then I was out the door, driving toward Boston's Logan Airport and my destination of choice, the Hyatt Boston Harbor.

AFTER MIDNIGHT ON A MONDAY NIGHT, most bars, even in a major city, were quieting down. But airport hotels exist in a timeless vacuum. People getting up, people going to bed, on so many different schedules, the actual hour ceases to have meaning. You can always find people drinking at an airport hotel's bar.

I took a table near the windows overlooking the Hyatt's fabled view of Boston's skyline. Dark harbor waters below, glittering city lights above. I ordered a Cosmopolitan, alcoholically aggressive, while still being appropriately feminine. Then I went to work.

I counted eight other occupants in the bar. One couple, six individuals. Of the individuals, two were older gentlemen, one clearly European, lost deep in his single malt, the other Asian. I discounted them as a reflection of my own lack of interest, not necessarily theirs.

Two guys at the end of the bar held my attention the longest. Both in blue suits. Clean-cut, short dark hair. Midwestern, I judged. On the younger side of middle-aged. The one to the right was larger, the dominant male, clearly at ease with himself and his surroundings. Sales would be my guess. The kind of man accustomed to life on the road, outgoing and energetic enough not to mind a new city every day, savvy enough to have developed a system for maximizing travel's upside while minimizing its inconveniences.

I sipped my fruity martini, feeling the hard rim of the glass with my teeth, my tongue. Letting my gaze find his back, linger.

Fifteen minutes later he appeared tableside, cheeks flushed, eyes sparkling. Alcohol? Anticipation? Did it matter?

I watched his gaze go to my left hand, note the ring that was a match for his own. Two consenting adults, same short-term needs, identical long-term constraints. His smile grew. He offered me a drink. I replied with an invitation to the vacant chair across from me.

He returned to the bar, ostensibly to order the drinks, while most likely informing his travel companion not to wait up. The traveling companion grinned, made his exit.

Then Salesman was back, introducing himself as Neil, admiring my sweater—nice color!—and we were off. Questions for me, questions for him. All easily answered, most of it probably lies. But kindly meant and prettily spoken. Just going through the motions, a third Cosmo for me, a fourth, fifth, sixth? whiskey for him. Then that delicate moment, as I watched him lick his lower lip, contemplate his next move.

I didn't like to make it too easy for them. Didn't resort to fawning giggles or suggestive touches. I had my own standards. The man had to come to me. He had to work for it.

Then finally, as worthy of a professional salesman, he made the ask. Would I like to retire someplace quieter? Maybe continue our conversation more privately?

In answer, I picked up my purse, rose to standing. His smile growing, as he realized it honestly was happening, the strange woman in the bar was really saying yes. And by God she was as good-looking standing up as sitting down and please oh please oh please let her be wearing a black thong beneath that tight-fitting skirt . . .

I followed him to his room, never having to give away that I didn't have one of my own, because in this day and age rooms required photo ID and these were not the kinds of evenings I wanted connected back to me.

Once inside, it was all pretty straightforward. Nothing special, nothing kinky. I always marveled at this. All these men, straying beyond the bonds of marriage to engage in the same old sex acts. A set repertoire on their part? Or maybe they didn't require variety as much as they thought. Even with a new partner, they instinctively sought out the routine they were most comfortable with.

My one request: Leave the lights on.

He liked that. Most of them did. Men are visual, after all.

I let him remove my tall leather boots. Unpeel my tight skirt to find the black lace thong. Then my fingers worked the clasp of his slacks, the buttons of his shirt. Clothes on the floor, two bodies on the bed, condom on the nightstand. I smelled his aftershave, probably applied right before he journeyed downstairs in search of conquest. I heard his guttural words of praise as his hands ran down my naked body.

I sighed, let myself go. The pressure of his fingers gripping my hips. The roughness of his whiskers against my nipples. The first, penetrating feel of him thrusting into my body. The sensations I could feel. A physical act I could register.

Then that suspended moment, his head arched back, teeth gritting, arms trembling . . .

I opened my eyes. I always did. I had to know, if even for an instant, that this person's ecstasy had something to do with me.

I touched his cheek. I buried my fingers in his thick brown hair. And I permitted him to see, for this second when he was aware of nothing, just how much this fleeting moment of contact meant to someone like me.

A woman who controlled all, having spent her entire life being told it would be physically dangerous to trust in what she could feel. A child, still trying to unravel the mystery of pain and still absolutely, positively terrified of sounds in the dark.

Afterward, he collapsed. I reached over, snapped off the light.

"I have an early morning flight," I said, the only words that needed to be spoken.

Reassured, he dozed off while I lay next to him, stroking the muscular outline of his upper arm, concentrating on the ripples of his shoulders and triceps, as if mapping the planes of his body with my fingertips.

I counted off the minutes in my mind. After five had passed and his breathing dropped to a slower, heavier tone, dulled by whiskey, sated by sex, I made my move.

First order of business, snapping on the bathroom light. I grabbed my purse, then moved into the lit space, closing the door behind me. Not thinking anymore. What I was going to do next defied rational thought or well-adjusted reasoning.

What had I tried to explain to my new patient, Detective Warren, earlier in the day? Without balance, difference pieces of Self sought dominance. Meaning even the strongest Manager mind couldn't run the ship 24/7. Sooner or later, the weak, hurting Exiles were bound to break out and wreak havoc for the Firefighters to handle next.

By engaging in various acts of self-destruction. By creating drama for the sake of drama. By ensuring for at least a brief period of time, the rest of the world felt their pain.

Slim black plastic kit out of my purse. Easing it open. Removing the square packages of lidocaine-soaked wipes. Tearing open the pack, removing the sheet. Holding it in my right hand, while picking up the slender, stainless steel scalpel in my left.

Cracking open the bathroom door. Adjusting until the glowing strip of white light fell across my target's sleeping form like a thin spotlight. Pausing, then, when he remained snoring lightly, padding naked to his side of the bed.

First, the lidocaine wipe. With light, even strokes, applying the topical anesthetic down the length of the salesman's left shoulder, slowly but surely numbing the surface of the skin.

Setting down the wipe. Counting carefully to sixty in order to give the lidocaine enough time to do its work.

My fingers, running along the contours of his left shoulder, mapping the muscles once more in my mind.

Then, picking up the scalpel. Positioning the blade. A slight prick to test for physical response.

Then, when my salesman remained snoring blissfully unaware, telling myself this was what set me apart from my family. I was not like my sister. I was not like my father.

I was not driven by a need to inflict pain. I just . . . Sometimes . . .

No sound mind would do what I was about to do. And yet. And yet . . .

My right hand moved. Four quick strokes. Two long, two short. Incising a thin ribbon of skin, approximately three inches in length and not even a quarter of an inch wide. Then, using the blade of the scalpel, wicking it away from the flesh, until it landed warm and wet in the palm of my left hand.

Blood welling up on the surface of the salesman's numbed skin. I picked up my own black panties and held them against the wound till the bleeding slowed, then stopped.

Moving quickly now, back to the bathroom. Ribbon of skin placed in an empty glass vial. Sealed, then labeled. Used anesthetic wipe, scalpel, everything, tucked into the plastic case, then slid once more into my purse. Hands washed. Face and mouth rinsed.

Heart starting to pound, fingers shaking, as I struggled with each article of my clothing. Finally, skirt on, bra, top, boots. Dragging a hand through my mane of brown hair before sweeping up the loose strands on the floor and flushing them down the toilet. One last glance in the mirror. Seeing my own face and yet feeling like a total stranger, as if I'd stepped outside my own skin. My sister should be standing here. Or my father.

Not the one who looked like my mother. The supposed innocent.

I reached behind myself, snapped off the bathroom light.

I stood alone in the dark. And I wasn't afraid anymore, because the dark was now my friend. I'd joined forces with it. It had told me what it wanted me to do, and I'd relied on it for cover.

Traveling salesman Neil would wake up in the morning with a raging headache from too much alcohol, a more pleasant soreness in other parts of his body, and a dull pain in the back of his shoulder.

No doubt, when he went to shower, he'd try to inspect his back in the bathroom mirror. At which point he'd spy a red stripe down his left shoulder blade, slightly puckered at the edges. He'd puzzle over it. Wonder if he banged into something. Except the wound would appear more like a broad scratch, meaning maybe he snagged himself on something, a belt buckle, a sharp strap.

Eventually, he'd shrug, climb into the shower. The wound would most likely sting for a second; then that would be that. It would heal, leaving behind a faint white line, the source of which remained forever a mystery.

Because who'd ever consider that his bar hookup had removed a strip of his skin with a scalpel while he slept? And even now, she kept it in a glass vial, part of a special collection she couldn't explain but was compelled to keep.

My adoptive father had obsessed over my genetic inability to feel pain.

Maybe he should've been more concerned with my genetic predisposition to inflict it upon others.

I WENT HOME, conducted a thorough physical exam to ensure I hadn't accrued any unsuspected damage, then collapsed into bed, sleeping without a single dream.

I woke up bright and early to a phone call from the prison.

Superintendent McKinnon's voice was firm and crisp. "Adeline, there's been another incident. Shana got her hands on a homemade shank. Apparently, spent most of the night working herself over. She's currently stabilized down in medical, but Adeline . . . it's bad."

I nodded, because when it came to my sister, there had never been anything good. I hung up the phone, swung out of bed and prepared to return once more to prison.

Chapter 6

ALEX MADE ALL THE ARRANGEMENTS. D.D.'s physical therapist plus Phil and Neil would meet them at the scene of the first murder and D.D.'s subsequent stair dive. Seven A.M., D.D. sat in the kitchen across from three-year-old Jack, plying him with Cheerios while engaging in their morning contest of who could make the most ridiculous face. As usual, Jack won, but D.D. felt she put up a fair fight.

Eight A.M., Alex drove Jack to day care, at a neighbor's house just down the street. D.D. told herself she was not nervous. Alex's idea to reconstruct the shooting incident of six weeks ago based upon the resulting trauma to her body made perfect sense. Forensic collision experts did it all the time, looked at smashed-up car A, smashed-up car B, then rendered stunningly accurate analyses of the auto accident, including who was to blame. If it could work on cars, why not the human body?

Eight thirty. Alex returned home and the real challenge began. Pulling on fresh clothes, despite the limited mobility of D.D.'s left arm and the excruciating pain that still radiated throughout much of her neck and shoulder.

"Melvin," she said, eyeing her tucked left arm in the mirror.

Her shoulder blazed instant pain. The kind that came from over-stretched muscles and inflamed nerves, she'd been told, and would require months to heal.

What had the shrink told her? Talk to Melvin. Let him know who was in charge.

"All right," she addressed her reflection. "Here's the deal. Got a big morning. Gonna do some real work, and part of that work is trying to remember what *you* made me forget."

Her shoulder remained . . . a shoulder, reflected in a mirror.

"Oh, for fuck's sake. This is the stupidest, most idiotic . . . Fine!" She scowled harder at her reflection. "These clothes are coming off. Then I'm going to shower so I feel like a real human being. And then I'm going to put on tight-fitting yoga clothes, because those are my instructions."

In fact, her physical therapist, Russ Ilg, had instructed her to arrive in black yoga pants and a tight-fitting black T-shirt. FYI, he was bringing chalk and she shouldn't be surprised if she became the blackboard.

"I don't want to hear it from you," she continued ruthlessly. "This is how it's gonna be. So just . . . take a break or something, Melvin. Because life goes on and I'm sick of being stuck in this house, wearing my husband's clothes and smelling like an animal in the zoo. It's been six weeks and I . . . I gotta do something. I'm not meant for lying around. If you are me, surely you know that, Melvin. Surely you understand."

Alex materialized in the mirror, appearing in the doorway behind her. "Is it working?"

"Fuckety fuck fuck fuck."

"I'm going to take that as a maybe."

"Fuck."

"Shall we?" He walked into their bedroom and gestured to her top, really his own oversize shirt, buttoned over her left arm.

"Fine."

He started with the top button and worked his way down. There had been a time in D.D.'s life when having this man slowly but surely undress her in front of a full-length mirror would've had her knees shaking in breathless anticipation. Now she mostly felt numb.

No, she felt broken, weak and useless. Which was worse than numb. Numb would've been a step up.

Alex eased the shirt from her shoulder. He unhooked her bra in the back, then carefully slid the strap down her injured left arm. A mere touch, and she hissed as inflamed nerves screamed their protest.

Her husband's blue eyes met hers in the mirror, quietly apologetic as he finished removing the top half of her wardrobe, then transitioned to the bottom. Her sweatpants were easier. Socks, underwear. They were in the homestretch.

Alex turned on the showerhead, offering her his arm as she climbed into the tub. His turn to strip; then he joined her in the narrow space. Again, an activity that two months ago would've been hot and sexy, and now was just a painful parody of what could happen to a couple in three seconds or less.

She wet her hair, but it took Alex's assistance to wash and rinse. Then, water still running, he assisted her out of the tub, wrapping a huge bath sheet around her shoulders for warmth, before leaving her to stand there, like a two-year-old waiting for parental assistance, while he finished his own ministrations, then joined her on the bath mat.

He dried her first, an act of chivalry, as it left him wet and cold. She should be grateful. Appreciative of her caring, compassionate husband. Knowing how lucky she was to have his help.

Mostly, she felt bitter, angry and frustrated. Worse, he knew it. Yet he tended her quietly and thoroughly, even as her ingratitude rolled off her in waves of impotent rage.

"You would do the same for me," he said finally, if only to ease the tension.

"No, I wouldn't. I suck at basic humanity."

"Not true. I've seen you with Jack, remember? You can be tough for the rest of the world, D.D. But you never have to be tough for me."

"The doctor says I've lost my true Self to a bunch of control-freak Managers running around my psyche."

"What do you think?"

"Fuckety fuck fuck Melvin," she whispered, but she didn't sound like herself anymore. She sounded dangerously close to tears.

"You're going to be okay." He kissed the top of her head.

"Don't lie. Your rule, right? I can lie to myself, but not to you. Well, ditto. I was in the room with the doctor. I heard him say I may not regain full use of my arm. And I've taken the BPD's yearly physical enough times to know what that might mean. Don't pass the field test, don't work in the field. Me, not on the job? Now who's crazy?"

"You're going to be okay."

"*Don't lie!*"

"I'm not. I know you, D.D. One way or another, you're going to figure this out. And you're going to be okay. And you know how I know that?"

"How?"

"Because you're not even on the job, and you're still about to spend your morning catching a murderer. Now, come on. Stop stalling. As long as you're this pissed off, we might as well pull a shirt over that lovely shoulder of yours. What's your pain's name again?"

"Melvin," she muttered.

"Well, Melvin, I'm Alex. Pleased to meet you. Now, fuck off."

PHIL AND NEIL WERE ALREADY WAITING at the scene. D.D. entered the town house self-consciously, as if expecting to be surrounded by shadows and assaulted by the stench of blood. Instead, the downstairs was pleasantly illuminated by natural daylight flowing through multiple windows, while the air contained the unmistakable tang of Lysol. The landlord must've finally been granted permission to tend his unit. She would bet he hired professional cleaners, one of those firms that specialized in exactly this kind of work. It made her curious to see just what sort of magic they'd wrought upstairs.

"Any news on cause of death?" she asked her squad mates.

"Good morning, D.D., good to see you, too. How are you feeling?" Phil asked dryly.

"Excellent. Like I could bench-press a boulder. Assuming, you know, I could move my arm. Neil." She gave an awkward half hug to the youngest member of their team, while Alex shook both men's hands. Neil, a lanky redhead who looked like he was sixteen but was actually thirty-three, was finally coming into his own. He'd even led their last investigation. Phil and D.D. still took all the credit, of course, having taught him everything he knew.

Neil had been an EMT before becoming a cop. He served as their liaison to the ME's office and was the person most likely to answer her question.

"Chloroform," he said now.

D.D. blinked. She and Alex came to a halt near the kitchen island. Christine Ryan's furniture had yet to be removed, but it seemed disrespectful to sit on a dead woman's sofa. Hence, all four of them huddled in the kitchen.

"The killer OD'd them on chloroform," Alex asked. "Is that even possible?"

"Not overdosed, but used it to incapacitate them. Frankly, Ben should've caught the smell on the first body, but as he put it, the whole skin flaying proved a little distracting."

"You can smell it on the body?" D.D. wasn't sure if that was fascinating or horrifying.

"Absolutely. The smell lingers around the mouth and sinus cavities. One of the first steps during an autopsy is to smell the body. Many poisons and toxins present that way. Like I said. Ben sends his apologies." Ben Whitley was the chief medical examiner, as well as Neil's former lover. The initial breakup had proved tough, but both seemed to be handling things better these days.

"So the killer first rendered both women unconscious," Alex stated out loud. His eyes were narrowed, mind churning. "And then?"

"Compression asphyxiation."

"Compression asphyxiation?" D.D. spoke up, startled. "Isn't that why doctors don't recommend co-sleeping with newborns? Because if a grown adult rolls over on the baby in the middle of the night, it can lead to compression asphyxiation?"

"Exactly. Asphyxiation occurs when the person's chest or abdomen is compressed to the point the person can no longer draw a breath. Hence, suffocation."

"So we're most likely looking for a larger perpetrator," Alex spoke up. "Someone with enough bulk to basically crush two women?"

"Not necessarily. Compression asphyxiation can also be a matter of strategically applied force. Say, a knee dug into the victim's diaphragm for the necessary length of time."

"Given that the victim is already unconscious," D.D. murmured, "I'm not convinced we're looking for a physically imposing subject at all. With size generally comes a feeling of power, right? Whereas, this approach—stealth, ambush, drugging, then immediate suffocation, followed by a highly ritualistic, postmortem main event—sounds to me like a guy trying to avoid any chance of confrontation. Someone not confident at all, maybe even a smaller, weaker male who's intimidated by real women; hence, his fantasy involves dead ones. Is there a chance the victims never even woke up? Never even knew what was happening to them?"

"There's a chance." Neil shrugged. "Ben determined COD based on the presence of petechial hemorrhages in the eyes and upper chest area. Interestingly enough, to learn more about the killer's asphyxiation technique, he'd generally map the bruising in the chest and abdominal area, an analysis that's complicated given the skin removal in exactly those areas."

"Meaning maybe he removed skin from the torso to help cover his tracks."

Phil grimaced, shook his head. "I think we're giving the guy too much credit. This kind of suffocation, hell, he basically climbed on board and crushed his victims, yes? That doesn't sound too sophisticated. In fact, seems like a guy looking for expedience, a no-fuss, no-muss murder, if you think about it."

"He enters the home," Alex filled in now. "Sneaks his way upstairs. Chloroforms his victims while they're still asleep in order to eliminate any chance of a struggle. Then he suffocates them, knee to diaphragm. You're right. It does seem . . . expedient. The quickest way to kill, at which point, he slows down, takes his time, lingering over each body for probably a matter of hours. Interesting."

"Why compression asphyxiation?" D.D. asked. "That's pretty unusual, especially adult to adult. I mean, why not just press a pillow over their faces, the more classic approach?"

Phil and Neil both shook their heads. Alex, however, had an answer.

"He sits astride the bodies, remember? We have the imprints of his shins on both sides of their hips. That position is not just how he mutilates them; it's how he kills them, too."

"A position that's obviously very dominating." D.D. glanced at Neil. "And yet still no sign of sexual assault?"

He shook his head. "Ben says no. Postmortem mutilation yes, sexual assault no."

"Any more information on the knife?" Alex asked.

"Nah, but you should see the pile of blades Ben has accrued for comparison. It's gonna take a bit."

"I thought about a hunter," D.D. announced. "The autopsy report on Christine Ryan categorized the ribbons of skin as being expertly cut. Only people I can think of who have a lot of experience skinning is hunters. So last night, I watched a bunch of YouTube videos on how to skin game, you know, rabbits, squirrels, deer, elk."

Alex was regarding her strangely. As if just now realizing his wife had gotten out of bed sometime after midnight. She wondered which was worse, not noticing her absence, or now picturing her padding through their darkened home to watch bloody home films of carved-up wildlife. The videos had disturbed her. She hadn't thought they would, given how much of her life she'd spent staring at carved-up humans.

And yet . . . She hadn't gone to bed for a while afterward. Instead, she'd sat in Jack's room, watching her son sleep peacefully in the comforting glow of his night-light.

"I'm not a hunter," she continued, "so I'll confess I didn't know anything about it. But having watched a dozen how-to videos . . . The experienced hunters don't even really use their blades. I mean, a couple of incisions around the anus, removal of the head; then most of them peel the entire hide from the animal's body using their bare hands. Which I gather is how it's supposed to be done, as you don't want to damage the skin. It's most valuable as one large piece."

Phil was staring at her blankly. "You did what?"

"I Googled skinning; then I watched some videos. Come on, we gotta start getting into this guy's head. You got any better ideas?"

"You're on medical leave."

"For an injured arm, not an incapacitated brain. Tell me the truth. For the past few weeks, you've been pulling hunting licenses and cross-referencing names."

Phil flushed, shifted from foot to foot. "Maybe."

"Exactly. Because you think of skinning, you think of hunting. Makes sense. Except I'm telling you now, I don't think this guy is a hunter. Their technique, it's totally different. Not to mention their blades. The knives of choice are large, fixed blades, at least an inch or two across in width. Hunters are purchasing for strength and durability, the classic Ka-Bar knife that can skin a deer, gut a fish and dig a hole. I don't see how you can excise fine strips from a woman's torso using such a blade, let alone wander the streets of Boston without gathering attention."

"I've seen hunting knives that fold," Phil countered. "And I've got some buddies who carry multiple blades. Ka-Bar has its uses, but they have smaller, lighter knives they also take into the field."

"But do they remove the skin of their catch in long, thin strips?"

"No," he admitted grudgingly. "That would be a new one. Though, after curing a hide, some guys will cut it into strips for making cords, that sort of thing. Given the current trend of paranoid preppers, God only knows the amount of people now studying pioneer-era survival techniques."

"He's not a prepper," D.D. stated.

"No," Alex agreed. "This is about domination, control. Not someone looking to practice fieldwork."

"And he's not practicing," Neil said dryly. "The use of chloroform, the unique manner of asphyxiation, the methodical removal of skin . . . This guy knows exactly what he's doing. Our killer's not learning as he goes. Our killer's already a pro."

THE FRONT DOORBELL RANG. The sound, so ordinary and mundane, happening at the scene of a murder made them all jump. They shared chagrined expressions.

"Russ Ilg, my physical therapist," D.D. guessed.

Alex went to let him in.

"Sure you want to do this?" Phil asked, the second Alex was out of earshot.

"Yes. Why wouldn't I?"

Phil and Neil exchanged a look. D.D. interpreted it correctly and shot them an annoyed one of her own.

"You don't have to cover for me," she bit out. "We go through this . . . reenactment, and the most logical conclusion is that I'm an out-of-control fruitcake who discharged her weapon for no good reason, well then, that's what you should report back to FDIT. I'm not looking for handouts. I want the truth."

"We're behind you," Neil murmured. "Whatever happens. Squad is family; you know that."

"Please, I've met your family."

That made them smile. Neil's family was a bunch of Irish drunks.

He often joked he wasn't the black sheep of his family for being gay. He was the black sheep for being the only one still sober.

Alex returned with a younger-looking guy, six feet, gym fit and clad in black sweats. D.D. did the honors. "Detectives Phil and Neil, Boston PD. Russ Ilg, my personal torturer, er, physical therapist."

Everyone exchanged handshakes. D.D. kept her own arms tight by her sides, where no one would see her hands tremble with growing nerves. Her first choice for this mission would've been her doctor. But MDs didn't keep schedules that allowed for last-minute field trips; hence, Russ agreed to do the honors. Besides, as he put it, doctors just diagnosed the damage. His job was to rebuild and repair, which provided him with a much more intimate knowledge of injuries both past and present.

As the lead detective, Phil brought them from the kitchen to the base of the stairs. D.D. could see the bullet holes in the drywall along the right-hand side. Three individual marks, sprayed across the surface. If she'd been aiming at the time, it didn't speak well of her marksmanship.

Phil cleared his throat. "So D.D., um, Sergeant Detective Warren was found unconscious at the base of the stairs. Given the, um, injuries she sustained, working theory is that she started at the top, fell down."

Russ nodded. He didn't look at D.D. but kept his gaze focused on the straight rise of the narrow staircase, for which D.D. was grateful. Suddenly, she didn't feel so great. Her stomach was churning, and she could feel sweat once more beading her brow.

Rockabye, baby . . .

She squeezed her eyes shut, as if that would make the feeling of foreboding go away. Her own nervousness angered her. She was here to remember. She *needed* to remember.

She forced her eyes open and locked them on the bullet holes instead. Her damage inflicted by her bullets fired by her gun. She owned them. One way or another, they would always be hers.

"So," Russ started, as if reading her thoughts, "first thing I'm noticing is that there's no right-hand railing on this staircase. Violates code, I believe, but not so uncommon in renovated older homes with narrow staircases."

They all nodded.

"Given that variable alone, D.D. was definitely falling backward down the stairs, facing the second-floor hall at the time."

He gestured to the stairs and they obediently filed into a single line, climbing up behind him.

"What's the first thing you do as you fall?" Russ asked now. It seemed a rhetorical question, so no one answered. "You reach out a hand to catch yourself. In this case, D.D.'s holding her firearm in her right hand, correct?"

She nodded.

"Given that you fired off three shots, you were still holding the gun in your right hand as you fell. That leaves your left hand to catch yourself, which would explain the damage to your shoulder." Russ had arrived at the top of the stairs. He indicated for them to take up a position in the hall. At which point, he backed down several steps, then grabbed the top of the left-hand railing with his left hand and abruptly let himself twist and dangle.

D.D. could see it immediately. The way his dangling posture rotated and strained the muscles of his neck, shoulder and left arm. She couldn't help herself; she winced, looked away, her arm held even more tightly to her side.

"D.D. falls backward," Russ stated matter-of-factly. "She reaches out with her left arm to break the force of her backward momentum. In turn, her arm is abruptly wrenched in abduction and external rotation as she grabs on to the railing. This leads to the avulsion fracture of the lesser tuberosity of her left humerus, where the tendons that connect the muscle to the bone end up tearing away a piece of that bone. Then, sequentially speaking, her head snapped away from her left shoulder due to the sudden halt in momentum, leading to the overstretching injury to her brachial plexus.

"At this point, given the sudden and excruciating pain to her neck and shoulder, she probably released the railing. Her momentum has been slowed, but she'd still be off-balance; hence, the rolling tumble onto her head at the base of the stairs. Which would explain the bruising to her back and the moderate concussion."

Russ glanced at D.D. "Did I miss an injury? I think that covers your file."

She shook her head. His gaze was kind, sympathetic even. It didn't help. She didn't want to be here anymore. At this house, in this hallway, with too many shifting shadows in her head.

"Why would you have your back to an open staircase?" Alex asked.

D.D. glanced around, realizing it was a fair question. She, Phil, Neil and Alex all stood at the top of the stairs. And each of them kept the opening in their line of sight, an instinctual habit, she'd guess, as well as a prudent one.

"I was looking behind me," she whispered.

They stared at her.

She turned, gazing down the hall toward the open bedroom door. The overpowering odor of blood. The long, dark fingers of night as she stood alone in the shadows. She hadn't wanted to see. She had wanted to feel. And then . . .

"I heard something."

"Something?" Phil asked gruffly. "Or someone?"

"I . . . I don't know. I turned. And then I fell."

"No."

"What?" She turned toward Russ, still standing halfway down the stairs. Fixed with the gazes of four cops, he suddenly flushed.

"I mean, not likely."

"How so?"

"Your injury, the avulsion fracture, is pretty rare. It only happens when enough force causes the tendon to break off a chunk of bone at the origin or insertion point. Bones are pretty strong," Russ continued, as if this should be obvious to them. "Tendons don't just shear off pieces under conditions of average force. We're talking a great deal of stress. As in, D.D. would have to have considerable momentum during her fall. Say, she ran off the top of the stairs, or she jumped. Except, given that she was facing backward at the time . . ."

"Oh my God," D.D. whispered. "I didn't fall."

"No." Alex wrapped his arm protectively around her waist. "You were pushed."

Chapter 7

DADDY USED TO SAY blood equals love. Then he would laugh. And press deeper with the razor. He liked to watch the blood well up slowly. 'No need to rush these things,' he'd whisper. 'Take your time. Enjoy the show.' "

Shana's slurred voice drifted off. My sister wasn't looking at me anymore but at some distant point on the bone-white wall. Prison medical ward. About as grim as a prison cell, except here the bolted steel bed came complete with wrist and ankle restraints.

They'd found her in her cell during the 6:00 A.M. roll call, Superintendent McKinnon had reported. Shana had been curled in the fetal position on her bed, which, according to the floor CO, was unusual enough. When she remained unresponsive to verbal cues, a security team armed with mattress shields had been summoned to forcibly enter her cell. More time lost, but my sister's own fault. To date, she'd killed two guards, plus one inmate, during her incarceration. When it came to an inmate with her reputation, nothing was left to chance.

Meaning the corrections officers had been more concerned with their own safety, even as my sister's blood had been slowly dripping from her shredded thighs into her mattress.

Another five minutes, according to the superintendent, and Shana probably would have bled out. I couldn't tell if Superintendent

McKinnon was proud of her officers' timely intervention, or regretful. When it came to my sister, nothing was ever simple.

Shana had fashioned a shank from a travel-size toothbrush. Very small, very sharp. Not the best weapon for harming others. But, in the dark of the night, perfect for etching multiple grooves into the inside of each of her thighs. I would've liked to have said I was surprised, but this made her fourth suicide attempt. They had all involved self-cutting, just as all of Shana's acts of violence had featured various homemade blades. I'd asked her once if she was really trying to die. She'd shrugged. Said it wasn't a matter of wanting to die, as much as simply needing to cut something. Given that she was confined to solitary, sometimes a girl had to make do. . . .

Shana was drugged now. Stitched up, doped up and slowly filling up with donated blood and fresh fluids. Soon enough, they'd have her back to her cell, caged twenty-three hours a day like a feral animal, but now we got to share a moment. When, thanks to the weakening effects of painkillers and blood loss, my sister was actually talking about our family. My job was to stand there silently and take mental notes.

"Harry used to cut you?" I asked now, referring to our shared birth father, keeping my tone deliberately casual.

"Blood is love, love is blood," she intoned now. "Daddy loved me."

"So that's what this is?" I gestured to her bandaged thighs. "Self-love?"

My drugged sister giggled. "Asking me if I got off?"

"Did you?"

"You can feel it. The skin bursting open, like overripe fruit. Then the blood releasing. Feels good. But then, you should know that."

"I don't feel pain, remember?"

"But it's not pain, little sis. Oh no, it's anything but."

"According to our father."

"You're jealous. You don't remember him."

"You were four. I don't believe you remember him."

"But I do. I do and you don't, which is why you hate me. Because Daddy loved me best."

My sister sighed, her glazed eyes far away. Probably seeing the tiny house where we'd once lived. Not having my sister's memory, I knew it mostly from the crime scene photos. My parents' bedroom, where the sole piece of furniture had been a dirty mattress placed directly upon the oak wood floor. The piles of dirty clothes, soiled linens, discarded food wrappings, that formed the perimeter of the space. Then a lone car seat, stuck in the corner, or at night, in the bedroom closet. The car seat where, according to the detectives' reports, I had lived.

While Shana had slept with our parents on that bloodstained mattress.

"I loved you," Shana stated now, her voice still dreamy. "Such a pretty baby. Mom would let me hold you. You'd smile at me, waving your pudgy little fists. I cut your wrist, very carefully, so you would know how much I loved you. Mom screamed, but you still smiled and I knew you understood." Her voice turned mournful. "You shouldn't have left me, Adeline. First Daddy, then you, and then it all went to shit."

After our foster mother had discovered Shana slicing up my forearm with sewing shears, my six-year-old sister had been sent to a locked-down mental institute where she was placed on antipsychotic meds, while spending most of her days physically restrained to a bed. The regimen worked so well she only managed to attempt to kill a fellow patient five years later. Given that clear level of success, they declared her magically stable on her fourteenth birthday and turned her loose on an unsuspecting foster family. In my expert opinion, that she finally succeeded in killing someone was less a matter of if, than when.

"What do you think of," I asked her now, "when you remember Daddy?"

"Love."

"What do you hear?"

"Screams."

"What do you smell?"

"Blood."

"What do you feel?"

"Pain."

"And that's love?"

"Yes!"

"So when we were kids and you cut me, you just wanted me to know how much you loved me?"

"No. I wanted you to *feel* how much I loved you."

"By cutting your baby sister."

"Yes!"

"And if you had a knife right now?"

"Blood is love," she intoned. "I know you know, Adeline. I know that in your heart of hearts, even you understand."

Then she smiled, so slyly it sent a shiver through me. As if she knew exactly what I'd been doing six hours ago, a beast, driven by her nature, even as all her nurturing warned her to behave otherwise.

"What if I told you that food is love?" I said now, keeping my tone steady, my mind focused. "That instead of cutting someone, you should offer them bread?"

Shana frowned, touching her temples with her right hand. For the first time, she appeared confused, even disoriented. "Daddy never offered food."

"What about Mom?"

"Mom?"

"Did Mom offer food?"

"Mom is not love," she informed me, her tone abruptly brittle.

"Mom is not love." We'd danced around this before, without ever making progress. Now, having this rare moment in time, I decided to press the matter. "Why not? Why can't Mom be love?"

Shana stubbornly pressed her lips together, refusing to answer.

"Harry loved her, married her. In turn, she loved him, took care of his house, raised children with him."

"He did not love her!"

"He loved you?"

"Yes. Blood is love. He loved *me*. Not her."

I leaned forward and stated quietly, "He hurt her. Every day, according to the detectives' reports. If pain is love, then our father loved our mother very much."

Shana growled back at me: "Don't be stupid! Anyone can beat someone. That's not love. Blood is love. You know this! Cutting requires thoughtfulness, even tenderness. To delicately slice through layer after layer of skin. To intentionally avoid the iliac or the femoral or the popliteal. To slice only the great saphenous vein and nothing else . . ." She gestured to her bandaged legs. "Blood is love. It involves great care. You know this, Adeline. You know this!"

I stared my sister in the eye. "It wasn't your fault, Shana. What our father did, what happened in that house, it wasn't your fault."

"You're a baby! A weak, useless baby. Mom used to tell him that just so he would leave you alone. But I showed you my love. I cut your wrist just so you wouldn't feel alone, and Mom beat the shit out of me for it."

"She hit you? Or Dad hit you?"

"*She* hit me. Mom is not love. And you're still weak and useless!"

I switched gears, leaning back. "Shana, who stitched you up? If blood is love, and he cut you each night, who repaired you in the morning?"

My sister looked away.

"Someone fixed you. Every morning, someone had to make you better again. And they couldn't take you to a hospital. That would've garnered too much attention. So every morning, someone had to clean your cuts, bandage the wounds, do their best to make you feel better. Who, Shana, did that for you?"

Shana, shoulders twitching, jaw working, kept her gaze fixed on the far wall.

"Mom did it, didn't she? She stitched you up. Every night he destroyed and every morning she rebuilt. And you've never forgiven her for it. That's why Mom cannot equal love. Daddy hurt you. But she failed you. And that was worse, wasn't it? What she did, that hurt worse."

Shana, suddenly staring at me, her brown eyes gleaming uncannily: "You are her. I'm Dad, but you're Mom."

"Do you think I am trying to rebuild you? My visits feel like the morning; then I go away and abandon you once more to the night?"

"Dad is love. Mom is *not* love. Mom is worse."

"You're Shana. I'm Adeline. Our parents are dead. It's not our fault what they did. But it is up to us to let them go."

Shana smiled at me. "Daddy is dead," she agreed, but her tone was sly again, almost gleeful. "I know, Adeline. I was there. What about you?"

"I don't remember. You know that."

"But you were there."

"A baby strapped in a car seat. That doesn't count."

"The sound of police sirens . . . ," she goaded.

"Harry Day panicked, realized the cops were on to him," I filled in evenly. "Rather than be taken alive, he slit his wrists."

"No!"

"I read the reports, Shana. I know what happened to our father."

"Blood is love, Adeline. I know you understand, because you were there."

I felt myself pausing, frowning. But for the life of me, I didn't know what Shana meant. Because I had been just an infant, and my knowledge did come solely from police reports.

"Shana—"

"She gave him the aspirin. Thins the blood." My sister's voice had turned singsong, almost like a child's. "Then she filled the tub. Warm water. Helps expand the veins. He took off his clothes. She told him to climb in. Then he held up his wrists.

"'You must,' he told her.

"'I can't,' she whispered.

"'If you ever loved me,' he said. He handed her his favorite razor, the old-fashioned kind with an ivory handle. A gift from his own daddy, he'd once told me.

"Bang, bang, bang on the front door. Open up, open up, it's the police. Bang, bang, bang.

"And Mom slit his wrists. Two strokes each, running down, not across, because across can be stitched up by doctors. Down is a killing stroke.

"Daddy smiled at her. 'I knew you'd do it right.'

"She dropped the razor into the water. He sank into the sea of red.

"'I will always love you,' Mommy whispered, then fell to the floor as the police burst into our home.

"Blood is love," Shana intoned. "And our parents are not gone. I'm Daddy, and you're Mom, and Mom is not love, Adeline. Mom is worse."

"You should rest now," I told my sister.

But she merely smiled at me.

"Blood will win out, Adeline. Blood always wins in the end, little sister mine."

Then she grabbed my hand. For a second, I thought maybe she'd smuggled in another blade and was going to do something violent. But she just clutched my wrist. Then the drugs finished taking hold. She eased back. Sighed. Her eyes closed, and my murderous older sister fell asleep, still holding my hand.

After a long moment, I eased my fingers free. Then I lifted my hand and studied the faint white scar I'd had for as long as I could remember across the pale blue veins of my wrists. Apparently put there by my sister forty years ago.

I could nearly hear my adoptive father's voice now in my head: *Pain is . . . ?*

Pain is remembering, I thought.

Pain is family.

Which explains why even an expert on pain, such as myself, turned away and walked out the door.

Chapter 8

UPON RETURNING HOME, the first thing D.D. did was call the medical examiner, Ben Whitley. Alex had had to continue on to work, so she was alone in the house, sprawled on the sofa, still wearing yoga clothes from the morning's analysis of her own injuries.

"I have a question," she said the moment Ben picked up.

"D.D.!" Ben's voice boomed in her ear. The ME wasn't necessarily the world's most outgoing personality, but during the years he'd dated D.D.'s squad mate Neil, they'd gotten to know each other personally and, even after the breakup, had remained friends. "Heard about the avulsion fracture. Leave it to you to injure yourself in the most creative way possible."

"I try."

"Left arm?"

"Yes."

"Icing? Exercising? Resting?"

"Yes. Yes. Mostly."

"You must be losing your mind."

"Yes!"

"Which is why you're calling me. Let me guess, you want to know about our latest skinning victim."

"No."

For the first time, Ben paused. D.D. could practically hear him thinking over the phone line.

"Not the second victim," she supplied graciously. "I figured you were just now getting to that exam."

"Slated for later this afternoon."

"Sounds about right. So I have a question about the first victim, Christine Ryan, as I'm assuming you've had more time with those remains. And given you're a savvy medical examiner, one of the best we've ever had—"

"Flattery will get you everywhere."

"And you've already examined the excised skin . . ."

"True."

"You may have some working theories on the blade used by the killer?"

"True again. Very thin, no nicks or damages to the edge. Question of the day, however, was it a knife edge, or perhaps a razor?"

"Oh." She hadn't thought of that. But now, considering . . . "Wouldn't a razor be difficult to manage through such an . . . involved process? I mean, as a cutting instrument, given the thin strips, okay. But factor in the *number* of thin strips, and to be blunt, wouldn't a razor become too slippery to handle?"

"Could be attached to a handle. Think of the classic straight blade used for shaving, or for that matter, a box cutter. My other thought for the day, perhaps it was a scalpel. But I'm veering away from knives. For one thing, I've tested dozens over the past few weeks and none provide the same results. At least in my tests, a larger, thicker blade has a tendency to pull on the skin, leading to puckering along the edges. Whereas, our subject . . . He is removing very fine, smooth-edged ribbons of tissue. Which, may I add, clearly indicates practice. Even with my own training, it took a number of tries to execute well. Of course, I was hindered in the beginning by poor weapons choices. Now that I have expanded my search to include surgical instruments, I seem to be coming closer to replicating his precise excise patterns."

"Okay." D.D. had to pause for a moment. She hadn't considered that the killer might have used a scalpel and could be someone with at least basic surgical training. But given her recent brainstorm, a scalpel didn't necessarily eliminate, and in fact . . . "I'm going to suppose," she continued now, "that an ME of your fortitude—"

"Already buttered up. Move along, D.D. It is a busy day."

"You tried to reassemble the skin strips. Re-create the whole."

"*Tried* being the operative word."

"You couldn't succeed." Her voice picked up, her heart quickening. Here it was, her middle-of-the-night stroke of brilliance: "Because it turned out, you don't have all the pieces. Some of the ribbons of skin are missing. The killer took them with him."

"Ding, ding, ding. Give the beautiful blond detective a prize. Tell me the truth, is it your golden ringlets that give you your edge?"

"Absolutely. How much skin is missing? Are we talking a little or a lot?"

"Say, approximately half a dozen ribbons of excised flesh. Enough a living victim would certainly notice the loss."

Which was what she had guessed. That the skinning aspect of the murders was more than just a fetish, but also a means of providing what the killer desired most; an extremely personal memento of his crime.

She returned her attention to the phone: "Last question," she stated to Ben. "The victim's skin. Was it treated with anything beforehand? Meaning it possibly tested positive for some interesting chemicals? Say alcohol, or even formaldehyde?"

"You're wondering if the killer attempted to preserve his trophy by first wiping down his victim with some sort of solution?"

"The thought crossed my mind."

"To answer your question: yes and no. The remaining skin on Christine Ryan's torso tested positive for basic antibacterial soap. However, her arms and lower legs did not. Now, assuming the victim bathed as part of her bedtime ritual, the skin on her entire body should retain traces of the same antibacterial residue. Given that's not the case, I think it's safe to assume the killer himself wiped down the victim's torso with a basic cleaning solution, most likely prior to the skinning process."

D.D. frowned. "Like a surgeon would do? Preparing the skin for incision?"

"True surgical prep would involve 'painting' the incision site with an official prep solution, most of which are alcohol based. The skin on our victim was washed but definitely not treated with a prep stick."

"So the killer made an effort to clean the target area but not sanitize it."

"I believe so. Also, to finish answering your previous question, I didn't find any traces of formaldehyde, so negative on a preserving agent."

"Okay."

"Though that doesn't preclude the killer from attempting to preserve his trophy after the fact," the ME continued, his voice warming to the subject. "A savvy killer could place the strips of skin in a glass jar containing a formaldehyde solution, or even dry the strips using a salting process. Really, the choices are endless."

"Good to know."

"You're the one who asked."

"Occupational hazard. So, to recap your findings: Our killer incapacitated the victim with chloroform, then asphyxiated her via compression. Then he removed the victim's clothing and wiped down her skin with basic antibacterial soap, before he proceeded with the main event, which involved delicately removing long strips of skin from her torso and upper thighs. A process you believe may involve a scalpel. Then the killer exited the scene, after helping himself to some of the victim's excised skin as a particularly morbid trophy. That sound about right?"

"Couldn't have summarized it better myself."

D.D., still thinking out loud: "Meaning our killer has some experience with surgery and/or prep, but also is comfortable with dead bodies. In fact, given the main elements of the crime occur postmortem, may even be *most* comfortable with dead bodies."

"Jeffrey Dahmer?" the ME supplied. "Wasn't he a necrophiliac who felt compelled to keep body parts from his victims? He claimed to be seeking the perfect lover—one who could never leave him."

"Except last I heard, our two victims didn't show signs of sexual assault?"

"No evidence that I could determine."

D.D. nodded to herself, then remembered to speak into the phone. "Okay, this has been most helpful."

"You've identified the killer?"

"Not yet, but I have an idea of possible occupation."

"You're going to investigate hospitals and/or medical schools?"

"I'm going to have Neil pursue hospitals and/or medical schools. Personally, I'm going to check out funeral homes."

The sensible thing to do would be to wait for Alex to return home after work. He could assist with proper wardrobe, then help load her into the car. But D.D. wasn't feeling sensible. She was feeling stubborn, not to mention as resentful as hell toward her arm, shoulder, Melvin. She was a strong woman. An independent woman. And a detective on a case.

She would dress her own damn self and Melvin could stick that in his pipe and smoke it.

Melvin, of course, had other ideas.

It started when she tried to remove her scooped-neck yoga top. She went to pull the spandex top up over her healthy right shoulder and somehow twinged her left. Then there was the matter of trying to slide the shirt down her left arm, once she finally got it over her head, let alone the matter of sliding off tight-fitting black exercise pants. Definitely no reason to be using her shoulder muscles to shimmy down yoga pants, and yet her left arm burned in response and she could feel sweat starting to bead her upper lip.

It was as if the more she tried not to jostle her left side, the more every movement jarred her neck, shoulder, upper arm. She gritted her teeth, grabbed dark-gray slacks from her closet and determinedly stepped into them. Then began the painful process of yanking them up, inch by inch, with only one good hand. She finally got them slid over her hips, only to be stymied by the fastening button. She tried it four times without luck.

Oversize top, she thought wildly. Or a jacket. She'd wear a long top to cover the open waistband of her slacks; no one would be the wiser.

It made so much sense, she sat on the edge of her bed and cried.

She hated this. Hated the feeling of uselessness and impotence and sheer frustration. She blamed her body for not healing. She resented her shoulder for aching and her stupid tendon for ripping away a chunk of her own bone. What if she never healed properly? It was a rare injury; no one had been able to provide an exact prognosis. Six months from now, would she finally be able to dress herself? Hold a gun? Pick up her child?

Or would she still be here, lounging around in her husband's clothes, relegated to telling stories of the glory days while secretly wondering about the might-have-beens? She couldn't be washed-up. Not yet. She was too young, too dedicated, too much of a cop. There was no next chapter for her. Not when she loved this job so damn much.

Even after it had hurt her. Turned her into a shadow of her former self.

She collapsed back on her bed. Half-dressed in pants, a bra and nothing else, she stared up at the ceiling. Then she closed her eyes, tried to see what she must have seen that final night, right before being shoved down the stairs.

Melvin. Paging Melvin. I'm here, I'm ready, I want to know. Come on, Melvin. Cut a girl a break and let me remember.

Wasn't that what Dr. Glen had said? If she would talk to her pain, directly ask Melvin to help her remember, the weak Exile would surrender. She just had to be ready for what happened next.

Melvin remained quiet. Or really, continued his normal, blah, blah, blah aching throb.

"I'm ready," she gritted out in the silent bedroom. "I can handle it, Melvin. Come on, you pissant, groveling son of a bitch. I want to know. Tell me."

Nothing.

"Was it the killer? Came back to relive his little fantasy, got a nasty surprise when he found me there?"

Except most killers hung out on the outskirts of their crimes. To actually pass under the crime scene tape, violate the police barricade, would expose them to risk. Next thing a killer knew, he was in jail for trespassing, not to mention subject to police interrogation. Now, maybe the perfect psychopath, the murderer who was secure in his superiority, would be attracted to such gamesmanship. But their killer? A man who attacked lone women while they slept? Incapacitated them quickly with chloroform, so even their death was a matter of simple, painless execution . . . ?

For a second, D.D. could almost picture such a man in her head. Small of stature. Low self-esteem, poor social skills, uncomfortable around authority figures, especially women. Never had a long-term relationship, probably lived in the basement of his mother's house. Except not the browbeaten son harboring a tidal wave of suppressed rage—that killer would explode upon his victims once they were suitably restrained. This killer . . . he was quiet inside and out. But obsessive, maybe. Had to do what he had to do, so was trying to at least do it with the least amount of fuss possible. The victims never even knew what was happening.

He got in, drugged, killed, carved.

Because that was what he really cared about. Skinning. Harvesting. Collecting.

He was a collector.

D.D. thought it and knew it to be true. They were looking for a collector. The murders weren't crimes of rage or violence, but crimes of obsession. A killer who was compelled to do what he had to do.

Or maybe, do what *she* had to do.

Because sexual sadist predators were almost universally male, but a collector . . . The lack of sexual assault. The use of chloroform to incapacitate the victims. Even the compression asphyxiation. What had Neil said? A person of any size could do it; it was simply a matter of pressing against the right spot for the right amount of time.

Meaning maybe they weren't looking for a small, socially submissive male after all. But a female. A woman who wouldn't appear as suspicious if spotted by the neighbors entering another female's apartment late at night. A woman who, even if she was found at the crime scene after dark, could more credibly claim to be a close friend of the victim.

Could it be? When D.D. had stood in Christine Ryan's apartment, maybe it hadn't been a man who'd caught her off guard. But a lone female, emerging from the shadows . . .

"Melvin. Come on, Melvin! Talk to me."

But Melvin refused to say a word.

D.D. had had enough. She sat up. Stormed across the room. Wrenched on an oversize cream-colored sweater before she could stop herself, then had to grit her teeth against the exploding pain.

"You want to complain, Melvin?" she muttered. "You want to be all pissed off? Then, come on. I'll give you something to be good and mad about. Let's go have some fun."

Sergeant Detective D. D. Warren hammered her way down the stairs, out the door and into her car. Ready to share her pain with the world.

Chapter 9

SUPERINTENDENT KIM McKINNON was a beautiful woman. High, sculpted cheekbones, smooth ebony skin, liquid brown eyes. The kind of woman who would be as stunning at seventy as she was at forty. She was also incredibly smart, relentlessly determined and phenomenally tough, all traits necessary to run the oldest female correctional institute still operating in the United States. Especially these days, when the MCI was facing record crowding and had just been written up for housing two hundred and fifty inmates in a space originally built for sixty-four.

The trickle-down theory of pain and punishment, the superintendent had informed me the day I'd asked her about it. Most sheriffs' jails were jammed up themselves, meaning they no longer had the space necessary to offer the sight and sound separation required by law between male and female offenders. Their solution: ship the women to the MCI, where they became Superintendent McKinnon's problem.

She got the bad press, the women got wedged into triple-bunked cells and the state still didn't authorize funds for building additional housing units.

Other than that, the superintendent had a dream job, I'm sure.

Now Superintendent Beyoncé, as the inmates called her, sat on the other side of her massive gunmetal-gray desk, hands clasped before her, and regarded me soberly.

"She's getting worse," she stated without preamble. "This morning's incident . . . Frankly, I've been expecting such an episode for days."

"Meaning you've conducted extra searches of Shana's cell, while asking your officers to be hypervigilant about her access to materials for making shanks?" I responded coolly.

Superintendent McKinnon merely gave me a look. "Come on, Adeline. You've walked these halls long enough. You know when it comes to an inmate like your sister, there's very little we can do. We may be the ones in uniforms, but more often than not, she's the one in control."

Which, sadly, was true. My sister was every prison administrator's nightmare: a highly intelligent, incredibly antisocial maximum-security inmate with nothing left to lose. She was already held in isolation, locked down twenty-three hours a day. With the sole exception of my one-hour monthly attendance, she didn't care about visitation privileges. Ditto with phone privileges, access to prison programming or even the few luxuries she'd managed to scrape enough funds together to purchase from the prison canteen. Time and time again, Shana acted out like a bad toddler, and time and time again the prison staff responded with loss of privileges and removal of toys.

Shana didn't care. She was angry, she was depressed and thus far, no amount of medication had made a difference. I would know, as I'm the one who'd prescribed her last three medical protocols.

My sister's suicide attempt wasn't a stain just on Superintendent McKinnon's record but also on my own.

"Has she been taking her pills?" I asked now, the next logical question.

"We've been supervising both her ingestion of the medication as well as searching her cell for undigested capsules. We haven't found anything, but that might just mean she's one step ahead. You understand, Adeline, I'm going to have to keep Shana in medical for at least a week as it is. You know what that's like."

I nodded, getting the message. If prisons were rife with mental illness, then the medical ward was the epicenter of the madness, where the deeply disturbed prowled their locked-down medical cells while howling their particular brand of crazy for all the world to hear.

If my sister hadn't wanted to kill herself before, a week in medical should do the trick.

"Is it the anniversary of her first murder victim?" I asked now. "Maria said some reporter's been trying to contact Shana, asking all sorts of questions?"

In response, Superintendent McKinnon yanked open a drawer and pulled out a banded bunch of letters. "Name's Charles Sgarzi. He first called my office six months ago. My staff informed him he should write to Shana directly with his request. I'm told she read the first few letters but never responded. Apparently, he got more serious after that."

She handed over the batch of letters. I counted more than a dozen, arranged in order of the postmark date. It appeared that as of three months ago, the reporter had started writing at least once a week. The envelopes had all been opened, but given the security protocols, that didn't mean anything.

"Same guy wrote all of these?"

"Yep."

"What newspaper?"

"Not a paper. A blog. Digital reporting, I don't know. They say newspapers are passé. Internet news will be the Pulitzer Prize–winning wave of the future. Of course, how do you line a litter box with that?"

"And Shana read every letter?"

"Only the first few. She's refused them all since."

"But you've read them?"

"The security team grew curious. Understand, your sister isn't one of our more popular inmates."

I nodded, knowing what she meant. Many inmates maintained

very active social lives while behind bars. If you were a beautiful young woman, that certainly added to the appeal. Shana, on the other hand, was midforties, prison hardened and mean ugly. Most men probably assumed she was a lesbian. Given the sexual nature of her homicides, I didn't believe she was, but then again, I'd never asked.

"When she started getting weekly mail," the superintendent continued, "we became suspicious the letters might contain more than social content."

I nodded again. My sister might not be pretty, but she did have a history of drug abuse, so I could understand the security team's concern.

"If it's code or contains some kind of hidden content . . ." The superintendent spread her hands. "It's better than anything we've ever seen. My best guess, this reporter is obsessed with your sister. Which, after I ran a background report on him, makes some sense; he's the cousin of Donnie Johnson."

I startled, glancing up. Donnie Johnson had been twelve years old when Shana had strangled him with her bare hands before taking a knife to his face and upper body. Though only fourteen at the time of the murder, she'd been tried as an adult given the "heinous" nature of the crime. During her trial, she'd alleged that Donnie had tried to rape her. She'd only been defending herself. As for the removal of his ear, the mangling of his face, the long strips of skin she'd excised from his arms . . .

Remorse, she'd stated deadpan. Classic disfigurement to repent for her crime.

As the DA had pointed out, Donnie had been a pale, scrawny little boy, the kind of kid picked last during gym class. The odds of this frail ninety-pounder sexually assaulting the bigger, wiser, street-tough foster girl next door . . .

The jury had needed less than two days to deliberate my sister's fate, and that was after the defense blocked any admission of my sister's prior bad acts, including another episode with a knife and a boy that had occurred while she was institutionalized at the age of eleven.

My sister had been branded a monster in every major media outlet at the time. Given that she'd killed three more people, including two COs, while incarcerated, I don't think the public's perception had been wrong.

In her own words, she was Daddy. A born predator.

And I was Mom. And Mom was worse.

I couldn't help myself. My thoughts drifted to glass vials and their floating dermal contents, tucked in a shoe box beneath my closet floor. What would Shana think to know that my life wasn't quite as bland and lily-white as she thought? That she, Dad and I had something in common after all?

I pulled myself together, refocusing on the letters.

"What does he want?" I asked now.

"To ask her some questions."

I held up the letters. "Did he?"

"No. He just keeps including information for her to contact him."

"And he doesn't admit that he's the victim's cousin. You found that out on your own."

"Exactly."

"So already, his motives are suspect."

"I'd be suspicious," Superintendent McKinnon agreed.

"Do you think Shana knows?"

The superintendent paused, regarded me anew.

"Why do you think she'd suspect a personal connection between the reporter and Donnie Johnson?"

I shrugged. "According to you, these letters upset Shana. Why? Just some reporter asking her to get in touch? You know Shana as well as I do. She's bored, she's clever, she's highly manipulative. I guess I would've assumed that she'd find this kind of outreach . . . intriguing."

"You ever talk to her about Donnie?" Superintendent McKinnon asked me.

"We've danced around it from time to time." But maybe not as often as other topics, such as our family.

"She didn't answer your questions."

"That's never been her style."

"She doesn't talk about him. Never has. In all her years here, the counselors and psychologists and social workers who've cycled through . . . Shana doesn't talk about him. The boy she stabbed when she was eleven, I know about him. The *ho*, in her terms, she had to gut when she was first incarcerated at sixteen, I know about her. But the Johnson boy. She never goes there."

I frowned, considering. Shana could be very explicit in her talk of violence. Fantasies about gutting this person, killing that person. There didn't seem to be anything too shocking, too graphic, too offensive, for her to say. Then again, if you boiled all her words down, parsed them away . . . She babbled. She offered forth exactly the kind of violent chatter you'd expect of a multiple murderer. Homicidal white noise that drowned out the rest of the conversation and kept you from continuing.

I could tell you now that if I asked Shana why she killed Donnie Johnson, she'd shrug and say because. Shana considered herself to be a superpredator, and superpredators didn't apologize. Superpredators didn't feel they owed their prey that much.

But it might be interesting to ask her why she didn't talk about the boy. Or why she hadn't responded to the journalist. Or perhaps even more interesting, why she had never mentioned any of the letters to me.

Thirty years later, what did she still have to hide?

"Can I take these?" I asked Superintendent McKinnon.

"Be my guest. Are you going to call the reporter?"

"I might."

"And you'll talk to Shana?"

"Would it be okay if I returned tomorrow?"

"Under the circumstances, yes."

I nodded, picked up the batch of letters, my mind already racing ahead. But just as I went to stand, I felt, more than saw, the superintendent's hesitation.

"Anything else?" I asked her.

"Maybe one last thing. Any chance you caught the morning's paper?"

I shook my head. Given my own evening's . . . activities, then the call from the prison, I hadn't had the opportunity to catch up on current events.

Now Superintendent McKinnon slid the *Boston Globe* across the smooth surface of her desk, one finger tapping a headline in the lower right-hand corner, below the fold. A local woman had been murdered; I gathered that immediately from the headline. It wasn't until my gaze skimmed down the next few paragraphs to the details of the crime, strips of skin, expertly removed . . .

I closed my eyes, feeling an unexpected shiver. But they couldn't . . . I didn't . . . I cut off the errant thought savagely. Now was not the time or place.

"If memory serves . . ." the superintendent began.

"You are correct," I interrupted.

"If I could spot the similarities between this murder and your sister's work, your father's crimes, others will as well."

"True."

"Meaning things for you and your sister could get worse."

"Oh yes," I agreed, gaze still locked on the desk and not meeting the superintendent's eyes at all. "Things are about to get much worse."

Chapter 10

THE COAKLEY AND ASHTON FUNERAL HOME had been serving
families in Greater Boston for more than seventy years. D.D. had
visited the establishment, a graceful, white-painted Colonial, twice
before. Once for the passing of a friend, and once to honor a fellow
officer. On both occasions, she'd been struck by the powerful odors
of fresh flowers and preserved flesh. It was probably not something
a homicide detective should admit, but funeral parlors creeped her
out.

Maybe she simply knew death too well, so to view it in this kind
of carefully sanitized venue made it feel alien to her. Like meeting a
long-lost lover who looked nothing like you remembered.

The funeral director, Daniel Coakley, was waiting for her arrival.
An older gentleman with broad shoulders and a shock of thick white
hair, he wore an impeccably tailored charcoal-gray suit and exuded
the kind of calm demeanor meant to soothe distraught family members and encourage close confidence.

D.D. shook his offered hand, then followed him through the
wood-paneled foyer, down the dark-red-carpeted hall to his office. In
contrast to the somber, old-world feel of the rest of the place, Coakley's office was surprisingly light and modern. Large windows overlooking a grassy common area, white painted built-in bookshelves,
a natural-stained maple-wood desk topped with a discreet state-of-
the-art laptop.

D.D. could almost feel herself start to breathe again, except, of course, for the ubiquitous floral arrangement that dominated the windowsill.

"Gladiolus," she observed. "Is it just me, or do they appear in most funeral arrangements?"

"The flower signifies remembrance," Coakley informed her. "So they are a popular choice for funerals. They also symbolize strength of character, honor and faithfulness, which can be equally relevant."

D.D. nodded, then cleared her throat, unsure of where to begin. Coakley granted her an encouraging smile. She had a feeling he was accustomed to uncomfortable guests and awkward questions. It still didn't help.

She started with the basics, establishing that Coakley and Ashton was a third-generation firm, with Daniel serving as both the funeral director and head embalmer. Turned out, embalmers had to attend mortuary school as well as complete a yearlong apprenticeship before earning their license. Good to know.

The business also included three full-time and five part-time employees who assisted with administrative duties, funeral preparations, might even fill in as pallbearers, that sort of thing. That grabbed D.D.'s attention.

"And these other staff members, how do you know them?" she asked, leaning forward. "What's bringing them to the job?"

Coakley smiled wryly. "You mean, why would they want to work at a funeral home?"

D.D. remained unabashed. "Exactly."

"My part-timers are older, retired community members. Many are at a phase of their lives where they've had a lot of experience with funerals, and I think easing the process for others appeals to them. They're mostly older men, interestingly enough. And I have to say, the majority of our families find their presence comforting."

"And the rest of your staff?"

"I have a secretary who has been with me for decades. I think she'd be the first to say when she showed up for the job interview, she was taken aback about working in a funeral home. But as she put it, answering a phone is answering a phone. Besides, the back-room embalming duties aside, we aren't so different than any other business. We maintain company cars, we manage a company office." He gestured around them. "We make payroll, we pay taxes. It's a business, and most of my employees probably work for me for the same reason they would work anywhere else. It's a good job, I treat them well and they feel valued."

D.D. nodded, understanding his point, even if she didn't completely agree. Coakley could say his company was a business like any other, and yet he dealt with death every single day. Most companies couldn't say that. Many people wouldn't be comfortable with that.

"Maybe you could walk me through the process," D.D. said. "You get a call. A person has died. Then what?"

"The deceased is transported to our facility."

"How?"

"A variety of means. We're qualified to pick up remains at local hospitals. Or there are professional mortuary service companies who specialize in transport, especially over long distances. For example, the funeral may be in Boston but the deceased passed away in Florida. So the body must be transported from there to here, which is out of our driving range."

D.D. made a note. Mortuary service companies. More people, employees comfortable with spending hours at a time in the company of a corpse. Maybe some of which even took the job precisely for that reason? "Then what?"

"I would meet with the family, determine their wishes for the funeral. Open casket, closed casket, cremation. Their choices, of course, impact the next significant step, the embalming process."

"How do you prepare the body?" D.D. couldn't help herself; she leaned forward, all ears and morbid curiosity.

Daniel Coakley smiled, but fainter this time. Clearly, he'd been asked the question before. No doubt at numerous cocktail parties by people who were equal parts fascinated and horrified.

"Essentially, the embalming process involves the transfusion of blood with embalming fluid. Several small incisions are made in major arteries. Then a formaldehyde solution is injected into the veins, pushing the blood out while replacing it with embalming fluid."

"Do you prepare the body before you start the embalming process?" D.D. asked. "Say, wash it?"

"No. Embalming can be rather messy. Personally, I wait till the end. Then I bathe the entire body."

"Are there any special cleaning solutions you favor? Trade products?" She was thinking of the clean crime scenes again. The almost impossibly clean bedrooms.

Coakley shrugged. "I use a basic antibacterial soap. Doesn't harm the tissue, while being mild enough to use on your bare hands."

D.D. made another quick notation. Antibacterial soap, such as traces of which the ME had found on the first victim's torso. "And afterward?" she pressed. "I imagine the room must also be cleaned?"

"The process takes place on a stainless steel embalming table, very similar to what medical examiners use for autopsies. It includes its own drain, of course. Afterward, we hose down the stainless steel surface, then disinfect with bleach. It's not that involved, which is helpful during those times when we're particularly busy."

D.D. pursed her lips, considering. In the middle of the night, she'd been fixated on the thought that their killer was most comfortable with the dead. And when she thought dead people, she thought funeral homes. Maybe an embalmer, someone with technical experience who'd trained with a scalpel as part of mortuary school. Not to mention, the killer's skill with cleaning the crime scene made her wonder about special products that might be used by funeral homes to eliminate all traces of blood and bodily fluids. Interesting.

"May I ask a question?" Coakley spoke up suddenly.

"Sure."

"Is this in regard to the Rose Killer case?"

"What?"

"The Rose Killer? To quote the front page of the *Boston Herald*, which maybe conscientious detectives never do."

D.D. closed her eyes. But of course. Boston PD had been doing good to keep the details of the first murder away from the press. She should've known they'd never get so lucky twice.

"Do I want to know what the *Herald* said?" she asked, peering out through one eye. "Or rather, splashed in graphic detail across the entire front page?"

Coakley granted her a look of compassion. "The article claims there have been two victims. The killer murdered them in their own beds, leaving behind a rose on their nightstands, like some kind of misguided lover."

"Anything else?"

"You mean other than they were skinned alive?"

"Not alive!" Too late, D.D. realized she shouldn't have responded. Then again, Coakley was a funeral director, not a reporter. "Wait, between you and me, I never said that. But the skinning occurred after the victims were dead. It's one of the reasons I'm here. Without getting too particular, our murderer . . . Let's just say, the majority of the time he spends with his victims is postmortem. It's almost as if the killing part is incidental. Mostly, he—or she—wants a corpse."

"Necrophilia?" Coakley murmured.

"No sign of sexual assault," D.D. granted. In for penny, in for a pound.

"Which is why you thought of funeral directors. Because clearly people who spend their lives embalming have an unhealthy fascination with dead bodies." Coakley stated the words calmly.

D.D. had the good grace to flush.

"I know," she said. "Just like people who spend their lives investigating murder must have an unhealthy fascination with violence."

"At least we understand each other."

"We do."

"Do you know what it takes to be a good funeral director, Detective Warren?"

"Probably not."

"Compassion. Empathy. Patience. Yes, one piece of my job involves preparing a body for burial, a process that has required years of technical training, but also, to be honest, art. Good embalmers have opinions on the percentage of formaldehyde, as well as the most realistic pancake makeup. But we're not working in abstract. Our goal is to take something sad, overwhelming and often frightening for a family, and make it cathartic. Every day, I deal with people at their most vulnerable. Some are prone to tears, but others are prone to rage. My job is to take each of these people by the hand and lead them gently through the beginning of their grieving process. Using a great deal of compassion, empathy and patience. Now, my comfort level with dead bodies aside, do I sound like a killer to you?"

D.D. flushed again. "No."

"Thank you."

"But—"

Daniel Coakley's eyebrows rose. For the first time, the funeral director appeared not only surprised, but as close as he probably got to annoyed. "But what?"

"The traits you described. Those are what it takes to be a good funeral director. Maybe I'm looking for a bad one."

Coakley frowned at her. "Or," he said abruptly, "a failed one. I can't say it happens often, but every now and then I've had an apprentice who clearly lacked the . . . interpersonal skills necessary for this job."

"What did you do?"

"Terminated the arrangement."

"Would you have records?"

"Please. I can only think of one such person, and last I knew, she'd changed to culinary school and was doing quite well. Given the scope of your investigation, I'd think you'd want to cast a wider net than going from funeral home to funeral home."

"What do you suggest?"

"The mortuary schools. There are two in Boston. See if they'd be willing to share the names of the students who failed. I could ask around as well. We're a close-knit industry. If there's a particular name, or what do you call it—a person of interest—you'd like to learn more about, I could probably make some calls."

"Thank you."

"We are not a bunch of ghouls," Coakley said quietly, as D.D. rose to standing.

"I didn't mean to imply that."

"But from time to time, we do attract those with ghoulish sensibilities."

"Story of my life," D.D. assured him.

Coakley smiled his faint smile, then quietly, but firmly, escorted her out the door.

Chapter 11

IN OUR ENTIRE TIME TOGETHER, my adoptive father and I had only one major argument: the day he'd discovered my sister's letters.

"*Don't be an idiot!*" he'd roared at me, clutching the stack of barely legible notes. "You've got nothing to gain from this and everything to lose."

"She's my sister."

"Who attacked you with a pair of scissors. And you're still luckier than her last few targets. Tell me you haven't written back."

I said nothing.

He thinned his lips, stern face radiating disapproval. Then, abruptly, he sighed. He returned the loose sheaf of papers to the top of my desk, then crossed to my pink ruffled bed and sat down heavily. He was sixty-five by then. A trim, gray-haired geneticist who'd probably been thinking he was too old for this.

"You remember there are two kinds of family," he said, not looking at me.

I nodded. This was familiar territory, trod by most adopted children. There are two kinds of family: those that are given, and those that are made. Birth families are given. Adopted families are made. At which point, most adoptive parents launch into an enthusiastic sales pitch on how much better it is to be made. Other kids only wished they could pick their parents, their siblings, etcetera, etcetera. Look how good it is to be you!

My adoptive father had spent my formative years reading me many books on the subject. *Child of My Heart. One-Two-Three-Family!* Except my father had extra credibility when he said he couldn't have loved me more if I'd been of his own blood; he didn't have any birth children. Or a wife. Dr. Adolfus Glen had been not just a perfectly content bachelor, but a perfectly content loner till the day he met me. And while he might not have been the most demonstrative father in the world, I never doubted his love. Even as a child, I recognized his rare integrity, his quiet dignity. He loved me, genuinely. And for a man such as him, that was everything.

"You don't have to choose her," he argued that day. "Shana might be the family you were given, but for very good reasons, she was also the family who was taken away. If this note were written by your father, would you still be reading it?"

"That's not the same!"

"Why? They're both killers."

"She was a just a little girl—"

"Who grew into a psychopathic adult. What's her body count these days? Three, four, five. Have you asked?"

"Maybe what she did, who she is . . . Maybe it wasn't her fault."

He regarded me steadily. "Meaning maybe if she hadn't been exposed to your father's insatiable appetite for violence? Spent night after night witnessing his depravity, while you were shut away in a closet?"

"The first five years of a child's life are the most important," I whispered, having just completed my undergrad degree. "I was only in that house one year. She spent four. Meaning the majority of her key development phase . . ."

"Nature versus nurture. You received the advantage of a caring home, versus your sister, who remained in the foster system. Hence, you're about to attend one of the most prestigious medical schools in Boston; whereas, your sister remains forever chained to the school of hard knocks."

"That's cruel."

"And you're lying to yourself, Adeline. This has nothing to do with nature versus nurture. It's survivor's guilt, pure and simple."

"She's my sister—"

"Who has a long history of committing acts of violence against others, not to mention yourself. Adeline, give me one good reason to choose Shana as family. One good reason, and I'll let it go."

I thinned my lips mutinously, looking away. "Because," I muttered.

My father threw his hands up in the air. "God save me from know-it-all college students. Tell me, have you sent her money?"

More silence. A second fatherly sigh.

"She asked, didn't she? Why not? She's a master manipulator and you're an easy target. She's locked in the big house, and you're living in one."

"Or maybe she's my older sister and I'm her little sister and this is the way sisters have always been."

"Nice sentiment. She write that?"

"I'm not naive!"

"Fine. Stop sending her money. See how long before the letters dry up."

"She wants to know me."

"And you?" My father, for the first time sounding less certain.

"I'm . . . curious. We both know my dad is infamous." I heard myself recite: "*The sick and twisted Harry Day just wanted to find a good lay. Grab 'em, stab 'em, whack 'em, hack 'em. He told each one he loved her best. Then buried her bones with all the rest.*"

I'd heard the rhyme for the first time in middle school. I'd never told my adoptive father, though. Because sometimes pain is knowing, and sometimes pain is sharing that knowledge with someone who loves you but can't do anything to help.

My father's shoulders came down. His brown eyes were kind. "True."

"My sister, too. Right? I come from a family of killers."

"Yes," he agreed somberly. "That is your gene pool."

"And despite what we would like to think, nature is a major factor in psychological behavior. Love alone cannot change the world."

"You are too young to sound so cynical, my dear."

I continued, "I don't think I'm a killer."

"Thank heavens."

"But I think I should know what I don't know, study what I can't remember. Because my birth family is my legacy and you always taught me there's nothing to be learned from denial. Confront, analyze, master—isn't that what you recommend?"

"I believe I have also advised caution. There are many kinds of pain, remember, Adeline. And family"—he pointed to my sister's handwritten letters—"any family, but particularly *your* family, Adeline, has a gift for inflicting pain. If you've read the file on Harry Day, if you truly looked at those photos, then you know that as well as I do."

"We're just exchanging a couple of notes," I said, glancing at my sister's letters. "Maybe once a month, like pen pals. It'll be okay."

"It won't remain letters. Sooner or later, your sister will ask to see you. And you'll go, Adeline. It's times like this, I truly wish you could feel pain. Because maybe then, you'd have better instincts for self-preservation."

"Everything will be all right, Dad. Trust me, I know what I'm doing."

Then I'd turned away from him. Conversation over. Conclusions made. Resolve strengthened.

And maybe I would've held out. Maybe I would've stuck to letters. Except then my father died. My family that had been made dissolved. I stood alone in the world, and even if I couldn't feel pain, I felt the ache of loneliness just fine.

Six months later, I paid my first visit to the Massachusetts Correctional Institute, sitting across from my sister. It turned out, as always, my adoptive father hadn't been wrong: My big sister did have a particular gift for inflicting pain.

But I liked to think, as most little sisters probably do, that I have my own special talents as well.

HAVING CANCELED OUT MY DAY upon receiving news of Shana's incident, I was surprised to show up at my office and discover Sergeant Detective D. D. Warren standing before my closed door.

For a moment, walking out of the elevator, office key in hand, I paused, feeling a shiver of dread. The detective's clothing, dark slacks and cream-colored sweater, were consistent with a woman on the job. And given the morning newspaper's graphic article regarding the two recent Boston murders, my own family's past . . .

Then I noticed the way Detective Warren stood, or really sagged against the wood-paneled wall, her pale face set in a grim mask of finely etched pain.

"Are you all right?" I asked carefully, resuming my approach.

"I'm here, aren't I? What do you think?" Her tone was harsh, her left arm tucked protectively against her torso. I judged the detective to have had a bad night and a worse morning. Given that the best defense was a strong offense, apparently D. D. Warren had decided to be as offensive as possible.

I kept my own voice neutral as I drew to a halt before her. "Am I confused? I don't remember us having an appointment. . . ."

"I was in the neighborhood. Thought I'd take a chance, see if you were available."

"I see. How long have you been waiting?"

"Haven't. Just got up here myself. Saw the dark windows, figured I was out of luck, when the elevator doors dinged, and here you are."

I nodded again, inserted the key in my office door, worked the lock. After another moment's consideration—resignation?—I said, "Please, come in."

"Thank you."

"Tea, coffee, water?"

"Coffee. If it's not a bother."

"You showed up at my office unannounced. Too late to worry about being a bother."

D.D. finally smiled, then followed me into the double-room suite as I snapped on the lights, hung up my coat, tucked away my purse.

"Where's your receptionist?"

"I gave her the day off."

"Don't you normally work Wednesdays?"

"Something came up."

D.D. nodded, walked around the space, seemed to study the framed degrees hanging on the walls while I got coffee brewing. I opened up the inner door that led to my space. D.D. sat down in the hard-back chair, sighing softly before catching herself. Her left hand was trembling. Discomfort, fatigue, hard to be sure, but I doubted the detective was the kind of woman who caved easily. That she'd actually sought out my services had to say something about her current level of physical distress.

"For insurance purposes," I informed her, "I'm going to have to count this as an official appointment."

"Okay." Then, "What does that mean?"

I smiled, took my usual seat behind my desk. "It means you get the full hour to tell me why you really showed up unannounced at the office of a pain specialist who just two days ago you accused of preaching bullshit."

"I didn't mean you personally," D.D. protested faintly. "Just, um . . . you know, the approach. Naming Melvin. Come on, I'm in real discomfort. How does a name change that?"

"Let's find out. Catch me up. On a scale of one to ten, how would you rate your pain as of this moment?"

"Twelve!"

"I see. And for how long has it felt like that?"

"Since this morning. I got a little frustrated getting dressed. Wrenched hard when I probably should've tugged delicately. Melvin's been pissed off ever since."

"Okay." I made a note. "What time this morning?"

"Ten A.M."

I glanced at my watch. It was now two o'clock. "So you have been suffering for the past four hours. What interventions have you tried?"

D.D. stared at me blankly.

"How about pain meds? Over-the-counter ibuprofen, prescription narcotics? Have you taken anything?"

"No."

I made another note, based on our last appointment, hardly surprised.

"Ice?" I asked next.

"Haven't been home," she mumbled.

"What about a topical pain-relieving ointment? Biofreeze, Icy Hot? I believe both products come in pads or gels for use on the go."

She flushed, looked away again. "Hard to apply. And you know . . . smelly. Doesn't go with the ensemble."

"By all means," I assured her, "let's not sacrifice the outfit."

She flushed again.

"What about nonpharmaceutical-based interventions? Have you tried talking to Melvin?"

"I've cursed him out a few times. Does that count as conversation?"

"I don't know. Does it?"

The detective smiled wryly. "My husband would probably say that for me, the answer is yes."

I put down my pen, regarded my patient steadily. "To recap, you're in extreme discomfort. You've said no to ice, anti-inflammatories, pain pills, topical ointments and meaningful conversation. So. How is that working for you?"

D.D.'s chin came up, eyes finally sparking to life as she replied in a heated voice: "And there it is: the ultimate shrink speak. 'How is that working for you?' It hasn't worked for me, obviously, or I wouldn't be right here, right now, feeling like my arm was on fire and my life is over and I'm never going to return to my career, let alone carry my kid or hug my husband. This sucks. Melvin . . . sucks."

"Which is why you came here. Because your life sucks, and frankly, you need someone to share that pain. How am I doing, Detective Warren? Why look in when you can lash out?"

"Don't fucking crawl inside my head!"

"With all due respect, I'm a psychiatrist; climbing inside heads is what I fucking do best. Now, would you like to continue yelling, or would you like your discomfort to dial down a notch?"

D.D. stared at me. She was breathing hard. Agitated. Enraged. But also distressed. Genuinely physically distressed. I leaned forward, stating more kindly:

"D.D., you have suffered one of the most painful injuries there is. Your own tendon ripped away a chunk of bone. And instead of being allowed to rest your arm to heal the break, you're being forced to move it every single day, because as I'm sure the doctors explained, immobilization could lead to a frozen shoulder and long-term physical disability. You're subjecting your broken humerus to daily physical therapy exercises, not to mention wrenching it through shirtsleeves and wrestling with car doors and doing dozens of other small, unconscious movements all day long that lead to instantaneous, teeth-grinding, mind-screaming pain. Welcome to a day in the life of Sergeant Detective D. D. Warren. You hurt, and you hate hurting. Worse, you feel helpless, which in turn makes you feel hopeless, and you are not a woman accustomed to either emotion."

D.D. didn't say anything, just continued to regard me stony faced.

"You don't trust shrinks," I continued briskly. "You're not even sure you like me. And yet, of all the interventions you could've done for your pain today, the only one you managed was to show up at my door. Surely that must mean something to you."

She offered a small nod of acknowledgment.

"All right, let's build on that. Have you done your physical therapy exercises today?"

"Not yet."

"I'm assuming at this stage of the healing process, you're limited to pendulums?"

"You know a lot about injuries and physical therapy."

"Yes, I do. Now I'd like to see yours. Fifteen pendulum swings. Please begin."

D.D.'s face paled. Her chin trembled; then she seemed to catch the motion, setting her jaw. "No . . . thank you."

"Yes, please."

"Look, my pain is already at a twelve. You make me do PT, and that's it. I won't be able to drive home, not to mention I'll probably puke all over your rug."

"I understand. Physical therapy is extremely painful for you. You start it in distress and end it in agony."

"Says the woman who can't even feel pain."

"True. I could break my arm and still do pendulums. In fact, I could break my arm and do back handsprings. I'd be destroying the rest of my bones, joints and muscles in my body, but I'd look really good doing them."

The detective fell silent.

"Pain is good," I stated quietly. "It's your body's primary technique for protecting you from harm. You can't see that right now. You're angry with your pain. You yell at it or try to ignore it altogether. In return, your pain growls louder because it *needs* your attention. It's doing what it's supposed to do to help you avoid further damage. Perhaps rather than curse at Melvin for speaking up, you could thank him for his efforts on your behalf. Tell him you understand what he's trying to do, but, for the next ten, fifteen or twenty minutes, you need him to understand that you must move your arm and shoulder. Even if it inflames your injury in the short term, your exercises are necessary for long-term recovery. Talk to him. Don't just curse."

"Now, see, this is where it starts to sound like bullshit again."

"Consider this: Ten years ago there was a study of major athletes and their pain thresholds. These were individuals who consistently performed at nearly inhuman levels of physical ability and had the training regimens that went with it. Now, the primary assumption of this study was that such athletes most likely had higher thresholds of pain than mere mortals—hence their ability to push their bodies to such extremes. Much to the surprise of the researchers, however, the opposite turned out to be true. In fact, most of the athletes reported significantly higher awareness of their pain, while showing more active central nervous systems than the control group. According to the athletes themselves, they felt their acute body-pain awareness actually helped them function at the levels they did. Success wasn't being unaware of physical limitations or injuries but acknowledging the constraints, then working with their own body to push through. Not mind over matter, per se, but a mind-body connection that enabled them to register, adjust and improve upon their functioning at all times. Does that make sense?"

D.D., frowning: "I guess."

"That's what I'm advocating here: Don't ignore your pain. Register, accept, then work with your own body to push through. Naming your pain . . . It's simply a device to help you identify and focus. If calling your pain Melvin makes you feel stupid, don't do it. Refer to it as Pain or don't call it anything at all. But acknowledge your pain threshold. Consider how your injury feels. Then work with your body to do what you need to do. Which, I believe, is fifteen pendulum swings." I gestured to the open space in front of my desk. "Please. Be my guest."

D.D. thinned her lips again. For a moment, I thought she might refuse. She hadn't been exaggerating before. I'd seen patients end PT sessions vomiting from the intensity. It wasn't just a matter of forcing a broken arm to try to move, but given the accompanying inflammation of the nerves surrounding it . . . An avulsion fracture was one of the most painful kinds of injuries there was. Or so I'd been told.

Now Detective Warren slowly moved to the edge of her chair. She bent at the waist and allowed her left arm to hang straight down, like an elephant's trunk, the physical therapists would say. Even that simple motion elicited an immediate hiss of pain. She breathed in, out, sweat already beading her upper lip.

"How do you feel?" I asked.

"Is this how you get your jollies?" she retorted harshly. "Can't feel any pain, so you feed off of others'?"

"Detective, on a scale of one to ten, please rate your pain."

"Fourteen!"

"Curse."

"What?"

"You heard me. Thus far, your primary coping strategy has been to lash out. So do it. Yell at me. Call me a bitch or a pervert or a sycophant. Here I sit, having never felt even the sting of a paper cut. And there you are, drowning in waves of physical distress. Rage, D.D. Rant to your heart's content. There is nothing you can say that I haven't heard before."

She did. She swore and fumed and shouted and roared. I let her go for several minutes, building to a full crescendo as she slowly but surely started swinging her left arm in small circular motions, like a dangling pendulum. More sweat beaded her brow. Between curses, she panted heavily as her fractured bone shrieked its own protest.

"Stop," I said.

"What?" She didn't even look up at me. Her gaze was locked on a spot on the rug, her eyes nearly glazed over from the stress of her exertions.

"On a scale of one to ten, rate your pain."

"What do you mean? You just had me do a dozen pendulum swings. I'm at a fucking fifteen. Or eighteen. Or twenty! *What the hell do you want from me?*"

"So has cursing worked for you?"

"What the hell?" She glanced up, ashen faced, bewildered.

I continued steadily: "For the past two minutes you have externalized your pain and vented your rage. Do you feel better? Has that coping strategy worked for you?"

"Of course not! I've been doing PT and we both know PT equals agony. Of course it didn't—"

"Stop."

Her mouth open, closed. She glared at me.

"I would like you to swing your shoulder in the opposite direction now. That's what you're supposed to do, right? Please reverse direction, and this time, instead of yelling, I want you to breathe with me. We are going to inhale for the count of seven, hold it in our lungs for a count of three, then exhale. Please begin. . . ."

She cursed, I held up a hand.

"Detective Warren, you came to me, remember? And we have forty minutes of our appointment left."

She continued to regard me mutinously, sweat trickling down from her hairline. Then, slowly but surely, she inhaled upon my command.

"Now," I said briskly, "I want to you to repeat after me: Thank you, Melvin."

"Fucking Melvin!"

"Thank you, Melvin," I continued. "I know this hurts. I know you're doing your job by telling me how much this hurts. I hear you, Melvin, and I appreciate you trying to help me protect my shoulder."

D.D. muttered under her breath, including a few terms that were clearly not words of praise. Then she gritted out:

"So, Melvin. Um, thanks for letting me know how much this sucks. But, uh, the doctors have said I must do this exercise. It will help me retain mobility. So, um, even though we both agree this feels like absolute shit, please help me out. We're in this together, right? And I gotta get through this, Melvin. I need my arm back. You need my arm back. Right?"

I had D.D. count to thirty. Then I had her change direction with her rotations for a second time and count to thirty again. We performed the exercise several cycles through. I spoke evenly, providing instructions for breathing, suggestions for words of praise. She followed more raggedly, until finally:

"Thank you, Melvin," I intoned for her. "Thank you for your help, thank you for your care of my body. Now we're done, and we can both rest. Job well done."

I stopped talking. After a second, D.D. straightened at the waist, once more sitting up. She appeared uncertain.

"No more pendulums?"

"No more pendulums. Now, on a scale of one to ten, please rate your pain."

She stared at me. Blinked several times. "It hurts."

I remained silent.

"I mean, it's not like it's magically gone away. My shoulder throbs, my entire left arm aches. I don't even think I can close the fingers on my left hand, everything's so swollen and inflamed."

I remained silent.

"Eight," she said finally. "I'd rate it an eight."

"Is that normally how you feel after your exercises?"

"No. I should be curled up on the floor right now. In the fetal position." She frowned, touched her forehead with her right fingers. "I don't get it," she said flatly.

I shrugged. "You've been externalizing your pain. You turn it into rage, which I imagine is a far more comfortable emotion for you. Then you lash out. At which point, your heart rate accelerates, your breathing shortens, and your blood pressure spikes, ironically enough, increasing your physical distress. In contrast, I'm trying to get you to look inward. Focus on steady breathing, slowing your heart rate and lowering your blood pressure, which in turn, eases your nervous system and increases your threshold for pain. Hence, the deep-breathing techniques used for centuries by laboring mothers and yoga devotees."

D.D. rolled her eyes. "I did natural childbirth," she muttered. "I remember the breathing exercises. But labor is a matter of hours. This . . ."

"In addition," I continued evenly, "by having you establish an ongoing dialogue with your pain, I'm attempting to move you beyond your current combative relationship with your own body. Acknowledging what you are feeling will lead to acceptance, which will lead to advancement. Basically, as you just experienced, when you talk with Melvin, you feel better. When you curse at him, you feel worse."

"But I don't *like* Melvin."

"Does that mean you can't respect him? Appreciate his role?"

"I want him to go away."

"Why?"

"Because he's *weak*. I hate weak."

I folded my hands. "Then you must love me. I feel no pain, ergo I can have no weaknesses."

"That's not the same thing," D.D. said immediately.

I waited.

"I mean, just because you can't feel pain doesn't mean you're strong. Maybe that's its own kind of weakness. You have nothing to overcome. No basis for empathy."

I waited.

D.D. blew out an exasperated breath. "Oh, bite me. You're trying to get me to say that Melvin is actually good. Pain has its usefulness, builds character, blah, blah, blah. You're using reverse psychology to do it, too. Is there nothing you shrinks won't do?"

"I like to think that in addition to being painless, I am heartless," I deadpanned. "But truthfully, does Melvin have value?"

The detective pursed her lips. "He's trying to protect me from further injury. I get that."

"Can you respect that?"

"Fine."

"Can you curse him less, maybe even offer him a moment or two of appreciation?"

"I don't know; will he send me flowers?"

"Better, he'll whisper softly in your ear, versus screaming in your shoulder."

"My left arm still aches."

"Your left humerus is still broken."

"But I don't feel as . . ." D.D. paused, clearly looking for the right words. "I don't feel as feral. Like I'm going to lose my ever-loving mind."

"You feel more in control."

"Yeah. That's it."

"As an advocate of the Family Systems model, I would say that's because you have acknowledged the piece of yourself that you were uncomfortable with, the Exile, resulting in your true Self being once more centered and in control."

D.D. gave me a look. "I'm going to say deep breathing is useful, and maybe talking to Melvin isn't so bad. Acknowledge, accept, advance. Okay. If it worked for a bunch of über-athletes, why not me?"

I smiled, unclasped my hands. "It's okay to nurture yourself, D.D. I imagine for a woman with your job and family, you often feel your attention is demanded elsewhere. But it's all right to accept your own needs. You know, ice your own damn shoulder, instead of waiting for someone else to buy you flowers."

D.D. finally laughed. She rose to standing just as her cell phone rang. She glanced at the number, then shot me a quick look.

"I need to take this; do you mind?"

She indicated the outer office. I nodded my permission. She was already talking as she passed through the doorway. I busied myself moving around a stack of files, shuffling more ubiquitous paperwork, but of course, I eavesdropped. I was born without pain, not without curiosity.

"ViCAP got a hit? Seriously?" The detective was talking excitedly from the waiting area. "Multiple victims, postmortem skin harvesting . . . In his own closet? Jesus, that's sick. Wait, hang on. What do you mean the guy's not even alive anymore?"

I felt the first shiver. My gaze falling to my desk, where the daily paper still awaited my attention. Two murders, shouted the front page, skinned in their beds. Never seen anything like it, claimed an anonymous detective. Except I had. In old crime scene photos, where the carnage had been inflicted by someone even better. Someone even badder.

Someone whose need for human skin had been passed along to both of his daughters.

I drifted to the inner doorway. I couldn't help myself. I stood there, meeting Detective D. D. Warren's narrow blue gaze as I whispered, a heartbeat before her, the name of the one and only person who could disturb a hardened detective so much: "Harry Day."

Chapter 12

D.D. ENDED THE CALL. She kept her gaze locked on her doctor as she slid her cell back into her coat pocket.

"How do you know that name?" D.D. asked, already suspicious.

"He was my birth father."

"Harry Day? The serial killer?"

"I was a year old when he died. Can't say I ever knew the man, more like over the years I've come to know of him. I saw today's paper, Detective Warren, including the article on Monday night's murder. I couldn't help but wonder."

D.D. continued studying her pain specialist. Adeline stood in the doorway between the two rooms, looking as cool and composed as ever. Muted brown slacks, cranberry-colored cashmere turtleneck. Her shoulder-length brown hair was worn down today, brushed to a high gloss that nearly matched her obviously expensive leather boots. Even at forty, fit, accomplished and with a string of initials after her name, the woman appeared more likely to be an Ann Taylor model than a notorious serial killer's daughter.

"We're going to talk," D.D. said, and crossed back to the office.

The doctor glanced at her watch. "You have ten minutes left."

"Not on my time. On yours."

Adeline merely shrugged. "Honestly, Detective, other than his name, there's very little I can tell you about Harry Day."

"Now, now, Doc. You have your expertise, I have mine. Shall we?"

D.D. gestured back to the inner sanctum. With another shrug of her shoulders, Adeline retreated as D.D. followed. D.D. was thinking fast, adjusting and readjusting her expectations. Given the ritualistic nature of the two murders, she'd figured they'd get lucky with the Violent Criminal Apprehension Program. But matching their current murders to a string of forty-year-old homicides, the killer long dead, was more of a complication than a true development. Perhaps they were talking a copycat; God knows serial killers seemed to rack up larger fan bases these days than most movie stars. Given the number of websites and chat rooms dedicated to glorifying psychopaths, anything was possible.

But then to have her new doctor, a pain specialist she'd seen only twice, automatically know the killer's name, even have a personal connection to him . . . That crossed over the line of coincidental in D.D.'s book and entered the land of creepy.

D.D. didn't take her usual seat but remained standing across from Adeline, her throbbing arm and shoulder tucked protectively against the wall.

"Tell me about your father," D.D. said.

"Dr. Adolfus Glen," Adeline began.

D.D. rolled her eyes, immediately holding up a hand. "Yeah, yeah, yeah. Got the point. You consider your adoptive father your real father. He raised you, loved you, gave you everything a daughter could need, including a golden ticket out of psycho express."

"Well, now that you mention it . . ."

"Tell me about Harry Day."

The shuttered look on the doctor's face relented. She sighed and sat back, not happy but apparently resigned to her fate. "I only know what I've read; I was still a baby when Harry's crime spree came to an end. The way I understand it, one of his victims, a young waitress, got away. She ran to the police station. By the time the officers mobilized and came to arrest him, Harry was already dead, multiple cuts to each wrist. My mother suffered a breakdown and was carted off to a mental hospital, while child services assumed care of my older sister and me. The police spent the next six weeks systematically dismantling our house, unearthing two bodies beneath the family room and six more beneath Harry's woodworking shop around back. Harry was a carpenter. He had a fondness for tools."

"He tortured his victims," D.D. said flatly, having been told that much by Phil. "Some of them took weeks to die."

"But that's not why his name came up in relation to these two murders, is it?"

"No, that's not why."

"The killer you're investigating skinned his victims, correct? The *Boston Globe* didn't provide many details, but based on your interest in Harry, I'm going to guess the skin was removed in long, thin strips. More to the point, you didn't recover all the strips at the scene. Meaning the killer took some of the flesh with him. As a trophy. And now, based on what you've heard about Harry Day, you're wondering if some of these strips aren't preserved in glass vials, suspended in a special formaldehyde solution Harry perfected for just such a purpose."

D.D. gave up standing, took a seat. She spread her hands before her, wincing as the unconscious gesture aggravated her left arm. "Gotta say, helluva coincidence. Two murderers, forty years apart, both with a fondness for excising and preserving their victims' flesh. How many women do you think Harry killed?"

"He's credited with eight."

"The eight bodies they found at your house. What did the press nickname it at the time? House of Horrors, something like that?"

Adeline shrugged faintly. She had an impassive look on her face; D.D. had seen it before, on family members distancing themselves from terrible truths about people they should've known better. Or on the faces of victims, resolutely telling a story about something that surely happened to someone else.

"Harry's trophy collection," D.D. continued now. "I'm told the police recovered thirty-three glass jars containing pickled human skin. He'd hidden them beneath the floorboards of the bedroom closet."

The doctor flinched.

"First dozen were small mason jars," D.D. said, "but it appeared Harry got more sophisticated as time went on. Not only improved his formaldehyde solution, but moved into glass vials, like the kind used for perfume. And he labeled them. Not with names but some kind of random detail that must've meant something to him. Hair color, a place, an item of clothing. A unique but completely dehumanizing identifier for each specimen in his collection."

The doctor flinched again.

"Did they ever finish identifying them?" Adeline asked. "I thought . . . I'd read a few years ago that a cold case team had the idea of analyzing the . . . preserved tissue . . . against a list of missing persons from the same time period. They were hoping to get DNA samples from surviving family members of some of the women who went missing in the late sixties, and look for matches."

D.D. hadn't heard that, but it made some sense. "Don't know," she answered honestly. "But it might explain why so many details from a forty-year-old case were in ViCAP."

"They were going to look at open rape cases, as well. Many sexual sadist predators start with assault, correct? Their twisted fantasies escalate over time, taking them from voyeurs to rapists to killers. Meaning Harry's total victim count is probably well more than eight."

"Those were just the ones he kept close to home," D.D. agreed. So he could spend more time with them, she almost added, but didn't. Because serial murder was an escalating crime, and by that point in his homicidal career, Harry Day would've been an accomplished predator with an arsenal of tools, private work space and flexible schedule. Meaning if that one waitress hadn't escaped . . .

Across from her, Adeline murmured: "Sooner or later, all adopted children fantasize about the true identity of their birth parents. *My real mom and dad were royalty, but they had to send me away me at birth to protect me from an evil sorcerer who wanted to take over the kingdom,* that sort of thing. My adoptive father was a geneticist. A good man but with a clinician's heart. Let's just say when I first asked him for the truth about my parents, he told me. And I had nightmares for the next ten years, incredibly vivid dreams where I would watch my own skin crack open and a monster burst forth."

"Your adoptive father took you in as a baby?"

"When I was three and first diagnosed with congenital insensitivity to pain. He was one of the doctors who handled my case. Given my high-risk medical condition, he didn't feel my needs could be adequately addressed by an inexperienced foster family. So he made arrangements to adopt me personally."

"Lucky you."

"Yes."

"And your older sister? You said there were two of you?"

"She didn't suffer from a rare genetic defect," Adeline said simply. Which apparently, in her world, said it all.

"What about your birth mom?"

"She died six months after Harry, never speaking a word. She'd suffered some kind of mental breakdown and was in basically a catatonic state."

"Do you think she knew what her husband had been doing?" D.D. asked. "Harry buried two bodies in the house. Ripped up floorboards, dumped them in the crawl space, covered them with lime. Can't tell me it still didn't smell."

Adeline shook her head, her gaze fixed upon the glossy surface of her neatly organized desk. "I don't know. My adoptive father had compiled a history on both of my birth parents. Family is legacy, and he wanted me to be prepared. I've studied the material a great deal over the years. There is significant documentation on Harry Day. The neighbors described him as engaging, clever, good with his hands. By all accounts, my parents didn't socialize a great deal, but if you ran into Harry on the streets, he wouldn't give you the cold shoulder or turn your hair on end. One of the neighbors, an elderly widow, even raved about what a nice young man he was, fixed a leaking window for her, helped out with a squeaky door. Wouldn't even accept any money, just wanted a piece of her homemade apple pie. Of course, those are the types of stories that become nearly legendary after the fact, the cold killer with the kind heart. But to be honest, I don't believe it."

"The elderly neighbor was making the story up?"

"No." Adeline looked up, regarded D.D. flatly. "Harry was making himself up. That's what superpredators do, right? Engage in camouflage. I suspect he probably had some poor girl chained to the workbench in his shop that same week. Ergo, he went out of his way to help a neighbor. So if the police did come sniffing around, they'd all get the same scoop: Harry Day, what a nice guy, why just the other day, he fixed my broken window . . ."

D.D. nodded. She'd run across the same phenomenon—the But He Seemed Like Such a Nice Guy killer—and she agreed with Adeline's assessment. Psychopaths were never nice. They were just good at playing the part when it suited their needs.

Now D.D. pressed: "You still haven't answered my question about your mom."

"Because I can't."

"Can't or won't?"

"Can't. Even my adoptive father, who was an award-winning researcher, couldn't find any information on her. She was a ghost. No extended family, no past. She migrated to Boston from somewhere in the Midwest; at least that's what she told people. Her marriage certificate listed her maiden name as Davis, which, frankly, is too common to effectively trace. She never answered any of the police's questions, and not even the neighbors seemed to know her. Anne Davis lived as a shadow. Then became a ghost."

D.D. couldn't help herself; she shivered slightly. "Maybe that just proves she knew what her husband was doing. Leading to the mental breakdown: survivor's guilt."

Adeline merely shrugged. "Irrelevant. As you know even better than I, Harry was the perfect psychopath, and that kind of predator is always the alpha. Even if Anne knew, there was nothing she could've done. Harry was the one in control."

"Your father," D.D. stated once again, for the sake of argument.

Adeline's expression never changed. "Given that I suffer from a rare genetic condition, no one knows the potential pitfalls of DNA better than I."

D.D. found this intriguing. She leaned forward. "Did Harry have your same condition—is it possible he also couldn't feel pain?"

"No. Congenital insensitivity to pain is caused by a double-recessive gene—meaning both parents must be carriers of the genetic mutation. Not to mention there are fewer than fifty cases known in the entire US, and half of the children diagnosed die before age three from heatstroke. Someone like me, grown to adulthood, with four fully functional limbs . . . I'm the exception, not the norm."

"Why is that?"

"As part of the gene mutation, we can't feel heat. Meaning we don't sweat. For infants and toddlers, this is particularly dangerous. On a warm summer afternoon, their bodies can overheat to critical levels without them ever showing signs of distress. By the time the parents rush their listless baby to the hospital, it's too late."

D.D. couldn't help herself. "So what do you during the summer?"

"Enjoy air-conditioning. Drink plenty of fluids. And I take my temperature multiple times a day. I can't trust what I feel, Detective, which means I must rely on external diagnostics to tell me if my body is all right."

"Melvin is useful," D.D. murmured.

"Melvin is useful. I've never lain on a beach or walked in the full summer sun. I don't even enter a shower without first checking the thermometer. And as for most athletic hobbies or fitness programs . . . It would be dangerous for someone like me to run or swim or play tennis or shoot hoops. I could blow out a knee, break an ankle, strain a shoulder and never be any the wiser. My health remains a matter of constant vigilance."

D.D. nodded. She thought the good doctor spoke very matter-of-factly when describing a lifestyle that must actually feel very limiting and isolating. Forget never being picked for someone's team in grade school; Adeline must have had to sit out the entire recess. Let alone never having the chance to walk hand in hand with a special someone on a sunny day. Or run hard and strong just because she felt like it. Or leap from point A to point B simply to see if she could make it.

A serious adult who no doubt grew up as a serious child, practicing constant vigilance. And realizing at a very young age that her rare condition inevitably set her apart, an outsider looking in.

Because Melvin wasn't just useful. Melvin was common, pain being the great equalizer that brought everyone together.

"And your sister?" D.D. asked.

"She doesn't share my condition."

"So your adoptive father didn't take her in."

"No."

"Must've pissed her off."

"I was three, she was six, too young to understand, let alone get 'pissed off.' "

"What happened to her?"

"She remained a ward of the state, bouncing around various foster homes."

"You in touch with her?"

"Yes."

"She got a name?"

"Yes."

"But you're not going to give it to me?" D.D.'s keen investigator's senses started to vibrate.

The doctor hesitated. "By the time I was fourteen, I was asking a lot of questions about my birth father. Unbeknownst to me, my adoptive father hired a private investigator to research all three members of my birth family. I'm guessing the PI was a retired Boston cop, as most of the information he gathered on my father was photocopies of the police reports. Maybe an old buddy on the force gave him access. Researching my mother proved more difficult, as I mentioned, and her file is thin. My sister . . ."

Dr. Glen paused.

"She would've been seventeen by then, I guess. Still a ward of the state. But even by that point, her file was thicker than my father's, her exploits even more legendary."

D.D. leaned forward, senses definitely humming.

"The most telling report, which I never read until after my adoptive father's death, comes from the social worker who came to my parents' house that day. The one who took us into custody, then sought immediate medical treatment for my four-year-old sister. According to her, my sister's back, arms and the inside of her legs were covered with dozens of thin lacerations. Some old, many new, but essentially her skin was striped continuously in long, even lines of dried blood."

"He was cutting her," D.D. filled in. "You believe Harry Day was cutting your sister."

Adeline looked at her. "It's not like she could've reached her own back."

"Did he remove skin?"

"Not that the doctors reported. But then, he wouldn't have to, right? Harry took trophies from his victims to remember them after they were gone. My sister wasn't a kidnapped girl who eventually would have to be disposed of. She was his own daughter. The victim who was always available to him. No doubt the perfect 'filler' option in between other sport."

D.D. studied Adeline. The doctor's gaze remained direct, her expression controlled. But there was a tightness to her jaw that hadn't been there before. The good doc was holding it together. But it was costing her.

D.D. asked the next logical question: "And you?"

"According to the hospital admittance papers, not a mark on me."

"Harry abused her but not you."

"Harry Day died one week prior to my first birthday. It might have proved interesting to see if the same still held true eight days later."

"You think your age saved you. You were a baby. Whereas, the moment you turned one . . ."

Adeline shrugged. "We'll never know."

"Could it have been your condition?" D.D. wondered. "Maybe he did cut you. But you wouldn't have cried, right? And that wouldn't have been very satisfying to him."

Adeline appeared surprised. "In all the years, I've never considered that."

"Really? Seems an obvious thought."

"It's possible, I suppose, but not probable. We didn't know about my condition yet. It wasn't discovered until I was three. Then it was my sister who did the honors. She cut me."

D.D. blinked. "Your sister, the six-year-old, cut you?"

"It's what she knew. A learned behavior drilled into her night after night: Blood is love. And in her own way, my sister loves me."

"I'm not attending any of your family reunions."

"She took scissors to my arms. When I didn't cry out, she cut deeper. Which might be further evidence my father couldn't have known. I have a feeling his first instinct would've been to cut deeper as well, and I don't bear those kinds of scars."

"Okay."

"So question of the day, Detective: Is evil born or made?"

"Nature versus nurture."

"Exactly. What do you think?"

D.D. shook her head. "No need to choose; I've seen both."

"Me, too. A good person can be warped into evil, and an evil person can be tempered by good."

"So your point is?"

"None of that matters when it comes to my sister; she got screwed by both."

"The daughter of a serial killer," D.D. filled in, "already subjected to years of ritualistic abuse, then turned loose in the foster care system." At which point, the light finally went on, and D.D. closed her eyes, not believing she hadn't connected the dots sooner. To give herself some credit, the case was thirty years old, meaning she'd been a teenager herself at the time and not a work-obsessed detective. Still, given the notoriety . . .

"Shana Day," D.D. stated out loud. "Your sister is Shana Day. Youngest convicted female murderer in Massachusetts, tried as an adult when she was only fourteen. Has spent the decades since picking off corrections officers and fellow inmates in the MCI. That Shana Day." Then, another lightbulb moment: "She mutilated him, right? It's been years since I thought about the case, but right after she strangled the kid, she worked him over with a knife. Removed an ear. And *strips of skin* . . ." D.D. stared at Adeline, nearly dumbfounded by the implications. "Where's your sister now?"

"Still a resident of the MCI, where she'll spend the rest of her life."

"I want to speak with her. Immediately."

"You can try. She's currently recovering in the prison's medical ward, however. Recovering from her latest suicide attempt."

"What's her condition?"

"Stable. For now." Adeline paused. "Next week will be the thirty-year anniversary of Donnie Johnson's death. I gather Shana's getting some unwelcome attention from it. At least one reporter has contacted the prison, wanting an interview."

"Does she talk about the case?"

"Never."

"What about friends, associates?" D.D.'s mind was already racing ahead. Shana might be behind bars, but it boggled D.D.'s mind how many convicted murderers carried out active social lives while supposedly imprisoned. They fell in love, got married. Why not seduce some burgeoning wannabe killer into finishing Daddy's—or her own—life's work?

But Adeline was shaking her head. "My sister suffers from severe antisocial personality disorder. Don't get me wrong; she's exceptionally smart and disturbingly clever. But she is not like my father. No elderly widow would ever let Shana inside the front door to repair a broken window. Nor does Shana herself have any interest in friends or followers."

D.D. couldn't help herself. "So your father is a serial killer, your sister is a proficient murderer—wait, she's passed the triple victim mark, making her a serial killer in her own right—and you suffer from a rare congenital condition making it impossible for you to feel pain. That's quite some gene pool."

"Every bell curve has its outliers."

"Outliers? Please, your family can't even be on the graph."

Adeline shrugged; D.D. switched gears.

"Your sister jealous of you?"

"You would have to ask her."

"But you two have a relationship?"

"I visit once a month. She'll tell you I come because I feel guilty. And I'll tell you she accepts my visits because she's bored. Detective . . You seem to think this so-called Rose Killer might have a direct connection to my family, may even be inspired by them. Speaking as a psychiatrist with some experience in deviant personalities, I wouldn't be so sure."

D.D. gave her a skeptical look.

"If you compare enough pieces of warped wood," Adeline continued, "some are bound to be warped the same way. Same with abnormal psyches. Many share the same obsessions, rituals and fantasies. Is it that this killer has read about Harry Day, or visited Shana? Or is it enough that he shares their primary belief?"

"Which is?"

"Blood is love. My sister took sewing shears to my arms not to hurt me but to demonstrate her affection. As for twelve-year-old Donnie Johnson, I think it's possible Shana's never spoken of that night for the same reason: She didn't hate the boy. She simply loved him too much and has missed him ever since."

D.D. arched a brow. "Your sister killed a twelve-year-old boy as a display of her affection?"

"I don't know. But something happened that night, Detective. Something powerful enough, or maybe simply personal enough, that not even a pure psychopath such as my sister has been able to speak of it since."

Chapter 13

Who am I? Average security company employee.

What do I look like? Nothing special. Tan pants, blue button-down shirt, baseball cap pulled low.

Primary motivation? Just doing my job.

Purpose of operation: Distract investigative efforts, confuse the issue.

Net gain: Everyone loves a villain.

The nondescript security company employee drove straight to the target.

No other vehicles in the driveway. No signs of life in the home. The security company employee parked on the street, grabbed a black computer bag from the passenger's seat, then pressed a navy-blue baseball cap lower onto head.

The khaki pants were baggy, same with the faded blue shirt. Flea market finds, hence the lack of perfect fit. But cheap clothes were disposable clothes. And excess fabric further distorted one's size, which would come in handy later, when nosy neighbors were inevitably called upon to provide a description.

Deep breath in and out. Hands flexing and unflexing on the steering wheel. This was it. Not a time to think but a time to do. Research had been done, plans debated, decisions made. Now the moment was at hand.

The first time, lurking outside the target's town house. Realizing after months and weeks of consideration that this was finally it . . . Then carefully positioning the package in the center of the walkway, far enough that she'd have to leave the doorway to retrieve it. Ringing the doorbell, then ducking behind the fake ficus tree in the corner of the front porch. The target opened the front door. The target sighed, spotting the delivery fifteen feet away. The target set out to retrieve her prize. Making it so easy to slip inside, taking up position in a hall closet until late that night, when the lights were finally out . . .

Who am I? Nothing. Nobody. No one. Or maybe I am just like you. The outsider, looking in.

What is my motivation? Financial security. Personal success. Call of the wild. Or maybe, just like you, I want to be someone. To finally feel as if I belong.

Now, the nondescript security company employee exited the van and headed straight for the home's front door.

Body angled, counting on bulky clothes to help further obscure the view, the nondescript security company employee picked the twin locks. Which, of course, triggered the home security system into its first round of wails.

Not rushing. In fact, now relaxing. Because with the alarm came further justification for the presence of a security company employee. All, in fact, was proceeding according to plan.

Striding into the house. Heading for the stairs. Locating the master bedroom.

Thirty seconds and counting now. Because while it might appear to nosy neighbors that the proper person was already on scene, a posse of security company operators were immediately placing calls to the local police as well as the responsible homeowner. Time mattered.

Now the nondescript security company employee studied the bed. Right-hand-side nightstand held a glass of water, faintly smudged with pink lipstick. Upon closer investigation, the pillow revealed several blond curls. Definitely her side of the bed. Did she sleep well? Or did she still remember that night, standing in the darkened hallway all alone, so completely vulnerable . . .

Rockabye, baby, on the treetop, the nondescript security company employee hummed. *When the wind blows, the cradle will rock . . .*

Attacking a homicide detective had not been part of the plan. But she'd heard, coming out of the bedroom, leading with her gun. Returning to the crime scene had been a rookie mistake, the nondescript person understood now. Giving in to the temptation to see it again, review each detail, had everything really gone just so? Plus, from the outside, the town house had appeared dark, empty, safe.

Then, the detective, suddenly appearing in the hallway. And a choice had to be made. Fight or flight. Really, it hadn't been so hard after all. Just as others had claimed, once you kill the first time, the rest really does come easy.

Improvisation. It had worked even better than imagined. So now, here stood a nondescript security company employee improvising again. While continuing to count the seconds: *Eighteen, nineteen, twenty . . .*

Time was a taskmaster. Must stay on plan.

Unzipping the computer bag, producing the first item. The bottle of champagne. Then, of course, the handcuffs, delicately lined with fur. Followed by a single red rose, placed directly upon her pillow.

Finally, the card. Purchased just this morning and the winning touch.

Stepping back. A final assessment of the scene.

Purpose of operation: Intimidate, scare, antagonize. Because then again, maybe I don't want to be you. I want to be better than you.

Net gain: Adrenaline rush.

Thirty-one, thirty-two, thirty-three . . .

The nightstand phone started to ring. No doubt the security company, checking to see if it was the homeowner who'd accidentally triggered the alarm, and could now silence the system by magically uttering the secret password.

Nondescript security company employee turned, walked steadily down the stairs, out of the house and back to the waiting van. A quick show of speaking rapidly into a cell phone, conscientious employee on the job. Face down, gaze averted, back to the nosy neighbors, who were now starting to look actively out their windows.

The home alarm continued to shriek.

As the nondescript security company employee climbed back into the vehicle. And drove away.

Leaving behind the tokens of affection for Sergeant Detective D. D. Warren. Including a very thoughtful card, which read:

Get well soon.

Chapter 14

A LEX PACED.

D.D.'s squad was assembled in their family room. Crime scene techs had arrived, inspecting their front door, dusting for prints, bagging the various tokens of the killer's affection. Uniformed officers had canvassed the area. Other detectives had interviewed the neighbors, establishing that a nondescript person in a nondescript white van bearing the name of a major home security firm had appeared in their driveway in response to their home alarm. Or maybe it had been there right before the activation of the alarm? But one way or another, Alex and D.D.'s home security system had activated, and an employee from their security company had been right there to handle it. Male, female, young, old, black or white, no one was sure. But a company employee. Definitely a company employee had been immediately on scene. Good thing, too, right?

Alex paced.

He'd been the one to find the note. Came home from work, pulled in the drive with Jack strapped into his car seat. He'd opened his car door and registered the screech of the alarm right about the same moment his cell phone had buzzed with their real security firm calling to check in with them.

Not having seen anything amiss from the outside, Alex entered their home. They'd had false alarms before. These things happened. And given the undisturbed front door, intact windows, quiet downstairs . . .

He'd just relaxed, he'd told D.D. tersely. Jack in his left arm, security company on the phone tucked against his right ear as he'd popped upstairs for one last, quick inspection . . .

The security company had contacted the Boston PD, while Alex had headed straight back out of the house with three-year-old Jack in his arms and driven him to his parents.

They would keep him for the night.

While the crime scene technicians processed Alex and D.D.'s home.

And Alex paced.

His hands were clasped behind him. He wore his academy clothes, khaki pants, a navy-blue shirt embroidered with the Massachusetts State Police logo on his chest. The hard line of his shoulders spoke of tension. Otherwise his set face remained expressionless, nearly impossible to read. If D.D. was an expert on externalizing her rage, then Alex was a master of internalizing his, maintaining a tightly reined control.

For the first time, it occurred to her how rough the past six weeks must have been for him. She was the one who gnashed her teeth and growled about feeling powerless. Yet, how much say had Alex had in the matter? One morning, his wife went to work. And she hadn't been able to dress herself, watch their child or do anything useful since.

He'd had to watch her suffer. He'd had to assist her with tasks that often increased her pain. And he'd had to shoulder the full load of parenting as well as household chores for the foreseeable future.

Yet he'd never once complained or snapped at her to get over herself.

He was there for her. Even now, he wasn't demanding to know what she'd gotten herself into, or how dare she bring the dangers of her job into their home. He was thinking. Analyzing. Strategizing.

Alex wasn't feeling sorry for himself, or for her. He was plotting how to get the son of a bitch who'd violated their home.

"So," Phil said at last. He was sitting on the sofa, notepad propped on his knees, gray blazer rumpled, dark-red tie askew. Of all of them, he appeared to be taking the break-in the hardest. With D.D. out, this had been his case. And not only had a second victim been murdered, but now the killer appeared to be getting closer to them, without them getting any closer to him.

"So," D.D. repeated. She'd moved a kitchen chair into the family room, where she sat with her left arm tucked against her ribs, an ice pack on the back of her left shoulder. After the impromptu physical therapy session with Dr. Adeline Glen, it seemed the least she could do. Plus, she was trying to prove to herself, if not to her pain specialist, that she wasn't a complete control freak. She could try other pain management techniques. Yes, she could.

"Neighbors don't have much to offer," Phil continued. "Basically, a *person,* very average-looking, entered your home."

Across from Phil, Neil shrugged. "Nothing we didn't already know. Killer has entered and exited two other crime scenes without arousing attention. Blending in is obviously something the perpetrator does well."

"But maybe we learned more about technique," Phil said. "The suspect was disguised to appear as a home security company employee. We can go back to the other two crime scenes, see if they had systems, if there were any calls that came in that night. Or ask about other common service companies. Maybe a van marked 'pest control' or 'plumbing.' You know, the kind of thing that really didn't stand out for the neighbors at the time, but if we return with more specific questions now . . ."

"Who is this guy?" asked Alex abruptly. He stopped pacing, stood in the middle of their modest, beige-carpeted family room and stared at them.

"Joe Average," Neil spoke up. "Or maybe Jane Average. Statistics would argue for Joe, given that most killers are male. But again, the lack of sexual assault, not to mention any kind of useful eyewitness account, means we can't rule out Jane. So maybe, just Average Person. We are looking for an everyday average person."

"No," Alex responded immediately. "Our suspect's a killer. That already makes him or her a member of an extremely small percentage of the human population. And a double murderer who's *not* a sexual sadist predator falls into an even smaller percentage of an already small percentage. So again, who *is* this asshole? Because right now, we're not understanding this killer. And yet, he, she or it is getting to us just fine."

D.D. thought she knew what her husband meant. "I paid a visit to a funeral home today," she spoke up. "Thinking along the same lines, that we're investigating a predator who commits incredibly macabre murders, except he doesn't seem that interested in the actual killing part. It's the postmortem mutilation that appears to drive him. Which made me think of someone who might feel more comfortable with dead people than living people, which made me think of people who work at funeral homes."

"The Norman Bates syndrome," Neil murmured from the love seat.

"Yeah. Except, when I interviewed the embalmer, he emphasized that successful funeral home directors excel at empathy. Not exactly how I'd describe our killer."

Neil sighed, sat up. "Much like you, I've spent the day contemplating necrophilia."

"This from the guy who spends all his time in the morgue," D.D. muttered.

Neil scowled, clearly not in the mood. "Here's the thing. On the one hand, our killer seems most comfortable with his victims postmortem. On the other hand . . . he or she or whatever is still not *that* into them. No sexual assault. Meaning by definition he's not a necrophiliac—which just for the record, once again does not exclude our perpetrator being female. I ran across five or six case histories of female necrophiliacs just to ensure my research was icky enough."

"Industry has a number of female embalmers, too," D.D. added. "Just saying."

"Meaning back to Alex's point," Neil continued. "We have two dead bodies and still no idea what's driving these crimes. If these aren't murders of pain, passion or punishment, what are they?"

"I think I might know the answer to that one," D.D. said. "Given the lack of pain and punishment, I think it's fair to say our killer isn't driven by bloodlust. I think, in fact, our killer is not that into killing at all. Instead, he, she, it, may be driven by compulsion. Say a deep-seated desire to add to a very unique, very personal private collection."

"What kind of collection?" Phil asked.

"Strips of human skin."

The room fell quiet. Then Neil made a face. "Ed Gein, anyone?" he muttered.

Now everyone grimaced; Ed Gein was a notorious serial killer who'd once made a lampshade from human skin.

"Earlier today," D.D. said, "when I pictured our unsub in my head, I kept seeing a lone guy, small of stature, limited social skills. If you think about his MO, ambushing his victims while they're still asleep, drugging them quickly, killing them expeditiously . . . Feels to me like our killer's primary goal isn't venting displaced rage or satisfying twisted sexual cravings but to carefully and judiciously harvest strips of flesh. Which, theoretically speaking, means we're looking for a socially awkward homicidal maniac with a fetish for collecting human skin. Sound good?"

Everyone nodded.

D.D. continued: "Except here's the problem: Two problems, actually. One, my shoulder. Meet Melvin," she introduced her injured left arm to her squad. "And two, the scene upstairs. Returning to problem number one and assuming for a moment our perpetrator is a male, since when does an antisocial skin collector have the balls to personally revisit his first crime scene? Crawling under the police tape, an act that would certainly call attention to himself, if not lead automatically to his arrest. Let alone, confront the female lead investigator of the case, and in some way I can't yet remember but someday will, shove said investigator down the stairs? Those are some pretty bold moves for a killer who only attacks sleeping women."

Alex pursed his lips. Slowly, Phil and Neil nodded.

"Same goes with the little scene staged upstairs. Suddenly, Mr. Antisocial is breaking into a cop's house? In broad daylight? Staging his wardrobe and vehicle to appear as if with a security company, waltzing right through the front door, then leaving his personal calling cards next to my bed? I mean, the level of social engineering, let alone pure gamesmanship . . ." D.D. scowled, twitched her icing shoulder uncomfortably in the hard-backed chair. "Seems to me the same predator who's interested in this level of direct confrontation and just plain *nah, nah, na, nah, nah, na* is not the same guy who'd be content to ambush women in their sleep. So I'm wondering, especially given the lack of sexual assault and detailed physical description, maybe our killer is a woman, a female collector obsessed with human skin." She couldn't help herself; she thought immediately of Shana Day.

"For a woman, attacking other women would be more of an equal playing field," Phil spoke up. "So not a socially awkward, low-self-esteem predator, but a female prepared to do whatever she has to do to pursue her compulsion. For someone like that, targeting the lead investigator, engaging in gamesmanship, wouldn't even be so much of a stretch—especially if she perceives you as threatening to come between her and what she wants most, which is additions to her collection."

"Except the card upstairs read, *Get well soon,*" Alex muttered. "If D.D.'s presence is a threat to our killer, why encourage her speedy recovery?"

"And the killer could be male," Neil spoke up. "Just saying, we shouldn't get ahead of ourselves on this one."

"The house was dark," Phil said abruptly. Then he flushed, and that's when D.D. understood what he meant. That house, the first crime scene, where she had plunged down the stairs. Phil had been one of the first detectives to find her. "When we got there," he continued awkwardly now, "lights were out. Scene was quiet. We didn't think anyone was there. Including you."

He glanced at D.D. "Maybe the killer didn't know you were there, either. He or she thought the scene was safe to revisit. Except, of course, it wasn't."

"I surprised the killer," she whispered.

"Who retaliated by pushing you down the stairs," Alex continued. "Who maybe even assumed you had plunged to your doom. Except no articles appeared in the paper about a dead detective found at the scene of a crime."

D.D. frowned at him. "No articles appeared about an injured detective, either, right? The fact I'm incapacitated, indeed, must get well soon . . ."

They all paused, the implication sinking in.

D.D. said it first. "The killer found me. Has been watching. Only way he or she could know about my injuries."

"No," Alex said, voice suddenly firm.

"What do you mean—"

"It's been six, seven weeks since your injury. Six, seven weeks where you've heard nothing. Till today. You tell me, what changed in the past twenty-four hours? Where have you been?"

And then she got it. "The second murder. A new crime scene—"

"Which you visited," he goaded.

"Which I visited," she agreed.

"The killer was there," Phil supplied. "Still watching the scene, still checking things out. Another note for the file." He turned to

Neil. "Our guy, or gal, is a watcher. That could help us, definitely help us."

Neil nodded, made a note. "But if the killer is a collector, why revisit the scenes? Isn't that something normally done by sexual sadist predators to recapture the thrill of the moment?"

"It could still be a thrill crime," D.D. said. "But it's the harvesting that's the thrill. The time postmortem, instead of the actual murder. But the same rules apply. The person wants to remember, recapture. That would be part of the whole value of the collection, the memories it evokes."

Alex was staring hard at her. "You're part of it now. The killer's fantasy, need, compulsion. Maybe you surprised him or her the first time. And maybe the killer reacted with the impulsive decision to shove you down the stairs. But then you come back. You reappeared at the second crime scene, not even on the job, but still on the hunt. . . . That triggered something. Made it personal. You, D.D., made it personal."

She caught it, just a whiff of blame, but it was enough. Her job had already caused her to injure herself. And now, her detective's instincts had endangered her entire family.

"Do we even know today's intruder is the same person as the killer?" she whispered, an exercise in wishful thinking.

Phil supplied what, deep down, she'd already known. "Same brand of champagne was left here as at the two murders, a detail that wasn't in the papers. We've considered it a minor victory. Got the damn media to omit at least that much."

"So it was definitely the killer who was in our house," D.D. summarized, looking up at Alex. "A predator obsessed with harvesting human skin and taunting injured detectives."

She didn't want to sound bitter, but she did. She didn't want to sound scared, either, though she still wasn't quite that lucky.

"So what kind of killer is obsessed with removing strips of skin?" Neil asked.

D.D. sighed heavily. "Oh, I have some ideas on that subject, too." They regarded her blankly.

"Introducing Harry and Shana Day."

SHE STARTED WITH HARRY DAY, walking them through Harry's spree of terror of forty years ago. The women he abducted, tortured and eventually killed. His own obsession for removing body parts, including the jars of excised skin found beneath the floor of his bedroom closet.

Alex and Neil remained blasé on the subject. Until she got to the last two tidbits. Harry Day's older daughter, Shana, was a notorious killer in her own right, currently serving life in the MCI. And, oh yes, his other daughter was none other than Dr. Adeline Glen, D.D.'s new pain therapist.

"What?" Alex exploded. "That can't possibly be coincidence. What if this doctor's the one who just broke into our house? She knows all about your injury, as well as details from both murders since you discussed them with her. A daughter of a serial killer, she has good reason to be obsessed with a cop. Maybe she even pushed you down the stairs of the first crime scene, just so you'd become one of her patients."

D.D. rolled her eyes, exasperated. "Oh, for the love of paranoid thinking . . . For starters, I was personally with Dr. Glen this afternoon—"

"What time?"

"I don't know. One to two."

"Break-in happened around three thirty. Doesn't count her out."

"Come on. I only started seeing Dr. Glen because Superintendent Horgan recommended her. And even then, if my fall had led to a minor injury or a different kind of injury, I wouldn't need her services. So to assume some malevolent shrink shoved me down the stairs at a crime scene just to get me into her office . . . large margin for error in that master plan."

"But Superintendent Horgan recommended her," Alex insisted. "Meaning she's known by the department, which has previously used her services. Meaning maybe not so unlikely that an injured cop would end up in her offices."

D.D. scowled at him.

"Did you say she was a psychiatrist or a psychologist?" Phil spoke up.

"Psychiatrist."

"So she's a doctor, right? Went to medical school, with full medical training," he continued, the skills-with-scalpel part being implied.

D.D. wanted to argue. She liked her new doctor. Adeline Glen was intelligent, tough, challenging. She was also . . . compelling. For all her composure, there was a sense of aloneness to the woman, of resigned isolation. D.D. would've thought not being able to feel pain would be the greatest gift in the world, especially lately. But having talked to Dr. Glen this afternoon, having had a rare glimpse into the woman's world . . . The doctor was forever set apart, studying her fellow man but never truly able to walk in anyone's footsteps.

And the woman knew it.

"Can we back up for a second?" Neil asked, raking a hand through his mop of red hair. "Our killer could be male or female. Possibly an embalmer, comfortable with dead bodies, or a hunter, comfortable with skinning, or even a licensed psychiatrist with a full medical background. Why not? What's throwing me is that you're saying these murders might have something to do with a guy who's been dead for forty years. Or, I guess, to be more precise, his surviving daughters?"

Phil nodded. "Gotta say, you lost me on that one, too."

"I'm not saying anything yet," D.D. clarified. "More like, here are some questions worth asking. Look, ViCAP exists to catch similarities in MO. According to it, our current killer has a match—Harry Day. Now, given that Day has been dead for four decades, I don't think we need to be concerned about him personally assisting our predator. Then again . . . in this info-mad day and age, where hundreds if not thousands of websites exist to idolize the careers of various serial killers . . . I wonder if it's as simple as our antisocial killer is a big fan. He researched Harry Day, and the way things work in the twisted mind of a psychopath, he read about jars of preserved flesh and his brain went ding, ding, ding. I want that!"

"He recognized Harry Day," Alex clarified. "Or at least, related to him."

"Wouldn't be the first time," D.D. observed, thinking again about Dr. Glen's point: Given enough pieces of warped wood, at least some were bound to be warped the same way.

"Does Harry Day have his own website?" Neil asked.

"I don't know. Haven't had time to look it up. But here's my second thought. If our killer researched Harry Day, his daughter Shana's name is bound to come up. And while he can't ask Harry any questions about his technique, Shana, on the other hand . . ."

"He might have reached out to her in prison," Phil supplied, making a quick note.

"More questions worth asking."

"What about your doctor?" Alex spoke up, laser focused. "Have any of her father's fans contacted her?"

"According to her, no. Her last name isn't Day, however, but Glen, meaning the killer would have to dig deeper to find the family connection. Plus, if the killer's inspiration is the personal . . . appeal . . . of preserving human skin, there's no reason for him to reach out to Adeline. Shana, on the other hand, would be a better source, having infamously sliced and diced during her first murder. Now, Dr. Glen says her sister doesn't receive visitors or respond to correspondence. But I don't know how much she's pushed the issue, either. Or how much her sister would admit to her."

"We need to interview Shana," Phil said.

"Dr. Glen said she'd be willing to assist with that," D.D. provided.

"You're going to be there, aren't you?" Alex stared at her, not really saying it as a question.

"If Horgan allows it, I'd like to be."

"Why?"

"Because. It's what I do. What I know best. And given I can't remember what happened that night, or if it was a man or woman or an asexual space alien who shoved me down the flight of stairs. And now *two* women are dead and I'm still stupid while the killer is walking through our home and thumbing his/her/its nose at us." Her voice picked up, though she didn't intend it to. "What if next time it's not champagne? What if next time, he/she/it leaves crime scene trophies on our pillows? Or ribbons of skin in the middle of our bed? It's going to get worse, Alex. What's the number one rule of serial killers?"

"Their crimes escalate."

"That's right. Their crimes escalate. Now, look at me! Look at my stupid fucking shoulder. Look at our house, where, let's face it, we both know we won't be sleeping tonight. This is my life. My family. And I can't even load my gun. I can't do anything and it's all my fault . . . Dammit!" Her voice broke roughly. "God dammit."

"I'll be posting a patrol car outside," Phil offered stiffly.

She nodded but didn't look up.

"And we got a lot to go on now," Neil offered. "These are good avenues of investigation. Given the publicity, you know Horgan will approve expanding the team. Pressure will be on to get to the bottom of this quick."

D.D. nodded again, her gaze still on the carpet.

Alex moved. He crossed the space, placing his hand on her right shoulder. The motion jarred her left arm, but she willed herself not to wince.

"*Our* family, D.D.," he said firmly. "*We* will handle this. Together. Side by side. Three good arms taking on the he/she/its of the world. Because this is what both of us do best."

"I still can't move my arm," she whispered.

He didn't talk anymore. He kissed her on top of the head. She closed her eyes and willed it to be enough.

Except it wasn't.

A killer had walked through D.D.'s home. And she didn't want her husband's love or her squad's protection.

She wanted revenge.

Chapter 15

I ENTERED THE SANCTUARY of my luxury high-rise condo building, oversize leather purse slung over my left shoulder, thoughts a million miles away as I considered my sister's latest suicide attempt, not to mention my discussion with Detective Warren regarding my homicidal family tree. One family, two killers, an infamous legacy of death and destruction. And I heard my adoptive father's voice once more in my head: *Any family, but particularly your family, Adeline, has a gift for inflicting pain.*

I wished I could talk to him now. I don't think I ever appreciated how much his crisp, analytic presence anchored me. Then he died, and I became adrift, a well-adjusted aspiring psychiatrist suddenly visiting her older sister in prison. A successful young woman, suddenly hanging out at the airport, armed with a scalpel and a collection of slender glass vials.

The two recent murders. A killer obsessed with removing human skin. Did it mean anything? Could it mean anything?

I stepped into the elevator, thoughts still churning. The car rising. Myself, contemplating things I didn't want to contemplate. The doors sliding open. Now telling myself I would not head straight for my walk-in closet, pry up the loose floorboards and check on my precious collection. Instead, I would take up yoga, pour a glass of wine, something, anything more befitting a woman of my education and success.

Finally arriving before my front door, still wanting what I knew I shouldn't have.

As a shadow peeled away from the far wall and a man suddenly materialized before me.

"Dr. Adeline Glen?"

Reflexively, I grabbed my purse strap, stifled a gasp.

"How did you get up here?"

He smiled, but it was a grim expression on his face. "Judging by the news this morning, that's about to be the least of your concerns."

HE INTRODUCED HIMSELF as Charlie Sgarzi. The reporter who, according to Superintendent McKinnon, had been calling and writing to my sister for the past few months. He was also the cousin of Shana's twelve-year-old victim, Donnie Johnson. Though interestingly enough, Sgarzi wasn't volunteering that information to me.

"I have a few questions," he stated now. "About your sister, Shana Day, and Donnie Johnson's murder, thirty years ago."

"I can't help you."

He gave me a look. He wasn't a large man, but heavyset, with a swarthy complexion and small dark eyes. I imagined he could be quite intimidating when he wanted to be. The question was, did he want to be?

"Oh, I think you can," he stated bluntly. "A professional shrink who meets with her sister at least once a month at the MCI? I bet you know all sorts of things."

I shook my head. "No. Not really."

"Aren't you gonna at least invite me in?"

"No. Not really."

He frowned, starting to look angry. Frustrated as well, because clearly this conversation wasn't going as he'd planned. But something else. I couldn't quite put my finger on it, but another emotion, dark and potent, stirring the pot.

Now he huffed, taking his hands out of his oversize Dick Tracy trench coat and making an imploring gesture.

"Come on. Cut a guy a break. Your sister was one of the first fourteen-year-olds ever prosecuted as an adult. Nowadays, it seems the news is filled with depraved teenaged killers. But Shana, what she did to twelve-year-old Donnie . . . that was a bad case. Can't tell me you don't think about it. Can't tell me, having her for an older sister, hasn't affected your life."

I said nothing, simply readjusted my hand on my purse. If I grabbed my apartment keys, then went for his jugular, or jabbed at his eyes, would that be seen as a woman protecting herself? Or would it simply prove that I was just as violent as the rest of my family?

"You care about your sister that much?"

I said nothing.

"I mean, it's not like you grew up with her. Nah, you were the lucky one." He rocked back on his heels. Giving me space, I realized, as if he knew what I'd just been thinking.

"I read all about you," he continued, voice matter-of-fact. "In a gene pool of freaks, you still managed to outfreak 'em all. Rare genetic condition, snagged yourself a rich doctor to play Daddy Warbucks. Way to go, Adeline. Bet your sister hates you for that alone."

He stared at me. I said nothing.

"Is it true you can't feel pain?"

"Hit me and find out."

His eyes widened. I'd called his bluff, and for the first time, he appeared uncertain. His shoulders came down, expression puzzled. I could nearly watch the wheels spin in his head as he rapidly reassessed. Then he steeled himself and I caught his look of resolve once again. One way or another, he was determined to speak to me. Because my sister had repeatedly blown him off? Because I was as close to her as he was going to get? Or then again, was there something darker, more potent, driving him?

"Were you relieved the prison guards got to her in time this morning?" he asked, going with a friendlier tone as if we were neighbors, meeting over coffee. "Or maybe a tad disappointed? You can tell me the truth, Adeline. I mean, a woman as accomplished as you, saddled with a sister as troubled as Shana. People understand these things. I'll understand."

"How are your aunt and uncle?" I asked quietly. "The thirty-year anniversary of their son's murder I imagine must be very difficult for them."

Sgarzi's face froze. For all his efforts, I'd hit the mark first, and he knew it. A spasm moved across his face. Faint but telling. And I got it then, the undercurrent of emotion swirling around the man as tangibly as his reporter's trench coat: grief. Charlie Sgarzi wasn't angry. He was grieving. Thirty years later, that night, my sister, still haunted him.

I felt myself falter.

"They're dead, thanks for asking." His voice, once again matter-of-fact.

"And your own family?"

"I'm not here about them. I'm here about your family. Stop avoiding the question."

"My question is equally relevant. I didn't know my sister when she killed your cousin. But you did. Meaning chances are my sister's actions have had a greater impact on your life than on my own."

"Donnie was a good kid."

I waited.

"He liked her, you know. She ever tell you that? During your sessions together, does she even talk about him?"

I remained patient. Charlie was just getting started. Sure enough . . .

"I found letters!" the reporter nearly exploded, his expression suddenly coming alive. Rage, sorrow, disbelief. Stages of grief, stamped into a man thirty years later, because pain can do that to a person. My sister can do that to a person. "Half a dozen letters I discovered stashed in the bottom of my uncle's bureau, and you know what they are? *Love letters.* Love letters your sister wrote to my cousin. He was twelve years old, just a lonely little guy without a friend in the world, and here comes this older, streetwise new girl saying what a cool bike he has, maybe they can get together sometime. Course he met her by the lilac bushes. She didn't just murder him. She lured him to his death."

"Blood is love," I murmured, but Sgarzi wasn't in the mood to listen anymore. He'd shoved himself away from the wall, pacing restlessly.

"My aunt never got over it. She spent the next ten years drinking herself to death, and there was nothing my mom could do to stop her. Because that's the lie they tell families of the victims; that it'll get better. Time heals all wounds. Blah, blah, blah. Thirty years. Thirty fucking years, and six months ago, my uncle got out his service revolver and shot himself in the head. Your sister didn't just kill my cousin. She destroyed my entire family. Now I have a few questions. Think you can pay me the courtesy of answering?"

"Why?"

"*Why?*" He stared at me, dark face nearly frozen in shock. "*Why?*"

"It's been thirty years, Mr. Sgarzi," I said gently. "There is nothing I can tell you that changes what happened to your family."

"Please. I know my cousin is dead. I know my aunt and uncle are gone and my mom has turned into a shut-in who won't even order takeout pizza because you never know about those delivery boys. I want access, okay? I want an exclusive interview with one of the most notorious female killers in the state of Massachusetts. After what Shana did to my cousin, hacking off his ear, slicing up his arms . . . At the very least, I think I deserve a seven-figure book deal. Maybe then, we'll call it even."

Despite myself, I was surprised: "You're cashing in on your cousin's murder?"

"No. I'm funding my mother's home health aid. My mom's dying of cancer, thank you very much, and she doesn't want to leave the house my father built for her. I'm a blogger; I don't make the kind of money my mom needs. But a book deal. An inside account of your sister, what she did to my family ... There's a decent-size market for true-crime novels. Especially something with a personal touch, say, written by the victim's cousin and including an exclusive interview with a killer as notorious as Shana Day. I've been fishing the idea around publishing circles, and there's some interest. Let's just say, thirty minutes of your sister's time, one-on-one, and my mom just might be able to die in comfort. My cousin was a good kid. He wouldn't mind helping out his aunt. Now, what's your excuse?"

"Mr. Sgarzi, you're assuming my sister listens to me. That having ignored your persistent written requests, Shana will magically change her mind on my say-so. To be blunt, we don't have that kind of relationship."

Charlie got that look again, all steely resolve and grim determination. Not just a man grieving, I realized now, but given his mother's deteriorating health, a man very much on edge.

"Manipulate her," he said.

I stared at him.

"You heard me. You're a sister as well as a psychiatrist. Stop dicking around and manipulate Shana into doing what you want."

"You mean, as you attempted to do with your relentless letter-writing campaign. And how did that work for you again?"

"Hey, I need this. My mother *deserves* this. Now, are you gonna make this happen or not?"

"Mr. Sgarzi—"

"Ask her about the Rose Killer."

My breath froze for the second time in a single day. "Excuse me?"

"You heard me. This new string of murders, some psycho running around harvesting strips of human flesh. You can't tell me that doesn't sound just like dear old Dad."

I remained silent, no longer trusting myself to speak.

"How does the killer do it, I wonder?" Sgarzi mused, tone mocking. "Know how to best slice down the length of the woman's torso, excising each precious strip. Then how to preserve them so the memories last forever. Why, it's almost as if he has inside information. . . ."

"You think my sister, who's been locked up for nearly three decades, has something to do with these killings?" I asked sharply.

"I think your sister has been dancing rings around you for years. All those hour-long visits, yet you've never asked the right questions. You wait and you wait for your sister to magically come to you. What are you afraid of, Adeline? You can't even feel pain. What do you have to fear?"

"I don't know what you—"

His voice dropped. "Take the kid gloves off. Tell Shana point-blank it's time to start cooperating. She knows more than you think."

"And you know this how?"

"Because I didn't just write letters to Shana. I wrote to several of her fellow inmates, including two that are no longer behind bars. And the stories they have to tell, about Shana, about the things she knows that she shouldn't possibly be able to know. The girl's connected, has a partner, a friend, I haven't quite figured out what. But she's not just moldering away in a cell like you seem to think. All these years later, she's still tending to business."

"Prove it."

"You want proof? Ask what she did to those two corrections officers. Exactly what she did, exactly how she did it. You think you can't feel pain, Adeline? Well, I think your sister is about to prove you wrong."

Charlie Sgarzi stormed off down the hall, heading straight for the elevators.

I remained rooted in place, watching as the downward arrow finally dinged to life, the car doors opening, swallowing the reporter, then carrying him away.

My hands were still shaking as I slowly slid my purse down my arm, then rooted around for the key.

Just a reporter, I assured myself. A man who would say anything to write an article, let alone profit from his family's tragedy.

But I couldn't quite convince myself. First my sister's suicide attempt, then the newspapers linking my father's forty-year-old murders to two recent murders and now this.

Oh, Shana, I couldn't help thinking as I finally walked into the quiet sanctuary of my condo. What have you done?

Chapter 16

THE CALL CAME while they were eating breakfast. Alex answered the phone, the two of them sitting across from each other at the kitchen table, pretending it was a morning like any other morning. Of course they'd slept well the night before, confident in the safety and security of their own home. Never jumping at unexpected sounds. Not getting up even once to double-check the lock, the security system, the Glock 10 Alex had moved to the top of his nightstand.

They were professionals. They didn't get unraveled by the thought of a killer walking through their bedroom, bearing the same gifts he'd given to each of his murder victims.

At 2:00 A.M., D.D. had said, staring up at the ceiling, "We should name him. You know, like Melvin."

"You want to name the intruder who broke into our house?"

"Sure. He's a pain in the ass. Or she's a pain in the ass. See, we don't even know that much, and saying he-slash-she-slash-it all the time annoys the shit out of me. Our intruder needs a name. Maybe, like Melvin, it will make it easier to manage him, too."

Alex was silent for a moment. "I vote for Bob."

"As in SquarePants? You want to name our personal murder suspect after Jack's favorite cartoon character?"

"Yes. Bob sounds very killable. How can you not be able to destroy a guy named Bob?"

By 2:05 A.M., D.D. had considered the matter. "What about Pat?

Equally killable, but, in keeping with the spirit of investigative truth, androgynous. Bob implies information we don't yet have."

"Pat from the *SNL* skits," Alex mused. "That works for me."

"Then Pat it is. Melvin, meet Pat. Pat, meet Melvin. Now, both of you go away."

Alex had reached for her hand. And they'd resumed their silent vigil, lying side by side in their shadowed bedroom, staring up at the blank ceiling, fingers lightly touching.

Now it was nearly 8:00 A.M. The phone rang, Alex answered and, a moment later, handed it to her.

"We have permission to interview Shana Day," Phil said without preamble.

"When?"

"Nine sharp."

"Where?"

"MCI."

"Who?"

"Her sister must be present—Shana's terms—plus one detective."

"Not Neil," she said immediately.

"Please, she'd eat him alive. I'll do it."

"Going with the kindhearted father figure?"

"Making it up as I go along." Phil hesitated. "It should be you," he said shortly. "Don't think I don't know that."

"It should be me," D.D. agreed. "She's not going to buy into the kindhearted father figure, either. In her world, understanding is weakness, and males are her murder victims of choice."

"I asked Horgan . . ."

"I'm not on active duty. I can't do it. I know that."

"Will you come anyway? I'm told the prison interview room has a viewing window. You can't go in, but there's nothing to say you can't watch."

"I'm there. Have you read her file yet?"

"Just pulling it up."

"Don't bother. I spent most of last night researching her and good ol' Harry Day. Take it from me, you need to remember just one thing."

"And that is . . . ?"

"Blood is love. And as the father figure, you're going to have to prove that you love her very much."

ALEX HELPED HER shower and dress. She was nervous, which surprised her. Her hands were shaking, and for a change, she barely noticed the ache in her left arm and shoulder. Alex helped ease a button-up silk shirt over her left arm. She winced; then the blouse was on, and Alex worked the buttons.

"For the record," he commented, "I much prefer the removal process. This goes against my grain."

She smiled but remained distracted.

"She's just another killer, D.D. How many have you interviewed over the years?"

"Dozens."

"Exactly. And this one's behind bars, meaning she can't even be that good."

"She was fourteen. Didn't have the maturity and foresight yet to better cover her tracks."

"She's just another killer," he repeated.

She nodded, but they could both tell it wasn't working. Then Phil arrived, looking even more hyped-up than she was, and Alex shook his head.

"You are the detectives," he informed them both. "You're smarter, more experienced and definitely more capable. Now, get out there, and learn what you need to know in order to destroy Pat."

"Pat?" Phil asked.

"It's a long story," D.D. supplied.

"Perfect," he said twitchily. "I could use one of those right now."

. . .

ADELINE WAS WAITING for them in the prison's lobby. She wore professional attire. Dark-brown slacks. A blue cashmere sweater. More respected psychiatrist than loving sister, D.D. noted. Girding her loins for what was sure to be a highly interesting conversation?

The doctor walked forward to greet them. She explained basic prison protocol, that all jewelry, bags, scarves, accessories, were to be checked into the available lockers. Phil also checked his sidearm; the MCI didn't permit firearms to be carried even by the corrections officers in order to minimize the risk of a weapon being seized by an inmate and used against them.

D.D. noticed Adeline kept her MedicAlert bracelet on. Another concession to her condition, D.D. figured. In case of emergency, any first responder would need to know that the patient couldn't feel pain and thus was in no position to judge her own condition. Plus that whole risk-of-overheating thing. On a hot summer's day, if Adeline collapsed in public . . .

D.D. wondered how many times a day Adeline was asked about that bracelet and what it signified. And she wondered how willingly and truthfully Adeline answered such questions.

By the time they'd divulged all personal possessions, a stunning black woman with gorgeous cheekbones had arrived. Adeline introduced her as Superintendent Kim McKinnon. She proceeded to lead them through security, down a narrow hall to where she said Shana was already ensconced in the interview room, waiting for them.

"She's still recovering from yesterday's incident," McKinnon informed them briskly, striding rapidly down the long, grungy white corridor. "She lost a lot of blood, so she tires easily. I'd suggest you get straight to the point while she can still answer your questions."

"She cut herself?" D.D. asked.

The superintendent nodded.

"Serious suicide attempt?"

"Serious enough she probably would've died in another few minutes."

"Has she done that before?"

"Shana suffers from severe depression, in addition to antisocial personality disorder. Think of it this way: She doesn't just hate your guts; she hates her own guts as well."

"Lovely," D.D. murmured. "And how long have you known Shana?"

"Since I first assumed the position of superintendent ten years ago."

"You think you can handle her?" D.D. asked curiously.

The superintendent arched an elegantly shaped brow. "Anyone who thinks she can handle Shana Day is a fool. The woman is too smart for her own good. And too bored for anyone else's health."

"You sound like you have a certain measure of respect for her."

The superintendent seemed to consider the matter. "Shana was incarcerated at the age of fourteen," the superintendent answered at last. "Only the first third of her life was lived outside these walls. Let's just say, I may run the MCI, but Shana is the expert here. I don't put anything past her, and in return, no officers have died on my watch."

The superintendent stated the last sentence matter-of-factly, a not-so-subtle reminder of Shana's full capabilities. Walking on the other side of the superintendent, Phil twitched again.

They arrived at their destination, a glass window overlooking a darkened room.

All of them halted, Phil nervously picking at a hangnail on his left thumb, while Adeline stared straight ahead, expression neutral. Her game face, D.D. figured. Whatever thoughts, feeling, emotions, the doc had about questioning her own sister regarding the two recent murders, she was carefully boxing up and putting away.

The interview room came equipped with an audio system. Super-intendent McKinnon helped Phil insert the earpiece into his left ear, which would enable them to communicate with him once he was inside the room. With the audio system flipped on, they'd also be able to hear everything said inside the cramped eight-by-twelve-foot space.

Phil and Adeline would enter the room. D.D. and the superintendent would remain on the other side of the glass, observing. Shana was also entitled to have her lawyer present but had declined.

Now Superintendent McKinnon glanced at Adeline, who stood slightly off to one side, then stared hard at Phil.

"Ready?" McKinnon asked him.

"Sure."

"You need a breather, just walk out of the room. Remember, you can come and go as you please. She's the one who has to sit there."

The pep talk seemed to work for Phil. He drew himself up straighter, nodded his understanding.

Superintendent McKinnon reached over, flipped on a light switch. Inside the room, Shana Day came into view, clad in prison orange, sitting at a small interview table, shackled hands clasped on top.

The inmate raised her head slowly as Adeline opened the door and led Phil into the chamber.

AT FIRST GLANCE, the aging female killer wasn't what D.D. had pictured. Photos online had been black-and-white smudges from a nearly thirty-year-old murder trial, meaning D.D. had been left to fill in the blanks. Given Adeline's sleek beauty, not to mention Shana's predilection for preying on men, D.D. had expected the juvenile murderess to have grown from a once-awkward fourteen-year-old girl into a passably attractive middle-aged brunette. Not even close.

Mouse-brown hair hung down in shoulder-length clumps. Washed-out skin, dark, puffy eyes, sunken cheekbones. Mouth set in a perpetually sullen line. Even beneath the oversize bulk of her prison jumpsuit, it was clear that the woman's body was too thin, nearly bony. Thirty years of incarceration had not been kind to Shana Day, and judging by the look on her face, she knew it.

She didn't glance over when Adeline and Phil entered but kept her gaze focused on the viewing glass, as if she knew both D.D. and Superintendent McKinnon were there.

Then she smiled.

A small, faintly knowing smirk that immediately set D.D.'s nerves on edge.

"Shana Day?" Phil began, approaching the table. "My name's Phil. I'm a detective with the Boston PD."

She didn't look at him.

"I'm here with your sister, per your request. As I believe Superintendent McKinnon has mentioned, I have some questions regarding a couple of recent murders."

Without waiting for her to respond, Phil pulled out one of the empty chairs and took a seat. Adeline stayed to the side, leaning against the doorjamb, arms folded over her chest. The support role, D.D. realized. She was doing her best to grant Phil center stage.

Shana finally roused herself enough to acknowledge Phil's presence. She looked him up and down, grunted once, then swung her attention to her sister.

"I like that color," Shana announced. "Pretty shade of blue. That cashmere?"

"How are you feeling?" Adeline asked.

"Does it matter?"

"Do you think I still ask questions just to be polite?"

"I think you wish you were anywhere but here right now. I think you wish you weren't adopted, and that doctor was your birth father, and you really were an only child."

Adeline made a show of glancing at her watch. "A lot of self-pity for first thing in the morning," she observed mildly.

"Fuck you," Shana said, but the words lacked heat, instead sounding dispirited. The depression, D.D. figured. She hadn't considered it before, but dejection made sense. The root of most rage was self-loathing.

Adeline finally moved. She pushed away from the door and calmly approached the table, moving around Phil until she could slide out the second chair and take a seat. The move forced Shana to confront both parties and, for the first time, truly consider Phil.

He remained silent, his face a study in patience. D.D. liked it. Draw the target out. Make Shana do all the work.

"How long you been a detective?" Shana asked abruptly.

"Twenty years."

"Why?"

"Good job."

"You like violence?"

"No. Personally, I'm a big fan of hands are for hugging."

Phil's easy admission seemed to throw Shana. She frowned again.

"You research me? You know what I did?"

"Yes."

"Think I'm guilty?"

"Yes."

"Well, at least you're not stupid."

"Do you like violence?" Phil asked her.

"Sure. All the time. What's not to love?"

"Prison," he said.

She gave an unexpected bark of laughter. "Sure as hell got that right. Then again, plenty of violence in here. In here, hands are for hitting. Or shanking. Personally, I prefer a quality homemade blade. My weapon of choice."

"Then why are you trying to escape?"

"Who said I'm escaping?"

Phil gestured to her hand, still bandaged from the IV needle. "Cutting yourself, nearly bleeding out. Sounds like a woman trying to escape to me."

"Nah. You heard wrong. Cutting isn't about the future. It's about enjoying the here and now. You look like a family man. The right age to have at least one or two teenagers. Ask your daughter about it sometime. How good it feels to watch the razor slide beneath your skin. Like masturbation. Bet she can tell you all about it."

Phil leaned forward, arms crossed on the table. "Who scares you, Shana?" he asked quietly. "Who do you know, what happened, to make a woman as tough as you slice open your own veins?"

The bluntness of the question surprised D.D. It seemed to catch Shana off guard as well.

She leaned forward as well, though her motions were more awkward due to her shackled hands and heavily bandaged legs. "You wouldn't understand," she informed him, tone equally solemn. "You don't know me, Mr. Detective Phil. And you can talk and talk, and ask and ask, but it won't matter. You don't *know* me, and no amount of time in this room can change that."

Her gaze shot to Adeline. "Same with you. All these monthly meetings, and what for? I'm nothing but a project to you. You don't see me as a sister, not even a person. You flutter in, do your good deed for the month, then flutter away to your respectable job and fancy home. Only reason you're here now is because you need something from me. Otherwise, I'd still be counting down twenty-nine days. That's what I get to do in here, you know. Count down the days. How often do you do that?"

"Stop," Adeline said calmly.

"Stop what?"

"The pity parade. That's between you and me. Sisterly resentment for us to discuss in—you're right—approximately thirty days. But this detective didn't drive all the way here to listen to us squabble. This visit isn't personal, Shana; it's professional."

Shana smirked. " 'Cause you want something from me. That's what it comes down to. *You* need something from *me*."

"So," Phil interjected briskly, trying to regain control over the conversation, even as his right hand resumed picking on his left thumbnail. "Let's talk. You agreed to the request, after all, and it's not like you have to."

"You mean I can get up and walk away?"

"Sure. Right now. Leave if you want to. I'm sure you're a busy woman. God knows I have plenty of things to do."

Shana regarded him suspiciously. "You're lying."

"Have you been advised of your rights, Shana? Do you understand you don't have to answer any of these questions? And you're entitled to your lawyer being present, if you want."

Now she snorted. "What's he gonna do? For that matter, what are you gonna do? I'm already here forever. Can't punish a woman any more than that."

"Is that why you cut yourself instead?"

"Shut the fuck up!"

Which D.D. took as a yes.

Phil leaned forward. He had his hands clasped before him, his expression still patient. A man with all the time in the world and who was still waiting to be impressed.

"You know what I see when I look at you?" he asked now.

"The future Mrs. Detective Phil?"

"A bright girl who once made a mistake. But you can't go back, can you? Thirty years later, no one knows that better than you. What's done is done. You can hate Donnie Johnson for dying on you. You can resent this overwhelming need you have to slice and dice human beings, but what's done is done. And here you are. Thirty years wiser, and still going nowhere. No, you're not trying to hurt yourself to escape the violence of prison, Shana. It's the boredom that's killing you."

She smiled slyly. "Gonna entertain me, Mr. Detective Phil?"

He glanced at his watch. "For another twenty minutes, maybe."

"Why only twenty minutes?"

"Because you're hurt, Shana. You need your rest. I won't interfere with that."

Shana blinked, clearly perplexed by his gentle tone. Phil didn't give her any time to recover.

"Tell me about your father."

"What?"

"Your father. I'm told you two were very close."

"No." Abruptly, her face shuttered up. She sat back. "I won't do it."

"Do what?"

"It's for her, isn't it?" She gestured at Adeline, plastic zip ties rattling. "Dad, Dad, Dad, tell me about Dad. She's the one who always wants to talk about him. Because she doesn't remember. She was just a *baby*."

"I don't remember him," Adeline agreed quietly, glancing for the first time at Phil. "I was only an infant. The few things I know come from memories Shana has shared with me."

Shana sat back, clearly gloating.

Phil ignored her, focusing his attention on Adeline instead. The skin around his left thumb had started to bleed from his picking, but he didn't seem to notice. "But you've researched your father, haven't you?" he asked Adeline.

"Yes."

"Did he have any close friends, known associates?"

Adeline pursed her lips, seemed to be considering the matter. "I could look it up for you. I have the old police reports—"

"What?" Shana sat forward.

"The police reports," Adeline said, not even looking at her sister anymore but continuing to address Phil. "From Harry's case file. I have them all. I could make you copies, Detective, if that's quicker than accessing them through official routes."

"That would be great."

"Hey!" Shana said.

"Is there other information you'd like?" Adeline continued, eyes still on Phil. Then suddenly, "Oh my goodness, what happened to you?"

She reached over, raised Phil's bleeding thumb.

"Oh, it's just a hangnail. Never—"

Phil's voice trailed off, as Adeline placed her index finger against the torn flesh and pressed hard. He stared at her pale finger with rapt fascination. As she slowly lifted it up, inspected his wound, then the tip of her carefully manicured nail . . .

"Oh dear," Adeline murmured softly. "I got blood on my finger."

Now she stared her sister in the eye. Raising the bloodstained finger in the air, then slowly but surely bringing it toward her own lips . . .

The result was immediately explosive.

"No! No, no, no. That's mine!"

Shana was up, chair rocked back, zip ties shaking around her wrists.

"It's not," Adeline retorted, low and fast. Professional psychiatrist was gone. This was a dark-haired, dark-eyed wild woman who seemed intent on pushing her own sister to the brink. "I earned it. I helped him. It's mine."

"You bitch—"

"You've done nothing! Sitting there, smirking, pretending to know it all. I bet you don't even remember our father; you were just a toddler, after all. Why do you think I ask so many questions? Because I know you're lying, making it all up. You can *claim* to remember Harry all you want. But I have the files. I know the truth, Shana. I've *always* known the truth!"

"One hundred fifty-three!" Shana declared abruptly. Her gaze was locked on Adeline's bloodstained finger, still suspended between them.

Phil had shoved back his chair slightly, hands braced on the table, as if preparing for fight or flight, except he wasn't sure which.

"One hundred and fifty-three what?" Adeline demanded.

"You're so smart, you figure it out!"

"No. This isn't about me. It's about you, Shana. It's about you finally proving yourself. Thirty years you've been wasting away in here. Detective Phil wasn't lying before. You're smart. You're capable. You could be someone, Shana, even behind bars. You could assist with a real murder investigation, do some good in the world. Maybe then you wouldn't be my pity project. Maybe then I'd call you sister instead."

"I know Daddy," Shana spit out. "You do not know Daddy!"

"Prove it!"

The two sisters glared at each other. Phil swallowed slowly.

"You want me to be *useful*?" Shana suddenly drawled.

"I think you might find it an interesting change of pace."

"Fine." Shana smiled. "Tomorrow morning, I'm going to be useful. I'm going to be the most useful person you know. In fact, I'm going to be so fucking *useful* that you will sign me out of this prison and take me home."

"Not likely."

"Oh, but it will happen. Mr. Detective Phil will even agree that you should do so." Shana gestured with her bound hands toward Phil. "And, since I'll be your *sister* and not your project, you'll let me stay in your house, Adeline. You'll even let me sleep in your bed. Forty-eight hours." She nodded. "That's what my *usefulness* is going to cost you. Forty-eight hours of me wearing your clothes, showering in your shower, living in your luxury high-rise. That will be the price of my usefulness."

"No."

Shana whispered: "One hundred fifty-three."

"Shana—" Phil began.

"Shhh," she informed him softly. "This isn't about you, Mr. Detective Phil. You be quiet now. This is about me and my sister. It's always been about me and my sister, and unfinished business."

"What is one hundred and fifty-three?" Adeline demanded.

Shana smiled again. But the expression was devoid of emotion and didn't do a thing to hide the cool, calculating gleam in her flat brown eyes.

She'd been pretending, D.D. realized slowly. Her show of belligerence. Her attempts to shock them with graphic details of her own self-mutilation. Even her awkward flirtations with Phil. Those hadn't been real emotions, but simply masks Shana slipped on and off the way other people changed clothes.

This was the real Shana Day. A stone-cold killer, whose gaze now lingered almost tenderly on her sister's bloodstained fingertip.

"One hundred fifty-three," Shana whispered. "That's my proof. I do remember Daddy. And I love him. I've always loved him. Now, go home, baby sister. Read your files. Talk to your little cop friends. Then lock your doors. Just because you can't feel pain, doesn't mean that when he comes for you, it won't hurt anyway."

Chapter 17

I LEFT THE INTERVIEW ROOM, struggling for composure, but in truth, rattled to the core. My adoptive father had been right; reconnecting with my sister merely returned me to the house of horrors I'd been lucky to escape the first time.

Now I dropped my bloodstained finger to my side, aware of D.D.'s gaze upon me, as Phil and the superintendent continued speaking in the background.

"Come on," D.D. said abruptly, gesturing to my hand. "Let's find a washroom, clean up."

She was already moving, so I followed. From a doctor's point of view, I thought D.D. appeared to be feeling better this morning. Whether that came from effective use of approved pain management techniques or simply the adrenaline rush of once more being a detective on the chase . . .

While the interview with my sister had wrung me out, D.D. seemed almost giddy.

"You played her," she said now. "First you were all cold clinician, then suddenly you were on the attack, belittling her memories, stealing her glory. Acting all, well, sisterly. Then, that whole bit, waving around Phil's blood on your fingertip. Pure genius."

I didn't say anything, but tucked my red-stained finger into my fist. The problem with talking to my sister was never her obsession with violence; it was the way her appetites called to my own. Beast to beast, family member to family member, until I really did want to lift my finger to my lips, take a quick, delicate taste . . .

We arrived at a single unisex bathroom, complete with a windowed door that eliminated any chance of an inmate's—or visitor's— privacy. I'd been hanging around the prison long enough to know the facilities. I stuck to washing my hands and nothing else.

D.D. waited in the corridor.

"Do you think she really knows something?" she asked when I re-emerged. "A connection between your father's forty-year-old crimes and these recent killings?"

I hesitated. "Do you know a reporter by the name of Charlie Sgarzi?"

The detective shook her head. We worked our way back to Phil and Superintendent McKinnon.

"He's the cousin of Shana's twelve-year-old victim, Donnie Johnson," I explained as we walked. "He's been writing to Shana for the past three months now, requesting permission to interview her for a book he's writing on his cousin's murder. Given how much damage Shana did to his family, he feels she owes him one."

"Okay."

"Shana never replied to his letters, so he showed up on my doorstep last night in order to plead his case in person. He also claims to have interviewed other inmates who once served time with Shana. According to him, they say she knows things she shouldn't know. As if she still has connections to the outside world and can manipulate things from behind bars."

"Like a crime boss?" D.D. asked, frowning.

"Possibly. Except here's the issue: Shana doesn't bond with fellow inmates, exchange notes with pen pals or entertain during visiting hours. I am her sole guest each month. Otherwise she spends twenty-three hours a day locked in the isolation of her cell. I can't picture her having the capability, let alone the opportunity, to forge the kind of complex social network required to reach beyond the prison walls. And yet . . ." My voice trailed off.

"Yet?"

"She does know things. Small, random things, say, the color of a new sweater I recently purchased. The kind of details that are slightly worrisome, but not significant. And easy enough to explain away. Maybe I mentioned the sweater purchase and just forgot. Except . . . There have been more and more of those kinds of observations lately. The past few months, each time I've visited, my sister has known something about me that, in theory, she shouldn't."

"You think she's watching you? Or, more accurately, having someone else watch you?"

"I don't know what to think."

"One hundred and fifty-three," D.D. prodded.

I shook my head. "I don't know what that means."

"Nothing about that number that reminds you of Harry Day?"

"No. I'll have to check the case files."

"That'd be great. God knows Phil wasn't lying in there; it takes about a pound of paperwork and a lifetime of patience to get old case files pulled from the city's archives. If we're lucky, we'll get access to the same info in a mere six weeks or so. Meaning it would be very helpful if you could just look the info up, at least for now."

"First thing when I get home."

"Perfect. In the meantime, let's speak with the superintendent. If anyone knows how your sister might be making contact with the outside world, it's gotta be her."

SUPERINTENDENT McKINNON WAS BLUNT on the subject:

"Communicate with the outside world? Please, most of these inmates are having sex in a no-contact facility. Talking is the least of our concerns."

According to the superintendent, the methods used for communication between inmates were numerous and ingenious. While Shana was confined to a maximum-security cell, she regularly checked out books from the roving library cart, ordered items from the prison commissary and received food trays three times a day. In prison life, each transaction was an opportunity to send or receive a message, whether a handwritten note, a hastily whispered word or a carefully crafted code.

"Sad to say," Superintendent McKinnon, "some of the inmates' communications are even assisted by the guards, in return for money, drugs, sexual favors. Now, Shana is hardly a favorite, as you can imagine, but the other inmate, the one she's in contact with, might be. And there are inmates willing to assist with these kinds of transactions if only to relieve their boredom. Bottom line: We have only an hour or two a quarter to evaluate our policies and revise our procedures, while the inmates spend twenty-four/seven, three hundred and sixty-five days a year figuring out how to beat the system. Why, there are women in here clever enough and capable enough to run Fortune 500 companies, if only they'd focused their powers on good instead of evil."

"Is there an inmate Shana's close to? A friend, either past or present?"

Superintendent McKinnon frowned slightly. "Not that I'm aware of, which is the more surprising piece of this puzzle. Most inmates forge relationships. Even a female as hardened as Shana . . . there are younger, more vulnerable inmates who'd look up to that sort of thing. And whether she identifies herself as straight or gay, most lifers end up with a partner. But to the best of my knowledge, Shana has never had even a girlfriend."

"She's never mentioned anyone to me," I spoke up.

"Nor to look at her commissary transactions—one of the first signs of a budding relationship is one inmate purchasing 'gifts' for another, just as you would see in the real world. A bottle of shampoo. A scented lotion. But Shana makes very few transactions, and they've been solely for herself. Nor has anyone sent her any gifts. If anything . . ." Superintendent McKinnon hesitated; her gaze slid to me.

I nodded my assent.

"I have been concerned about Shana's nearly total social isolation," Superintendent McKinnon continued. "Despite what you may think, unhappy inmates are not in our best interest. Depression leads to anger, which leads to an increased chance of violence. As I've discussed with Dr. Glen, I've been troubled about Shana's state of mind for the past several months. It's been clear to me that she's been deteriorating, meaning yesterday's suicide attempt wasn't a surprise."

"Hang on," D.D. spoke up. "You mean there's been a marked change in Shana's behavior? Starting when?"

"Maybe three or four months ago? I'd assumed it had to do with the approaching anniversary of her first murder, but of course I can't know for certain. While Shana is entitled to mental health resources, she's refused all overtures."

"Who manages her care?" Phil asked.

I raised a hand. "I do. I'm a licensed psychiatrist, as well as one of the only people Shana will speak with. While it's not completely . . . kosher . . . to be diagnosing a relative, Shana and I hardly have a traditional relationship. For most of our lives, we haven't even lived as family."

"But she calls you her little sister," D.D pushed.

"Only when she's trying to push my buttons."

"Which sounds like a sisterly thing to do."

"Or a patient hostile to the possibility of change." I regarded D.D. drolly. "Why, you'd be amazed some of the things my patients say and do in order to resist my efforts."

She flashed me a grin, clearly unrepentant. Then she returned her gaze to the superintendent. "Does the number one hundred and fifty-three mean anything to you?"

Superintendent McKinnon shook her head.

"Do you think it's possible Shana could be in contact with this so-called Rose Killer? Or the killer be in contact with her?"

"Oh, it's possible. I'd like to know how, though. The thought of an active killer communicating with an incarcerated murderer doesn't exactly make me sleep well at night."

"If I may?" Three pairs of eyes turned to me. "Maybe now is not the time to worry about the how. Perhaps the more relevant question is why? Shana committed a horrible crime, but it was also nearly thirty years ago. The case hasn't even been on the news, enabling Shana to maintain a pretty low profile for years. Maybe next week, the anniversary week, that will change, but to date . . ."

"She doesn't have any pen pals or known admirers," Superintendent McKinnon supplied. "Which is uncommon. Generally, the more infamous the killer—male or female—the larger the volume of mail. And/or," she added dryly, "marriage proposals. As far as most notorious murderers go, Shana lives a quiet life."

"What if it's about Harry Day?" D.D. said. The detective focused on me. "If someone was, say, an admirer of your father, and he wanted more information on your father's—"

"Harry's," I corrected. I couldn't help myself.

"Harry's techniques," D.D. continued smoothly, "he wouldn't very well ask you, would he? I mean, you're a respected psychiatrist."

"I get letters," I heard myself say.

"What?" Two homicide detectives, gazes now fixed on me.

"I get letters," I repeated slowly. "Not often, but from time to time. Harry's crime spree was a long time ago, but as you can imagine, there are people who are fascinated by serial killers, regardless of time frame. Hence, the enduring mystique of Bonnie and Clyde. Given that my rare genetic condition has made me the subject of several write-ups, and in those articles, I'm identified as the daughter of Harry Day . . . I receive mail. Probably three or four letters a year regarding Harry. Sometimes it's people who have questions—what was he like, how does it feel to be his child. More often, it's requests for memorabilia. Do I still have any personal items of his and would I be interested in selling them."

"Seriously?" D.D. asked, expression appearing half-horrified, half-fascinated. Which was Harry Day's overall effect on people. One part terror, two parts morbid curiosity.

"There's quite a market for serial killer memorabilia," I informed her. "Several websites dedicated to selling letters from Charles Manson, or a picture painted by John Allen Muhammad. I looked them up when I received the first request. The big-money items are from the truly infamous—Manson, Bundy, Dahmer. Harry Day doesn't carry the same level of name recognition. In a list of items ranging from ten dollars to ten thousand dollars, a signed letter from him would be much closer to the ten-dollar mark."

"Do you keep the letters sent to you?" Phil asked.

"I shred them. They aren't worth my time or attention."

"Repeat writers?" D.D. pressed.

"Not that I recall."

She turned to Phil. "What if our guy started by writing to Adeline? Then, when she didn't reply, located Shana Day and contacted her next. She's gotten some mail, right?" D.D. glanced at the superintendent.

"Sure. Shana has received some letters, just not a lot of them."

"And in the past year maybe?"

"I'd have to ask."

"Meaning it's possible she got a letter. And maybe Shana even decided to reply. Except, she realized that the second she wrote back and finally adopted a pen pal after all these years, you guys would take an interest."

"True." The superintendent nodded.

"So she took it off-line, so to speak. Reached out through a different communications channel. Maybe with the help of another inmate or guard. Or her lawyer?" D.D. eyed both me and the superintendent questioningly.

"Shana has a public defender," I supplied. "She doesn't like him, and I don't even remember the last time they met."

"Two years ago," Superintendent McKinnon provided. "Shana bit his nose. We took away her radio. She claimed it was still worth it."

D.D. nodded. "All right. We're getting somewhere now. We have a killer who identifies with Harry Day and who has possibly forged a relationship with Day's equally homicidal daughter. Cool."

"The daughter who's already predicted that we'll let her out of prison first thing tomorrow morning," Phil added more slowly. "I'm gonna guess that's what's in it for her."

"Not gonna happen," D.D. said.

"Agreed," Superintendent McKinnon stated firmly. "My prisoner, my facility. Period."

I gazed at both women. And I wished I could share their certainty. Instead, I heard myself murmur, "One hundred and fifty-three."

"You figured out what that means?" Phil asked immediately.

"No. But knowing my sister like I do, I think we'll be sorry soon enough."

Chapter 18

Who am I? Someone who cares.

What do I look like? Nothing special, just myself.

Primary motivation: To offer help to someone in need.

Purpose of operation: It must be done.

Net gain: ~~She won't feel a thing.~~

Net gain: ~~She won't feel a thing.~~

Net gain: ~~She won't feel a thing.~~

Stop thinking. It's time.

This would be tricky.

Taking a deep breath, practicing once more before the full-length mirror:

Slender glass vial tucked up the tight-fitting sleeve. Then sliding it down into the palm of the hand. Uncorking and pouring as a single deft motion. Then slipping the vial away into left pocket . . .

Too slow. Stupidly slow. Her back would need to be turned, her attention distracted for at least a full minute.

Couldn't count on that. Not with this target. She would be the most ambitious to date. A woman who trusted no one and suspected everyone. Life had already hurt her once. She wasn't planning on giving it a chance to smack at her again.

No, this latest endeavor would demand perfection. Genuine smile, steady eye contact, all the right words. Then, when the opportunity arose . . . Fast and fluid. Palming the glass vial in no more than the blink of an eye, while stirring the contents into her drink in less than a heartbeat.

Then, even more challenging, sitting and waiting. Level out the natural adrenaline rush, control the breathing, while resuming a genuine smile, steady eye contact, all the right words, as the contents of the vial slowly but surely went to work.

More practice. Smile. Eye contact. All the right words.

Slip up, slide down, uncork, pour, dismiss.

Too slow, too slow, too slow.

Practice. Practice. Practice.

Who am I? A master of pain.

What do I look like? Anyone you've ever met.

Purpose of operation: I can do this!

Net gain: . . . We all have to die sometime.

Palm the vial, uncork the contents, quick pour, slip it away.

Smile, make eye contact, say all the right words.

Again and again and again.

Because any single misstep and she would know. She'd spent too many years expecting the worst not to recognize it the moment it happened. Everything had to be smooth, controlled, perfect. Right up until the final moment.

No fuss, no muss. Just the way murder should be.

Primary motivation: A painless death.

Net gain: The gift that keeps on giving.

Who am I? ~~Harry Day's legacy.~~

Who am I? ~~Shana Day's legacy.~~

Who am I?

Chapter 19

CHARLIE SGARZI WAS A SOUTHIE KID, born and raised. Had the wary expression and set jaw to prove it. Of course, somewhere along the way, he'd traded in calloused knuckles for the smooth hands of a guy who mostly attacked keyboards, not to mention the tough guy's leather jacket for the classic reporter's trench. He still maintained the shuttered expression of a former hood turned cynical journalist who'd seen it all. Then again, given what had happened to his cousin when they'd both been just boys, maybe he had.

They'd come upon him as he was exiting his third-floor apartment. He'd glanced up from locking his door, saw D.D. and Phil approach from down the hallway and grunted in acknowledgment.

"Took you long enough," he said.

"For what?" Phil asked.

He'd tried to get D.D. to wait in the car. Actually, he'd tried to convince D.D. to let him take her home. It had been a big morning, she should be resting her shoulder, focusing on recuperation.

Like hell. She was pumped up, feeling the best she had in weeks. They were onto something. She could feel it in her bones. Shana Day held the key to finding their killer, and Charlie Sgarzi was yet another link to the puzzle that was Shana Day. No way she was sitting this one out.

"Dr. Glen call you?" Sgarzi asked, hand still on his doorknob.

"Accuse me of harassing her? Because I'm not. I just want what's owed to me and my family."

Fun, D.D. thought, and practically skipped down the hallway.

"So you didn't threaten Dr. Glen?" she asked now.

While Phil added, "How about we go inside, Mr. Sgarzi. Talk where it's more private."

Sgarzi sighed heavily, then unlocked his door and led them inside.

Cramped one-bedroom, D.D. observed. Definitely a bachelor abode, given the ratio of TV size to non–garage sale furniture items. Tidy enough, though. Sgarzi might be living lower on the economic ladder, but he'd made some effort with the space. Countertops were clean; no dirty underwear littered the floor.

State-of-the-art Mac laptop was set up on a TV tray in front of the threadbare brown sofa. His office, she was guessing. Where he could brave the new frontiers of digital reporting, while keeping up on the Bruins.

"You talk to Shana Day yet?" he demanded to know, coming to a halt in the middle of the living space.

"Why don't you take off your coat and stay a while?" Phil suggested.

Sgarzi shrugged. "Sure, I got nothing to hide. Fact, you guys want something to drink? Water, beer? Hell, let's hang for a bit. We can talk crime. You know my uncle was a cop? At least till he ate his gun. Does Shana Day get that mark on her record? Still killing, after all these years."

Sgarzi shed his coat. Then, true to his word, he crossed four steps to the kitchen, banged on the faucet and poured two glasses of tap water. He handed them over without ceremony, then stared at them expectantly.

Without his coat, he shrunk in size, like Superman without his cape. Not a tall guy, probably just a hair over five-nine, but he still carried himself a certain way. Like he was steeling himself for a blow that had yet to come, and was determined not to flinch. Had he always been like this? D.D. wondered. Or was this what losing most of one's family did to a man?

"How old were you when your cousin died?" she asked.

He shot her a glance. "You mean was murdered? Fourteen. I was fourteen."

"Same age as Shana Day."

"Are you asking if I knew her? Because of course I knew her. I lived in the same neighborhood as Donnie. That's how it was back then in Southie. Families, even extended families, lived close. Grew up together. Took care of one another."

Sgarzi's tone was intentionally flat, but D.D. still caught a faint trace of emotion. Nostalgia. Regret. Back in the day when he'd felt secure in his place in the world. His family, his neighborhood, his world.

"You hang out with Shana?" Phil asked evenly.

"Nah. She was trouble. Everyone knew that. And not the good kind of trouble, either, you know, a reputation worthy of street cred. Shana . . . She was freaky scary. Like a dog gone bad. Kids . . . Most of us who had any sense stayed clear."

"Except Donnie."

Sgarzi grimaced, shrugged. "Donnie was . . . different. He liked books, science, math. Hell, if he'd survived, he probably would've become another Bill Gates and my mother wouldn't have any worries now. But a twelve-year-old geek in Southie? The other kids were hard on him. If I heard of things, or if I was around, I made them knock it off. He was my cousin, you know. I tried to take care of him. But he didn't fit in. And Shana may be freaky, but she was clever. Even back then . . ." Sgarzi shook his head. "My cousin never stood a chance."

"You follow the trial?" Phil asked.

"Nah, my parents wouldn't let me. I got my news the way the rest of the neighborhood did, by listening to gossip. Besides, this was a long time ago. Not like today, where there's twenty-four-hour cable and constant media blitzes. The local news followed the case, of course, particularly when the DA announced he was trying Shana as an adult. But her defense didn't put up much of a fight. Whole thing was over and done with pretty quick. Then everyone went back to their everyday lives. Except for my aunt and uncle, of course."

"And you?" D.D. asked curiously. "Thirty years later, still writing letters to your cousin's killer? Stirring the pot?"

"Still?" asked Sgarzi in clear bewilderment. "Who says still? Letters I sent three months ago were the first time I've initiated contact. I mean, Donnie was a good kid, but so was I. Hell, I had bigger plans than spending my life as a murdered boy's cousin. I got out of the neighborhood. Went to NYU, majored in communications, became a reporter. I'm no schmuck."

"And yet, here you are . . . ," Phil prodded.

"I returned to look out for my mom," Sgarzi replied sharply. "Or didn't Dr. Glen tell you that part? My mom's dying of cancer. She needs hospice, a home health aide, someone more capable than her journalist son. Which costs money. And given how financially lucrative it is to be a writer these days, I don't have a whole lot. Then it occurred to me, digital reporters might not make much money, but some of these true-crime books . . . I mean, we're talking six-figure, seven-figure advances. I'm capable of doing the work. I just need the right material. You know, such as an exclusive interview with a notorious female killer. Now, you tell me, is that too much to ask? Thirty years later, maybe Shana might even like a chance to make amends. Course, given how she's never replied to a single letter, I'm gonna guess not."

"So you went after her sister?"

"Sure. That's what reporters do. One source says no, find another source that'll say yes. I need a yes. My mom needs a yes."

"When was your mother diagnosed with cancer?" D.D. asked.

"Six months ago."

"And you sent the first letter to Shana . . ."

"Three months ago, give or take."

"And the first woman was killed by the Rose Killer," she filled in, "what, six, seven weeks ago?"

Sgarzi stiffened. His hands had fisted unconsciously by his sides. His eyes narrowed warily. "What do you mean?"

"I mean, here you are, ostensibly trying to sell a book that features a thirty-year-old case very few people—no disrespect to your family—even remember, and all of a sudden, a fresh string of murders occur with ties to your book subject. Interesting, if you ask me. Might even say convenient."

"Wait a minute—"

"Where were you Sunday night?" Phil asked.

"Fuck you!"

"You invited us in," D.D. said mildly. "Said we could talk crime."

"I'm a reporter! I look for the truth. Something you might want to give a try. I mean, unless you don't really mind women being murdered in their own beds."

"How do you know that?"

"Please, that detail is common knowledge. What you should know, without me having to tell you, is that Shana Day is just as crazily clever now as thirty years ago."

"How would you know? She never wrote you back."

"She didn't. But again, trick to this trade is to keep on digging. I tracked down some of her fellow inmates—"

"She's in solitary."

"They all share a corridor. Think they don't talk across the hall? Let alone cross paths in medical, or on their way to visiting hours. There are opportunities enough to socialize, even in solitary. It's not like they have anything else to do."

"Who did you talk to?" D.D. asked, eyes narrowing.

"Please, like they'd even be willing to talk to you. As you can imagine, they're not so partial to law enforcement. Whereas, a good-looking guy like me . . ."

"Just tell us what they said," Phil spoke up.

"Shana has a friend."

"Who?"

"A fan. From way back. Maybe even someone she knew in the neighborhood, or foster care. No one really knows, but a supporter from all those years ago, who keeps in touch, even performs small favors for her."

"Such as?"

"For starters, spies on her sister."

"Dr. Adeline Glen?"

"Yep. Shana's obsessed with Adeline. Her sister's job, apartment, car. Adeline has everything Shana's ever wanted. Course she can't let it go."

"And how do Shana's former fellow inmates know all this?"

Sgarzi shrugged. "Things Shana said, alluded to. But also . . . Things Shana would know. Including about her fellow prisoners. Apparently, her little friend would research for her, because if anyone got in an argument with Shana, suddenly she would start making very specific threats. You know, stop humming that same goddamn song, or the next time your drunken whore of a mother takes your six-year-old son to Billy Bear's day care, they'll both be sorry. Crap like that. But very detailed crap. Enough so, the other girls did what Shana said. She spooked them then, she scares them now. I'm not kidding. Research among yourselves. Shana's rep reaches far beyond prison walls. She may have her sister and all the prison officials thinking she's some depressed lonely soul, but take it from me, it's all an act. She's running the biggest con in MCI history. Pathetic prisoner by day. Homicidal genius by night."

D.D. stared at Sgarzi. She didn't know what to say. She didn't know what to think.

"One hundred and fifty-three," Phil said.

"What?"

"One hundred and fifty-three. You're the supposed expert on Shana Day. Tell us what that number means."

Sgarzi frowned at them. "Hell if I know."

"You research Harry Day, Shana's father?"

"Course."

"Then, what did it mean to him?"

"You mean, like a lucky number?"

"Was it?"

"Beats me. I've never run across mention of a lucky number before."

"Address?" D.D. asked. "Significant to him or his victims?"

Sgarzi shook his head, looking as confused as they felt.

"What about for Shana?" D.D. pressed. "Your cousin, her foster family, where did they live?"

"Not at one hundred and fifty-three anything." Sgarzi's gaze suddenly sharpened. "So what's the significance? Is it a clue from the Rose Killer? A code you have to crack? I can work on it. First dibs on the story, though. Full quid pro quo."

"Please," D.D. informed him. "You gotta pay to play, and so far, you haven't told us anything we didn't already know."

"I gave you Shana's friend."

"What friend? You mean her imaginary friend? The one she talks to but no one has ever seen? You might as well have told us to track down Casper the Friendly Ghost."

"She's got eyes and ears beyond prison walls."

"Already knew that."

"She spies on her sister."

"Knew that, too."

"Really?"

"Dr. Glen isn't as dumb as she looks. Wait, she looks plenty smart. And she is a professional psychiatrist with few illusions about her own gene pool. Come on. We want something good. Why do you think Shana is connected to the Rose Killer?"

"For starters, the whole removal of skin. And not just because Harry Day was known for keeping such things as trophies, but because I know what Shana did to my cousin. Come on, fourteen-year-old boy. Of course I had to sneak in my uncle's study and look at the photos. I mean . . ." Sgarzi's voice broke off. For all his bravado, thirty years later, his composure grew strained. "When I read the details of these latest two murders in the paper, first image that flashed through my mind was the picture of Donnie's arm, his stomach. I . . . I knew what had been done to those women. Because I'd seen it before. In the photos of my cousin's body. Tell me I'm wrong, Detectives. Look me in the eye and tell me I'm wrong."

D.D. and Phil couldn't do it. For once, they were the ones to glance away. Because both had reviewed Shana's thirty-year-old handiwork in the past twenty-four hours, and Charlie Sgarzi was right. The parallels between what she'd done to her victim, what her father had done to his victims and what the Rose Killer was doing now . . .

"Shana Day didn't kill those women," Sgarzi continued now. "And obviously, Harry Day didn't kill those women. But if skinning is the signature mark of the crime as well as the calling card of both father and daughter . . ."

Sgarzi paused. D.D. already knew what he was going to say next.

"Well, there's one family member left. . . ."

Chapter 20

MY FIRST ISSUE WAS properly disposing of the formaldehyde solution.

After the interview with Shana, I'd called my receptionist and told her to cancel my remaining appointments for the week. Pessimistic? Preparing for the worst? My adoptive father had been right; just because I didn't feel pain didn't mean my family couldn't hurt me.

My sister knew something. The interview request, the Boston detective's questions, none of them surprised her. That was my biggest impression from the morning. The police could pat themselves on the back, even congratulate me for getting Shana to "volunteer" the mystery number 153. But I knew my sister better than that. This was a game for her. And she had willingly shown up to play, which already told me it was her match after all. We were the ones catching up.

I'd been honest; I didn't know what 153 meant. But Shana did, and if she said we would be letting her out of prison in the morning, at which time she'd be staying in my condo, sleeping in my bed and wearing my clothes, I believed her. The prediction was too specific to simply dismiss.

And it terrified me.

Formaldehyde. I possessed an entire collection of vials filled with the preserving agent and single strips of skin. It all had to go. Now.

Would the fact I kept my "collection" tucked beneath the floorboards of my closet surprise you? I can tell you as a professional that even the smartest people are driven by forces more powerful than logic. Compulsion. Obsession. Addiction.

Now I headed into my massive walk-in closet. The left-hand bureau, made of cherrywood and appearing built-in, in fact pulled straight out. I squeezed myself behind it, then went to work on the exposed floorboards, each with telltale scratches around the edges. I'd created this hidey-hole myself, the first weekend after I'd moved into my new, luxurious high-rise apartment. My first homeowner's project. Does that tell you something?

Tucked beneath the floorboards was an ordinary shoe box. Nothing special. Black lid, faded gray-blue sides, brand name long since worn off. The kind of battered old box that might contain faded photographs or other precious family mementos. I pulled it up, holding it in two hands, then weaseled my way back out, clutching my treasure tight against my chest.

In my bathroom now. A modern white marble, chocolate cabinets, gray and blue glass-tiled affair. I placed the box on the creamy marble countertop, next to the second sink, the one that should be used by my husband or live-in companion, or the long-lost love of my life. The sink that for the entire time I've lived in this unit has never had a drop of water in it.

Now I removed the black top of the shoe box to reveal a padded, silk-lined interior completely at odds with the exterior. Vials. Numerous slender glass vials, each one the approximate size of a test tube, each with a rubber-stoppered top. No mason jars for this daughter of Harry Day. The gene pool had been moving on up.

It occurred to me I'd never counted the vials. Even now, I had a tendency to take it in as a whole. The collection. I didn't count individual pieces, amassed on and off over nearly ten years. The psychiatrist who didn't want to know what she didn't want to know.

I closed my eyes. Pretended I was my own patient. How many vials did I think were in the box? A similar exercise to asking the alcoholic how many drinks she thought she'd had last night.

I went with twelve. An already shockingly high number. Rounding up, I told myself, because the answer on the tip of my tongue had been eight. So again, like the alcoholic who somewhat understands she has a problem—I want to say I had three drinks, but it was probably more like five . . . Forced honesty. If I'm not really in denial, then I don't *really* have a problem.

I opened my eyes, counted the glass vials.

Twenty-one.

I swayed on my feet. Had to grab the smooth edge of my bathroom countertop to catch myself.

Twenty-one.

No. How? Not possible. Couldn't be . . .

I counted again. And again.

And a curious sensation washed through me. Like my soul, taking in the awful, horrible truth, literally drained from my body. Sank from my head down to the heels of my feet, onto the bathroom floor, where it disappeared down the shower drain. Not a soul at all, but a dark spirit returning to the netherworlds from which it came.

I couldn't . . .

I picked up a vial at random. *Computer Tech,* it said. I suffered a sudden image of a police snapshot from my father's closet. *Flowered Shirt,* that mason jar had read in the forty-year-old police photo. A single, random detail that had been all that was left to tie the contents of the jar to the young woman who'd once lived in that skin.

My body started to tremble. I wanted to sit down, but I fought the instinct. Better to remain standing, to force myself to confront my own guilt.

"But no pain," I heard myself whisper. "The lidocaine. They didn't even know . . ."

Because after denial comes rationalization. I'm not really a monster like my father. He butchered young women, held them hostage and tortured them for days. So I removed a very small sliver of skin from my sleeping partners. They never even flinched, rolled over, felt the loss. An innocent token of our single night together. For the record, some might even have agreed willingly to such terms: I'll give you one night of mad, passionate sex, no commitments, no obligations; all you have to surrender is a thin noodle of derma, which you'll grow back in a matter of days. . . .

I held up the vial marked "Computer Tech." Then stared at my reflection in the bathroom mirror. Look at that nice-looking, obviously successful middle-aged woman. I wonder what she's holding in her hand . . .

Then I remembered the sight of Detective Phil's blood on my finger. The feel of it. The smell. The overwhelming desire to taste.

My knees gave out. I sank to the cold tiled floor. Because being someone who suffered from a rare genetic condition, I knew firsthand that nurture would never be enough. We were all products of nature as well. And this was my nature. This glass vial, clutched protectively to my chest.

Filled with formaldehyde and human skin.

My sister could not discover this. No one, absolutely no one must know. I had failed, been weak, succumbed to some kind of genetic obsession. But I could beat this. Sure. Why not? Except, of course, first I had to survive this strange, frightening week where the ghost of my father once more roamed the streets of Boston, and young women died and my crazy sister knew things she shouldn't.

First order of business, dispose of the evidence. The box, the vials, the formaldehyde solution, the strips of skin. All of it must go.

Except how? Formaldehyde is actually a colorless gas, primarily used in aqueous solutions for preserving specimens. In addition to being poisonous in high enough concentrations, it can negatively impact the upper respiratory system and irritate the skin and has been linked to several kinds of cancer. Needless to say, safe disposal of formalin solutions generally involved identifying the solution as a hazardous waste and following proper protocols.

But I couldn't risk being documented turning over hazardous waste.

The easiest thing would be to dump the clear solution down the drain, or flush it down the toilet, relying upon the city's water system to successfully dilute the relatively small amount of formaldehyde. Unfortunately, I wasn't sure if that was foolproof from a forensics point of view. For one thing, the pungent smell might linger, a particular odor no one would mistake for toilet bowl cleaner. Also, later on, should my sister's scheme lead to a law enforcement sweep of my home, would they be able to still determine even a trace of formaldehyde in, say, the ring around my sink, or trapped in my pipes? I honestly didn't know; such things never came up in medical school.

I would have to remove the solution from my unit. Take it elsewhere for disposal. As well as the strips of skin, the glass vials, the box.

A mall. A large public space where I could visit many stores as well as public bathrooms without arousing suspicion. Maybe discard one item here, one item there. Then maybe a trip to the grocery store. A woman, just running her errands.

It could work. As long as I was calm and inconspicuous, and remembered there were cameras everywhere. If there was one thing I had learned from my sister over the years, the best deceit was covered in layers of truth. Of course I went to that mall with the Ann Taylor store. Of course I picked up milk and bread. Why wouldn't I do those sorts of things?

A rough plan forming in my mind, I took a calming breath and got to work.

Latex gloves. A larger, single glass container to hold all the formalin solution, maybe a mason jar? But that would look strange. Anyone who saw a woman walk into a public restroom with a glass jar filled with a mysterious liquid, especially in Boston, post–marathon bombings . . . Not going to work.

Stainless steel water bottle. I had four or five in my kitchen cupboard. I picked my least favorite, an innocuous metallic blue with black top, which I placed on the bathroom counter to my right. Added to that a quart-size sandwich bag, opened to my left.

Single strip of skin placed in the ziplock bag. Couple of tablespoons of solution poured into the water bottle. Quick work, really. A decade of collecting dismantled in less than fifteen minutes.

I sealed up the bag, then the bottle, both of which would fit easily in my oversize purse.

Of course, I now confronted the matter of the twenty-one empty glass vials.

I could wash them. Run them through my dishwasher, then remove them to my office. Glass vials in a psychiatrist's office, not too strange. But would a trace of the formaldehyde remain in the rubber stopper? Not to mention my fingerprints . . .

Gallon-size freezer bag this time. Two of them. I removed the rubber stoppers, then double-bagged the glass vials. Then got out a stainless steel meat mallet and proceeded to pulverize the contents of the freezer bags, reducing the empty tubes to glass fragments small enough to flush down a toilet, at another stop along the routine errands/evidence disposal field trip.

The gallon-size bag also went into my purse, as well as a bag of rubber stoppers, to be tossed in a random Dumpster. The box was easy. It was, after all, only a shoe box. I removed the silk scrap, folded it up and placed it in my closet. The foam cushion I threw away. The box I broke down for deposit in my apartment building's recycling center.

If any of those three items were traced back to me, what did it matter? *Yes, Officer, I recognize that empty box. Used to have it in my closet. But I recently tidied up the place, throwing it away.* End of story.

Done at last, I stripped off the latex gloves and placed them in my purse. I would throw them away as well, but at a separate location.

Like a trail of guilty bread crumbs, scattered across the greater Boston area.

Then I washed my hands. Again and again and again. And I watched my fingers tremble and I told myself it was okay, I was doing the right thing, I did not have to be this person; I would not be this person.

Anyone could change. Even the deepest compulsion could be overcome with time and effort.

Then I walked into my bedroom, sat on the edge of my bed and cried.

Because my collection was gone and I didn't know what would ever fill me up, get me through the bad nights, quite like that again.

I was alone.

A baby, strapped into a car seat and trapped in a dark closet, the entire world reduced to nothing but a thin sliver of ominous light . . .

Nothing to see but plenty to hear.

Understanding little but absorbing all, like little hobgoblins now stuck in the back of my mind.

Please, Harry, not the baby.

Suddenly . . . I scrambled up off the edge of my bed. Raced into my home office. Knocking over a book, yanking open the filing cabinet, searching, searching, searching.

There. The binder my adoptive father had compiled so many years ago on Harry Day's case. Quickly flipping through the pages, the photos, hastily skimming the various detective notes. Until I found it. A report from the coroner's office.

One hundred and fifty-three.

Just as my sister had predicted—remembered?—known.

Our father's own collection. One hundred and fifty-three preserved strips of human skin contained in nearly three dozen mason jars.

I picked up the phone and dialed Detective Warren.

Chapter 21

You THINK SHANA DAY, an inmate who's been locked up for nearly thirty years, is somehow connected to this so-called Rose Killer? In fact, Shana may even be the one calling the shots?"

"Yes."

"Even though she's in solitary confinement? Has no fan base? No pen pals. Not even a fellow prisoner who claims to like her?"

"Exactly."

"All right." Alex took a seat across from D.D. at the kitchen table, where she was currently icing her shoulder. "I might be just a lowly crime scene analyst, but color me confused."

D.D. had just returned home from the morning interview with Shana, followed by her and Phil's chat with reporter Charlie Sgarzi. Glancing around the house it was clear Alex had been equally busy while she was out. Brand-new state-of-the-art locks gleamed on the front door, while the windows had been reinforced and a wooden dowel now effectively blocked the back sliders. He'd also taken the liberty of updating their home security system with several motion-activated cameras they could access from their smartphones. D.D. felt a little bit like a contestant on a new reality TV show, but given that they were due to bring Jack home in just a matter of hours . . .

"Okay," was all she'd said.

Alex had nodded in satisfaction.

So this was their new world order. Living like prisoners/TV show contestants till they caught the murder suspect who'd broken into their home to personally deliver a get-well-soon card.

"Of course you're confused," D.D. stated now. "You're an evidence junkie, and at the moment, that's kind of what we're lacking. Actual, you know, evidence."

"Yes," Alex agreed.

"Here's the deal: The obvious smoking gun would be a note from Shana Day to our murder suspect, the supposed Rose Killer. Based on what Superintendent McKinnon told us, however, written correspondence is hardly necessary for open and honest communication from behind prison walls. Chances are, Shana has developed some kind of coded system based on library books, or socks in her window, or the number of bites left on her food tray. Beats me. It's been done, though, many times and by many inmates. Given how smart Shana is, no reason to assume she's *not* able to reach beyond her cell door."

"Fair enough," Alex granted. "But . . . who? You're saying this reporter guy claims she has a helper from before her life in prison. Meaning a thirty-year-old never-before-seen friendship?"

D.D. shrugged. "By all accounts, Shana hasn't made any contacts while in prison. Thus, it makes some sense her lone ally is from before her life behind bars."

Alex shot her a look, obviously skeptical. "And this person spies for her?"

"We have numerous reports of Shana knowing things she shouldn't."

"So Shana gets information and power. And her imaginary friend? What's in it for him?"

D.D. pursed her lips. "Shits and giggles? Thrills and chills? How am I supposed to know? I'm sane. The kind of people who form attachments to incarcerated murderers, not so much so."

Alex rolled his eyes. "How's Melvin?" he asked, gesturing to her icy shoulder.

"Oh, you know, he's his normal cranky self. It's possible I might have pushed it too hard today."

Alex shot her a glance.

"Then again, turns out playing head games with one of the most notorious female killers in Massachusetts is very distracting, which has at least helped me ignore the pain. Who knew?"

Her husband sighed heavily. Chances were, right about now he was wishing he'd married a cupcake baker, or maybe a very nice librarian who ran amazing programs for educating kids. Then again: "All right," he said briskly. "Have it your way. As long as Melvin isn't too cranky and you're not too tired . . . I have another issue with your theory of the crime."

"Which is?"

"Why now?"

"What do you mean?"

"Why now?" Alex repeated. "Assuming Shana and her mysterious partner have had a relationship for thirty-plus years, why was the first murder only seven weeks ago? Don't all killers have—what do you call it?—an *inciting* incident? What then, basically three decades later, elevated their relationship to this whole new level?"

"The upcoming thirty-year anniversary of Donnie Johnson's murder," D.D. guessed.

"Really? Because what about the ten-year anniversary of the boy's murder? Or the twentieth, or the twenty-fifth? What makes thirty the magic number?"

"How am I supposed to know?"

"And why you?"

"What about me?"

"Exactly. The Rose Killer, the supposed protégé of Shana Day, who's now spent thirty years learning from a master, finally graduates, kills his first victim and targets you, Sergeant Detective D. D. Warren. Pushes you down a flight of stairs. Delivers love tokens to your home. That's deliberate, D.D., don't tell me that's not deliberate—"

"I'm not saying—"

"So why you?" he insisted. "You weren't even a cop thirty years ago, when Donnie Johnson was murdered. You have no connection to him or Shana Day. Why bring you into this mess? Why bring any investigator into this mess?"

D.D. scowled. "If you're going to keep grilling me, I'm going to require take-out Chinese."

"Deal."

"Okay, then. First off, it's not like we're done investigating. We know the theory has more unanswered questions than answered ones. Which is why Phil is contacting the parole officers of any released inmates who once shared a unit with Shana Day. Who knows? Maybe one of them was released three months ago and, having spent quality time talking shop with Shana, has decided to embark on her own reign of terror, collecting skin. Maybe I even have a connection to that inmate. It's possible. I'm already guessing it's going to be a long list of interview subjects."

Alex stilled. Across from her, his eyes took on a thoughtful gleam. "We're back to the possibility the Rose Killer is a woman. Which takes on additional weight, given the number of female criminals who've come into contact with Shana Day over the years. If Shana is the key and has brought someone under her wing, so to speak, it seems most probable you're looking for another female inmate, now out in the free world."

"Again, lack of sexual assault, compression asphyxiation as COD . . . We're still looking for Pat, not Bob," D.D. agreed. "As for why target me . . . maybe we're back to our first theory. I was there at the first crime scene, I surprised the killer, and even after being shoved down the stairs, I keep turning up. If our killer is a super-villain, well obviously I'm a supercop. We're meant for each other."

Alex gave her a look.

She ignored it. "Finally, you're right about an inciting incident. There must be a reason these murders are happening now. Parole, frankly, of a female inmate who's familiar with Shana Day is as good a one as any."

"Timeline," Alex stated. "I want timeline, I want motive, I want evidence. Then I want my wife to be safe. And not necessarily in that order."

"Fine. Now, I want General Tso's chicken. If not for me, then for Melvin."

"Fucking Melvin," he said.

She smiled, said softly, "I love you."

He didn't say it back. He didn't have to. He kissed her, full on the lips.

Then picked up his keys and departed for take-out Chinese.

THE PHONE RANG five minutes later. D.D. was surprised to see that it was Adeline calling.

"Hey, I have a question for you," D.D. stated immediately.

"About your shoulder?"

"No, your sister."

The line was silent for a moment. When Adeline spoke again, her tone was more cautious. "Yes?"

"We've been operating under the assumption that your sister has some kind of partner beyond prison walls. And this partner has now taken up murdering victims in a style reminiscent of your father, Harry Day."

"It's a theory."

"Why now? Your sister has been incarcerated for three decades, but the murders only started seven weeks ago. What was going on in between?"

"Shana met someone new?" Adeline spoke up slowly but didn't sound convinced. "Or . . . this Rose Killer . . . his or her homicidal instincts have been brewing for quite some time. The killer finally reached out to Shana, and her response lit the fuse."

"But how do the Rose Killer and Shana find each other to even begin communicating? Her only visitor is you, right? And her only new mail has been from Charlie Sgarzi, to which she never replied. That's why he tracked you down."

"True."

D.D. waited a heartbeat. She was curious if Adeline would pick up on the point that she was Shana's only visitor. A woman who shared the same twisted gene pool. A psychiatrist who'd attended four years of medical school.

When Adeline said nothing, D.D. moved on, voice still brisk, asking for information, not sharing suspicions.

"When Superintendent McKinnon was talking," she continued, "she mentioned that Shana's mood changed a few months ago. She grew more depressed. Do you know why?"

"No, but Shana is hardly the type to sit around and talk about her feelings. From a clinical point of view, my sister suffers from depression. The condition is ongoing. Some periods of time are simply better than others."

"But given that she suffers from depression, something could have happened that triggered the down cycle?"

"That's possible."

"But you don't know what?"

"No. Her life is very . . . contained. Though"—Adeline's voice picked up—"the thirty-year anniversary of Donnie Johnson's murder is approaching, combined with Charlie Sgarzi reaching out and demanding an interview . . . That certainly could've triggered an emotional response in Shana. Despite what you might think, her feelings regarding Donnie are very tangled. She won't talk about him, even now, which is almost a sure sign that day still bothers her. If she was truly remorseless, she would speak of him and/or what happened that day easily and often. But she doesn't."

"Okay." D.D.'s mind was still churning. Alex had raised a good point. Timeline mattered. All killers had an inciting incident. So two, three months ago, what had happened to suddenly spring the Rose Killer onto the world?

"What do you know about so-called partner killings?" D.D. asked now, given that she was speaking to a trained psychiatrist. She continued: "Such relationships are rare. There have been a handful of husband-and-wife or otherwise 'romantically linked' killing teams. Couple of male cousins who killed together. Either way, there's always one partner who's the alpha, and one who's the submissive."

"You think Shana and the Rose Killer are partners?" Adeline asked sharply. "She gives the commands, he performs the deed?"

"Maybe she performs the deed," D.D. said, then waited again.

Adeline simply sounded confused. "My sister? She's the one behind bars."

"No, the Rose Killer. What if he is a she?"

"That's extraordinarily rare," Adeline said immediately. "Most serial killers are male, as men are much more likely to externalize their rage than women. The few women who have been serial predators mostly fall into the category of black widows—they aren't motivated by sex or violence but by financial gain, making hired killers or poisons their MO of choice. The Rose Killer, personally assaulting, then skinning victims, well . . ."

"Sounds more like your sister?"

Silence. Then: "In fact . . ."

"No sexual assault," D.D. provided. A risk. That detail hadn't been revealed in the paper; she was now officially releasing privileged information to someone outside the case team. But D.D. was fishing, and she had to use something for bait.

"I see." Adeline's tone relented, turned more contemplative. "So maybe the Rose Killer is a fellow inmate. That's how she got to know Shana, where they came into contact. It would certainly explain how Shana could meet someone without having had new visitors or fresh pen pals. Then again . . ."

D.D. waited. Adeline sighed heavily.

"I just can't picture it," the doctor said at last. "And not just because my sister is so antisocial, but because if such a thing had happened—Shana took a friend, even had a lover—Superintendent McKinnon would know. Don't let her modesty from this morning fool you. As directors of major incarceration facilities go, McKinnon is more than up to the task. There's nothing going on behind those walls she doesn't know about. Meaning if such a relationship had happened, she would've told us about it."

"Unless she didn't want anyone to know," D.D. said. Couldn't help herself. The words just came out.

"What do you mean?"

"What if it wasn't an inmate? What if it was a guard? Male guard, female guard, it wouldn't matter. Such a thing wouldn't look good for anyone, especially for Superintendent McKinnon. She obviously takes a great deal of pride in the fact that Shana hasn't killed any more COs on her watch. If word got out that's because Massachusetts's most infamous female killer had taken to sleeping with them instead . . ."

Adeline sighed heavily. "I don't know. I suppose, when it comes to my sister, the honest reply is, anything is possible."

"Let's assume there is a relationship. Male, female, guard, inmate, whatever. For someone like Shana, how would that work?"

"Shana would be the alpha," Adeline provided without hesitation. "She has no empathy, no ability to bond with others. Meaning if she's in a relationship, the other party would have to do all the work to keep her happy. Without ongoing incentive, Shana would simply end the relationship."

"Does that include her relationship with you?" D.D. asked curiously.

"Actually, she made the initial contact. She wrote me a letter."

"When?"

"A long time ago, Detective."

"So . . . she does pursue some relationships?"

"Given that lone example over a span of three decades . . ."

"But she's into you, Adeline. Anyone can see that. If you suddenly stopped visiting, ceased all contact, do you think she'd simply accept your absence, sit quietly in her cell?"

The phone line was silent for a long time now. "No," Adeline said finally. "Shana would do something. Act out, most likely, in an egregious manner until I returned again."

"She's manipulative. She can leave you, but you can't leave her?"

"Exactly. It's a matter of power. As the older sister, she considers herself the alpha in our relationship. She would not permit me to walk away without her permission. That would be perceived as a slap in the face."

"I don't suppose, three months ago, you threatened to stop visiting?"

"No. I don't make such threats to my sister, Detective. That would only reduce myself to her level. We have our . . . squabbles. But I try to keep us on a more typical sisterly level of engagement, and not disintegrate into needless power plays."

D.D. nodded. "So Shana needs to be the alpha in a relationship. Meaning if she has a relationship with someone beyond prison walls, she's the one calling the shots. But how? She's living in solitary confinement. How does she keep the other party in line, ensure the person is following her orders, etcetera?"

More silence. "She would have to have something the other party wants. Something she could hold over him or her. The threat of exposing the relationship. Or maybe just plain threats. My sister can be very scary. It's possible, this other person, the Rose Killer, is in her sway. She's doing what she promised to do because Shana both frightens and fascinates her that much."

"Your sister is Charles Manson," D.D. filled in.

"Heaven help us all." Adeline sighed. "But no. Shana is not charismatic. Far from it. But that doesn't preclude, in the way love works, that one person out there isn't entranced by her. And one is all it would take."

D.D. nodded, digesting.

"I've made progress," Adeline continued now, "on the number one hundred fifty-three. I went through Harry Day's file. According to the coroner's report, all told in his collection of mason jars, he had harvested one hundred and fifty-three strips of human flesh."

D.D.'s eyes widened. "That's our connection? Harry Day once collected one hundred fifty-three strips of skin and that's your sister's new favorite number? How do you think she learned that number? Looked it up, or maybe got it from some reporter researching her father years ago?"

"I checked. There's not actually a lot written about Harry. And none of the articles I found contained that level of specificity regarding the crime scene. I even Googled his name combined with the number one hundred fifty-three. No hits."

"Did your sister get her hands on the police report? Have her own copy?"

"Doubtful. We could check with the prison librarian, of course, see what kinds of subjects Shana was prone to researching."

D.D. pursed her lips, feeling more confused than ever. "At the end of the day," she said slowly, "Shana provided us with a number that relates back to her father. But that's it, right? So she knows how many pieces of skin he collected. Now we do, too. Doesn't necessarily mean it's something to be too concerned about yet."

Silence. Long silence. Long enough that D.D. suffered a sudden, acute feeling of foreboding, while Melvin began to ache.

"The Rose Killer," Adeline started, and D.D. no longer wanted her to continue. "He's removed strips of skin from his victims. I don't suppose your ME knows how many?"

D.D. closed her eyes, said nothing.

"It's only a guess, of course, but if those numbers match . . ."

"Your sister offered up a tangible connection between her and the Rose Killer. Proving she's involved in this mess once and for all."

"I'm assuming you'll call the ME next."

"Oh, I would assume that."

"Detective, Shana does nothing without a reason. The question isn't, what does her partner get out of this relationship. The question is, what does Shana get out of it? What's in it for her? And I can tell you, the answer to that question won't be simple. It would be easier for all of us if my sister were just a homicidal maniac. But she's not. She's smart, she's strategic, and she's . . . complicated. She's also already lost thirty years of her life behind bars. If all of this is some gambit for her to get out, a brief furlough in return for her cooperation, as she alluded to this morning . . ."

"Yeah?"

"She won't go back, D.D. I know that much about my sister. In her mind, she made one mistake when she was just a kid—"

"You mean killing another kid?"

"No, I mean getting *caught* killing another kid. Inside prison, Shana's life is over. Outside . . . Whatever is going on here, whatever Shana's looking for, we can't give it to her. She will win and we will lose."

"Is that your opinion as a professional psychiatrist or as a little sister?"

"Do you have any siblings, Detective?"

"Nope, I'm an only child."

"For most of my childhood, so was I. So I'm sticking to professional psychiatrist. You'll call the ME's office?"

"I'll do that. In the meantime, we're not going to jump to any conclusions. And we are absolutely, positively *not* going to let this mess with our heads."

D.D. could practically feel Adeline's tired smile over the phone line. "Let me know how that works for you, Detective. As for myself, I'm going shopping. A little retail therapy can ease the burden of any woman's soul."

The doctor hung up. D.D. called the ME's office. She had to wait ten minutes for Ben to pick up the line. As a matter of fact, he'd just finished arranging and analyzing the strips of skin from the first victim earlier in the afternoon. He'd counted 153.

"I'm actually guessing one hundred and sixty were removed," he continued briskly. "With seven being taken away as souvenirs. I don't have any proof, of course. Only that one hundred and sixty is a nice round number, and it's clear to me that some amount of derma remains missing."

D.D. thanked him for his report, disconnected the phone, hung her head. It didn't matter, she thought. Whether the Rose Killer had removed 160 strips of skin total, or 155, or 161. What mattered was the precise number left behind for the investigators to find and catalogue. One hundred fifty-three.

A numeric homage to Harry Day. As predicted by his daughter Shana.

"I absolutely, positively will not let this mess with my head," she muttered. Then: "Shit."

Chapter 22

WHAT DID IT FEEL LIKE to open your eyes in the middle of the night and find a killer standing in the middle of your bedroom? The split second when you blinked your eyes owlishly, because such a thing, the silhouette of a man now at the foot of your bed, couldn't be. It just . . . couldn't be.

Did you scream? Or did the terror squeeze your throat, compress your chest just as quickly and easily as his hands would soon do. Denial. An innate inability to process. This couldn't be happening. Not to me. Not here. I'm not this kind of person, I don't lead this kind of life, I wasn't meant for this kind of death.

Then the gleam of the finely honed blade moving in the dark . . .

My thoughts scattered. Jumping and leaping as I roamed the overbright shopping mall, surrounded by a sea of humanity and judiciously avoiding all eye contact as I clutched my oversize purse and went about my business.

At the Ann Taylor store. Dutifully trying on a new cream-colored blouse, a pair of camel-colored wool pants. Glancing once at the name tag of the chirpy young sales clerk. Then noticing her pale left hand, devoid of rings, and wondering if she had her own place, a confident single woman with her own apartment. She had brown hair like me, a quick smile.

I wondered if she was the Rose Killer's type. I'd never thought to ask about hair color, physiology. Ted Bundy had preferred blondes. And my sister's possible friend?

I fled the store to the women's restroom, which was thankfully empty. In the end stall. Metallic-blue water bottle out. Clear formaldehyde solution pouring into the toilet. Flushing.

Then back at the sink, rinsing out the bottle more energetically than most. A mother walked in, juggling three large shopping bags and two young kids. She gave me a weary smile, then disappeared into the handicap stall with her charges.

I made a show of refilling my water bottle just in case. Then tucked it in my purse, nestled against a gallon-size bag of crushed glass. Or maybe it was the quart-size bag of human skin.

I left the mall, drove to Target, where at least I had a shopping list.

Six P.M. now. The sun gone, the evening biting. Huddling along with the rest of the postwork commuters, head down, as we performed our final errands before marching home.

The ladies' room in Target was much more crowded. I had to wait in line for a stall, feeling increasingly self-conscious. Finally, one opened up. I stood before the toilet, fumbling with my purse, then realized belatedly that the waiting patrons would notice my feet facing the wrong way; in that stance, I couldn't possibly be sitting.

Rearranging myself quickly, purse now on my lap. Waiting for someone to flush so the noise would cover the sound of me working the zipper. I stood at the last minute, dumping half the bag's contents into the toilet. The bloated strands of flesh had become one congealed mass, floating on top of the water and looking almost exactly like a dead goldfish, before sinking to the bottom of the toilet.

I thought I might vomit. A curious sensation, so far removed from myself, it occurred to me that while harvesting human skin somehow allowed me to sleep better at night, disposing of evidence made me ill.

Another sign of genetic mutation? My adoptive father had had it all wrong. He'd studied me for signs of pain, when he should've been analyzing me for signs of violence.

I flushed the toilet. The bowl emptied, refilled.

And three tendrils of human flesh floated back to the top.

I nearly screamed. Had to catch myself, bite my lower lip.

Hands shaking, breath panting, I flushed again. Control, control. Nothing here that couldn't be managed . . .

Second time was the charm. The toilet bowl emptied, then refilled devoid of human tissue.

I turned, carefully composed my features, then unlocked the stall door and proceeded to the sink.

Not a single waiting female so much as glanced at me. At least, I didn't think so.

I washed my hands twice. Just . . . because.

I wondered, not for the first time, how my father had done it.

Was he so cold that he felt nothing when either targeting his victims or, inevitably, cleaning up afterward? Or was the difference that this was the only time he felt anything at all? It was the nervous energy, combined with the corresponding adrenaline rush, that urged him on. Oh, and of course, his need to inflict misery. A miswired sexual circuit board that made him feed off pain instead of pleasure. Until doing the worst felt the best to him.

I often thought if my father were still alive, he would be the first to tell you it wasn't his fault. He'd been born that way. It was simply his nature. Which he'd graciously handed down to his older daughter, Shana, while apparently saving some pieces for me.

Except I didn't want to be Harry Day's daughter. I didn't want to be Shana Day's sister.

And I wondered about my mother again. A mere shadow of a woman, who didn't even exist on paper, and yet had been the one to take our father's life.

Dad is love. Mom is worse.

As D. D. Warren and I had discussed, in any relationship there could be only one alpha. In my family, clearly my father had called all the shots. Meaning if my mother had fed him aspirin before slitting his wrists, it was only because he'd told her to. He'd commanded, and she'd obeyed.

Which Shana held against my mother, because she had sensed the submissive in her, the weak female, which Shana despised. Shana identified with our father, the alpha hunter, living on his own terms. I often wondered if she envied his decision to die rather than be captured.

If Shana and I had still been in the same home, like true sisters, when the police had come for her thirty years ago, would she have climbed into the tub, then silently handed me the razor?

And me?

Maybe I would've accepted the razor. Then leaned forward and delicately removed a single strip of skin before running away.

My sister was wrong. I was not our mother, any more than I was our father. Somehow, I was both. A submissive predator who both harmed and felt remorse. A terrible person some nights, while holding strong even more nights.

We can all be both good and bad. Heroic and evil. Strong and weak.

I shivered again, seeing things in my mind I didn't want to see, and unable to shake the relentless feeling of dread. My sister had spoken. She'd given us a number tying our long-dead father to a new and improved killer.

My sister, all these years later, still determined to make me bleed.

From Target, I went to the grocery store. Another stop in the restroom. The last of the human skin flushed down the toilet. On the first try, this time. Apparently, the grocery store had better water pressure.

I crumbled up the bag in my fist, then deposited it beneath a pile of crushed paper towels in the trash, along with the rubber stoppers.

More hand washing. My skin dry and chapped from such stringent cleaning. I couldn't feel it, of course. Just note the red, inflamed skin stretched over my knuckles. I made a mental note to apply Aquaphor later tonight. I should also take a magnifying glass and inspect myself for slivers and broken bits of vial. In my earlier rush, it was possible I'd somehow maimed myself, and the wound was even now starting to fester. It wasn't as if I would know.

After all, what would I feel if I woke up in the middle of the night and found a killer standing in the middle of my bedroom? It wasn't as if he could cause me pain. Surprise, yes. Shock, rage and even shame. But no pain.

Never any pain.

And I thought, rather wildly, that my father had to have known. I bet he did cut me when I was a baby, because why would he have cared about my mother's pleas? No, I bet one night he casually reached over and sliced a razor across my pudgy fist.

Except I hadn't reacted. I'd remained rooted in the same spot, little arm still outstretched, blood welling, staring at him with perfectly solemn, baby eyes. Practically daring him to do worse.

I bet I'd unnerved him. I might have even sparked fear in the heart of the alpha. Until he'd picked up my baby carrier and stuck me in the closet. Anything to keep me from studying him with my all-knowing gaze.

I was not my mother. I was not my father. I was not my sister.

I was my family's conscience.

No wonder they'd kept me in the closet.

All alone.

Eight P.M. The temperature had fallen even further, and I shivered inside my wool coat as I trudged back to my car, two grocery bags in hand. I wanted to go home, but I still had the crushed vials. Where could you dispose of broken glass and no one would notice?

Then, it came to me. Recycling. Of course. Glass recycling.

I loaded my twin bags into my car, then returned to the front of the grocery store and its blue-plastic recycling center. Sure enough, one bin marked glass. I glanced around, waiting for a lull in pedestrian traffic.

Then I quickly opened my purse, grabbed the gallon-size bag, yanked it open and dumped out the glass. One, two, three, done.

Mission complete, I headed once more for the automatic doors, looking up only at the last minute to spot the security cameras directly overhead. Pointed at the recycling bin.

Go, go, go, I instructed my suddenly frozen muscles. Move!

Back outside into the bitter night. Nearly fleeing to my car, where I put it in gear and raced out of the parking lot. Two, three, four blocks down before I got my breathing under control and forced myself to focus.

Grocery stores had security cameras to protect against shoplifting. I hadn't taken anything illegally; ergo, I had nothing to fear. In fact, I'd dumped glass into glass recycling, so I *really* hadn't done anything wrong.

Just go home, I ordered myself. It had been a long and trying day, dealing with my sister, the riddle of 153 and the terrible possibilities that now loomed ahead.

But time was on our side. The Rose Killer had struck only two days prior. Given the cycle of six weeks between first and second victim, odds were the police had at least another month before the killer attacked again. Plenty of time to figure out the best way for handling Shana and her manipulative games.

Plenty of time for me to get my head on straight.

Nine P.M. Finally entering my condo, where I dropped various shopping bags on the floor.

I walked straight into my bedroom. Turned on a lone bedside lamp. Stripped off my clothes.

Then moved into my closet, where I curled up on the floor, huddled in the pitch black, arms wrapped tight around my knees, as I gazed at the faint sliver of light formed along the edge of the door.

And finally succumbed to wave after wave of nameless fear.

How would you feel? What would you do? If you woke up in the middle of the night and found a killer standing in the middle of your bedroom?

"Daddy," I whispered.

While out in the bedroom, my phone began to ring.

Chapter 23

CHARLIE SGARZI LOOKED DESTROYED. Set jaw, obstinate chin, solid shoulders, all gone. Instead, he sat on his mother's sofa, a gutted version of his former self, and regarded D.D. and Phil with red-rimmed eyes.

"You don't understand," he said thickly. "She never opened her door without first checking the peephole. And she sure as hell wouldn't let a stranger into the house. Even in broad daylight. When do you think my cousin was killed?"

D.D. nodded. She remembered Sgarzi having said that his mother basically lived as a shut-in.

And yet, sometime roughly between two and four this afternoon, according to the ME's initial assessment, the Rose Killer had entered Janet Sgarzi's home. At which point the killer had drugged Charlie's ninety-pound cancer-ravaged elderly mother, carried her to a back bedroom and proceeded according to plan.

Charlie had discovered the scene shortly after seven, when he'd shown up at the house with dinner. Having Phil's card from their earlier discussion, he'd dialed the older detective direct. In turn, Phil had summoned Alex to assist with the crime scene analysis and D.D. to serve as an "independent consultant."

They'd been driving to Alex's parents' house to pick up Jack. Instead, they'd turned around, notifying his understanding parents as they'd headed straight to the Rose Killer's latest crime scene. A tiny, perfectly appointed home in South Boston that reeked of old memories and fresh blood.

"It's possible the killer poses as a security company employee, pest control, etcetera," Phil said. "Would your mother have opened her door for a deliveryman, that kind of thing?"

"Why hasn't that been in the paper?" Sgarzi exploded.

"Because we haven't found any witnesses to corroborate our theory," Phil supplied gently. "Right now, it's just our best guess based on the ease with which the suspect is accessing his victims' homes. You say your mother was cautious—"

"Yes!"

"Could she have been asleep in the middle of the afternoon?"

"She naps, yeah. Hell, she's getting near the end now. More bad days than good and nothing the doctors can do . . . I mean, could've done. Ah geez. I need a fucking minute, okay?"

The tiny front parlor allowed little space for privacy. Sgarzi stalked over to the fireplace and stood staring at the mantel.

The house reminded D.D. of Sgarzi's apartment. Small but well kept. Freshly dusted surfaces, vacuumed rugs. She wondered if Janet still maintained her own home or if it was something Sgarzi did for his mom. Most likely the latter, given the woman's drastically declining health. Just like Sgarzi had brought his mother dinner tonight. Soup from one of her favorite local restaurants, he'd said, as swallowing solid foods was becoming increasingly difficult.

D.D. couldn't imagine what it must've been like to walk through the door, call his ailing mother's name and receive no reply. Then, already starting to worry, moving to the back bedroom, only to discover his deepest, darkest fears had never been deep enough or dark enough to picture what he'd found there.

Now Sgarzi's hands clenched and unclenched spastically down by his sides. D.D. wondered if he was going to punch the brick fireplace or drive his fist through the aged yellow drywall. With obvious effort, the reporter seemed to pull himself together. One last shudder, then he turned, staring at them with a haggard expression.

"Shana Day did this," he stated, jabbing the air with one finger.

"Now, Charlie," Phil began.

"Don't 'now, Charlie' me. I'm onto her, and she knows it. I thought I was just sifting through old dirt when I started asking questions about her. Except first thing I learned is that she's got eyes and ears beyond prison walls. And now she's using them. Got herself a little killer puppet who can do all the work out here, while Shana sits in her cell pulling the strings. Perfect alibi, right? Shana couldn't have killed my mother; she's already locked up! But she did it. She slaughtered my mom to get back at me, and worse, she's laughing her ass off because she knows there's nothing you can do about it. This is what thirty years of incarceration has taught her—how to perfect her own goddamn crime."

"Would your mother have opened the door for a deliveryman?" Phil asked again.

"I don't know. Probably."

"Does she have a home security system?" D.D. spoke up.

"Yeah, the house is alarmed."

"Cameras?"

"No. Just wired the doors and windows."

"Name of the company?"

Sgarzi supplied it; Phil wrote it down.

"Did your mother mention noticing anyone new in the neighborhood? A stranger she'd spotted lurking around? New tenant on the block?"

"No."

"Feeling as if she was being watched?" Phil asked.

"My mom didn't leave the house and kept the blinds down. How the hell could anyone watch her?"

Fair enough, D.D. thought. "What about a visiting nurse, some other kind of health professional?" she spoke up.

"Yeah. Twice a week, Nurse Eliot. My mom needed more help, course, but that's all we could afford."

"Nurse Eliot? Male, female?"

"Older woman. Nice enough. My mom liked her."

"And it was always the same nurse?"

"Most of the time. But if Nurse Eliot couldn't make it, they'd send someone else. But they always called and notified us ahead of time. Besides, Nurse Eliot worked Tuesdays and Fridays, so no one was due to show up until tomorrow. Did the neighbors see anything?" Sgarzi jumped ahead. "I mean, the guy would've had to stand on the front porch, in full view of the street. . . ."

"We're canvassing now," Phil assured him, voice still soft.

"Which means you got nothing!" Sgarzi accused. "One of your plainclothes had anything good, you'd have heard it by now. Son of a bitch!"

He whirled back around, returned to staring at the fireplace.

"You said you brought food back for your mom," D.D. said. "What about lunch?"

"She does one of those nutritional drinks for lunch. Ensure, something like that."

D.D. eyed the reporter's back. "What about midafternoon snack? Because there are two plates and glasses in the sink."

"What?"

Sgarzi turned around again, eyes wide. Before they could stop him, he barreled past them, into the kitchen.

"Don't touch anything!" Phil's voice boomed behind him.

The reporter's arm froze right where he was already reaching into the stainless steel sink for the first glass.

"Evidence," D.D. chimed in more directly.

Sgarzi returned his arm to his side. "She had a guest," he said, and his voice sounded funny, almost confused.

"What do you mean?"

"Ma hasn't eaten much in weeks. Side effects of the drugs, pain, who knows. I bring her dinner, she has a little breakfast, then one of those drinks for lunch. But two plates, two glasses. And these are her good plates. She brought them out for special occasions. You know, like a guest."

"Charlie," D.D. said quietly, "is it possible your mom knew who came to her door this afternoon? That's why she let the person in?"

"I don't know," Sgarzi said, and his voice sounded dazed, far from his certainty of before.

"If she had a guest, what would she offer?" Phil asked.

"Fig Newtons. Tea and cookies, you know?" Sgarzi opened a cupboard, pulled out a yellow cellophane package. It appeared to have been freshly opened, with two cookies missing.

"Son of a bitch," Charlie said again.

"We're going to need a list of your mother's friends and acquaintances," Phil began.

"No, you don't. My mother was dying of cancer. The people who knew her didn't come here looking for cookies; they brought her food. This was a stranger guest, you know? The kind of person you're still getting to know, putting your best foot forward, that kind of thing." Sgarzi frowned down at the yellow package, as if the cookies could tell him something. "A friend of a friend would do it," he murmured. "Someone who claimed to know me, or an old acquaintance returning to the neighborhood. Someone who knew Donnie," he concluded abruptly. "Someone claiming to know something *about* Donnie." He glanced at them. "She'd open her door for that person. Invite him in. Offer him refreshments on her nicest plates. She'd make an effort for someone who once knew Donnie. I'm telling you, Shana Day killed my mom. And you're fucking idiots for not having stopped her sooner."

D.D. didn't bother with a reply. Lack of evidence to support his theory, due process, investigative 101—these were not topics that interested Charlie Sgarzi. What he really wanted was the one thing they'd never be able to give him—his mother back.

Phil got the man to return to the front parlor, while putting a crime scene tech to work fingerprinting the items in the sink, as well as everything else in the kitchen. Phil had just gotten Sgarzi started making a list of his mother's friends and neighbors when Alex appeared.

He had a look on his face D.D. had never seen before; not just very grave but also deeply troubled. He made a gesture for her to follow him.

Not one word of warning. Not a single expression of encouragement.

Which was how D.D. knew it was going to be awful before she ever entered the room.

THE BACK BEDROOM WAS VERY TINY, probably originally intended to be a rear study in the quaint Colonial-style house. Most likely the room had been converted when Janet Sgarzi's health had deteriorated to the point she could no longer climb the stairs.

A single hospital-style bed with metal railings dominated most of the space, pushed up against the far wall and blocking what was probably a rear exit. Next to the bed was an old oak nightstand, topped with a pitcher of water, numerous orange pill bottles and, of course, a champagne bottle and a single red rose.

D.D. stared at the two items for a moment, because knowing she was about to see didn't make it any easier.

"No fur-lined handcuffs," she murmured.

"No," Alex said from beside her, where he currently blocked her view of the bed. The two of them were tucked tightly together, crammed into the remaining space in the room. For her to step forward, he would have to fall back, and vice versa. "There are some differences this time around," he continued. "With both the victim and the MO. Though the differences in the MO may have to do with differences in the victim."

"Start from the beginning?"

"The victim is sixty-eight-year-old Janet Sgarzi, lived alone, also in the end stages of cancer. The living-alone part is consistent with our victim profile. Her age and health, however, make her distinct. We've gone from a predator who targets relatively young single women, to the murder of an ailing elderly mother."

"Daylight attack," D.D. supplied. "Higher risk for our predator."

"Yes. Pat is getting bolder. Then again, this particular victim had a reputation for caution and probably wouldn't have answered her door after dark. Also, while she lived alone, sounds like Charlie often stayed over, given the state of Janet's health. Meaning a nighttime attack might have actually proved riskier in this particular case."

"The Rose Killer watched her first. Must have to account for all those variables."

"Which we figured," Alex said. "Pat does his or her homework, plans ahead. That's why we can't get a bead on him/her, even after four break-ins."

"Four?"

"Three murders, plus our own home. Which was also midday."

D.D. straightened. "Pat was practicing! I bet you anything the son of a bitch was practicing. Toying with us, yes, but also practicing! Pat had already selected the next victim, Janet Sgarzi, who would have to be approached during the day. So Pat worked on technique while scoping out and entering our house. Dammit!"

Alex placed a hand on her right shoulder. Not to soothe but to still her.

"D.D.," he said, and there was a wealth of gravitas in that word. Immediately, she fell silent.

"To continue our analysis," he stated formally.

"Okay."

"Pat plans ahead. In this case, the Rose Killer had to approach the victim during the day. Given the victim's age and health, however, Pat probably wasn't worried about overpowering her even if she was awake and fully conscious. Just to be safe, however, the killer appears to have brought a colorless, odorless and tasteless sedative; Ben recovered a vial from the trash can with traces of Rohypnol. Most likely, Pat drugged Janet Sgarzi first."

"There are dishes for two in the sink," D.D. reported. "As if Janet shared refreshments with a guest beforehand. Fig Newtons."

Alex grimaced.

"Chances are, Janet Sgarzi never felt a thing," Alex said quietly. "Compared to what the cancer was doing to her body, perhaps you could argue this was . . . easier. At least, a less painful way to die. And yet . . ."

He stepped back, revealing the oversize, metal-framed hospital bed. And despite herself, D.D. gasped.

Postmortem, she reminded herself. Postmortem, postmortem, postmortem. And yet, as Alex had said, it didn't help.

True to the first two crime scenes, the Rose Killer had flayed the skin from Janet Sgarzi's torso and upper thighs. Unlike the first two victims, however, young, relatively healthy females, Janet had already been wasting away from a terrible disease. She'd been nothing but skin and bones. Meaning once the killer had removed the skin . . .

D.D. put a hand over her mouth. She couldn't help herself. As crime scenes went, this one would leave a mark.

"There are hesitation marks," Alex said.

"What?"

"Along the edge of her outer thigh, and ribs. You can see . . . The skin is jagged, not evenly sliced. Third time out, a killer should have less internal resistance. He/she should be growing even more adept and elaborate with his handiwork. Instead, our killer struggled with this one."

"Her age?" D.D. guessed. "Harder to attack an elderly woman?"

"No fur-lined handcuffs," Alex said. "Which are the most blatantly sexual objects left behind at each scene. If we're thinking a female killer obsessed with attacking young women in order to collect ribbons of unblemished skin—"

"An elderly woman doesn't fit. She's not the Rose Killer's type. Are we even sure this is the Rose Killer's handiwork and not a copy-cat crime?"

"Yes," Alex said.

"But the hesitation marks, lack of restraints—"

"Janet Sgarzi is his third victim," Alex interrupted her. "One hundred and fifty-three, D.D. That's what I've been doing. Counting flayed strips of human flesh. And I hope to God I never have to do that ever again in my lifetime, but it did yield the magic number: one hundred and fifty-three ribbons of skin."

D.D. didn't answer right away. She couldn't swallow, much less talk. No wonder Alex had appeared so . . . somber. Of all the scenes he'd ever had to analyze . . .

"I'm sorry," she said at last.

"Janet Sgarzi was the Rose Killer's victim," Alex continued steadily. "She wasn't, however, the killer's preferred victim type. Meaning something else must have made her a target."

"Charlie Sgarzi believes Shana Day did this," D.D. supplied. "She ordered the Rose Killer to murder his mother to get back at him for investigating her. Or maybe to warn him off, in which case, I don't think it worked, because he's mostly vowed revenge."

"Or she knew something," Alex said.

"What do you mean?"

"Shana Day has been quietly sitting in solitary for nearly thirty years, yes?"

"True."

"And now, suddenly, you believe she's engaged in some kind of coded communication with a serial killer who's magically appeared in Boston and seems to be emulating another long-dead predator, Harry Day."

"True."

"Except, returning to the question of the day, why now? What's the inciting event? The thirty-year anniversary of Donnie Johnson's murder? Because that seems rather arbitrary as anniversary dates go."

D.D. gave him a look. "We discussed this. And trust me, you doubted my intelligence just fine the first time."

"I'm not doubting your intelligence. I'm offering a theory. Janet Sgarzi wasn't just Donnie Johnson's aunt; she was Charlie's mom— the reporter who, only a matter of months ago, started asking fresh questions about his cousin's death."

D.D. looked up at him, frowning. "You mean . . ."

"A thirty-year anniversary date is subjective. Reopening an investigation into an old murder, on the other hand . . . What if Shana really does have a friend from back in the day? And what if that person knows things, or did things, that all these years later, he/she/ it still can't afford to come to light?"

"The Rose Killer's true motive isn't a macabre string of murders deliberately staged to recall shades of Harry Day," D.D. murmured. "It's a cover-up. Because there's no statute of limitations on homicide. Pat's still got everything to lose."

"And one very real weakness," Alex offered grimly. "Shana Day."

Chapter 24

SUPERINTENDENT MCKINNON CALLED just after 6:00 A.M. Having yet to fall asleep, I found it easy enough to pick up the phone, then murmur the appropriate words as McKinnon explained that my sister wanted to speak with me. But of course, I said. I could be there at eight.

Then I hung up the phone and crawled out of the depths of my closet, where I'd spent the night after D. D. Warren's phone call notifying me of the Rose Killer's latest attack. I spent long minutes under the stinging spray of a lukewarm shower. I still didn't feel quite human.

What to wear for this latest battle of wits? I went with the fuchsia cardigan. It seemed the obvious choice. It felt that for years my sister and I had been engaged in a dance. One step forward, one step back, swaying side to side. The music was changing now. Speeding up, moving toward a pounding crescendo, where, at the end, only one of us would be left standing.

I contemplated checking in with D.D. or Detective Phil as I drove south to the MCI. But I didn't. I already knew what I would say to Shana, what I had to do. And when it came to my sister, I was the expert. It was only appropriate that I should be the one calling the shots.

I entered the sterile, gray shaded lobby. Showed proper ID, then checked my purse into an available locker. I went through the tasks on autopilot, a ritual I'd performed too often lately. If my sister was the one who had committed the crime, then why did I feel like the one who was spending all of her time in prison?

Superintendent McKinnon was already waiting for me. She escorted me through security, down a back hall, her low-slung black heels clicking briskly.

"No BPD?" she asked.

"The day is young. How is Shana?"

"Same old, same old. That reporter, Charlie Sgarzi . . . Paper says his mother was murdered last night. Latest victim of the Rose Killer."

"So I'm told."

"You think Shana's involved, don't you?" The superintendent stopped walking, turning abruptly, arms crossed over her chest. Dressed in an impeccably tailored black suit, hair pulled tight, high, sculpted cheekbones pronounced, her intimidating look worked well for her. "I called an emergency meeting of my COs yesterday. Demanded to know if any of them had caught so much as a whiff of Shana communicating with anyone inside or outside of the prison. According to them, there's no way, no how. Least they haven't suspected a thing."

I kept my voice neutral. "Not the kind of thing the guilty party would admit to, though. As you mentioned yesterday, if a corrections officer is the one serving as the messenger, it would be for a price."

"Except no price is high enough to help your sister. She's killed two of our own. Behind these walls, that kind of thing is taken personally."

"Are you sure? Those killings happened a long time ago, before many of your current COs started working here. For that matter, before you came here."

McKinnon stared at me, gaze hard. "What are you getting at, Adeline?"

"Shana hasn't had any new visitors. And according to you, she definitely hasn't been engaging in any outside communication. Which makes me wonder if that simply means she doesn't have to: Her new friend isn't from outside these walls. Her new friend is already on the inside. Inmate. Corrections officer. Staff."

McKinnon didn't speak right away. When she did, her words were clipped. "You suspect me in that list? I fall under staff? Because to be fair, I have to include you in that list. You're not a new visitor, and yet you're here often enough. The kind of regular all of us are so used to seeing, sometimes I bet we don't even notice you."

"Why are you letting Shana and me talk?" I asked. "We're way over our monthly allotment. Yet she made the request and you allowed it."

The superintendent frowned, appearing troubled again. "I want to know what's going on," she said. "Yesterday . . . Shana convinced me. I don't know how, but in some way, she's connected to these murders. The question remains: Is Shana some criminal mastermind, ordering murders from the solitude of her cell? Or is she simply laughing at our expense, creating a macabre game where now I suspect you and you suspect me, and the BPD probably suspects both of us. I need to know what's going on, Adeline. As the superintendent of this prison, hell, as a supposedly intelligent woman who used to sleep at night, I want to know what's really happening in my facility. Now, I expect the Boston detectives will visit again soon enough to press the matter. But, all suspicions aside, my money's on you. If anyone gets the truth out of Shana, it's going to be you."

We resumed walking, not toward the visiting room Shana and I usually shared, but toward the interview room used last time by the Boston detectives. Apparently, Superintendent McKinnon planned on listening in. All part of her pursuit of truth? Or to make sure Shana didn't reveal too much?

And me? What did I want, think, feel about all of this?

McKinnon was right. We were all twisted up. Jumping at shadows, suspecting everyone, frightened of everything.

I thought of what Charlie Sgarzi had said just the other day. I couldn't feel pain, meaning what did I have to fear?

I remembered my disposal project yesterday. The way I had flushed strings of human flesh down a public toilet. The way three had floated back to the top, mocking me.

And I realized, for the first time in my life, I had never been so afraid.

Once again, Shana was already waiting inside the room, shackled hands resting on the edge of the table. She glanced up as I walked in, dark eyes lasering in on my fuchsia top, and I suffered my first moment of uncertainty.

My sister didn't appear anything like I'd expected.

Her face was gaunt; if anything, even paler than yesterday, with deep bruises under her eyes. As if she had yet to sleep, her shoulders bunched with tension.

I'd imagined a gloating Shana, smug in her newfound powers that enabled her to meet with police officers and myself at the snap of her fingers. Her prediction had come true, and now here I was, answering her summons, while waiting for her to dictate her terms.

Instead, if I didn't know better, I would say my sister appeared deeply stressed. Her gaze went from my cardigan to the one-way viewing glass.

"Who's there?" she asked sharply.

I hesitated. "Superintendent McKinnon."

"What about Detective Phil?"

"Did you want to speak with him?"

"No. Just you."

I nodded, crossed to the tiny Formica table, took a seat.

"I suppose you've heard that the Rose Killer murdered another woman last night?"

Shana didn't say a word.

"Flayed one hundred and fifty-three strips of skin from her cancer-ravaged body. Must've been hard to do. Some of those treatments leave a person's skin so thin and translucent, it's like the skin of an onion. Difficult to remove without tearing."

She didn't say a word.

"How are you doing it?" I asked at last.

She looked away from me, lips pressed firmly into a thin line, eyes locked on the wall behind my head.

"One hundred and fifty-three," I said lightly. "The number of pieces of skin our father collected forty years ago. The number of strips the Rose Killer leaves behind now. Proof that you really are exchanging notes with a killer? Feeding him information about our father? Does it feel the same, Shana, to kill long-distance? Or is it not as good as you imagined? You're still the one sitting here, and your puppet is the one out there, actually gripping the blade, smelling the blood."

"You don't know what you're talking about," she muttered at last.

"Really? I'm wearing your favorite-color sweater."

A muscle flexed in her jaw. She glared at me, and I could see for the first time just how enraged she truly was. But she'd stopped speaking again.

I leaned back. Rested my hands on my lap. Studied the woman who was my sister.

Prison-orange scrubs today. A color that jaundiced her complexion, further washed out her skin. Her hair still appeared lank and unwashed. Or maybe it was simply the best she could do given the notoriously low water pressure in the prison showers.

A hard woman. With a thin, sinewy build like our father. I bet she worked out in her cell. Push-ups, sit-ups, lunges, plank exercises. Plenty of ways to keep strong in an eight-by-eleven-foot space. It showed in the harsh lines of her face, the gaunt hollows of her cheeks. All these years later, she'd not allowed herself to go soft or fatten up on processed prison food.

All these years later, she was still waiting.

Somehow, someway, for this very day.

"No," I said.

"No what?"

"No to whatever it is you're asking for. No to any deals, negotiations or exchanges of information. If you are in communication with the Rose Killer, if you have knowledge that would help catch a murderer, then volunteer it. That's what people do. It's called being a member of the human race."

Shana finally looked at me. Her brown eyes were hooded, hard to read.

"You didn't come all the way down here to tell me no," she said flatly. "No is a phone call, not a personal visit. And you've never been one to waste your time, Adeline."

"I came because I have a question for you."

"So now you're the one who's going to negotiate?"

"No. I'm going to ask. Answer or don't answer as you'd like. When did Daddy first cut you?"

"I don't remember." Her words were too automatic. I already didn't believe her.

"When did he first cut me?"

Now she smirked. "Didn't. You were just a *baby*."

"Liar."

She frowned, blinked her eyes.

"He did. I know he did. And I didn't cry, did I? Or flinch or pull away. I just stared at him. I stared and that scared the shit out of him, didn't it? That's why I lived in the closet. Not to keep me safe. Not because our mother magically loved me more, and not because I was *just the baby*. I was stuck in that goddamn closet because he didn't want me looking at him like that."

"Seriously?" my sister drawled. "*That's* what you're angry about? Being stuck in a closet? Because take it from me, I got bigger things worth raging about."

She started rolling up her sleeve to show me her collection of scars, ones my father, and even Shana herself, had inflicted over the years. Fat scars, thin scars, rolling pink lines, thin white streaks. All of which I'd seen before. All old news.

"I know your pain, Shana," I said quietly. "I can't feel it, but I *know* it. That's my role. I'm our family's conscience. I have been from the very beginning. That's what scared Daddy so much forty years ago. He looked into my eyes, and instead of seeing the terror and anguish and misery he was accustomed to, he saw himself. Just himself. No wonder he kept me in a closet after that. It's easy to be a monster. It's much harder to see yourself as monstrous."

"That doctor talk? Kind of thing you bill out by the hour? Because real people, we call that bullshit. Just so you know."

"Good-bye, Shana."

"You're leaving already?" Then, as the silence dragged and the full meaning of my words sank in: "Seriously? You came down here . . . all the way down here . . . to, like, break up with me?"

"I loved you, Shana. Honestly, when I first got your letter, all those years ago . . . It was as if I'd spent twenty years locked in that closet, just waiting for you to open the door. My sister. My family."

Shana thinned her lips, drumming her fingertips restlessly on the tabletop.

"I told myself I could handle these monthly conversations. I assured myself I had the training necessary to manage a relationship with a convicted killer. But mostly, I wanted to see you. I wanted one hour a month when I could have a sister. We're the only ones left, you know. Just you and I."

Shana's fingertips, drumming faster.

"But we don't really have a relationship, do we? The bottom line is, you suffer from severe antisocial personality disorder. Meaning I'm not real to you. Nor is Superintendent McKinnon, or any of the corrections officers or your fellow inmates. You will never love me or care about me. Such emotions are as impossible for you as feeling pain is for me. We both have our limitations; it's time for me to accept that. Good-bye, Shana."

I pushed back my chair, rose to standing.

And my sister finally spoke, her tone so low, her words sounded more like a growl than a sentence. "*You are a fucking idiot!*"

I moved toward the interview room door.

"He told me to take care of you! That's what Daddy said that day. Sirens coming down the street. Daddy, stripping off his clothes, climbing into the bathtub, clutching his goddamn aspirin. And smiling. Fucking smiling as he handed over the razor blade.

"I was scared, Adeline. I was a four-year-old kid and Mom's crying and people outside are shouting and Daddy's just smiling, smiling, smiling, except even I knew that wasn't the right kind of smile on his face.

"'Take care of your sister,' he tells me as he climbs into the tub. 'No matter what happens, you're her big sister and it's your job to keep her safe. Take it from me, Shana girl, if you don't have family in this world, then you got nothing.' Then he stuck out his arm, and Mom brought down the razor. . . .

"The shouting men heaved a battering ram against our door. Because they'd knocked and rung the bell and screamed at us to open up, but Dad was too busy dying, and Mom was too busy killing him, and I didn't know what to do, Adeline. I was a scared little kid, and all the grown-ups, the whole world, had gone crazy.

"Then I heard you crying. You, the baby who never cried, who simply watched us all the time with your big dark eyes. You were right, Adeline. You unnerved Mom and Dad. But not me. Never me. I went to you. I opened the closet door and I picked you up and held you close. And you stopped crying. You looked at me. You smiled. Then the door burst open, and shouting men poured into our house. And I whispered to you to close your eyes. Just close your eyes, I told you. I'll keep you safe. 'Cause you're my baby sister, and if you don't got family, then you got nothing at all.

"I didn't mean to hurt you that day in foster care. I did what I was taught and they took you away from me and I was alone. You have no idea, Adeline, just how alone. But I didn't forget you. I remembered what I'd promised Daddy, and I found you so I could watch over you and keep you safe. I'm the big sister and I won't ever let anyone hurt you. I promised, and regardless of what you think of me, I've always been a person of my word."

My sister's voice trailed off. I'd stopped moving toward the waiting door. I stared at Shana instead. Her face held the strangest expression I'd ever seen. Not just earnestness but sincerity.

"You're in league with a killer," I whispered.

"How? I can't communicate with the outside world. Someone inside here would have to like me enough to help. No one likes me, Adeline. We both know that."

"You know things. My fuchsia sweater."

"I see things. That's what thirty years of solitude does to you. That day, you had a fuchsia-colored thread stuck to your top. It stood out against that stupid gray shirt. It made sense that you had been wearing a brighter color but changed so you wouldn't stand out while visiting prison. And that . . . angered me. That this place makes even you depressing."

"One hundred and fifty-three," I said.

My sister sighed, her face falling. "I remember everything," she whispered. "Maybe I shouldn't. Maybe that's my problem. If I could just forget . . . I looked up Daddy when I was old enough. I dreamed of blood. All the time. Things I could see, always clear as day, as well as smell and taste. The things I already fantasized about doing . . . Except they weren't really fantasies. They'd be . . . reenactments. Daddy ruined me, Adeline. And not just with his DNA but with his appetites. I am him. He died in that goddamn tub, just to regrow under my skin. So, yeah, I looked him up. Went to the library, read every article I could find on microfiche. His collection reached one hundred and fifty-three strips of human skin, labeled and preserved in jam-size mason jars. You gotta admit, not bad for a life's work."

"But the Rose Killer—"

"Clearly looks up to Daddy. Meaning he's done his own homework. As long as you are studying a master, wouldn't you pay homage?"

"You're saying you have no personal connection with the Rose Killer. You merely . . . think like him? Or like her."

Shana smiled. "Is that really so hard to imagine?"

"Did you know the killer would strike again last night?"

"I wouldn't have picked last night. But sooner versus later. Once you know what you can do . . . it's harder to fight the cravings."

"Male or female, Shana? If you're such a great expert, which is our killer?"

She shrugged. "I don't know, haven't really thought about it. Most killers are boys, so I default to that. Not every woman, you know, can be as good as me."

I stared at her. "Maybe it's still you. Maybe it's all about you."

But my sister shook her head. "Nah. It's you, Adeline. I'm locked up, tucked away, moldering after all these years. No one even remembers me—"

"Charlie Sgarzi—"

"Arrogant little shit. Always was, even back then. No one cares about me, Adeline. But you . . . The killer knows you. You're the daughter of his idol, all grown up, pretty, successful. Interesting, too, with that whole can't-feel-pain thing. Of course the Rose Killer's looked you up, learned your name. Probably also visited your office and found where you live. I bet he's walked through your bedroom, placing his hand upon the pillow where you sleep. He'd pose as a maintenance person or pest control to get inside, something so ordinary that all these weeks, months later you've still never suspected a thing. But he *knows* you, Adeline. He or she. The Rose Killer has researched you, watched you, obsessed over you. He has to. You're Harry Day's magical daughter who can't feel pain. You're like catnip for serial killers. Of course he can't walk away."

I couldn't help myself; I shivered.

"But I know you, too," my sister continued now, her voice matter-of-fact. "I understand not feeling pain actually works against you. It means you've never been able to take self-defense or engage in any kind of physical training because of course you can't risk hurting yourself. You don't know how to handle a blade, fire a gun, even throw a punch. You're vulnerable, Adeline. I know it; bet the killer knows it, too."

"Stop." I meant the word to sound forceful. It didn't.

"Rose Killer's gonna come for you. You call to him. And your call will only be silenced when you're dead and he's proved his superiority by murdering his idol's daughter. He'll kill you, Adeline. Slowly. Because he or she will have to test out this whole theory of you not feeling pain. My best guess: He'll skin you alive. Because he'll want to see how you react. He'll want to look into your eyes as he flays every inch."

I couldn't face my sister anymore. I glanced sharply away, staring at the floor, because her words spooked me, no doubt just as she intended. She manipulates, I reminded myself. This whole conversation, I had to keep asking myself, what is in it for her?

My sister continued. "I sit in my cell, Adeline. Day after day. I hear things. I read things. And this is what I see. Some Daddy wannabe picking off my baby sister. Boy, girl, who the fuck cares. The Rose Killer is gonna come for you. The Rose Killer is gonna kill you. And then I'll be all alone.

"Course, you don't care about all this right now, do you? You came today to tell me good-bye. To prove to yourself you're stronger and wiser than me. But I didn't leave you, Adeline. All those years ago, I got you out of that closet. I honored my vow to Daddy. I held you close. I kept you safe. And I'd do it again—"

Shana's voice broke.

I glanced up, just in time to catch a spasm of sorrow cross her face. Unexpected emotion? Particularly powerful acting?

"If . . . somehow, someway, I got a twenty-four-hour furlough from this joint, I could get this killer for you, Adeline. I'll agree to any terms, follow any rules you want. What matters is that you let me at him, give me a chance to keep my little sister safe." My sister smiled. A cold baring of her teeth that sent shivers down my spine. "As Daddy said, if you don't got family, then you got nothing at all. You're my family, Adeline. Get me out of here, and I'll kill for you. You know I'll get the job done right."

Chapter 25

D.D. WAS SURPRISED by the midmorning knock on her front door. Her gaze went automatically to Phil and Neil, who sat across from her in the living room. Both had notepads on their laps, not to mention the enormous flipchart, propped up in the center of the space and now covered in black marker.

"Want me to get it?" Phil offered.

"No, I can handle it." She got to her feet slowly, removing the bag of ice from her left shoulder. Alex had left her bright and early to teach his morning classes at the academy. Afterward, he planned on swinging by his parents' and picking up Jack. This was the longest they'd been away from their son, and both missed him terribly.

Now D.D. approached her front door with growing trepidation. She'd made Alex leave behind his Glock 10, fully loaded. She could fire it one-handed. Maybe not with her best aim, but as long as she went for center mass, she ought to be able to hit enough to slow her opponent. Then it was simply a matter of continuing to squeeze the trigger. Her friend and former sniper, Bobby Dodge, might believe in one shot, one kill. D.D. didn't really care, as long as she was the person left standing.

She arrived at the door. No gun in hand, because she had two trained police officers at her back, but still, flexing the fingers of her right hand nervously as she brought her eye to the peephole and carefully peered out.

Dr. Adeline Glen stood on her front porch.

Surprise, surprise, D.D. thought, and went to work on the bolt lock.

"Sorry to bother you," Adeline said without preamble. "But I just came from visiting my sister, and I was hoping to speak with you."

"You talked to your sister without us?"

Adeline's gaze went past D.D. to the family room, where D.D.'s squad mates sat in plain sight. D.D. tried not to flush guiltily.

"We're trained investigators," she said defensively, because for her and her fellow detectives to continue investigating without Adeline was clearly different than Adeline continuing to investigate without them.

"Oh? Your shoulder's better? You've been cleared for duty?"

"Ah hell." D.D. gave up. "Come on in. Yes, we're comparing notes on last night's murder, and no, I'm not on the job, though I swear that's not why Phil and Neil decided to pay me a visit. Has nothing to do with my lack of official capacity. Coffee's simply better here, right, guys?"

Phil and Neil both nodded. Phil rose to standing, shaking Adeline's hand, then introducing her to Neil. D.D. wasn't surprised by the uncertain look on the doctor's face as she regarded their youngest squad mate. With his lanky build and mop of red hair, Neil appeared perpetually sixteen. Came in handy when interviewing suspects, however. They rarely took the veteran detective seriously until it was too late.

Then the doctor's gaze took in the easel-size flipchart, divided into three columns, one for each victim. She didn't pale, as much as her expression set. Clinical. Already distancing herself from the graphic details listed there.

"So." D.D. couldn't help herself. "What's up, Doc?"

"Is that coffee? I would love a cup of coffee."

Phil did the honors of pouring. When D.D. had tried it earlier, she'd missed the mug. Shooting a firearm one-handed, okay. Pouring coffee one-handed, not so great.

"You call your sister, or did she call you?" D.D. asked. She took a seat in one of the kitchen chairs Neil had dragged into the room, then indicated for Adeline to make herself comfortable on the sofa.

"She contacted the warden with her request to speak with me first thing this morning. I assumed it was to wheel and deal. Shana had heard of the latest murder and was willing to offer up additional information in return for a furlough from prison life."

"Not gonna happen," D.D. said. "Didn't you mention that to her yesterday?"

"Can't blame a girl for asking. Anyway, that wasn't . . . exactly how the conversation played out."

"Okay." D.D. sat forward, waiting expectantly. Neil and Phil did the same.

"Shana claims she hasn't been in contact with the Rose Killer or anyone else. No secret network of spies or adoring fans beyond the prison walls. She would need inside support to pull off such a feat, and as she put it, she has no friends. We all know that."

D.D. frowned. Certainly not what she'd been expecting. "Denial, of course, is in her own best interest. How does she explain knowing what she knows?"

"The powers of observation."

"Say what?"

"Thirty years in solitary. She's had nothing better to do than observe her fellow man. She's not a criminal mastermind. She's Sherlock Holmes."

Phil made a disparaging noise in the back of his throat. "How'd she know the magic number?" he asked with clear skepticism.

"As a teenager, she researched our father at the local library. According to her, she determined he'd collected one hundred and fifty-three scraps of skin simply by reading articles in the local papers. No reason the Rose Killer couldn't go through the same effort—I'd tried a basic Google search but only cursory. According to my sister, the information is out there; you just have to be willing to dig for it.

Furthermore, since the Rose Killer is obviously emulating our father, it makes sense he'd include some sort of grand gesture, say, removing precisely one hundred and fifty-three slivers of skin, as an homage to the master. Shana claims she didn't *know* that he was doing such a thing. She merely anticipated it. Possessing, after all, a unique insight into the criminal mind."

"You can say that again," D.D. muttered.

"Thing is, she also went on to say the killer would've looked me up, too. The daughter of Harry Day, who also happens to suffer a unique genetic condition. My very presence calls to him. Meaning he'd be driven to visit my office, even enter my home, possibly under the guise of a deliveryman—"

"What?" D.D. interjected sharply.

"I called my condo building after leaving Shana and asked them if anyone had been inside my unit in the past few months. Mr. Daniels wanted to know if I meant in addition to the worker from the gas company. Apparently, four weeks ago, a uniformed gas company employee showed up, claiming there'd been complaint of a possible leak on my floor. Of course they let the worker inside my condo. Given the risk, Mr. Daniels didn't enter my unit but stayed outside in the hall . . . He claimed the person didn't stay inside my home too long, but then again, couldn't tell me with any specificity how long 'not too long' constituted. I called the gas company right afterward. They have no record of receiving such a call or sending someone to my unit."

"But Mr. Daniels saw the person?" Phil asked immediately. "He can give us a description? Such as we're definitely looking for a male suspect?"

Adeline paused.

"Oh no," Phil murmured, already seeing the answer on her face.

"It turns out," she began.

"Oh no."

"Upon further examination, Mr. Daniels isn't exactly sure who he saw. The gas company worker was wearing a hat, pressed low, while carrying a clipboard held high. In fact, he's not even sure he saw the person's face."

"So gas company worker could be a gal or a guy?" D.D. asked, confused.

Adeline shrugged. "Mr. Daniels had the impression of a male. I tried to press as delicately as I could, without influencing his recollection. Not a large person, so height and build could go either way. But a gruff voice. That's what decided his gender impression. Not the look of the person, but the sound of the fake gas company employee's voice."

"Oh geez," Phil muttered.

Adeline nodded. "Exactly. Gruff voice could be a man. Or it could be a woman disguising her voice."

"You think this person was the Rose Killer," D.D. stated.

Adeline's turn to appear confused. "Don't you?"

"And based upon that," D.D. continued slowly, "your sister predicting such behavior from the Rose Killer, you now believe your sister is using her superpowers for good instead of evil?"

"Such thoughts have crossed my mind. She's my sister. It's in our nature to assume the best about our families. So, yes—"

"Or she set it all up," D.D. interjected. "Your highly manipulative sister, who we have reason to believe might be in cahoots with the Rose Killer. She told the person to enter your unit. Told her puppet exactly what to do. Then went to spring the information when it would be most to Shana's advantage. Say, when you were beginning to doubt her. What better way to bring you around?"

Adeline blinked, then stated quietly, "Or there is that possibility as well. I *want* to be objective when it comes to my sister, but I doubt that I am. Hence, I am here, sharing this information with you. Maybe you can tell me what to believe."

"Posing as a gas company employee fits the Rose Killer's MO," Phil spoke up. "We already know that he or she is using social engineering to access people's homes, including posing as a security company employee to break into D.D.'s house—"

Adeline stared at D.D.

"Killer left me a very thoughtful note," D.D. supplied. "'Get well soon.'"

"Bottom line is," Phil continued, "D.D.'s right: Your sister could know all this *because* she's in contact with the killer. Not despite her lack of communication."

"Have you been able to determine how's she reaching out to the killer?" Adeline asked. "Code, letter, messenger?"

D.D. shook her head. "But your sister's clever; you're the one who keeps saying that. Not to mention, we've been a little busy with yet another murder to process. You know who the victim is?"

"Charlie Sgarzi's mother."

"Who, for the record, doesn't fit the killer's type. First two vics were young side of middle-aged, single women. Janet Sgarzi was an elderly widow, already dying from cancer. Serial killers rarely change victim type. It's all part of the fantasy for them. Change out the victim and you might as well change the whole crime. Which makes this murder the outlier, especially as it happened so quickly after the second homicide. Maybe this attack wasn't in response to some deep-seated compulsion, but a matter of cold, hard calculation. Janet Sgarzi needed to die. And according to Charlie Sgarzi, it's your sister's fault."

"Shana doesn't target women."

"No, but this was a helluva way to target Charlie. Get revenge on a reporter who's asking a lot of nasty questions about your sister, including accusing her of continuing her life of crime while behind prison bars."

Adeline set down her coffee. Sighed heavily. "Prove it," she said simply.

"Well, that's kind of what we're working on right now. Until you interrupted, of course."

"Why did your sister ask to talk to you?" Phil spoke up. "If not to negotiate for her freedom, then what?"

"Oh, she still believes we should furlough her from prison and set her up in my apartment—"

"Aha!" D.D. exclaimed.

"But it's not in return for her helping catch the killer. It's so she can protect me. And, well, kill the killer. In her own words, she's good at getting such jobs done."

Another moment of silence.

"What does that mean?" Neil spoke up nervously.

"I asked the superintendent for more information on my sister's alleged incidents behind bars. My sister has killed three times. The first occurred shortly after her incarceration and involved a female inmate who allegedly attacked Shana first. That death was ruled self-defense. Then life was quiet for nearly a decade, until Shana attacked and killed a male CO, apparently quite . . . savagely. Weeks later, she took out a second officer and officially earned the rest of her life in solitary. Superintendent McKinnon was clearly trying to be circumspect, but when I pressed her on the details of those deaths . . . Both guards were under investigation at the time of their deaths. For 'consorting' with female inmates. Of course, any sexual relationship between a guard and an inmate is considered inappropriate, but for at least the first officer, the allegations were pretty nasty and included two female inmates in Shana's cellblock. There was some question that maybe the guard had entered Shana's cell to target her next when she resisted. Vigorously."

"She shanked the guy who was about to sexually assault her?" D.D. asked.

"It's possible. Shana refused to say. In the end, with the officer dead and the investigation inconclusive, the case disappeared, no doubt because it would also cast a negative light over the prison's officers. Of course, then Shana struck again, just weeks later, which sealed her fate, even though that guard also had a reputation for being 'physically aggressive' with his charges."

"Hang on," Neil interjected. "Your sister is now basically saying the victims made her do it? I mean, age-old defense, right? Blame the victim."

Adeline nodded. She remained clear-eyed, D.D. thought. Still seeking that objectivity, as she'd claimed.

"But what about Donnie Johnson?" Neil spoke up. "Twelve-year-old boy. By all accounts, a geeky bookworm. No way had he posed a threat to her. You look at those old police photos, she's bigger than he is. And definitely tougher."

"I can't explain Donnie Johnson," Adeline admitted. "And Shana won't speak of him. Thirty years later, it's a topic non grata."

"He's the outlier," D.D. murmured. And suddenly, she had her coffee mug down and herself up as she moved to the flipchart. "For the sake of argument, let's compare: the Rose Killer and his three victims with Shana Day and her four. Because we already know the Rose Killer has one outlier: Janet Sgarzi. While Shana has one outlier, Donnie Johnson. Which wouldn't normally be such a big deal, but what are the odds that the outliers from two different crime sprees would belong to the same family? A nephew and an aunt. You can't tell me they aren't connected."

"To Charlie Sgarzi," Adeline said with a frown, clearly not getting it.

D.D. beamed triumphantly. "Who is doing what?"

"Asking questions about his cousin's thirty-year-old murder," Phil supplied.

"Which means?" D.D. prompted.

"I'm going to be pulling more ancient files from the archives," Neil intoned. He was still working on the Harry Day files. Latest report was they might have been lost in the move from the old HQ to the new digs. Such was the fate of much precomputer-age casework.

"Ding, ding, ding, give the detective a prize. That's our connection. The murders may be happening now, but whatever set them in motion occurred thirty years ago. Donnie Johnson, Shana Day, and

I'll bet you anything, the Rose Killer, all crossed paths back in the day. We need the names of neighbors, witnesses, known associates. Work that list and we will find ourselves a killer."

"Or," Adeline said, rising to standing, "we can simply wait, and the killer will find us soon enough. According to Shana, he or she won't be able to help it. My existence calls to murderers everywhere."

"Are you concerned for your safety?" D.D. spoke up. "We can assign you an officer."

"Can you shoot a gun one-handed?"

"Yeah. Part of our basic firearms training, and these days, color me grateful."

"I can't. Rare genetic immunity to pain, remember? Means engaging in dangerous activities, even for training, could lead to harmful results. I can't fight, shoot or run. You could assign me an officer. But as strange as it sounds, I'd prefer my sister. Police only practice going on the offense. Whereas, Shana has it down to a science."

D.D. rolled her eyes. "You seriously want us to furlough your sister? You understand, of course, that she's probably going to do more than borrow your favorite clothes?"

Adeline moved toward the doorway. "Just because my sister's offer is highly aggressive and extremely violent doesn't mean it's not worth considering. You have to admit, it's the last thing the Rose Killer would see coming."

"Unless, of course," Phil offered up quietly, "it's exactly what the murderer's been working toward all along."

Chapter 26

Who am I? Excited new tenant, friendly new neighbor.

What do I look like? Nice, educated, professional. I might ask to borrow a cup of sugar, but I would never contemplate the texture of your skin and how it might look floating in a mason jar.

Primary motivation: Just so happy to meet you.

Purpose of operation: Up the ante, heighten tensions, twist the screws.

Net gain: All good things must end.

Happy New Neighbor was struggling. The clothes were right. Recently purchased from Goodwill, which in a city like Boston carried as many designer labels as Saks. Tailored, professional, but subdued. A disguise, like the others, designed to form an impression of a person, while leaving the actual details hazy. *How did the person look? Nice. What do you mean nice? I don't know. Nice.*

The clothes were right. Next up came posture and gait. More time spent practicing in front of the mirror. Not slouchy, but comfortable and confident. Shoulders rolled back, limbs loose. It was harder to do than it looked. It meant controlling the adrenaline rush, not leaning too far forward, not giving in to the constant hum of now, now, now, I gotta do, do, do.

But once again, practice made perfect.

Clothes were right. Body language acceptable.

Yet still. Standing in front of the full-length mirror, running through it again and again, Happy New Neighbor wasn't . . . happy.

Killing her had been hard.

That had been the risk, of course, from the very beginning. The first two subjects had been easy, selected at random from local coffee shops. That recon work had been conducted as Everyday Average Person, the role that had been practiced the longest and was the easiest to pull off. Everyday Average Person had actively sought out two pretty single women. The victims had to be arbitrary; that would be the key. With no connection to each other or Everyday Average Person. It had actually taken more than a dozen tries. Women selected, then carefully followed, only to discover they lived with a husband or roommates or two-point-two kids. It took time and effort, as the research had suggested.

Murder was not for the faint of heart.

But eventually, the hard work had paid off. Two victims selected, fully vetted, then officially targeted. The first phase of operations had launched, marking the transition from Everyday Average Person to Accomplished Killer. Even earned a nickname, the Rose Killer, which had yielded a surprising sense of accomplishment.

Who knew that of all the personas tried on and discarded over the years, the one of murderer might actually fit the best?

Who am I? Your worst nightmare.
What do I look like? Just like you.
Primary motivation: Recognition, infamy, success. Fuck Harry
    Day. Fuck Shana Day. I will be the best.

Except, of course, last night's murder hadn't felt like that.
Last night's deed . . .
Just thinking about it was agitating. Happy New Neighbor lost the hard-sought approachable vibe and started pacing restlessly instead.

Last night had been necessary. Logically it was understood. Rationally, the Rose Killer had proceeded according to plan. The quick slip of Rohypnol into her tea. Watching her eyelids grow heavy, her words slur.

When she'd slumped over, the Rose Killer had leapt into action, catching her gracefully, slightly surprised and impressed by the quick reflex. Then lifting her nearly weightless frame . . .

Her eyes had opened. She'd looked at her own killer. No, she'd stared *into* her killer's soul. She'd seen her own death and acknowledged it.

And her gaze had held clear and open pity.

Then the drug had taken hold, conquering the last of her worn-out body's defenses as she'd slumped unconscious. Hard part was over. Now carrying her to the back bedroom. Stripping off clothing, climbing aboard, scalpel in hand. Then . . .

The Rose Killer had faltered. Alone at last with the chosen target, most difficult part of the mission accomplished, the great and terrible killer had just wanted to flee the scene. Run away and never look back. She was dead; wasn't that enough?

Except it wasn't. Maybe the attending physician would assume she'd succumbed to her cancer, but maybe the doc wouldn't. Meaning there'd be tests and tox screens, the finding of Rohypnol immediately muddying the waters.

Best to make everything consistent. Victim number three. An older victim, to be sure. Clearly not the Rose Killer's usual type. But victim number three. Proving once and for all the Rose Killer's terrible legacy, because what kind of monster attacks a cancer-stricken elderly lady? Not even Harry Day had been so merciless.

Once again, murder wasn't for the faint of heart.

Who am I? I don't know. I've never known. How can any person really figure that out?

What do I look like? A shell of normalcy. Because all kids learn quickly that normal is important, meaning if you're *not* normal, you'd better go out of your way to look like it.

Primary motivation: To feel just like everyone else. Which, of course, is the one thing I can never feel.

Purpose of operation: If I can't be like everyone else, I will be better than everyone else. I will hone my powers. I will be you. I will be me. I will be death. I will be salvation. I will be all things. And then I will finally have everything I want.

Net gain: Freedom at last.

Happy New Neighbor turned away from the mirror. Happy New Neighbor had been fretting long enough. No more thinking. Time to do.

Happy New Neighbor moved into the closet, kneeling down, then working carefully to pry up the three loose floorboards. A minute later, the shoe box came into view.

Removing the lid, gazing down at the contents. Knowing what must come next. And feeling the strength that comes with resolution.

Purpose of operation: To see what a pain specialist who couldn't feel pain is really made of.

Net gain: Winner takes all.

Chapter 27

CHRISTI WILLEY WAS EXACTLY WHAT D.D. had pictured. It depressed her a little. There had been a time in her policing career when she'd promised herself the moment her job became a cliché, she'd hang up her hat. And yet here she was, at the Pru Center food court in downtown Boston, meeting with a former inmate and her parole officer, and yeah, Christi Willey was mostly what you'd expect, down to the overgrown bleached-blond hair, slumped shoulders and darting blue eyes.

Christi's PO had called Phil while they were all still brainstorming in D.D.'s home. Per Phil's request to meet with any parolees who'd once served time with Shana Day, the parole officer had a candidate: Christi Willey, released last year after serving twenty years in the MCI for a variety of offenses, including accessory to murder. The former inmate had agreed to answer their questions in return for one request: that Adeline be present.

Not Shana's sister. Nor Dr. Adeline Glen. But Adeline.

The request had piqued D.D.'s curiosity. Fortunately, it had piqued Adeline's as well. So here they were, Phil, D.D. and Adeline, sitting at two hastily combined cafeteria tables with PO Candace Proctor and her charge, Christi Willey, in the middle of a space that smelled overwhelmingly of fried food. In particular, spicy orange shrimp. It was making D.D. hungry.

So far, Adeline was playing it smart; she had yet to say a word, letting Phil and D.D. do all the talking.

Yes, Christi Willey had once shared a cellblock with Shana Day. They'd also spent some time together in solitary, after, you know, the incident.

Christi Willey's rap sheet included half a dozen drug-related charges, including armed robbery to help fund her habit, assault to protect her habit, and accessory to her boyfriend killing a rival to further enable their habit. . . . Given the woman's jittery movements and ping-ponging gaze, D.D. wasn't convinced Christi had given up the lifestyle just yet, prison being one of the easiest places to score drugs. On the other hand, Christi was meeting with them of her own accord, with her parole officer present, and given the mandatory drug testing that was no doubt part of the terms of her parole . . .

Who knows? Maybe the woman was clean. Maybe this was simply your brain even after several years of no longer being on drugs.

It was possible.

"Yes, I knew Shana Day," the twitchy informant was saying now. She wore a tank top, very much not in season, which showcased rail-thin arms. Candace, the PO, had brought over a large basket of fries, maybe to tempt her charge. Christi had yet to touch them.

D.D., despite her deep and abiding love for food courts, had restricted herself to a bottle of water. Phil as well. Adeline had splurged on a fruit smoothie. Something about having never eaten breakfast. So far, Christi wasn't paying much attention to the doctor, for which D.D. was grateful. Technically speaking, Adeline shouldn't even be present. Then again, neither should D.D.

"They had this game," Christi was saying now, her gaze fixed on the table. "It was called the Hooker Olympics. Frankie, Rich and Howard would play it anytime they all worked together. They'd pick three girls, line us up in front of them, then unzip their flies. Whichever one of us got the guy off first won a prize. Maybe a bottle of lotion. Or a couple of extra minutes in the shower. Stupid shit like that."

The PO reached over and patted her charge's hand. D.D. had

never worked with Candace before, but she seemed to genuinely care about her clients.

"So three COs were involved in this?" Phil asked.

"In the beginning," Christi mumbled. She still wasn't looking at them. "But they didn't all work together very often, and Frankie, you know . . . he had appetites. So sometimes, he'd act on his own. Just appear in your cell. Suck and tuck, he'd call it. He'd whip it out. You'd suck. Then when it was over, he'd tuck it away and return to duty. Like nothing had happened. Like . . . you were nothing."

"How many inmates did he target?" Phil asked.

"I don't know. Three or four of us."

"Did you file a complaint?"

The woman looked up, her expression still bleary after all these years. "How? Who? I mean, these were our guards. Who the hell were we supposed to complain to?"

Phil didn't say anything. Mostly because there wasn't an answer to that sort of question.

"What happened?" he asked next.

"Howard wasn't so bad," Christi answered. "He even said thank you on occasion, smuggled in some gifts, chocolate. I don't think he had a girl. He seemed . . . lonely. But Frankie and Rich . . . The more they got, the more they wanted. There were cameras, so they'd take turns covering for each other. One would, like, flip this switch or something. I don't know. I guess it caused the cameras to blink. Then, while the cameras were resetting, the other would enter your cell. Once inside, the cameras couldn't see him, so it didn't matter. He could stay as long as he wanted, do whatever he wanted . . . Then, when he'd had enough, he'd give a signal, and the other guy would hit the switch, and alakazam, the guard was back in the halls, on duty. They thought they were pretty damn clever. Bragged about it all the time."

"How long did this go on?" Phil asked.

"I dunno. Months. Years. Fucking eternity."

"And they also assaulted Shana Day?" D.D. spoke up.

Christi looked at her funny. "What would they want with Shana? I mean, she'd hacked the ear off a little boy. Who the hell wants to fuck that?"

D.D. took that to be a no.

"She kept to herself, nasty piece of work. That's what made it all so strange, what happened next."

D.D., Phil and Adeline leaned forward.

"It was Frankie's night off. God help us, we were relaxing. Bastard was gone, we could finally breathe. Then there he was. In street clothes. Blabbering something about he'd figured it out. He wasn't even working, meaning he could stay all night. Then he looked at each one of us, smirking, while he waited for us to fully understand. Richie had the desk. Meaning all Richie had to do was flick the camera switch once, then Frankie would be safely in place, and yeah, we could serve as his sex slaves. All night long. Lucky us.

"He chose me," Christi said, flat blue gaze fixed on the fry basket. "He chose me."

None of them spoke.

"I screamed at one point. Not that it mattered. I mean, it's just a unit full of convicted offenders and a lone corrections officer who didn't give a flying fuck. At one point, I heard the other girls making a fuss. Whacking shoes, books, toothbrushes against the bars. Prison protest. But the cameras can't do justice to that. So Frankie stayed. He did everything he wanted to do. Again and again and again. Must've taken Viagra ahead of time, the goddamn son of a . . . Not a thing I could do about it. When he was done, he put on his clothes, zipped up his pants and handed me a travel-size bottle of shampoo. You know, like from the Holiday Inn. He fucked my . . . And that's what I got. Cheap motel shampoo.

"I didn't get up the next day. Couldn't even walk. But Richie had already left a note that I'd 'worn myself out' causing a ruckus the night before. Day officer didn't even bother to check in on me.

They're all in cahoots, you know. We're the inmates, but they're the monsters."

D.D. didn't have anything to say to that.

"Frankie was on the next night. Left me alone. Went after one of the new girls instead. She cried. Poor stupid thing. Cried and screamed and cried some more. I didn't care. That's what it's like. If he's not fucking me, then I'm down with it. I get a night off, hallelujah, praise the Lord. But we're not animals, you know."

The woman looked up sharply, her hands skittering across the table. "It's just, you get treated like one long enough . . .

"Frankie had Friday night off. We all knew it. Waited on pins and needles. The whole unit. Because we knew he was coming. He was our devil, our curse, and sure enough, ten P.M., he sauntered onto the floor. Blue jeans, a Red Sox sweatshirt. And I fucking liked the Red Sox! Then he looked straight at me and grinned. Like it was something special to be his date. Like the fucking new girl wasn't still bleeding from both ends after what he'd done to her.

"He came over. What the hell was I gonna do? What was, was. Then . . ."

Christi paused, stared at them. "Shana spoke to him. Clear as day. Stood at her cell door and asked him how the divorce was going. What was it like to know some other guy was fucking his wife, raising his kids. And oh yeah, didn't it just figure his own dog didn't even like him anymore. I mean, talk about a loser. Look up the word in the dictionary and Frankie's picture would be *right there*. . . ." Christi shivered slightly, shaking her head. "Shana kept talking and talking. And she *knew* things. All these things about Frankie's personal life. I mean, how the hell? At first, Frankie tried to ignore her; then he told her to shut up, she didn't know jack shit. But she just kept going and going, and next thing you knew, Frankie was standing in front of her cell, shouting that she was a stupid fucking cunt, and she'd better shut her mouth before he shut it for her. But she didn't. She smiled, man. She smiled right at him, fucking freakiest damn smile I ever saw.

" 'Make me,' she said. Just like that.

"I thought that was it. She'd signed her own death warrant. Frankie wasn't just going to beat the shit out of her; he was gonna kill her. For talking to him like that. For *looking* at him like that, like he wasn't nothing but a poor pathetic loser, probably couldn't even keep his dick up.

"Frankie gestured for Richie to open the cell door. Which he did. Then Frankie exploded into Shana's room, all jacked up and ready to kill. I could see the whites of his eyes as he went for her. But she stood her ground. Then she smiled again. He faltered. You could almost see some very tiny part of his brain try to sound the alarm. Except it was too late. Frankie charged, and Shana shanked him right in the stomach. I still hear it, sometimes, in the middle of the night. This heavy wet sound. Followed by a sucking noise when she pulled the blade back out. It was a short blade. Maybe a sharpened comb? I'm not sure I ever found out. She must've stabbed him dozens of times, the happiest I've ever seen a person, while Frankie gurgled, then fell to the floor, and she kept going after him. Squish, squish, squish.

"Richie finally got off his fat ass and sounded the alarm. The response team arrived, all geared up for business. But Shana wouldn't retreat. She stood over Frankie's body and bared her teeth at them." Christi turned unexpectedly toward Adeline. "You gotta understand. The whole place is going nuts. Sirens are going off. Women are freaking out. The corridor is filled with pumped-up guards wielding mattress shields and heavy batons. They're screaming at Shana to stand down, drop her weapon, fucking face plant. But Shana won't give it up. She was like some lioness, I don't know, protecting her kill. Then, while they're all yelling at her, she licked the blood dripping down her wrist. I thought two of the guards were gonna pass out cold.

"They took her down hard. And she fought them. To the bitter end, she was slashing and kicking and punching. I thought they might kill her. I almost yelled at them to stop. But I couldn't. Even after what she'd done for me . . . I couldn't.

"When they finally dragged her from the cell, she was barely recognizable. Nose smashed, eyes already swelling shut. But she turned toward me. As they carted her down the hall, she gazed straight at me and said, 'I'm sorry, Adeline.' That's what she said. 'I'm sorry, Adeline.'

"Two weeks later, she was out of medical. They moved her to solitary, where ironically enough, I gotta live across the hall from her again. Apparently, when I'd reported that Frankie had raped and sodomized me, the powers that be took that to mean I'd been consorting with a guard, so I needed reprimanding. I got sent to solitary, where Richie had also arranged to work. Mostly to keep his eye on Shana, of course. The things she knew about him . . .

"'Gotta sleep sometime,' he'd whisper through the slot in the door. And she'd just laugh and say, '*Back at you, fucker.*'

"I don't know how she did it. But one night, I woke up to the sound of whispering. A low, urgent mutter, almost like a chant. Shana was murmuring softly to Richie, something like, really important, over and over again. He didn't talk back, but he also didn't walk away. He kind of just stood there, right outside her cell, shaking his head, no, no, no. . . . Then she stopped. The place fell silent, and let me tell you, prison ain't *ever* silent. It's like everyone was listening. More we couldn't hear, the more we wanted to know. But Shana didn't speak again.

"Instead, Richie . . . sighed. Like . . . like the world's most exhausted guy, finally setting down his load. Then he unlocked Shana's door. I watched him do it. He opened her cell door and walked straight into her arms. You would've thought they were lovers. When she drove her blade into his heart, he didn't even appear frightened. He was . . . grateful. He sank to the floor and she sat beside him, stroking his hair until central command realized a guard had disappeared from view, and more alarms sounded and once more the response team arrived.

"She didn't fight them this time. She looked over their shoulders straight at me. Then lifted the shank and slit her arm, wrist to elbow. Zip. I might have gasped, but she didn't make a single sound. She'd just switched her knife from her right hand to her left when the guards reached her, took her down before she got the job done. Otherwise . . ."

Christi's voice trailed off. She shrugged, which appeared to conclude her story. No one else spoke. Adeline, D.D noticed, appeared nearly dumbstruck.

"And the third CO?" Phil asked at last. "What was his name, Howard?"

"Never returned to work. Heard he died months later. Ran his truck off the road. I don't know much about it, but I bet you Shana does. Bet you, if he killed himself, it was because she told him to."

"Who else knows this story?" D.D. asked.

The woman shrugged again. "I don't know. I mean, I answered questions at the time. We all did. Bits and pieces. But did they hear? Did they care? You don't know what it's like. Inmates aren't humans. We're animals, baaing and bleating for all they care. Course they swept it under the rug. COs got their funerals, the widows got their pensions. We got new guards. Just another day in paradise."

"And the superintendent?"

"You mean the boss? We never saw the boss. Not until Superintendent Beyoncé at least. She pretends to like us, even visits the units on occasion. But Boss Wallace? No way."

Superintendent McKinnon, aka Beyoncé, had been at the MCI for only the past ten years, meaning Christi's story had happened under her predecessor's reign. Which might explain why McKinnon didn't seem aware of all the grim details.

"You ever speak to Shana?" Phil asked now.

"Never saw her again. I got out of solitary while she was still recovering in medical."

"But the guards," Adeline spoke up, "Richie, Frankie, Howard, never targeted her? You're sure about that."

"Yep."

"So why, then, do you think she chose to get involved?" Adeline asked.

"For Adeline," Christi said. Her gaze focused on the doctor, expression openly curious. "You're Adeline, aren't you?"

Adeline nodded.

"You're her sister?"

Another nod.

"You've never been in prison, though. You look too nice."

A faint smile.

"I had a brother," Christi said abruptly. "Five years younger. When I was a kid and our father had been drinking . . . I tried to make sure my father didn't see Benny. Or if he did, then my father maybe got distracted, noticed me instead."

"Did that work?" Adeline asked.

"For a bit. Then Benny turned twelve, started drinking himself, and it didn't matter anymore. They were both mean-ass drunks."

"I'm sorry."

"I loved my baby brother. The before-twelve Benny. I would've died for him. Coupla times, I nearly did. When Shana looked at me, when she whispered, 'Adeline,' I knew what she meant. She was really saying 'Benny.' She was saving you."

"Maybe."

"Are you worth saving?" Christi asked intently. "Or are you the same ungrateful piece of shit my brother turned out to be?"

"I don't know. Like most sisters, our relationship's . . . complicated."

"I'm glad she killed Frankie. I don't care if that's wrong or not. He was just like my father. Different man, different uniform, same son of a bitch. Shana knew that. She saw him for what he was, and she used it against him."

"How did she know all those things about him?" Phil asked. "His divorce, kids, dog. Was that all true?"

"I don't how she knew, but after Frankie's death, we heard the COs whispering. According to them, his wife had left him two weeks before for another guard. That's why he started spending the night."

"But you never heard the gossip until *after* Frankie's death?" Phil repeated.

Christi shrugged. "Not that I remember. Shana knew things about Richie, too. Like, like his own private thoughts, innermost secrets. I think that's what she was whispering to him that night. She was telling him that everything he feared the most about himself was true. That's why he wanted to die. I mean, once you understand that you're not just a worthless piece of shit, but the whole rest of the world knows it, too? Dying doesn't seem such a bad option. He walked straight into her arms and she was . . . nice about it. Almost tender. Girl's got voodoo. That's what I think."

"You tell all this to Charlie Sgarzi?" D.D. asked.

"The reporter? Yeah, he came sniffing around, coupla months ago. Working on some big 'bestseller' involving Shana." Christi used the term *bestseller* mockingly.

"You answer his questions?"

"He offered me dinner," Christi said, as if that should explain things, "at the Olive Garden. Hey, a girl's gotta eat."

"He ask you about his cousin's murder, Donnie Johnson?"

"Yeah, but I couldn't answer those questions. Shana never spoke about it. Never even heard her say his name."

"But you knew what she'd done, right? Her case was a big deal back in the day. Surely other girls must've asked her about it," Phil pressed.

Christi looked at him in surprise. Then she laughed. "You've never even met her, have you?"

"I have."

"Yeah? And how many questions did you survive? You can't just . . . talk . . . to someone like Shana. She's serious fucked-up shit. Not the cute kind of cuckoo, or the lights-on-but-nobody's-home loony. She's really, genuinely, sold-my-soul-to-the-devil crazy. She don't care about me or anyone else in the place. I mean, sure, she killed Frankie. And *maybe* she wanted to save the rest of us or whatever. But *mostly,* she just plain wanted to kill him. I mean, she stabbed him like a zillion times. Then licked his blood. I don't remember Wonder Woman ever doing that at the end of an episode."

"But then she called you Adeline," D.D. pointed out, because she found that curious. That Frankie's assault of Christi had seemed to trigger something inside Shana. She'd slaughtered him; whereas, the death of the second guard, Rich, had been much more subdued, almost gentle, as Christi said.

"She's Adeline; ask her." Christi gestured to the doctor.

D.D. turned to Adeline.

"Basic projection," Adeline supplied, her voice sounding rough, not quite her usual composed self. The doctor cleared her throat. "Shana spent four years in an abusive household before moving to a series of foster homes that probably offered little in the way of personal security. For such people, a younger sibling often comes to represents the person's own inner child. In trying to rescue a younger sibling, the older child is really trying to go back and save herself. Shana fixated on guarding me as a proxy for protecting herself. Likewise, in prison, looking out for younger, less experienced inmates would be one way of trying to preserve some sense of self."

"Yeah?" Christi asked. "And where does the blood licking come in?"

"Genetics," Adeline said, and there was a grim smile around her lips.

"What did Sgarzi tell you about his book?" Phil asked.

"Not much. Shana killed his cousin. He was writing about it and he wanted to interview her and people like me in order to get the inside scoop."

"What did he think of this story involving the corrupt COs?"

"Honestly? He seemed a little shocked. I mean, if the guy's gonna write a true-crime book, don't you think he's got to get a better stomach for gore?"

"Was it news to him?" Phil asked.

"Seemed like it."

"He asked you about friends, fans of Shana's?"

"Yeah. But that's a short answer. She doesn't have any."

"You keep in touch with her?" Adeline asked. "After you were paroled?"

"Nah. I hardly ever talked to her when we were both still in the joint. Why would I talk to her outside of it?"

"But inmates can communicate inside the prison."

"Sure." Christi squirmed in her seat, looking at her parole officer self-consciously.

The officer got the hint. "How about I fetch us a couple of bottles of water?" Candace suggested brightly.

"Sure."

The moment the PO was out of earshot, Christi leaned forward. "People pass notes all the time. Between cells, between floors. Inmate to inmate, guard to inmate. Sometimes, just to have something to do. Other times, in return for favors, you know. Chocolate, sex, drugs. Depends on the message, depends on the messenger."

"But not Shana?"

"Guards don't trust her. She killed two of them. And even if you weren't a fan of Frankie or Richie, the *way* she did it . . ." Christi shivered slightly. "MCI's own girly Hannibal Lecter," she muttered. "You know she once cut her own finger and stirred the blood into her applesauce?"

D.D. and Phil shook their heads; Adeline didn't.

"Now, maybe if she were into drugs," Christi continued briskly, "then she'd have currency for bribing guards or paying for friends. Or if she weren't so fucking scary, she could offer a quick BJ, something. But Shana is . . . Shana. Guards fear her. Inmates stay clear of her. Like hell anyone's gonna pass notes on her behalf; they don't even offer up a *Hi, hey, how you doin'*. That's the truth of it, plain and simple."

D.D. nodded. Sitting across from her, she could see Adeline's strained expression. She wondered how much the doctor had ever fully contemplated her sister's life behind bars. It was one thing to know your sister suffered from antisocial personality disorder. It was another thing to know your sister *suffered* due to her antisocial personality disorder.

"You think Shana's smart?" Phil asked now. D.D. regarded him curiously, unsure where he was going with this.

"Sure."

"Think she could catch a killer?"

"If she wanted to." Christi shrugged. "But you probably wouldn't get him back in one piece."

"And she never spoke of Donnie Johnson?"

"Nope."

"What about at night?" Adeline spoke up. "Did she suffer from nightmares, ever talk in her sleep?"

"Oh, I'm sure she had nightmares. We all do."

"But did she say anything?"

"Only ever heard her whisper one name."

"Which was?"

Christi regarded the doctor, her gaunt face intent. "Adeline. In the middle of the night, whatever your sister dreamed about, it always involved you."

Chapter 28

Y OU DON'T NEED TO FEEL SORRY FOR HER," I said briskly. We'd departed the food court, leaving behind the queasy scent of deep-fried foods as we headed down the escalator and out of the Prudential Center. "My sister isn't like you and me. She doesn't bond, feel empathy or receive comfort from other human beings the way you and I would. Just because she's alone doesn't mean she's lonely. Technically speaking, she would feel the same standing in a crowded room, or even in the arms of a man who claimed he loved her. It's part of her personality disorder."

"Meaning solitary confinement is hardly punishment for someone like her?" D.D. asked.

"Yes and no. It's not the company of people she misses; it's the stimulation. Shana may not feel lonely in her cell, but she does grow bored."

"Not bored enough to change her ways," Phil stated.

"The kind of change required is too deep-rooted. Bonding disorders are very challenging. Best odds of success are when the subject is younger than five. Given that Shana has spent her entire adolescence and now adult life behind bars . . ."

"She really stirred blood into her applesauce?" D.D. asked.

"Shock value," I informed her. "Superintendent McKinnon had assigned Shana a new caseworker, which, given Shana's limited social life, was basically the equivalent of handing her fresh meat.

Shana told the man she was a servant of the devil, and mixing blood into applesauce revealed patterns that helped her foretell the future. For example, the caseworker would be dead by the end of the month. Then, when he had a heart attack just three weeks later . . ."

"No way!" D.D. stopped walking.

"Not a heart attack," I assured her. "But a panic attack. Most likely brought on by spending three hours a week in the company of my sister. Needless to say, the caseworker retired. And my sister went back to plotting new ways to entertain herself."

"Like contacting a killer?" Phil asked.

I didn't know what to say anymore. I felt suddenly exhausted, worn-out. The things I understood professionally about my sister, versus the things I wanted to feel about her personally.

Such as, just because I couldn't feel pain didn't mean my family couldn't hurt me.

She dreamed of me, whispered my name. My big sister. We'd spent only a few years together, one with our parents, two in various foster homes. And yet our lives seemed forever intertwined.

"Have you ever played the bar game?" I asked now.

Both detectives had stopped walking. We were outside the Prudential Center, standing in the middle of a bustling sidewalk, streams of humanity splitting around us. Midday in downtown Boston. Commuters, tourists, residents, all going about their very important business. While we discussed murder, with the late fall air sharp against our cheeks and the sun already contemplating its decline.

"The bar game," I repeated. "We did it all the time as psych students. Go to a bar, gaze around the tables and deduce the life story of each of your fellow barflies. As soon-to-be-doctors, we prided ourselves on interpreting body language. You're detectives; I imagine you'd be equally good."

D.D. and Phil were frowning at me. "Okay. We like bar games, too," D.D. said at last. "What of it?"

"Bet you could always pick out the fresh divorcé."

"Sure."

"And so can my sister."

They paused as I watched the implication of this sink in.

"You think," Phil said, "Shana guessed that Frankie was going through a divorce, simply by studying him."

"It's not so hard. He used to bring a bag lunch—packed by his wife—now does not. He used to wear a freshly cleaned uniform—laundered by his wife—now does not. Not to mention a change in pattern, such as staying all night at the prison during his time off. Someone as misogynistic as Frankie was reputed to be no doubt was married to a stay-at-home, see-to-all-of-my-needs wife. A woman who cleaned, cooked and otherwise tended him. Meaning when she escaped, the impact on Frankie's world would be readily visible. In a crowded bar, I'd be able to read him, and so would you. Why not my sister, who had nothing better to do, day after day after day?"

They considered the matter. "But sounds like she knew more than the recent split," D.D. said.

"Perhaps she gleaned choice tidbits from the prison rumor mill. Others dropped hints; she picked them up. Not to mention, it's all about the delivery. Not knowing what you know, but *sounding* as if you know what you know. Christi called it voodoo. More likely, my sister is simply very adept at basic parlor tricks. She listens, she analyzes and then she strikes."

"She listened and analyzed the second guard, Richie, into letting her kill him?" Phil asked dubiously, still looking troubled.

"I think she pegged him as having a conscience. After that, the rest wouldn't be so hard."

"Meaning you could do it," D.D. said, her tone challenging.

"Except I have a conscience," I reminded her. Reminded myself.

"You think Christi might be telling the truth," Phil said. "Your sister outmaneuvered both those guards, maybe even got the third, Howard, to kill himself in a car accident, except it wasn't because she had access to outside information. She simply manipulated them."

"I think we shouldn't imbue my sister with too many superpowers. She has enough superior attributes as it is."

"Which leaves us with what?" D.D. asked.

I took a deep breath. "She didn't do it."

"Which it?" D.D., again, already disbelieving. "Kill Donnie Johnson, murder an inmate, shank two guards, manipulate the Rose Killer or all of the above?"

"She didn't murder Donnie Johnson," I said, and the moment the words were out of my mouth, I knew them to be true. "Basic projection, right? The three murders in the MCI, the crimes we know the most about, all had motive: to protect. That's Shana's trigger. Someone stronger attacking someone weaker. In which case, she identifies with the weaker victim and is driven to intervene. Save this kid today, save the child she used to be. Even the attack on herself, the inmate she killed in self-defense, fits that pattern. It was in the early days of Shana's incarceration, and that inmate was larger and more experienced. Again, someone strong assaulting someone weak."

"Except Donnie Johnson wasn't someone strong," Phil said.

"No. In fact, Donnie Johnson represents the kind of person she'd be driven to protect."

"So what happened?" D.D. asked.

I shook my head. "I don't know. Shana claimed self-defense, alleging that Donnie had tried to rape her. Frankly, it's never made sense, then or now. Not given the size difference between her and Donnie, and certainly not given their character references. He was cast as a kindhearted, socially awkward science geek, while Shana became the hardhearted street kid who manipulated him into meeting her just so she could slaughter him. The first thrill kill, so to speak. Given the heinous nature of the crime, the jury took less than a day to sentence a teenage girl to life in prison. It was that kind of case. Shana was that kind of defendant."

"You're talking thirty years ago," Phil said cautiously. "Your sister was a kid. Impulsive, hormonal, reckless . . . Maybe the reason that murder is different is because your sister was different."

"Triggers are triggers," I said simply. "We only wish we could change them so easily."

"Then why didn't she protest it more?" D.D. asked.

"Because she's Shana. Because she really does suffer from antisocial personality disorder, meaning she doesn't relate to people well, whether they're her lawyer, a judge or a jury of her peers. It's possible she already suffered from depression back then as well. I don't know. I didn't meet her for another ten years, so I don't know the fourteen-year-old Shana. But if that's the case . . . she would've expected the worst. Then when it happened, what's the point in fighting it?"

Phil nodded. He appeared troubled. Locking away my forty-four-year-old psychotic sister didn't bother him. Contemplating who she'd once been, the young girl with a troubled past. That was harder. As it should be.

"What about her lawyer?" D.D. asked. "He must've put up a fight, a fourteen-year-old client."

"The best no money could buy," I assured her.

D.D. rolled her eyes.

"Now, Charlie Sgarzi claims he found love letters from Shana to his cousin, but I don't believe that, either. Shana abhors submissive types. No way she'd be attracted to a smaller, younger, weaker boy."

"He has letters?"

"Found them after his uncle's suicide."

"Think he made them up? Maybe to sell a novel?"

I shrugged. "Or there really are notes, but he misunderstood them. The letters are really a form of coded communication or not intended for Donnie at all. He was the delivery boy, or . . ." I paused thoughtfully. "Donnie was smart, a bookworm, right? Maybe he was helping Shana write them. Shana wasn't exactly a model student. To this day, her handwriting, spelling . . . Let's just say, a handwritten note from her doesn't do her natural intelligence justice."

D.D. was still frowning.

"You think she planned this?" she spoke up suddenly. "I mean, all of this." She made a churning motion with her hand. "You heard Christi. Shana's basically rotting away in the MCI with no hope of ever seeing daylight. She's clever, she's bored, she's got plenty of time on her hands. Why not concoct an elaborate series of murders, then position herself to emerge as the hero. It's been more than a decade since she got to save the day by stabbing Frankie what's-his-name a hundred times. Now she can take on the Rose Killer. Like you said, fresh meat."

I shook my head. "I think you were right this morning: There is a connection between the Rose Killer and my sister. But it's not Harry Day; it's Donnie Johnson. It's what really happened thirty years ago. It's whatever secret the Rose Killer doesn't want Charlie Sgarzi to dig up."

"So we return to Charlie Sgarzi," D.D. stated, looking at Phil.

"No," I corrected her, earning a hard glance. "He hasn't learned the secret yet; that's the whole point. We need to find the person who has. And I might be able to help with that. Shana's foster mother from back in the day. They lived by the Johnsons. Chances are, she remembers a thing or two about the kid. And I happen to have her name and phone number."

BRENDA DAVIES STILL REMEMBERED ME. We'd met only once, nearly six years ago, when I'd first started taking over my sister's mental health care and had interviewed Brenda as part of basic fact-finding into my patient's history. At that time, our conversation had been focused solely on Shana. She didn't appear surprised by my call, or that I had fresh questions regarding the murder of Donnie Johnson. According to Brenda, her busy social calendar was currently clear if we wanted to come right over.

We headed into South Boston, Phil doing the driving. Along the way, I had him stop at one of the local Italian delis for fresh pastries. It seemed the hospitable thing to do, given we were intruding on a now elderly woman's life to talk about a time she most likely had spent the past thirty years trying to forget.

Now Brenda opened the door of her run-down triple-decker, blinking her eyes against natural daylight, though in fact the sun was setting, the day drawing to a close.

"Dr. Adeline Glen," she said immediately.

Mrs. Davies seemed to have shrunk since the last time we'd met. Her rounded frame was hunched, her gray hair sticking out, giving her a bristly look in her floral green housecoat. I introduced her to the detectives. She nodded respectfully but was already wringing her hands.

I handed over the box of pastries. Her faded blue eyes sparked in appreciation; then she led us down the dark hall of her bottom-level unit to the family room that occupied the rear of the narrow triple-decker. She gestured to a faded brown love seat, then busied herself fussing over stacks of papers that crowded the top of the coffee table. She moved the pile to the floor, where it joined many similar piles. Both Phil and D.D. were looking around cautiously.

I remembered Brenda Davies's home as being cluttered six years ago. Now she was venturing into hoarding territory. The loss of her foster children? The void created when her husband died, and she now faced the waning days of her life all alone?

I looked around the overflowing kitchen, the cramped family room, and I already felt sorry for the questions we would be asking this nice woman. She'd been one of the good foster homes. Proud of it, too. That was why they'd sent my sister to her and her husband. Except instead of helping my sister find her happily-ever-after, they'd simply become more debris left behind in Shana's wake, the murder of Donnie Johnson destroying their standing in the neighborhood, not to mention their faith in their work.

It occurred to me that maybe Charlie Sgarzi was onto something.

The full story of that one murder had yet to be explored. All the lives it had impacted. Brenda Davies's. The Johnsons'. Their extended family, the Sgarzis'. My sister's. And now my own.

One terrible act. So many ripples in the aftermath.

"Coffee, tea?" Mrs. Davies asked. She'd been busy in the kitchen, moving around stacks of dirty dishes, empty jugs of water, until she seemed to have found one clean plate. She loaded the collection of cream puffs, cannoli and macaroons onto it, then carefully carried the platter toward the coffee table, feet shuffling.

Phil graciously took the plate from her. He and D.D. declined coffee. Then, given her crestfallen expression, recanted and agreed coffee would be lovely.

Mrs. Davies's face once more brightened, and she returned to the kitchen to resume bustling about a space that probably hadn't seen a mop or sponge in years.

Phil and D.D. sat stiffly on the love seat, D.D. with her left arm tucked protectively against her ribs. I took the ratty recliner at the head of the coffee table. An orange tabby appeared from nowhere and jumped onto my lap. Then two or three more cats started to show their faces. But of course.

D.D. ended up with a black-and-white-spotted cat with bright green eyes, who shoved his nose aggressively against her injured shoulder. She hissed at him, and he leapt down, stalking away with his tail twitching.

"Now, Tom," Mrs. Davies called from the kitchen. "Stop bothering our guests. No sense of manners, that one. I took him off of the streets as a baby, and he has yet to be grateful! Now, here we are."

Mrs. Davies reappeared, one coffee mug of instant coffee at a time. Phil leapt to his feet, most likely to dodge further advances from Tom, and assisted. When we were all situated again, Mrs. Davies sat across from me.

She didn't have a cup of coffee, nor did she touch the pastries. She simply sat, her hands clasped on her lap, with an air of anticipation.

Two of the cats joined her, one on each side, like flanking guards. And I saw it then. The sorrow in her eyes, deep and penetrating, that no amount of cats or clutter would ever ease. She suffered, and she accepted her own suffering. She gazed at us now, knowing these questions would hurt, and resigning herself to her fate.

"Thank you for seeing us on such short notice," I said.

"You said it's about your sister?"

"Some new questions have come up, regarding the death of Donnie Johnson—"

"You mean his murder?"

"Yes. These detectives, they'd like to ask you about that time. About Shana, Donnie, your neighbors. All of it."

Mrs. Davies cocked her head to the side. She frowned, seeming unsure, then relented with a short nod. "Well, it's been a while now, you know. Lucky for you, though, seems with age, my memory prefers the past to the present. Ask me about last week, I don't know that I could help you. But thirty years ago . . ." She sighed. "Thirty years ago, I still remember things I'd rather forget."

"Tell us about Shana Day," D.D. spoke up.

Mrs. Davies shot me a look, as if she wasn't sure how to proceed in my presence.

"It's okay," I assured her. "I have no illusions regarding my sister. You don't need to worry about speaking ill of her in front of me."

"She's soulless," Mrs. Davies stated immediately. No emotion, just matter-of-fact. "Oh, the number of kids Jeremiah and I had taken in by then. Troubled kids, sad kids, angry kids. Boys and girls, all ages. We thought we'd seen it all, could handle anything. We were arrogant. Pride is a sin, and the devil sent Shana to be our undoing."

"Did you have other kids at the time?" Phil asked.

"Three others. An older boy, Samuel, who was seventeen and had stayed with us for three years. Jeremiah had taken him under his wing, had taught him carpentry. It's an issue with the system, you know. The kids turn eighteen, and that's that. The state turns them loose, ready or not. The older boy, Sam, he was nervous about what was to come. But Jeremiah thought he could get him a job with a friend. And we'd told him he could stay with us; he was like our son. Didn't matter what the state had to say. We weren't turning our backs on him."

"Do you still hear from him?" D.D. asked.

"Yes. He lives in Allston now. Comes by when he can. Course, everyone's so busy these days. And carpentry's not the job it used to be. He travels a lot, to find work. I don't see him, maybe, as often as I used to."

I noticed that on her lap, Mrs. Davies was clutching her hands so tightly, the knuckles had gone white. One of the cats, a gray one, nudged her. She obediently stroked its back. On my own lap, the orange tabby was purring away, a strangely soothing backdrop for such a troubling conversation.

"And the other kids?" Phil continued.

Mrs. Davies rattled them off. A little girl, eight, most beautiful mocha skin, who'd been there for only two months, then had bounced back to her crack-addicted mother. Plus a five-year-old boy, Trevor, whose parents had died in a car crash. The state had been working on locating other members of his family who might be willing to take him in. In the meantime, he was set up with the Davieses.

"And then Shana, of course. The state had warned us she was a problem child. She'd already been in six or seven homes in the past two years, which is never a good sign. Problems getting along with other kids, problems with authority. A cutter." Mrs. Davies paused. "You know what that is, right?"

"She used razors to cut her arms and legs," D.D. supplied.

"Well, yes. That was the most about it I knew, too. But Shana, um, cut a little higher on the legs than strictly necessary. More, like"— Mrs. Davies's voice dropped to a whisper—"up there," she said meaningfully. "I thought she was having her girl time and offered her appropriate products. But no, she was bleeding from her own hand.

First time I brought it up, she just stared at me. Not, thank you for offering assistance, no appreciation for someone else trying to look out for her, just . . . nothing. I asked why she hurt herself like that. She shrugged, said why not.

"And that was Shana. There was nothing you could say or do. . . . I'd catch her stealing red-handed, her fingers in my purse. She wouldn't deny it, just shrug and say, I need the money. Sam, the seventeen-year-old. I caught Shana in his bedroom, twice. They were . . . you know. That's not allowed, I told them. Sam, now, he got all embarrassed, couldn't even look me in the eye. But Shana could've cared less. She liked sex, she wanted sex and who was I to tell her otherwise? No shame, no remorse, just me, me, me, me, me.

"Within two weeks we were ready to throw our hands up. You couldn't punish her, you couldn't reward her. Jeremiah had a schedule for the whole household. Nothing too hard to follow, but enough to provide the kids with a sense of order and consistency. Not Shana. She got up when she wanted, left when she felt like it, came home when she pleased. We tried to ground her. She laughed in our faces and walked out the door. We called the cops on her for theft, she spent the night in jail, then sauntered home no worse for the wear. Nothing we said or did had any impact on her.

"We thought if we just gave it a little more time. We were a good home. Clean house, good meals, attentive parents. And Trevor liked her, as strange as it sounds. I always watched them when they were together—don't look at me like that! But she was actually good with him. She'd read him stories or draw pictures with him. He was hurting, this sad little boy who'd lost his whole family in a single afternoon. When Shana was with him, that awful smirk would leave her face, and for a bit, she'd seem nearly human. The girl she could be, we kept thinking, if we just tried harder."

"When did she first meet Donnie Johnson?" Phil asked.

Mrs. Davies shook her head. "I didn't know that she had. Donnie lived in the neighborhood, of course, but so did twenty or so other kids. They all ran around. We never thought much of it, back then. The kids went out to play. When it was time for dinner, you called out the front door, and they came home again."

"Were there some kids in particular she seemed to hang out with more than others?" Phil tried.

"Donnie's older cousin, Charlie. Charlie Sgarzi. He and some of the bigger kids had a bit of a, I don't know, *gang* would be too strong of a word. But they were always hanging out. Black leather jackets, cigarettes, pretending they were tough."

"Charlie was friends with Shana?" My turn to speak up, as this was news.

"Friends?" Mrs. Davies repeated with a frown. "Oh, I don't know that Shana had friends. But for a bit, we saw her hanging with that crowd. I was concerned about it. They were a bunch of aspiring hoodlums, and she had enough problems. I tried to talk to her about it, but she just laughed. *Wannabes* is what she called them. Then later, I heard from one of the other moms it wasn't those kids she was interested in, but one of them had a twenty-four-year-old brother who dealt dope. That's who she was really spending time with. A fourteen-year-old girl, getting involved with a twenty-four-year-old . . ."

Mrs. Davies shook her head. All these years later, she still sounded dismayed.

"How long did Shana live with you?" Phil asked.

Her expression changed, abruptly sobering up. The lines appeared deeper in her face. "Three months," she whispered. "Three months. That's all it took. And then we were done."

"What happened that day, Mrs. Davies?" D.D. spoke up gently.

"I don't know. God's honest truth. Shana got up around eleven, left the house. We fed the other kids a snack around four, when they got home from school, but still no sign of Shana. Then, sometime around five. Yes, five; I was about to put dinner in the oven. I heard screaming. Mrs. Johnson, her house is just a few doors down. She was screaming and screaming. My baby, she kept crying. My baby . . .

"Jeremiah ran out the door. By the time he got there, someone had already called an ambulance. But according to Jeremiah, nothing for the EMTs to do. Just looking at the young boy's mangled body . . . Mrs. Johnson never got over it. That family, that poor, poor family . . ."

Mrs. Davies's voice trailed off. Then she offered quietly, "An hour later, Shana walked in through the back door. She was covered in blood, holding a knife. I gasped. I asked her if she was all right. She just walked over and handed me the blade. Then she turned and went upstairs. When Jeremiah went up, he found her sitting on the edge of the bed, still covered in blood, just sitting there.

"He knew. He told me, looking at her, the expressionless look on her face. He asked her if this had something to do with the Johnson boy. She didn't answer; she reached into her pocket, drew out what looked to be a wad of tissue and handed it to him. Donnie Johnson's ear. She handed my husband the boy's ear. Jeremiah called the cops. What else could we do?

"George Johnson, Donnie's father, arrived first. He'd heard the news over some other cop's radio and ran straight down the street. I didn't think we should let him in. I worried what he might do to the girl. But he held it together when Jeremiah led him upstairs. He asked Shana point-blank if she'd killed his son. But she still wouldn't talk. Just kept staring at us with flat eyes. Finally, the other officers arrived all huffing and puffing. One officer took the ear, bagged it as evidence. Then they read Shana her rights and took her away.

"She never returned to our home. But it didn't matter. The damage was already done. Neighbors didn't want to talk to us after that. We'd taken in a monster, then unleashed it on our friends. Jeremiah never got over it; he seemed to break, losing all interest in the kids, our home, our life. Samuel moved out six months later; I think it was too hard for him to be in a house that had become so . . . shadowed. Pretty little AnaRose was returned to her birth mom, while the state moved Trevor to another home. Didn't tell us why, but we knew.

That hit the hardest, you know. Shana, we never stood a chance. But those two little ones we could've saved. I never had the heart to find out what happened to them. AnaRose, a beautiful little girl returned to the care of a crack addict. God only knows what happened to her next time her mom became desperate for a fix. And Trevor most likely ended up in one of those . . . other homes. You know, where the people take in kids just for the monthly stipend, then pile them in, four to a room, where the biggest three abuse the littlest fourth, and no one cares. I probably should've asked more questions, but I don't think I could've handled the answers. Maybe, after all that happened, I broke a little, too."

Mrs. Davies resumed stroking the cat on her right, settling herself.

"Can you tell us what happened to the Johnsons?" Phil asked.

Mrs. Davies shrugged. Her eyes were red rimmed. "Martha, Donnie's mom, took up drinking. That's what I heard. She wouldn't see me after that, talk to me. I started staying in more, as it seemed to upset the neighbors when I showed my face. But that household . . . Donnie was their pride and joy. Bright young boy, especially gifted in science. His father used to brag that he might be a cop, but Donnie would one day be the director of a crime lab. I heard George shot himself. Parents weren't meant to outlive their children, plain and simple."

"Mrs. Davies," I spoke up, "were you present when they searched Shana's room?"

"Yes."

"Do you remember if they found any letters, any communication between Shana and Donnie? Maybe personal notes, love letters."

Mrs. Davies made a funny face. "Shana and a twelve-year-old boy? I don't think so. Frankly, the twenty-four-year-old dope dealer was much more her style."

"Could she have simply befriended him? Taken him under her wing, like her relationship with Trevor?"

"I don't know. She kept to herself, that one. But . . . maybe. I always thought there was more to Shana than met the eye. Which maybe simply proves I'm naive after all."

"What about the Sgarzis?" D.D. asked. "Sounds like Donnie's murder was hard for them, too."

"Sure, Janet and Martha, the two sisters, had always been close. I heard Janet stayed over for long periods afterward, as Martha took up trying to drown her sorrows. Couldn't have been great for Janet's own marriage or family. Unfortunately, it didn't save Martha either, who drank herself to death sooner versus later."

"Meaning Janet Sgarzi lost her nephew, then her sister, then her brother-in-law," D.D. filled in quietly. "What about Janet's husband, Mr. Sgarzi?"

"I don't know much about the husband," Mrs. Davies said. "Being a fireman, he kept odd hours. But, now, Charlie, their son, he got himself in some trouble in the years that followed. I don't know if it was the shock of his cousin being killed like that, or his mother disappearing to tend her sister, but he got involved in petty theft, vandalism, that kind of thing. His parents finally arranged for him to get away. New York, maybe. Must have worked; last I heard, Janet was bragging about him becoming a reporter, making something out of himself. I think he's back these days, taking care of Janet. Her health isn't good, you know. Cancer. Bad, I'm afraid."

We all nodded, realizing belatedly that Mrs. Davies hadn't heard of Janet Sgarzi's murder. Maybe she didn't know anything about the Rose Killer at all. It seemed kinder to leave things that way.

"Anyone else you can think of who was directly affected by Donnie's murder?" Phil asked.

"Not that comes to mind."

"Friends of Donnie's? The kids from back then who knew him best?"

Mrs. Davies shook her head. "I'm sorry. I didn't know that much about Donnie. He was just one of the kids. You should ask Charlie; he'd remember the younger crowd better than I."

Phil nodded. He asked for the full names of the other children who'd been staying in the home while Shana was there. Samuel Hayes, AnaRose Simmons, Trevor Damon.

We rose to standing, the orange tabby leaping gracefully from my lap.

For all the strain and remembered sorrow of our conversation, I could tell that Mrs. Davies was sad to see us leave. I wondered what it must feel like, still living in the same neighborhood after all these years, and still feeling like a pariah.

I leaned over instinctively and kissed her on her papery-thin cheek.

She squeezed my hand.

Then she escorted us back down the long, narrow hallway to the front entrance. The last I saw was her deeply lined, sorrowful face, right before she closed the door.

Chapter 29

How's your shoulder?"

"Fine," D.D. grumbled, though in fact, her shoulder was killing her and she knew she had to be moving even more stiffly than usual. She should be at home, resting, icing, delivering impassioned soliloquies to Melvin. Instead, she'd pushed it too hard today, and now her shoulder, arm and neck were paying the price.

She didn't care. At least, she didn't want to care; she was a detective on a case. And things were finally getting interesting.

She glanced over at Adeline, who was walking on one side of her, Phil on the other, as they headed back to Phil's car. Parking was a bitch in Southie; they had a ways to go.

"Do you know you're bleeding?" she asked the doctor now.

"What?" Adeline stopped walking.

D.D. regarded the doctor curiously as Adeline took a quick inventory of her body, finally discovering the three gouge marks on her wrist, probably left by the cat as it'd leapt down from her lap.

"Are you allergic to cats?" D.D. asked, because in addition to bleeding, the scratches appeared swollen.

"I don't know. I don't spend time around animals. For just this reason."

"You can't feel that?" Phil spoke up.

The doctor's features remained expressionless. She shook her head.

"I have a first aid kit in my car," he offered.

"Thank you."

"I bet if we clean the marks with an antiseptic wipe, that'll do the trick."

"Thank you," Adeline repeated. They continued walking, the doctor appearing more troubled than before.

"You still think Shana didn't kill Donnie?" Phil asked. "I mean, that whole arriving home covered in blood, then pulling the boy's ear out of her pocket. Sounds pretty convincing to me."

"I think my sister doesn't honestly know what happened that night. Hence, her terrible job defending herself. She may have killed Donnie. She may not have. She doesn't know, which is the other reason she probably never speaks of that night. She doesn't remember it."

"Umm . . .what?" Phil asked.

"The symptoms Mrs. Davies described are consistent with a psychotic break—an episode of acute primary psychosis when reality becomes unbearable and the brain shuts down. Probably Shana had been suffering symptoms for a while, but no one put the pieces together. Most psychotic breaks are triggered by extreme or sudden stress. Say, a battlefield experience, new parenthood or trauma."

"Such as killing a twelve-year-old boy," Phil said.

"Or witnessing his murder."

"Hang on," D.D. interjected. "Why didn't Shana's defense lawyer figure this out? I mean, the way you describe it, a psychotic episode would be the perfect defense. She wasn't in her right mind."

Adeline shrugged. The night had fallen, the air fulfilling its earlier promise of icy chill. The doctor, in only a thin sweater, wrapped her arms around her waist.

"Shana wouldn't be in a position to say what happened. Most people suffering psychotic episodes can't remember them. Given her troubled past, maybe her lawyer felt such a defense wouldn't hold up. Shana already had a history of violence. Why would the jury believe this single incident was different than all the rest?"

"But that means she could've killed Donnie Johnson," Phil said. "And the reason he doesn't fit the profile of her other victims is that she was out of her mind at the time. I mean, how else to explain the bloody knife, the ear in her pocket? That sounds like she did a bit more than stumble upon a murder in the neighborhood."

Adeline didn't answer, but D.D. had the impression the doctor's mind was already made up. She didn't believe her sister had killed the boy. Wishful thinking from someone who really should know better? Or something else she wasn't willing to share with them yet? It bothered D.D. still, Charlie Sgarzi's offhand observation. That if skinning was the signature element for both Harry Day and Shana Day, and if they couldn't be the Rose Killer for obvious reasons, well, there was one family member left.

"You said you and your sister didn't grow up together," D.D. said. "So when did you meet again?"

"About twenty years ago. She wrote me a letter."

"She initiated contact?"

Adeline's voice was dismissive. "Yes."

"Why?"

"I don't know. Because she was bored? Because I'm the only family she has left? You'd have to ask her."

"She wrote to you because she wanted something," D.D. deduced.

Adeline smiled. "Now you sound like my adoptive father."

"But you've hung in there with her. All these years, various suicide attempts later. You're her single longest relationship. Right?"

"True."

"To what end? According to you, your sister doesn't feel empathy, doesn't bond, doesn't even understand a real relationship. So what does she want from you, Adeline? You and she have been talking for two decades, for what?"

"We haven't been talking regularly for that long. It was only six or seven years ago that Superintendent McKinnon started permitting the monthly meetings."

"Still, why? What does Shana want from you? I mean, this is a woman who's destroyed how many families, how many lives? No repentance, no remorse. Biggest emotion she sounds capable of is boredom. So why keep you coming back? Two decades later, what does she *need* from you?"

"She needs to keep me safe, Detective. It's a promise she made to our father forty years ago. And if you don't have family, you don't have anything."

"Seriously? Keep you *safe*? Seriously?"

Adeline kept her gaze fixed down on the sidewalk, her footsteps quickening, as if she could outwalk the skepticism in D.D.'s voice. It occurred to D.D. that when it came to her sister, Adeline suffered a giant blind spot. She didn't think she did. She dished up clinical evaluations, offered frank statements to the likes of Mrs. Davies: *Don't worry about me. I harbor no illusions about my sister.*

But Adeline did. All these years later, some part of her still wanted a big sister.

Making her the perfect victim-in-waiting for Shana Day. Question was, what was Shana waiting for?

"Sounds like Janet Sgarzi was close to her sister, Martha Johnson," Phil spoke up. "Meaning if there was something more to Donnie's murder, some relationship or secret friend his mother knew about but never thought to mention after Shana pulled her son's ear out of her pocket . . ."

"Janet Sgarzi could've known something about the crime," D.D. agreed, "whether she realized she held the key or not. Which leaves the Rose Killer feeling a need to dispose of her after all these years."

"I think we should check out Samuel Hayes," Phil announced as they finally reached his vehicle. "Seventeen-year-old boy at the time of the murder. Clearly had some kind of relationship with Shana given that the foster mom caught the two of them together. Probably has his own past, being a teenager in the system. Definitely old enough and big enough to kill a twelve-year-old. And maybe still thinking about Shana after all these years. His first girl, the one who got away, the one he can never forget. He researches her obsessively, learns everything there is to know about her infamous father, Harry Day. . . . Embarks on his own crime spree. Hell, maybe the rose and champagne aren't for the victims at all. Maybe they're really for Shana. These murders are his love letters to her."

"That's creepy!" D.D. said, but she was shivering, and from more than the night air.

Phil's phone rang. He paused in the process of unlocking the doors to take the call. D.D. and Adeline waited patiently on the curb, as Phil nodded, listened, nodded some more, then exclaimed, "Shit!"

D.D.'s eyes widened. Family man Phil hardly ever swore. That was generally her contribution to their squad.

"Charlie Sgarzi has organized a protest in front of the MCI," Phil announced, ending the call and pocketing his phone. "Apparently, he wrote some blog this afternoon, giving away all the details from his mother's murder—"

"Shit," D.D. moaned.

"Including the removal of skin, the possible homage to Harry Day, a serial killer no one could even recall until about four P.M. this afternoon. Except now, thanks to Sgarzi, all the major news stations are leading with we have a copycat predator, imitating a legendary serial killer as he picks off vulnerable women all over Boston. And, oh yeah, Harry's equally infamous daughter Shana Day seems to have insider's knowledge of the crime, including knowing ahead of time how many strips of skin had been removed from the bodies—"

"How did Charlie know that?" D.D. exploded. "We never told him that."

Phil shrugged. "He's a reporter. I imagine he did some investigating. And you know the ME's office . . ."

"Shit!" D.D. said again. Because lately, the ME's office had been leaking like a sieve. Ben Whitley hadn't pinpointed the leak yet, but he'd better figure it out soon, before the higher-ups had all their heads.

"Well, Charlie's now at the MCI, and apparently he's whipped into quite a frenzy demanding justice for the victims. Are you up for one last field trip?" Phil asked Adeline, as they'd left her car downtown.

"I'll go."

"I fucking hate reporters," D.D. muttered as she climbed gingerly into the car.

"Shit," Adeline agreed.

CHARLIE SGARZI APPEARED TO HAVE ORGANIZED a candlelight vigil. A crowd of maybe 100 or 150 people had gathered outside the main building of the MCI, bearing poster-size photos of the three murder victims, including Charlie's mother, beneath the glare of the prison's perimeter lights.

When Phil pulled in, the crowd was singing "Amazing Grace," while a line of heavily padded corrections officers stood between them and the facility. When Charlie Sgarzi spotted Phil and D.D. getting out of the vehicle, he grabbed the bullhorn and started a chant of "Justice, justice, justice!"

Phil sighed heavily. D.D. didn't blame him. Moments like this, policing wasn't fun. Taking on violent offenders, good. Confronting grieving loved ones . . . not so much so.

She let him take the lead. Finally, her injured shoulder was useful for something.

Adeline brought up the rear. What the doctor thought of this circus, D.D. could only guess.

"Charles," Phil said, greeting the reporter.

"Did you come here to arrest Shana Day?" the reporter demanded. His eyes appeared bloodshot, almost glazed over, as if he'd been drinking.

"Would you like to talk about that?" Phil suggested graciously. He'd always been good at this.

"Damn right!"

"All right, let's take a quick walk. Get on the same page."

"No."

"No?"

"You got something to say, tell it to all of us. Have you met Christine Ryan's parents? Or Regina Barnes's grandparents? Their families, neighbors, friends. We all deserve answers. We all *demand* justice."

"Shit," D.D. muttered. She just couldn't help herself.

Charlie's gaze swung wildly to her. "What'd you just say? What? What?"

"Hey, Charlie," she said, all done with diplomacy. "Hear you got some letters Shana wrote to your cousin. We got a search warrant for them in the car." Small lie, but effective. "Now, hand them over."

Charlie lowered the bullhorn. He regarded her blearily. "Huh?"

"The letters, Charlie. The letters you claim Shana wrote thirty years ago to your cousin. We want them. Now."

He swayed on his feet.

"There aren't any letters, are there, Charlie?"

"This isn't the time—"

"Search warrant."

"But—"

"Search warrant."

He glared at her.

"Let's take that walk, all right, Charlie?" Phil interjected soothingly. "We're here to help. So come on, let's have a chat and figure things out."

Charlie handed over his bullhorn to a bystander.

He fell in step with them, his gaze not totally focused. Up close, D.D. couldn't detect any smell of alcohol. So maybe he wasn't drunk after all. Just completely emotionally devastated.

Phil waited till they were fifty yards from the madness. "Why didn't you tell us about the letters, Charlie?" he asked. "You claim to want justice, but you're the one holding back."

"I need them," Charlie mumbled, not making eye contact. "For my book. Gotta have original material. You know. Exclusive content."

"Are you really writing a book?" D.D. pressed.

"Yeah!"

"But you don't have letters. We know that, Charlie. Because Shana wasn't into your cousin. She was into you." D.D. had been contemplating the theory ever since leaving the foster mom's house. No way a girl with Shana's reputation would be attracted to a geeky twelve-year-old. But Charlie, leader of the local pack, with his fire-fighting father and cop uncle . . .

Charlie stared at them. Then his face melted. His body sagged, and for a moment, she thought he might collapse from the weight of the guilt he'd been carrying on his shoulders.

"I liked her. So help me God, I knew she was trouble. But I was fourteen and stupid and trouble sounded good."

"Were you two dating?"

He grimaced. "These days, I think the proper term would be *fuck buddies*. We got together. You know, when the mood struck."

"Are there letters? Ones she wrote to you."

"No. I lied." He cleared his throat uncomfortably, glanced at Adeline. "I was just trying to get your attention. I mean, seriously. After everything my family's been through, first your sister, then you, blow me off. Is wanting to know the truth about what happened to my cousin really asking too much?"

His voice picked up again, his rage straightening his frame, lending him strength.

"Donnie was your go-between," Adeline said, her gaze boring into Charlie's. "That's the truth, isn't it Charlie? You used your younger cousin to relay messages to Shana. Where and when to meet. That way, you wouldn't be seen with her—the crazy girl—too often."

D.D. thought he might deny it, then Charlie muttered hoarsely: "Yes."

"What happened that night?" D.D. asked, though at this stage, she figured she knew.

"Shana was becoming more . . . freakish. I mean, in the beginning, I'd never met a girl so frank about sex. When she wanted it, she wanted it. No apologies, no pretenses. Hell, she started the whole thing by turning to me one day and asking me if I wanted to fuck. So we did.

"But then I heard about Mrs. Davies, her foster mom, catching her with Samuel, not once, but twice, and that started to creep me out a bit. How many boys in the neighborhood was she screwing? Not like she'd say. So I decided it was time to cool things off. We were supposed to meet that evening. Five o'clock, at the lilac bushes. Maybe hang out, grab a pizza.

"I asked Donnie to meet her instead." Charlie paused. His voice had grown thick. He swallowed, continued. "I asked Donnie to, um, break things off."

"You sent your twelve-year-old cousin to break up with your fuck buddy?" D.D. asked, voice incredulous.

Charlie Sgarzi gazed down at the dark pavement. "Yes."

"And then?"

"She killed him." Charlie looked up. "I was stupid. Sent my cousin to do what I didn't have the courage to do, and she got mad and killed him. Then my aunt drank herself to death, and my uncle swallowed his own gun, and my parents fell apart. 'Cause I was a coward. Spent all my time trying to look so tough, when in the end, I was simply an asshole. And everyone I loved paid the price."

"You didn't see anything that night?" Phil pressed.

"Wasn't even in the neighborhood. Had met up with some buddies of mine and hightailed it over to the mini-mart. Wanted to be far away . . . just in case."

"That's why you're working on the book, isn't it?" Adeline asked quietly. "Because it's finally time to tell the truth."

A muscle twitched in Charlie's jaw. "Probably. I hadn't gotten that far with confronting myself. But yeah, I figure there's a reason I decided to write the book after my mom was diagnosed with terminal cancer; I'd never want to embarrass her while she was still alive. But if I coulda gotten the advance now, to help out with her care. Then finish up the book . . . afterward. I could tell the truth. Just . . . lay it all out there. No one to hurt but me, and who the hell knows, maybe the truth can set a man free.

"I don't sleep so well at night," he finished up softly. "I mean, it's been thirty fucking years, and I still can't fall asleep without having nightmares of Shana prancing around with my cousin's bloody ear. I'm an asshole. I know that, okay? But she's still the monster here."

"Who did she hang out with back then?" Phil asked. "Other than you?"

"Sam, of course. He was into her, too. And not in a good way. He, like, actually thought they were an item. Boyfriend, girlfriend, long-lost souls. At least I was never that crazy."

"Anyone else?"

"One of my friends, Steven, had an older brother, Shep. Rumor was, Shana and Shep would hook up, smoke dope. Shana wasn't one to talk. She more like demanded. I want. I need. When you're a fourteen-year-old boy and the demand in question is sex, you don't think much of it. But in hindsight . . . She was scary. None of us mattered. It was always just about her. Until I said no. At which point, apparently she lost it. Maybe no one had ever told her no before."

"Did you really release the details of your mother's death in your blog?" D.D. asked.

"The public has a right to know." Charlie's voice grew heated. "You're holding things back. Like, the whole social engineering. And Shana Day having some kind of connection to this new killing machine. Three women are dead in seven weeks. And you don't even have a suspect."

"I thought we were supposed to arrest Shana Day," D.D. said innocently.

"Fuck off!" Charlie informed her. "I realize she's already behind bars and there's nothing more you can do to her. But maybe if the killer understands you got the connection, he'll spook, or drop all contact, or go underground or something. . . ."

"None of which helps us catch him."

"Well, it might save some lives!"

"Grieve," Phil ordered the man. "Give yourself a day or two to be Janet Sgarzi's son. While you do that, we'll do our jobs. Then we'll talk again. But giving away our case in the paper—"

"Internet."

"Whatever. Doesn't help us. We're making progress. We're closing in on a suspect."

"Can I quote you?" Charlie perked up.

"Nope, because you're honoring your mother, remember?"

Phil escorted Charlie back to the crowd, which had grown quiet in his absence.

Standing alone with Adeline, D.D. stuck her right hand in her pocket for warmth.

"Still think your sister didn't kill Donnie Johnson?" she asked Adeline.

The doctor didn't say a word.

Chapter 30

RETURNED TO MY CONDO tired and worn-out. What I wanted most was to kick off my shoes, pour a large glass of wine and stare at a blank wall till the whirlwind of fresh revelations and old fears regarding my sister finally quieted in my mind.

What I discovered was my front door, unlocked and slightly ajar.

I froze in the hall, my grip tightening unconsciously on my purse.

I didn't have friends or associates. No neighbor had an emergency key to my place. No, in Charlie Sgarzi's lexicon, fuck buddies had ever met me here.

The Rose Killer.

I stepped back, got out my cell phone and dialed the front desk. Mr. Daniels was on duty.

"Did you let anyone up to my unit?" I inquired. "Maybe a deliveryman, or a long-lost friend."

"Oh, no, no, no," he assured me. "I got the message loud and clear after the gas company man . . . woman . . . person. All requests should be run by you first. It's been a busy day, of course, with guests for other units, a new tenant moving in and a couple of prospective buyers. But no one for you, Dr. Glen. I would've directly contacted you if that'd been the case. You have my word."

I said thank you, then hung up. Multiple guests, prospective buyers requesting tours. Any of them would serve as adequate coverage for the Rose Killer. Requesting my specific condo a second time would've drawn suspicion; whereas, requesting to visit an apartment, say, one floor above mine, just a quick stairwell hike away, would work just as well. Or going on a tour ... *Can I have a moment alone, maybe walk around the building? I'd just like to get a feel for the place.* Then make a quiet sprint for my condo.

I should call Detective D. D. Warren. Take her up on her offer of police protection.

Instead, I pushed the door and let it fall open into the dark, hushed space.

"Honey," I called out, barely a warble in my voice, "I'm home."

I snapped on the main light, illuminating the broad sweep of living space. The front door of my apartment opened into a tiled foyer, kitchen to the left, open door to the master bedroom straight ahead, family room to the right. My low-slung black leather sofa appeared the same as always, not a single accent pillow out of place.

I stepped into my condo, left hand on my purse strap, right hand still clutching my cell phone.

The Rose Killer attacked sleeping women, or a cancer-ravaged elderly woman. No direct confrontation but a game of finesse. Watching and scheming behind the victim's back. Then, the final ambush, armed with chloroform.

Well, I wasn't asleep. I wasn't elderly. And I'd be damned before I let some murderer scare me out of my own home. I'd been born into a family of worse predators, and I knew it.

Snapping on more lights. Moving toward the kitchen with my back to the wall and my gaze on open territory. Nothing appeared amiss. My sleek furniture, modern décor, offering the same upscale comfort as before.

I should get a weapon. Maybe retrieve a baseball bat or a golf club from my hall closet, except being a woman who'd spent her life avoiding athletics, I didn't have either one. I could grab a knife from the kitchen. The proverbial butcher's blade to carry around like the plucky heroine in some horror movie. Only I didn't trust myself with knives. It would be too easy to cut myself and never know it.

Like the three cat scratches I now bore on my wrist, after it had been nice to sit with a cat on my lap for a change. The soothing hum of its purr. The soft feel of its fur. I'd actually enjoyed the moment, even thought maybe I should get a kitten.

Right up till I walked outside and D.D. announced I was bleeding.

A cat, for God's sake. All these years later, I still couldn't even trust the comfort of a goddamn kitty.

And suddenly, I was pissed off. At my gene pool, which had cursed me with a condition that would forever set me apart. Until I spent my days with patients suffering from the one sensation I would give anything to feel. Because there was no Melvin in my life to keep me safe. Meaning I had to say no to everything. Hobbies, walks on the beach. Love. Kids. Kittens.

I lived like a shrink-wrapped toy, forever on a shelf, never taken down to be used and enjoyed, in order to avoid breaking.

I didn't want to be a toy. I wanted to be a person. A real, live person. With cuts and bruises and battle scars and a broken heart. Someone who lived and laughed and hurt and healed.

I might as well wish for the moon. What was, was. What you couldn't change, the intelligent, high-functioning person learned to accept.

I looked around my shadowed apartment, and it occurred to me that for once, my unique condition might be my best self-defense. Ambush relied on stunning your victim with an unexpected attack that delivered disabling amounts of pain. But I didn't feel any pain. The Rose Killer could clock me over the head, punch my stomach, twist an arm. None of it would do my attacker any good. I would just keep coming, no longer my family's conscience, but now its vengeance, as I chased a killer around my own home with my dark, unblinking eyes.

I checked the pantry. The hall closet. The lavette. Finally, my bedroom. A flip of a switch. My king-size bed coming into view, my gaze dashing immediately to the nightstand . . .

Nothing.

No champagne, no roses, nor fur-lined handcuffs. Not even the rumpled shape of another person's body having laid upon the mattress.

I frowned. Not much left to check. The walk-in closet, the sprawling master bath . . .

Nothing.

The Rose Killer had been here. I didn't doubt that. Whether to satiate curiosity or stoke obsession, I had no idea. But the Rose Killer had walked through my condo, maybe rifling my delicates, checking out my favorite foods, before exiting, leaving the front door open just to show off.

I conducted a second sweep of my unit, footsteps steadier, gaze more focused.

After the second pass failed to reveal any monsters lurking under the bed or masked intruders tucked inside a closet, I finally set down my purse, sank down on the edge of my bed and released the breath I hadn't even been aware I'd been holding.

The Rose Killer had come to see me again. Just as my sister had predicted. This monster, somehow tied to my sister and a thirty-year-old murder.

I didn't know what to think anymore. If I'd been capable of it, I imagine I would've had a headache. Instead, I was tired deep down to my core, as if I couldn't think another thought, take another step.

Then it occurred to me that the killer had probably sat on my bed. Maybe even laid his or her head upon my pillow, just to see what it would feel like.

I got up, stripped off the top covers, then my sheets. I carried the first bundle down the hall to the stacked washer and dryer. I went heavy on the detergent and even heavier on the bleach.

Then it was into the master bath, where I finally confronted my-self in the mirror. I looked paler than I had just this morning. Features gaunter, eyes shadowed. I looked more like my sister. Jail life, living in fear, apparently had the same effect on people.

I switched my attention to my wrist, the three gouges I'd treated in Detective Phil's vehicle. The scratches appeared shallow, the skin not too ragged around the edges. The wound remained slightly inflamed; I would need to monitor my temperature to help protect against an infection. Now I unbuttoned my fuchsia cardigan to reveal a thin white shell beneath. Then I removed the shell as well, taking in the pale expanse of my shoulders, arms and stomach. I pivoted, this way and that.

A bruise. I didn't know how, let alone when, but a bruise darkened the back of my left arm. And another abrasion, just above the waistline of my slacks. The cat? Myself carelessly brushing against random sharp objects?

Things I would never know. I just got to log the damage, not necessarily identify the source.

I stepped out of my slacks, letting them puddle to the floor. I found another bruise, this one on the inside of my right thigh. Apparently, playing with two cops wasn't great for one's physical well-being.

My fingers ran slowly through my hair, checking my scalp. Then I felt each joint, testing for swelling, because maybe I'd stepped funny off a curb or twisted my ankle getting into a car. I finished by checking my eyes in a magnified mirror, then taking my temperature. The final few checks were fine. Other than the fact a serial killer was stalking me, I was good to go.

I belted on a long silk robe, then plodded out to the kitchen. Went ahead with that giant glass of wine. Then I stared at my front door and realized I'd never be able to sleep like this. If the Rose Killer had picked the lock once, he or she could do it again. Or maybe it hadn't even been that hard; maybe the killer already had a copy of my key. Why not? The killer already seemed to know everything about me.

I was too tired to call a locksmith, so I settled for wedging a chair beneath the handle. Then, feeling vindictive, I covered the floor with round glass Christmas ornaments, like the boy had done in that *Home Alone* movie. If it had worked for him, why not me?

Empowered, I took my glass of wine and retreated to the master bath, where I indulged in a temperate shower, the glowing red numbers of the thermostat's digital display assuring me I wouldn't burn.

Then, at long last, I finally confronted the biggest question of the day, the true cause behind my rage and restlessness.

Hurricane Shana.

My big sister. Who claimed she'd taken me out of the closet, so many years ago, and held me close.

Because if you don't have family, you don't have anything at all.

I wanted her to love me. It was terrible. Illogical. Weak. Frail sentiment from a woman who knew better.

And yet I did.

When she'd talked of that last moment we'd had together in our parents' house . . . For a moment, I could almost remember it. The sound of shouting men, pounding against the door. My father's voice in the bathroom, my mother's hushed reply.

Then Shana. My big sister coming for me. My big sister picking me up in her arms. My big sister telling me she loved me and would always keep me safe.

I loved her, too.

The water seemed thicker on my cheeks. Was I crying? Would there be any point? The four-year-old child who'd existed forty years ago was not the same woman incarcerated now. Grown-up Shana used people. Destroyed Mr. and Mrs. Davies's lives, let alone the Johnsons' and the Sgarzis'. And what about the other children who'd been in the home? Mrs. Davies had been right. Chances were, little Trevor had gotten shipped out to some terrible place where he'd been beaten or raped or otherwise corrupted by the relentless hopelessness of foster life, while pretty AnaRose had been pimped out to earn money for her mother's desperate habit.

And Shana never even mentioned their names. Entire families, vanquished by her actions. It was as if they no longer existed for her. Because they didn't. She had needed. She had wanted. Then she was done.

I pulled myself together, shutting off the shower.

This morning, my sister had gotten to me, because that was what she did best. I showed up to break up with her, as she put it, and suddenly she had this story she'd never told me once in twenty years. Standing there, listening to her talk, I'd been swept up in her spell. Just as that first prison guard, Frankie, or maybe the second one, Rich.

She was manipulative. Not being able to feel sentiment herself, she suffered no blinders when it came to human nature. She could observe, analyze, collect. The perfect predator.

And Donnie Johnson, thirty years ago, trudging to the lilac bushes to deliver his older cousin's message? Had he been scared that night? Nervous about Shana's reaction? Or at twelve, had he been too young to fully comprehend the dangers of breaking a teenage girl's heart?

Right until her face had changed into a snarl. And she'd turned on him, lashing out with a knife. Impulsive. Wild. She was angry, and so she acted enraged.

My sister, who weaved a story to make me stay. Who talked at least two, if not three, men into their own deaths.

I frowned, finding a towel, drying myself off.

Words. Those were my sister's weapon as well. And no less dangerous. But, if you were into patterns—and psychiatrists loved patterns—my sister's MO was to talk first. Engage. Seduce. Coerce the desired behavior.

If she could do that with trained guards, why would she not have tried that first on a twelve-year-old boy? Sold him some story devised to make him fetch Charlie for her right away. She was sick, she needed Charlie, she wasn't mad at all; she just needed to give him something back.

She would. I knew it. She would've talked to Donnie first. Because my sister wouldn't have wanted to waste her wrath on the twelve-year-old messenger. No, Charlie had rejected her, and her razor-sharp mind would've gone straight there, lasering in on target.

My sister hadn't killed Donnie Johnson.

Someone else had. But had she seen it? Maybe arrived toward the end of it? A person . . . A girl, I thought, a girl bending over a boy with a blade in her hand, like my mother with my father all those years ago.

Instant psychotic episode.

My sister had never stood a chance.

But the ear in her pocket?

She could've taken it. Maybe even done the mutilation herself. At that point, she would've been on autopilot, the episode having triggered not only all of her deepest, darkest desires but also her deepest, darkest memories. Had my father ever removed some poor girl's ear? I'm sure if I went through the files, I'd find at least one instance.

Someone else had killed Donnie. Maybe even looked up in shock when Shana appeared. Except my sister hadn't responded with outrage. Instead, she'd stepped forward, already captivated by the smell of blood. . . .

That person had found his or her perfect patsy. One person to do the crime but another to serve the time. And my sister hadn't been able to fight back, because she lacked all memory from that night. Not to mention, the murder looked exactly like something she knew, deep down inside, she would do.

She was the daughter of a serial killer, accused of murder, who went on to become a serial killer. Destiny, I think Shana would say. She simply got tired of fighting it.

So what did she want from me?

And what could I realistically offer her?

I stepped into my closet, seeking pajamas. I didn't realize it until after I opened and then closed the top drawer of the bureau. Then it nagged at me. The closet wasn't right. Something was off. Something . . .

The movable cherrywood bureau. It wasn't where it should be, safely positioned over my hidey-hole. Instead, it was forward at least a couple of inches. As if someone had moved it and not gotten it back in place.

My heart, starting to accelerate.

I could've done it. Last night, removing vials, my frantic bid to dispose of evidence. Except I always returned it precisely to position, a paranoid habit developed from years of trying to hide the worst of myself.

He'd been here. In my closet. He'd . . .

Then I knew.

I moved the dresser myself, exposing the desired floorboards. On my hands and knees, prying up the first, then the second.

My recently emptied hiding place wasn't empty anymore. Instead, it contained a shoe box. A perfectly ordinary shoe box, just like one I used to have. Or the one I'd seen in my father's crime scene photos.

I knew. Even as I lifted it out. Even as I placed it on the floor.

I knew what I would find inside. The true horrors that could lurk in the most ordinary of boxes, tucked beneath a closet floor.

The Rose Killer inside my home. The Rose Killer bearing gifts. The Rose Killer bringing me the one thing he or she knew I would want most, hidden in a place no one, not even my sister, knew existed.

I removed the lid. Set it aside.

Then gazed down in horrified fascination at three brand-new mason jars filled with fresh ribbons of human skin, the replacement for my collection.

I screamed. But there was no one around to hear.

Chapter 31

"WE'RE BEING STUPID," D.D. said.

"*We* as in you and me, or *we* as in your case team?" Alex asked.

"All of the above."

"Okay, what have we been stupid about?" They were sitting on the sofa in the living room. D.D. had returned home in time to put Jack to bed, a ritual she'd needed after all the intensity of her day. Now she had her feet on Alex's lap and a large ice pack on her left shoulder.

"For starters, we don't have a killer. I was hoping by now we would."

"Well, you can't just conjure up these things."

"Oh, I was prepared to use deductive reasoning. No conjuring required."

"Wanna catch me up?"

"Okay." D.D. repositioned the ice pack on her shoulder while composing her thoughts. "First question we had: Could Shana be communicating with an outside friend/ally/killer, and if so, how?"

"Survey says?"

"Probably not. The biggest evidence that suggested she did have an outside ally was the fact she seemed to know things she shouldn't. However, Adeline believes Shana is simply more observant than most. Basically, Shana doesn't possess special knowledge, as much as she's adept at using social engineering skills to manipulate others. Turns out, she may have talked three corrections officers into their own deaths. At least they weren't very nice corrections officers."

"Okay. But if she isn't communicating with the Rose Killer, what is her relationship with the killer?"

"That one is harder to answer. More and more, we think this all has to do with Donnie Johnson's murder thirty years ago. Adeline doesn't believe anymore that her sister killed the boy. I'm not willing to go that far just yet, but there's definitely more to that night than came out at trial. Charlie Sgarzi earned the title of biggest loser of the day by revealing he most likely sent his own cousin to his death."

"Seriously?"

"Yeah. Apparently, twelve-year-old Donnie served as the messenger between Charlie and Shana. Meaning when Charlie decided his girlfriend was too slutty or, possibly, too scary for him—I'm not sure which—he sent his younger cousin to deliver the news."

"Nice."

"Charlie agrees he is an asshole, but Shana is still the monster. Now, get this. Talking with the foster mom, we learned Shana was involved with two other boys. One was a twentysomething drug dealer called Shep, the other a seventeen-year-old kid who lived in the same house, named Samuel. Mrs. Davies apparently caught Shana and Sam together at least twice, and according to Charlie, Sam's interest in Shana was intense. She might've been love 'em and leave 'em, but he considered her the real deal."

"Ooh, a wounded teenage boy. But still sounds like Shana is the only one with motive to murder Donnie. Kill the messenger and all that."

D.D. shrugged, then immediately wished she hadn't. Melvin was currently quite annoyed. She'd tried speaking to him, but apparently her inner Exile was capable of having a snit. Maybe because she'd been a bad Self and pushed too hard today.

Wow, D.D. sounded loonier all the time.

"Adeline thinks Shana didn't kill Donnie," she continued, "but maybe saw what happened, which triggered a psychotic episode, erasing her memories from the evening and setting her up to take the blame."

"But Donnie didn't have any enemies, right? He was the good kid."

"By all accounts. Only thing I can think, and it fits with your kill-the-messenger theory, is that this Sam was an even bigger dope than Charlie thought, and didn't realize Shana was sleeping around. Then he's passing through the shortcut with the lilac bushes, and he overhears Donnie breaking up for Charlie. But what Sam really hears is that Shana had another boyfriend in the first place. And that sends him into a frenzy."

"Did anyone see him that night?" Alex asked reasonably. "Witnesses that spotted Sam returning home bloody, or maybe the foster mom found blood-soaked clothes?"

"Nada. Whereas, Shana wins on all those accounts. So again, I'm liking Shana for the murder of Donnie Johnson. However—"

"Excellent. I enjoy a good investigative *however*—"

"I think there's something we still don't know about thirty years ago. Hence, my problem, because I can't know what I don't know, right? But you raised an important question the other night."

"Thank you."

"Why now? What's the inciting event? Shana's been locked up thirty years, Harry Day's been dead forty years. Why all this madness now?"

"And the answer is?"

"I think it's Charlie Sgarzi. He decided to write this stupid book about his cousin's murder, apparently to cleanse his own conscience, and as a result, he's been dredging up old business. And that got someone's juices flowing."

"Someone who never even met you but decided to push you down a flight of stairs?"

"I can't know what I don't know," D.D. assured him.

"Interesting alibi. Do you remember anything yet?"

"No." She rubbed her forehead. "Just Jack's favorite lullabye, *Rockabye, baby, on the treetop* . . ." She started humming it; she couldn't help herself. "I can hear it all the time, playing in the back of my mind. Like a radio song you get stuck in your head. Except I don't think it came from the radio. I was humming it at the scene, and then . . . a sound. I heard something. Then I must've done . . . something? Maybe confronted the killer somehow. But my gun was out, right? I couldn't have drawn after I started falling. The gun had to come first. Meaning I did see something that night, engaged in some kind of altercation. Rather than run away, however, the killer decided to give me a giant shove off instead."

Alex smiled at her sympathetically, massaged her feet. "How's Melvin?"

"Oh, we're getting more used to each other. At least investigative work is distracting. I know they'd never clear me for duty yet, but I swear, Alex, if I didn't have this case to occupy my mind . . ."

She was thinking of his earlier point, that faint whiff of blame that while being pushed down the stairs might not have been her fault, her actions since had basically drawn a murderer even closer into their lives.

Alex smiled at her now, blue eyes crinkling with understanding. "You are who you are, you do what you do. And you're tougher than you think."

"Isn't that from *Winnie-the-Pooh*?" she asked him.

"Hey, I happen to like a tubby little cubby all stuffed with fluff. What do you think Jack and I do with our free afternoons?"

She rolled her eyes. He smiled again, and for a moment, life was good.

"All right, back to the case," Alex said. "Male or female killer. Have you decided yet?"

She made a face. "Tricky. Odds would still say male. Shana Day aside, not many female killers would engage in this level of postmortem mutilation. Of course, Shana Day is involved, meaning all bets are off."

"The use of chloroform strikes me as girly," Alex said. "Not to mention, women arouse less suspicion than men, especially when walking a neighborhood late at night or visiting a cancer-stricken elderly woman. It might be one of the reasons your killer has been operating beneath the radar screen."

"True. But what motive? I like someone such as foster brother Sam, who was once involved with Shana, had some kind of attachment. Shana doesn't have, and apparently has never had, any girlfriends. Only female bond in her life is with her sister."

Alex stared at her. "You mean the one who shares the same homicidal gene pool, not to mention a medical school background that must've involved scalpels?"

"Yeah. That one."

"Have you looked at her?"

"Please, she's pretty much part of the case team. As tactics go, we're keeping our friends close and our enemies even closer."

"Does she have alibis for the nights in question?"

"Nope. Phil asked. Apparently, Dr. Glen spends most of her nights alone."

"Meaning . . ."

D.D. shrugged, winced again. "It's possible Adeline's involved. It would be naive of me to assume otherwise. But . . . I think Adeline's trying to figure this thing out, too. I think her sister is as much a mystery to her as to the rest of us, except in her case, it hurts more. Shana is her only living family, and while Adeline talks a good professional game, you can tell she's vulnerable when it comes to her Shana. She does want some sort of relationship, even as the clinician in her understands that's never gonna happen; Shana isn't capable of it. Besides," D.D. added more briskly, "if you believe this all has to do with Donnie Johnson's murder thirty years ago . . . Adeline wasn't around back then. Didn't even know what had happened to her sister."

"Why the graphic nature of the murders?" Alex asked. "If this all has to do with covering up a thirty-year-old crime, why the postmortem mutilation?"

D.D. didn't have to think. The answer came to her immediately, from the back of her mind. "Because the murders are staged."

"What?"

"Staged. Everything about the crime scenes, the rose, the champagne, the handcuffs, the flaying . . . It's the killer making us see what the killer wants us to see. So we won't notice the rest of the details. For example, the victims were asleep, their deaths quick. It's not a crime of passion or bloodlust. It's calculated. Staged. Frankly, I'm beginning to wonder if the first two murders weren't simply a ruse to cover Janet Sgarzi's death. To make it look like she was the random victim of a serial killer instead of a targeted prey."

"Except she was already dying of cancer."

"Maybe not fast enough. Charlie's asking questions now, not later."

"I can tell you one winner from all of this," Alex said with a sigh. He moved her feet off his lap, rose to standing.

"Who?"

"Harry Day. Thanks to Sgarzi's blog comparing the Rose Killer to Harry Day, news stations are going nuts resurrecting details from Harry's homicide spree. Frankly, he's gone from a nearly forgotten serial killer to front-page news. Not bad for a guy who's been dead forty years."

D.D. looked at him. "Told you we were stupid!"

She scrambled off the sofa, jarring her shoulder, further aggravating Melvin. But he was gonna have to live with it, because she needed her computer tablet—now.

Alex went to the kitchen to fetch a glass of water. By the time he returned, she was already Googling *merchandise from murderers*. Four sites popped up. She went with the top one on the list and started scrolling.

Alex came to stand behind her, as she remained rooted in the middle of the family room.

"What is that?" he asked in horrified fascination, as the page loaded up with images of skulls, bloody daggers and yellow crime scene tape.

"A website for murderabilia. Incarcerated killers write notes, paint pictures, and other people hawk it to collectors online. Apparently, when the Night Stalker died last year, purchase prices tripled for a month."

"Are you buying or selling?"

"Window shopping. Check it out. Handwritten confession letter from Gary Ridgeway, aka the Green River Killer. One hundred percent authentic, the seller assures. Or, get this, a letter from Jodi Arias. With sexually explicit details. Holy crap, that's going for six grand from some seller in Japan with a five-star rating."

Alex made a face. "Seriously?"

"Face it, the Internet is nothing but a giant shopping mall. Given these kinds of items are banned on eBay, they were bound to find another outlet."

"A signed confession letter, original art, *Christmas cards*," Alex was now reading over her shoulder. "A dozen custom-designed cards from your favorite killers. Because nobody says Merry Christmas better than Charles Manson? How does someone even *get* such stuff?"

"Ummm . . ." D.D. was still skimming. "Based on what I'm reading, a lot of these 'vendors' have forged relationships with the killers in question. I guess you establish trust, then request custom Christmas cards?"

"But convicted killers can't profit from their crimes, meaning there's nothing in it for them."

"Not money but time, attention, diversion. According to Adeline, boredom is a major problem when you spend the rest of your life behind bars. Maybe for the killers, that's what they get out of it. Someone who writes to them regularly as well as a small purpose to the week, paint this portrait, design this card. I don't know. It all looks creepy to me. Hang on, here we go: Harry Day."

She clicked on his name, and a fresh page loaded.

"Two items," she announced. "One is an alleged floorboard from his house of horrors. Another a handwritten invoice he gave to a neighbor, billing for custom bookshelves. He was a carpenter, re-member? Now check this out." D.D. tapped the screen. "Price for invoice has gone from ten bucks to twenty-five. The real winner, however, is the floorboard from his house, which has gone from one hundred to two thousand dollars in the past four hours. Now, there's a happy seller."

"A floorboard from Harry Day's house? Meaning a forty-year-old piece of wood?" Alex already sounded skeptical. "How does the seller authenticate such a thing? Why, that could be any old floorboard."

"As the website puts it, buyer beware. But, in this case, the seller claims the artifact comes with a corresponding police evidence entry log and detailed description."

"You mean some of these items are from *cops*? Police depart-ments?"

"Looks like it. That might explain the autopsy report I saw for sale on the home page."

"Oh my God." Alex appeared ill.

"Remember, I'm just window shopping." But she didn't blame him. Coercing a convicted killer into sketching a self-portrait was one thing. But many of the items listed seemed to be a clear violation of victims' rights, not to mention the criminal justice system. Crime scene photos, a coroner's report. From a cop's perspective, it was nearly sacrilegious.

"Maybe leaked by disgruntled employees," she mused out loud. "I hope ex-employees, because God, some of this stuff just isn't right."

"But Harry Day killed himself, right? No arrest, trial or incarceration. Meaning there shouldn't be much for ex-employees to leak, and there's no living serial killer to befriend."

"Yeah. Well, I've only found two items, where some of these killers have dozens of entries." She paused, considering. "In other words, if you happen to be one of the lucky few owning anything related to Harry Day, this week is a good week to be you. The value of your sales inventory just jumped thousands of percent, and given the serious dollars attached to some of these items . . ." She eyed Alex. "Assuming our killer has a treasure trove of Harry Day items, maybe he or she had financial motive to make Harry Day front-page news again. Could it be that simple? The external motivation we've been looking for is financial gain. Cash, pure and simple."

Alex frowned. "But who would be in a position to have personal mementos from a serial killer dead and gone for the past four decades?"

"His surviving heirs. Shana and Adeline were just kids, though. The house probably sold at auction. Maybe money was put aside for their care or future college funds. Someone might have set personal items aside for them. Maybe a social worker or even the DA. I've seen it in other cases where a small child is the lone survivor."

"Did the foster mom mention anything?"

"No, and I can't see her hanging on to any of Shana's personal belongings. Not after what happened. Adeline claims she's kept far away from her father's legacy. She's mentioned a case file her adoptive father made for her but no family heirlooms."

"So, again . . . ?"

"It's not Shana and Adeline. Can't be. But what if . . ."

D.D. turned to Alex. "What if Shana, the older daughter, once had a few of her father's belongings? Items she'd dragged from foster home to foster home. She's the one who apparently worshipped him."

"Where'd they go?"

"She gave them away? A friend? A boyfriend? Or someone knew

about them. She bragged or confided in another person in the neighborhood. Who, after the police took her away, snagged the items out of her room. Quick, let's check the other websites."

D.D. pulled up all four murderabilia sites, with their various disclosures. Second site didn't even list items by Harry Day, but on the third site, they got lucky. Two letters, so-called love notes, written from Harry to his wife. Both items had gone from twenty bucks to more than a thousand in the course of the day.

"If you were trying to salvage something for a couple's surviving daughters?" she murmured to Alex.

"That would be the kind of thing to stash away," Alex agreed.

She clicked on the seller. Instead of a name, however, she got a list of random numbers attached to a Gmail account.

"Trying to cover his tracks," Alex said. "If I was hawking things to people who were obsessed with serial killers, I'd do the same."

"Can you trace it for me?" D.D. implored. "I could have Phil run it through the department experts, but you know that'll kill at least twenty-four hours; whereas, if memory serves, you have a friend at the academy. . . ."

"Who is the very best at computer forensics. All right, I'm in."

Alex made the call. Given the late hour, Dave Matesky was at home. Alex read off the e-mail address. Matesky did whatever it was computer techs did, and within a matter of minutes, they had a name.

Samuel Hayes.

Shana's former foster brother.

"Hot damn." D.D. got on the phone with Phil.

Chapter 32

I STARTED MY PREPARATIONS as the sun first peeked over the horizon. I hadn't slept, but the gaunt look of my face, the deep bruises under my eyes, would only help in the hours to come.

I began with my hair, wrenching it back in the most severe hairstyle I could imagine. No foundation, powder, mascara. Dr. Glen would be unpolished this morning. Showing her true face to the world. Given my current level of stress, I didn't think anyone would question this new look. If I appeared on the verge of a breakdown, well, I had a couple of things worth breaking over, didn't I?

Three mason jars. Set inside a shoe box. And fitted neatly into the hidey-hole where just the day before I'd emptied out my own collection of human skin.

Sometime yesterday, the Rose Killer had graciously refilled my supply. The victims' flesh hidden neatly in my condo. A murderer's atrocities in my closet.

Had the Rose Killer imagined me sleeping there? Harry Day's daughter, once more curled atop precious trophies?

It had taken me another fifteen minutes to find the cameras, little electronic eyes. One in my closet, one in my bedroom, one in my living room. That was how the killer had known about the hiding space. Because the killer hadn't just been visiting my condo; the killer had been spying on me. He or she must've been in my unit more often than I'd realized to set up such an elaborate system.

In the middle of the night, I didn't try to understand it. I simply placed strips of masking tape over each tiny lens, blinding the eyes. Then I sat on my sofa, armed with only my rage, and waited for the killer to come do something about it.

I didn't call the police. I didn't notify D. D. Warren or Detective Phil. Yes, I had evidence in my house. Items they most likely needed for pursuing the Rose Killer, from the skin collection to the home electronics. But it didn't matter anymore. This game wasn't about cops and robbers.

It was business. Family business.

Now I chose my wardrobe with care. Basic brown slacks, long-sleeved black shirt, dark-brown loafers. Plain and simple. Next I packed a bag filled with an assortment of casual clothes, then lined it with cash before adding makeup, scissors and a couple of hats.

No breakfast. I couldn't eat.

Seven A.M. I was on the phone with Superintendent McKinnon. I needed to speak to my sister immediately. About our father. Please, if she would just permit . . .

She agreed I could visit after nine.

That gave me plenty of time for the drive to Walmart. Disposable cell, disposable razors, a few other necessities. I finished with more than an hour to spare. I didn't know what to do with myself, so I sat in the parking lot, flinching at every noise. Was the Rose Killer watching me, even now? Had the murderer followed me from my condo building? I tried to pay attention to the vehicles around me, but I was no 007. I was merely an exhausted, stressed-out psychiatrist, engaging in a one-way ticket to self-annihilation.

Rigging my shoe took longer than I'd expected. Finally, the clock hit eight thirty and I drove to the Massachusetts Correctional Institute, hands trembling on the wheel.

Upon entering, I forced myself to breathe slowly and evenly. Nothing here I hadn't done a million times before. Sign in. Check my bag. Greet officers Chris and Bob by name. Walk through security. The machine buzzing as usual due to my medical bracelet.

Officer Maria was so accustomed to the drill by now, she didn't even bother with the wand.

A quick pat down, and we were done. Could she have inspected me more thoroughly? Should she have? Then again, I was a familiar face, well-known to all of them after six years of monthly visits. They knew me, they trusted me and they let me carry on.

Officer Maria led me down the corridor to the private visiting room where Shana and I usually met, versus the interrogation room that had been favored recently. I exhaled a quick sigh of relief at this second lucky break.

My sister was waiting for me, hands bound before her, per protocol. Officer Maria took up position outside, where she could see us through the glass window, though she couldn't hear us. These so-called privacy rooms were generally assigned to inmates meeting with their lawyers. Outsiders could not hear what was said inside, to protect an inmate's legal rights, but corrections officers could still keep tabs on the inmate, which would pose my first challenge.

All in due time.

For now, I entered the room. I walked to the empty chair. I took a seat.

My sister looked like she'd had the same night I had. Sleepless. Troubled. Agitated. For once, we almost matched.

Perfect.

She frowned as she took me in. "New look for you? I don't recommend it."

I ignored her, glancing at my watch. Five minutes, give or take.

Her frowned deepened. "What, I'm boring you already?"

"Tell me about Donnie."

Her expression blanked. Just like that. Went perfectly smooth. She thinned her lips, said nothing.

"Was he one of your fuck buddies, too?"

She arched a brow at my language. "Barely knew the kid." A grudging admission, but an admission nonetheless.

"He was the messenger. Charlie Sgarzi used him to set up time and location to meet."

She turned away.

"Is that why you never answered Charlie's letters? Because he's more than a reporter, right? He's more like a former flame."

She still didn't say anything.

"You slept with him," I continued briskly. "Samuel Hayes as well."

No answer.

"I met with your former foster mother, Mrs. Davies. You ruined her life, you know. She and her husband took equal blame in the eyes of the neighbors for Donnie's death. She was a good foster mother, Shana. Until you came along."

Finally a response. An obstinate look I knew too well.

"And Trevor's life as well," I said quietly.

She jerked back slightly, the name seeming to catch her off guard.

"Five-year-old boy," I continued, my voice merciless, for that matched my mood. "Lucky enough to get it right the first time and land in a good home. You remember him, right? You spent time with him, read him stories, painted pictures. He liked you. He was the only person in that house who had any faith in you."

Shana's jaw, setting.

"And the state yanked him. Overnight, Mr. and Mrs. Davies went from two of their best foster parents, to people non grata in the system. Trevor was bounced, probably to one of those homes where he was beat up every night, or worse."

It wasn't my imagination; her face had paled.

"You remember Trevor, don't you, Shana? He became the object of your internal projection. The child you felt compelled to try and save as a proxy for saving yourself. Like the inmate Christi, and once upon a time, me."

"Adeline." Her voice was slightly pleading. "Let it go."

"But you can't remember Donnie, can you? That night. What happened with Donnie Johnson. You can't remember any of it."

"Go away." She straightened abruptly, pushing back her chair. When in doubt, lead with rage. "I don't know why you even came here. Aren't we over with, all done? You don't love me and I'm not capable of feeling love. Run along, Adeline. Run away from me."

"You are a fucking idiot."

Her own words, thrown back at her, drew her up short.

"What the hell—"

"Sit. There's not much time left. I have one last question: Do you know who the Rose Killer is?"

My sister stared at me. Something about my intensity had finally gotten through. Slowly, she shook her head.

"But the killer will find you, right? Or really, the Rose Killer will find me. And when that happens, you'll kill him or her. Like you did with that corrections officer, Frankie."

My sister, still staring at me: "Okay."

"Afterward, I'll give you what you want, Shana. What you've always wanted."

"How do you know what that is?"

"Because I'm your sister. Who would know better than me?"

My sister staring at me. Myself staring back. I'd been honest with D.D. before. The trick to dealing with my sister was to never fool yourself. The relationship would always be dependent upon what was in it for her. I would like to think she would help me out of love. But far more likely, she would keep her promise to get the one thing I could give her, at last, at very long last.

Slowly she nodded again. "Pinky swear," she said, and her voice sounded rough, not at all like herself.

"Pinky swear," I promised back. Then I smiled because the childish promise, with its hint of sisterly cahoots and summer days and girlish innocence, nearly broke my heart.

"Any second now," I said steadily, "there's going to be an outside disturbance. When that happens, Officer Maria is going to be distracted. I need you to ambush me. Take me down and out. Then jam a chair under that doorknob and kill the lights."

My sister, still staring at me.

"They'll get in, though, right?" I continued. "Guards train for this kind of thing."

"They'll take out the window. It's bulletproof glass, but you can still hammer out the frame."

"How long?"

"They'll alert a tactical team, grab gear, get in place. Five to seven minutes."

"Then we need to be quick."

"Adeline—"

But she didn't get to answer, because at that moment, the sound of shouting came from the corridor, followed almost immediately by a shrill siren. Officer Maria turned her head down the hall. And my sister leapt across the table and drove against me with her shoulder. One second, I was sitting in a chair. The next, both the chair and I fell back. I heard the crack against the wall, registered the pressure of my sister's interlaced fingers pressing hard against my windpipe.

But of course, I didn't feel a thing.

More shouting. Much closer. Officer Maria yelling, though it was hard to hear her above the din of the prison's alarm. Then the room went dark as Shana hit the light switch. She slammed a chair beneath the doorknob then flipped the table up in front of the window, further obstructing the view. Five seconds, ten? My sister moved even faster than I'd expected.

I was already sprawled on the floor behind the flipped-up table, hastily grabbing my right shoe.

"Quick," I gasped, still breathless from my fall. "Hold out your wrists."

"Adeline."

"Shut up, shut up, shut up. This is the locker number. Second they release you, walk out to the lobby, go to this locker. This is the combo. Repeat it back."

She repeated it back as I finally got my fingertips clenched around the barely protruding razor and ripped it out from between the top and the base of my shoe. The razor that had set off the metal detectors earlier, only Officer Maria had assumed the disturbance had been caused by the usual suspect, my medic alert bracelet.

Now I studied Shana's wrists, which were restrained with thick plastic zip ties. A small box-cutting razor was hardly optimal, but it was the best I could do.

I started sawing, tucked against my sister, her shoulder to my shoulder, her hands on my lap. In all these years, it was the closest we'd ever been to each other. So close I could hear the sound of her shallow breath, smell her sweat-encrusted skin. When we were little, had we ever huddled together like this, maybe keeping each other safe after one of Daddy's outbursts? Or just two lost little girls, trying to survive.

I detected a new scent. Fresh, coppery. Blood.

I didn't feel any pain, of course, but I understood the implications of the wet sensation growing between my fingertips, making it harder and harder to grip the razor. I'd cut myself. Maybe even lost a fingertip, removed an entire knuckle. It wasn't like I would know.

I just had to get the zip ties off. The next act would be Shana's.

"Stop this!" she commanded now, voice low. "It's not going to work. I'm never walking out of here. This just puts you behind bars."

"I didn't do anything," I assured her, feeling the ties starting to give. "I'm the victim here."

"What the fu—"

"Listen! Inside the locker is my purse, which includes the keys to my car. White Acura SUV. Fifth row of the parking lot. Eventually, you'll want to swap it out for another set of wheels—one the police won't be on the lookout for—but the Acura will get you started.

Inside the car, you'll find a bag with several changes of clothes, a thousand in cash, the keys to my office and a disposable cell. Don't call me. First chance I get, I'll call you."

More noises in the hallway. Pounding footsteps intermingled with the pulsing siren. I was counting on the outside disturbance slowing mobilization. With so many officers running in one direction, how many would understand there was a second threat that demanded equal attention?

The zip ties gave. I sagged, already feeling wrung out from the exertion.

"Strip," I ordered. "Quick, quick, quick."

I went to work on my pants, then pulled off my long-sleeved top. Bra and underwear, too; I was leaving nothing to chance. I threw it all at Shana. The fabric was probably bloodstained by my mutilated fingertips, and I was happy I'd gone with dark colors, which would help minimize the stains. Soon enough, a little blood would hardly matter.

Shana was moving. Whether giving way from shock or bewilderment, she drew on my dark-brown slacks, even as I made my first attempt with prison orange.

"Don't go to my apartment or my office," I instructed now. "Those are the first places they'll look. Find someplace to hole up, sit tight. There's a bag of fresh clothes, as well as some tools and scissors. Change outfits, cut your hair, dye it, do what you need to do. When the dust settles, I'll bring you home."

"All this to catch a killer?" Shana grunted.

"No."

"Then why?"

"Because I need you."

"Why?"

I stopped moving. In the dark, smelling blood, my sister's nervousness, I felt a deep calm set over me. This was it. The conclusion of the dance. The place we'd always been heading toward.

My sister and I together again, as shouting men once more pounded against the door.

"Dressed?" I asked.

"Yes."

I handed her my medic alert bracelet, slipped from my wrist onto hers.

Next my hair tie. "Pull it back, tight as you can."

Then, while she struggled on the floor with her hair, I attended to the final detail of Shana's disguise, finding her face with my bloody fingertips. Gently, tentatively, I drew wet lines across her nose, down her cheeks. Eradicating my sister. Creating a new, blood-covered Adeline in her place.

It occurred to me this was the first time I'd touched my sister, truly touched her, in forty years. We'd talked. We'd sat across tables from each other. But the planes of her face, the bump in the bridge of her nose . . . She felt both alien and familiar. The nature of family.

The first crack as the window began to give way. Not much time left.

"You are Adeline," I informed her. "You are a successful, well-educated woman who was just violently attacked by your older sister. Hence, the blood on your face, your uneven steps. When Superintendent McKinnon questions you, keep your answers short, while modulating your voice the best you can. Just remember it all happened so fast. You don't know what set your sister off, you didn't expect the attack. No, you're not that injured. You simply want to go home and rest. Flash the MedicAlert bracelet a lot. It's a detail they associate with me and will lend your disguise that much more credibility, whether they're aware of it or not."

"But you don't look like me," Shana burst out desperately, nose nearly touching mine. "Maybe with these clothes, the hair, the bloody face, I can almost pass for you. But they're never gonna believe you're me."

"You're right. One last step." I held up the razor. Placed its edge against my right cheek. "Your history of self-mutilation is about to become your salvation. Untouched, I can't pass as you. But once my face has been shredded to ribbons . . ."

I started to slide the razor. No pain, not even a sensation of cold, as by now, the razor was prewarmed by my own blood.

"Wait!" Shana grabbed my hand.

Guards, voices louder now, as the glass window surrendered to the constant assault and displayed the first array of spiderwebs.

"I'll do it. You don't have enough experience. You'll cut too deep, leave behind a scar. It wouldn't be right."

She stopped talking, taking a deep breath. Then her fingers plucked the razor from mine.

Shana, leaning closer, trying to see in the dark. I could feel her eyes, fixed on mine. One second. Two. She placed the razor against my right cheek. Three seconds. Four.

"It's okay," I whispered. "Remember, I won't feel a thing."

My sister drew the first line down my face. I could feel her breath wash over me, a sigh, both mournful and ecstatic. I wonder if she had looked like this all those years ago, marking my arm with scissors in the foster home. Or if she was being true to her word now, trying hard not to cut too deep and disfigure me permanently.

" 'Kay?" she asked after the first cut, her voice thick.

"More."

"Jesus, Adeline."

"More. Make them believe, Shana. For both our sakes, they must believe."

Another cut. Across my nose, I could feel the razor like a pen tip, someone drawing across my face. Then the sensation of wet raining down my cheeks.

"Forehead," I commanded. "Nothing bleeds like a head wound."

My sister's eyes glistened. Unshed tears? Unwanted emotion? But she didn't stop. I was handing her freedom. Why would she stop? After this, she would walk out the door, Dr. Adeline Glen. Fulfill her deepest fantasy of taking over my life. My car, my condo, my office. I had handed her everything.

Shana Day. The most notorious female killer in the entire state. Who had ruined Mrs. Davies's life. And the Johnsons' and the Sgarzis', before talking three men to their own deaths.

And yet she'd saved her fellow inmates and still mourned a five-year-old boy.

My big sister. The monster I was releasing upon the world.

I reached out, placing my fingertips against her cheek, even as she continued to draw the razor across mine.

"I'm sorry," I whispered, though I wasn't sure why. I was the giver; she was the taker.

Yet I could see in her eyes, positioned so close, this was costing her, too. Shame, because she was hurting me, combined with an unholy glee, as some part of her reveled in it. Her nature and her nurture. Just like mine.

My sister drew a fifth line, and I tasted blood upon my lips.

The last edge of the window frame gave way, the entire panel collapsing with a shatter of glass. Then they were upon us, men in black armored suits screaming at me—Shana—even as others jerked Shana—Adeline—away, and I heard my sister cry, high-pitched, distressed:

"Help her, please, help her. She smuggled in a razor somehow. I think she may have cut her throat. Dear God, please help!"

A big man loomed over me, visor down, face obscured as he shouted.

"*Hands, fucker. I wanna see your hands!*"

I merely smiled, picturing the sight I must make, with the red blood rimming my white teeth.

A Shana-worthy moment to be sure.

Then I was grabbed and hustled away.

As my sister, Dr. Adeline Glen, staggered into the hall, still inside the prison but already on her way to freedom.

Chapter 33

WHEN D.D. SAW PHIL'S NAME appear across her call screen, she snatched up her cell phone, fully expecting to hear that he'd finally located Samuel Hayes. Instead:

"Shana Day has escaped."

"What?"

"Shortly after nine this morning. Attacked her sister with a razor, then swapped their clothes so that Adeline was dressed in her prison jumpsuit, while Shana appeared to be Adeline. After that, it was a simple matter of walking out the door."

"What?"

"Yeah," Phil sighed. "That sums it up nicely. Adeline is still in the prison infirmary, getting treated for her injuries. I'm heading over there now to talk to Superintendent McKinnon—"

"I'll be ready in thirty minutes," D.D. answered quickly.

She could nearly see Phil's smile across the airwaves. "See you then."

He ended the call. She flung down the phone and bolted off the sofa.

"Alex, Alex! I gotta shower and change. Help, please. Help!"

SUPERINTENDENT MCKINNON MET THEM in the MCI's lobby. Given the big doings for the day, D.D. was surprised that the place looked much the same as usual. Other than the armored guards standing out front, of course, and an occasional helicopter conducting a flyby overhead.

"The perimeter team has already been activated," Superintendent McKinnon informed them briskly, the immediate response team being the go-to unit for prison escapes. "They found Adeline's vehicle badly damaged several miles down the interstate, but still no sign of Shana."

"Badly damaged?" D.D. asked.

"Shana hit several other cars attempting to exit the parking lot, let alone what she might have done on the freeway. She's been locked up since she was fourteen, remember? Most likely, this was her first time behind the wheel."

D.D. blinked. She hadn't even considered that fact. They were basically searching for an institutionalized lifer. A woman who'd never owned a cell phone, driven a car, let alone experienced the full frenzy of the modern world. Shana might as well be a cavewoman, suddenly freed from a block of ice.

"She have computer experience?" D.D. asked now.

"Shana's taken several continuing ed classes. Depending on her behavior, she's sometimes had a radio in her cell. She also reads a lot, meaning she may know a lot, she just hasn't . . . *done* a lot."

"Our best odds are to catch her now," Phil muttered. "Before the learning curve sets in."

Superintendent McKinnon escorted them back to her office. "I'm assuming you will want to speak to Dr. Glen."

"Absolutely."

She nodded. "Adeline is in the infirmary. The cuts to her face are mainly superficial, but given her inability to feel pain, doctors are worried about her wounds becoming infected. In particular, there's significant damage to her hands. They're pumping her full of antibiotics now."

"Her hands?" D.D. asked.

"They were badly slashed, including a severed tip on her left index finger. Defensive wounds, I would guess, as she tried to block the razor."

D.D. looked away. Cuts were hard for her to take. She didn't know why. Gunshots wounds, rope burns, acute poisoning, not so bad. Slicing and dicing, on the other hand, gave her the heebie-jeebies.

"From the beginning?" Phil asked, whipping out his recorder.

He set it on the desk, and the superintendent began.

Adeline had set things in motion, shortly after 7:00 A.M., by requesting a visit with her sister.

"Regarding the Rose Killer?" D.D. interjected.

"Personal business, she said. Something to do with their father."

D.D. and Phil nodded.

Upon arrival, one of the corrections officers had escorted Adeline to the private visitation room normally used for her and Shana's meetings. About eight minutes into their conversation, however, there was a disturbance outside.

"What kind of disturbance?"

Superintendent McKinnon sighed heavily. "Firecrackers. Rolled underneath one of the vehicles in the rear of the parking lot. At first, of course, it sounded like gunfire. A guard sounded the alarm, then mobilized the tactical unit."

"You got cameras on the parking lot?" Phil asked sharply.

"Covering the first few rows. Unfortunately, the car in question was parked too far away. According to my chief officer, the fireworks were planted sometime before; someone had attached a long, slow-burning cord. His initial impression was that it was simple criminal mischief, perhaps related to the vigil last night. Of course, given what happened next . . ."

"What happened next?"

"Officer Maria Lopez turned just in time to see Shana tackle Dr. Glen. Apparently, Shana leapt right over the table and slammed into Adeline, taking her down—"

"Hang on," D.D. interjected. "Aren't Shana's hands normally restrained?"

"They were. Everyone had followed protocol. Everyone was doing their job to the best of their ability." McKinnon uttered the words tersely. "Of course, we're duty bound to follow the same patterns and procedures. Whereas, someone like Shana has spent years with nothing better to do than think of ways to outsmart the system."

"What did she do?"

"She jammed one of the chairs under the door, then killed the lights. Officer Lopez immediately alerted the tactical unit, but given that they were already responding to the incident in the parking lot . . . It took several minutes. Five, I'm told, until the full team was assembled outside the visitation room."

"During which time?"

"Officer Lopez couldn't see that far into the room given the lack of lighting and the table blocking the lower part of the window. It appeared to her that Shana and Dr. Adeline were in some kind of struggle on the floor. She could just see bits and pieces as they rolled around. When the response team arrived, they went to work on the shatterproof window, popping it from its frame.

"Upon entering the room, they found Dr. Adeline Glen—they presumed—leaning over Shana's body. Both women were covered in blood. Dr. Glen's wounds, however, appeared superficial; whereas, the inmate, Shana, had deep cuts all over her face. Dr. Glen—they presumed—claimed that Shana had attacked her with a razor, before turning on herself. Given Shana's long history of suicide, that story didn't arouse immediate suspicions. A razor blade was recovered from the scene—"

"How did Shana smuggle a razor into the room?" D.D. again.

The superintendent shot her a look. "We don't know, Detective. Officer Lopez swears she conducted a thorough physical exam, internal as well as external, before escorting Shana to the visiting room.

Then again, how has Shana gotten any of her assorted blades, shanks and razors? For the record, I feel strongly that my staff is among the best there is. They do a tough job brilliantly. Only Shana can make us look like idiots."

The superintendent's voice broke off harshly. Up until this moment, D.D. hadn't realized just how personally the woman was taking this. But this was her facility, her staff, her domain. And yeah, thanks to Shana's latest escapade, Superintendent McKinnon didn't look so good.

"So," Phil interjected smoothly. "Your team does the logical thing: They cart off the injured woman in jailhouse orange to the secure medical ward. While, Shana, posing as Dr. Glen . . ."

"I personally came down to debrief her. She assured me she was physically fine; the blood covering her face belonged to her sister, not her. She was merely shaken, and wanted to return home immediately. She kept twisting her MedicAlert bracelet, however, so I could tell she was rattled. Of course, I questioned her further. What had happened, what had set Shana off? She claimed she didn't know. She'd mentioned the name Donnie Johnson—"

Phil and D.D. exchanged a look.

"And Shana attacked her. The whole thing happened too fast. There wasn't anything she could tell me. I offered her additional medical treatment, even an ambulance ride to the hospital of her choice. She declined. As a friend—" The superintendent's voice broke slightly. She caught herself, got her chin up. "I offered to drive her home. I also suggested she contact either of you, as you all seem to be working together, in order to request additional security now that her sister was on the loose. Obviously, she declined."

D.D. couldn't help herself. "How long did you speak with her?"

"Fifteen, twenty minutes."

"And you never figured out it *wasn't* Dr. Glen?"

The superintendent's dark eyes gleamed. "No."

Phil made a sound in his throat, the one he usually made when he wanted D.D. to back off. She leaned back in her chair, adjusting her position for better comfort.

"When did you figure out the switch?" he asked now.

"Not for another forty-five minutes, when Adeline finally recovered enough to talk. I immediately activated the tactical unit, as well as notifying all major law enforcement agencies, and now here we are."

"How did Shana get the keys to Adeline's car?" Phil asked.

"From Adeline's purse, which she'd stashed in the lobby locker. According to Adeline, Shana threatened to kill her unless she gave up the combo."

D.D. considered the matter. "Okay, we have an escaped murderer, most likely now on foot, since you've recovered the vehicle. Plus, she doesn't have enough experience driving to make stealing a new vehicle useful to her. We have a description of her clothing, which are really Adeline's clothes, not to mention they're pretty gory."

"Yes."

"I wouldn't think it would be too hard for Joe Public to spot someone that conspicuous," D.D. said, "which begs the question, four hours later, why haven't there been any sightings?"

"She had help," Phil stated quietly. "The person who set off the firecrackers in the parking lot. She drove down the freeway to meet him. Not so far away she'd have to drive for too long but far enough the security team or cameras wouldn't catch her making the switch."

"But who?" Superintendent McKinnon quizzed. "Shana doesn't have friends or fans."

"Oh, she may not have a friend," D.D. said, "but I think she does have a fan."

Phil glanced at her. "The Rose Killer."

"Meaning we're not looking for just an escaped murderer or just a serial killer. Now, we're looking for a killing team, squared."

. . .

ADELINE WAS SITTING UP when D.D. and Phil followed Superintendent McKinnon into the infirmary fifteen minutes later. Her face was covered in white bandages, making it nearly impossible to determine her features. But she had a determined look in her eyes as she swung her legs over the edge of the bed.

"What do you think you're doing?" Superintendent McKinnon demanded sharply.

"Leaving."

"Now, wait a minute—"

"Don't make me yell," Adeline gritted out. "It'll pull my stitches."

Superintendent McKinnon thinned her lips, crossing her arms sternly over her chest. D.D. didn't know how she did it. For a gorgeous black woman, the superintendent was one of the most imposing people D.D. had ever met.

She stepped around the superintendent's planted form, Phil coming around the other side.

Adeline regarded their approach, then sighed heavily. "I just want to go home."

"Think that's wise?" D.D. asked. "Your sister has the keys to your condo."

"If she'd wanted to kill me, she already could have." The doctor fingered her bandages. "Not so hard, you know, to go from slicing one's face to slitting one's throat."

"So why didn't she?"

"You'd have to ask her."

"Still think she's protecting you?"

"I have dozens of stitches in my skin. I'm missing a fingertip. *Protective* isn't the word I'd used to describe my sister right now."

D.D. nodded. She stood on one side of Adeline, Phil on the other, effectively blocking the doctor's escape. Once more, the woman sighed.

"What do you want?"

"Why did you meet with your sister this morning?"

"I wanted to ask her about our parents."

"And Donnie Johnson."

Adeline skewered her with a look. Or tried to. The doctor's eyes were slightly glassy, the remnants of shock, fear or painkillers, D.D. thought, before remembering Adeline wouldn't have needed any painkillers. She wondered how much that had freaked out the attending doctor, stitching up the face of a fully conscious, fully lucid patient as she stared back at him.

Adeline licked her lips. "I have a theory about Donnie Johnson. I wanted to test it."

"What's your theory?" Phil asked.

"I think Shana suffered a psychotic episode—"

"You mentioned that yesterday."

"Yes, but the more I thought about it, the more I'm convinced. . . . Do you know what happened to our father? The last moments of Harry Day?"

"He killed himself," D.D. said.

"Not exactly. According to Shana, our mother did it. Harry climbed into the tub, handed her the razor, and she did the deed. While Shana watched. Can you imagine how traumatic that must have been for a four-year-old girl? Literally, a defining moment in her development. Anything related to that, any kind of reenactment of that scenario, would hit a person such as my sister like a mental hammer."

"Wait a second." D.D. held up a hand. "Are you saying you think that's what Shana saw that night? A girl attacking Donnie? Like your mother with your father all those years ago?"

"I think something like that definitely would've been powerful enough to trigger a psychotic episode."

"A female killer," D.D. murmured, "becoming, thirty years later, a female serial killer."

"So what was the answer?" Phil asked with a frown. "What did your sister say?"

"I never got an answer. I said Donnie's name and . . . all hell broke loose. Sirens went off, men were shouting. And Shana jumped me. Just like that."

Adeline blinked, still appearing faintly surprised.

"She cut you pretty bad," D.D. said.

"She had to. Otherwise no one would mistake me for her."

"Still defending her?"

"I'm alive. In Shana's world, that's showing restraint."

D.D. shook her head.

"Where do you think your sister would go?" Phil asked.

"I don't know. She hasn't been out in the world in nearly thirty years. Frankly . . . I would consider her vulnerable. Finding me would have made some sense, but given she slashed me in return for her freedom . . . I'm sure she understands I'm not likely to assist her now."

"We think she had help," D.D. challenged.

"She doesn't have any friends."

"But she has a fan. The Rose Killer."

For the first time, Adeline faltered. "No," she breathed, but the word didn't come out strong enough.

"Shana and the Rose Killer," D.D. said. "The Rose Killer and Shana. Now, where would those two crazy homicidal maniacs go for fun?"

Then, in the next instant, she didn't have to ask Adeline anymore; she already had a hunch. They'd go back to the beginning. To where this had all started, thirty years ago.

She turned quickly to Phil.

"Mrs. Davies's house," she stated urgently. "The old neighborhood."

Chapter 34

SUPERINTENDENT McKINNON INSISTED on driving me to a car rental agency. The police had already impounded my vehicle, she informed me. Given that it would now be processed as a crime scene, no telling when I'd get it back. Or if.

We drove over in awkward silence. Myself, thinking of all the things I couldn't reveal. And McKinnon with an intent look on her face that was hard to read. As if she had her own secrets she didn't trust herself to speak.

It occurred to me that in all the years we'd been working together to best manage my sister, the superintendent and I had become more than colleagues; we'd become friends. I wondered if Officer Maria Lopez or Chris or Bob thought the same. I wondered what it would do to them when, if, they discovered I was the one who'd broken my sister out of prison. I was the one who'd betrayed their trust.

I thought I should say something. An outreach of sorts, a cryptic apology she might not understand now but that might give her comfort later. But then she turned and looked at me with such blazing dark eyes I couldn't help but lean away.

"A smart woman would change her locks, Adeline," she stated, her tone less helpful than challenging. "Are you a smart woman?"

I didn't answer.

"A smarter woman would go on vacation. Say, to Bermuda. Someplace far, far away from here."

"If my sister wanted to hurt me, I'd already be dead," I replied steadily.

She eyed me with that intent expression again. "You're assuming your sister is all you have to fear."

"What do you mean?" I asked sharply.

But she'd turned away, was watching the road, and we didn't speak again.

At the car agency, the desk clerk took one look at my heavily bandaged face, my oven mitt of a left hand and immediately recoiled. McKinnon, however, wasn't having any of it. She started barking commands, and in twenty minutes or less I had a midsize sedan in deep blue.

"I'll follow you home," she announced briskly. "Help get you settled."

"No, thank you. I'll be fine. I just need rest."

"Can you even open your front door with that thing? Work a key, undo a lock?" She gestured to my heavily wrapped and padded left hand, which looked more like a baseball glove than a body part. "Let alone drive the car, change into comfortable clothes, fix yourself some food."

"I'll be fine."

"Adeline—"

"Kimberly."

She huffed at the rare use of her first name. She tried her stern glare again. Then, when that didn't work: "Don't take this the wrong way, Adeline. But when it comes to Shana, you can be a damn fool."

I touched the bandages on my face. "And this is my punishment?"

"I'm not saying that. Shana is clearly the one in the wrong here, but . . . You are her sister. And you seem determined to find some good in her, whether any exists or not."

"Duly noted."

"I've supervised her for nearly ten years, remember. You're not the only one who knows her, who can anticipate her every move.

I'll come with you to your apartment. Between the two of us, she'll never stand a chance."

An offer of help, graciously given. But McKinnon's eyes were overbright again, making me uncomfortable. A wronged prison superintendent's zealous desire to make things right, correct the one inmate who'd gotten the better of her? Or something more? Something I couldn't quite put my finger on yet.

"I'll change my locks, first thing, I promise."

McKinnon scowled, studied me harder.

And I started to think of things I didn't want to think. D.D.'s growing conviction that the Rose Killer might be female. And that my sister couldn't have been in contact with someone outside the prison; whereas, someone inside those same walls, say, a fellow inmate, or a corrections officer, or even the prison superintendent . . .

"I need to go. I need to rest."

McKinnon hesitated, expression still inscrutable.

"You're sure?"

"Yes."

"What about that vacation?"

"I'll take it into consideration."

"You'll keep me posted?"

"Of course," I lied.

"If you need help, Adeline, please don't hesitate to call. I realize our relationship has always been about Shana, but given the number of years . . . If you need anything," McKinnon finished stiffly, "I'd be honored to assist."

"If it's any consolation," I said, already moving toward the rental car, "I doubt Shana's enjoying her freedom right now. After thirty years behind bars, I imagine she's feeling mostly overwhelmed if not downright anxious."

The superintendent grunted, dropping back, giving us both space to breathe. "I can take some solace in that. But I'd take even more solace in a SWAT team nailing her sorry ass."

My turn to smile, but it felt strange, my skin rubbing against the rough bandages.

"Kimberly," I heard myself say, hand on the car door.

"Yes?"

"I'm sorry. For this morning. For all that my sister's put you through. For . . . everything."

"Not your apology to make."

I smiled again and thought that for someone who didn't feel pain, the sensation in my chest felt curiously like a slow, aching burn.

I made it back to my high-rise building, parking the rental car in the subterranean lot. I'd driven around the block three times first, counting four police cruisers in the vicinity, three Boston, one state. My condo would remain under watch for the near future, I figured, which made it imperative to plan ahead for what would happen next.

I entered my unit carefully, not sure what I feared the most: detectives, crime scene techs or the Rose Killer him- or herself.

I found only empty rooms. For the moment, the police still considered me a victim. They were watching my building for a sign of my sister's approach but didn't yet have reason to intrude upon my personal space, given the last sighting of Shana had been roughly twenty miles south of here and they considered her on foot.

Shana couldn't drive. I'd forgotten about that. Which immediately made me wonder what other details I'd screwed up.

I conducted a quick search of my entire condo. The cameras were still in place, masking tape over the lenses. So the Rose Killer had not yet had the opportunity to fetch his or her toys. Too busy stalking the next woman? Or simply savoring this lull in the storm before descending and wreaking havoc on my life again?

I wasn't afraid anymore. Mostly, I just wished the Rose Killer would hurry up and get it over with.

In the bathroom, I carefully removed the taped patches of gauze from my face. No time like the present. I took a deep breath. Looked up. Stared.

If the white bandages had seemed conspicuous, then the bloody patchwork quilt that was currently my visage was beyond shocking. Six, seven, eight, bright red lines. Across my forehead. Slashing down over my right eye. Across my nose, down both cheeks, a jagged gash slicing across my chin. I looked like Dr. Frankenstein's monster; not a real woman but a macabre imitation sewn together with random pieces of skin.

And yet . . . I fingered one shiny red line, then another. Only three of the cuts had required stitches, and then only in certain places. The majority of the damage, true to Shana's word, was superficial. The doctors had cleaned the wounds, then coated them with a skin adhesive to aid in healing.

No, the far greater damage was to my left hand. And I'd done that myself, most likely while sawing through Shana's wrist restraints.

My sister had done as she'd promised. Didn't that mean something? Honor among thieves and all that.

No going back, I informed the woman in the mirror. No going back.

I would've liked to shower, but I wasn't supposed to get my hand or face wet. I settled for a sponge bath, the best I could do with only my right hand. Then I awkwardly pulled on a loose-fitting pair of jeans, plain cable-knit sweater.

Fortified, I crossed to my closet. I had a safe in the back where I stored my nicer pieces of jewelry. Now I opened it and pulled out a phone. A prepaid cell, the twin of the same phone I'd left for my sister in my purse. I'd memorized her number first thing this morning. Now I dialed it.

The phone rang. Two, three, four, five, six times.

Just when I was beginning to panic, my sister picked up.

"Where are you?" I asked.

"Fanueil Hall."

"Faneuil Hall? How did you get there?"

"I can't drive," she said, voice flat.

"Then how?"

"Guy stopped. Saw the car broken down, offered me a ride. I'd cleaned my face," she said, as if this explained everything.

I couldn't help myself: "And this man, is he . . ."

"I didn't kill him." For the first time, I caught exasperation in her voice. "I didn't know where to go. I said Boston. He brought me here. It's crowded. I'm blending in."

"Cops?"

"Not bad."

Most likely because they were currently focusing their efforts elsewhere.

"I'll be there in fifteen minutes," I told my sister. "I'll find you at the Starbucks. That's the coffeehouse at the end of the food court."

"I know what Starbucks is," she said, exasperated again.

"I'm sorry. I didn't realize you were such a connoisseur of non-prison foods."

"Fuck off," she said, but her voice lacked heat.

I couldn't help myself; I smiled. For a moment, we sounded almost like sisters. I hung up the phone, retrieved the largest sunglasses I could find to help disguise my savaged face, then went downstairs to hail a cab.

I WALKED RIGHT BY Shana the first time. Slender, middle-aged guy in jeans and a plaid shirt sitting casually at a table. No reason for a second glance. It wasn't until I'd perused the entire crowded space that I realized my error. Why that one person stuck out from all the others I'd seen.

When I returned to the table, Shana was smiling at me.

"I did good," she said, with a trace of genuine pride.

She had done good. She'd done great. Gone were the long, lank locks. She'd shorn her hair right off, a boyish cut that changed the lines of her face, made her appear more youthful as well as masculine, given her slightly broader shoulders, flat chest and nonexistent hips. I'd packed sweats, but she must have used some of the money to buy new clothes, because she sported a pair of distressed jeans as well as a button-up flannel shirt. She could've been an ad for Gap or Old Navy. The earth-tone plaid suited her complexion better than bright orange ever did, but she'd also played with the makeup. Foundation, I would guess. Maybe some powder. Enough to even out her skin, take years off her age.

I felt as if I was in some perverse makeover show. How to look twenty years younger and no longer incarcerated!

She had a baseball cap in front of her on the table, as well as a cup of coffee; the duffel bag I'd left for her in my car decorated her feet.

I took a seat across from her, feeling dowdy in my hastily thrown-on clothes, conspicuous with my injured hand and face. We wouldn't be able to linger here. We wouldn't be able to linger anywhere without commanding attention.

My sister took a sip of coffee. On the table, she was rhythmically tapping the fingers of her left hand, a sign she wasn't as calm as she was trying to appear.

"How is it?" I asked, gesturing toward her drink.

She grimaced. "Tastes like cat pee. And impossible to order. Some kid in line yelled at me."

"Starbucks is a cultural thing. You'll get used to it."

She grimaced again, set down the cup. Picked up the hat, twisted it in her hands.

"Now what?" she asked.

"Is there anything special you want to do? Something you've dreamed about all these years?"

She regarded me funny. "Adeline, I was a lifer. Lifers don't dream. We don't have someday."

"But is it as you remembered, the outside world?"

"Kinda." She shrugged. "Louder. Crazier. Like the memories were faded, now here's the real deal."

"It's overwhelming."

She shrugged again, striving for nonchalance, while continuing to twist the hat. From thirty years in solitary to midday in downtown Boston. It would be too much for most people.

"You could go," I said evenly. "Leave me. Just walk away."

My sister didn't take the bait. Instead, it was her turn to regard me steadily. "Go where? With who? To do what? I don't know how to drive. I've never held a job. I don't know how you find an apartment or house, let alone how to cook a meal. For most of my life, the state has taken care of me. I think I'm a little old to change that now."

"I'm sorry," I said. My theme for the day.

"Why? None of it had anything to do with you. What happened, happened. Aren't you the professional shrink? Because sometimes, you seem a little dense to me."

"You'll help me?" I asked. Because now that she was on the outside, I wasn't so sure.

"I checked out my pressing social calendar. Looks like I can squeeze in one confrontation with a serial killer today. But that's it. Any more killers, and we're gonna have to negotiate payment terms. Hell, maybe I'm employable after all."

"You seriously don't know who the Rose Killer is?"

"No."

"You haven't been talking to anyone?"

She gave me a look.

"The killer came to my condo last night," I whispered. "Brought me a present. Three mason jars filled with human skin."

My sister didn't even blink. "Why would the killer think you'd like something like that?"

I didn't say anything. I could've, but I didn't.

"Scared, Adeline?"

"Aren't you?"

"Never. Don't even understand the emotion. You can't feel pain. Seems you should be fearless, too."

"I have nightmares sometimes. I'm in a very dark place. All I can see is a strip of yellow light. And I'm terrified. I wake up screaming every time. It puzzled my adoptive father for years. That a girl who couldn't feel pain could still experience fear."

"You dream of the closet," my sister said.

"I think so."

"Well, then, you do have things to fear. Adeline, I don't want to talk about the past. You started this game. I sure hope it wasn't just for a trip down memory lane."

"I need you to do as you promised; I need you to protect me."

She looked at my cut-up face, and even I got the irony. But then she shrugged and went with a breezy, "I'm here, aren't I?"

"And afterward . . ."

"You'll give me the one thing I've always wanted," my sister mused, and for once, I could catch the wistfulness in her voice.

This was the trick to managing my sister. You could want love and loyalty. But far more reliable was to appeal to her basic narcissism. Assure her there was something in it for herself. My sister, who after thirty years of institutionalization, would never make it in the real world.

"I'm going to take you to my place," I informed her now.

"Is it safe?"

"As safe as anywhere."

"But the cops'll be watching."

"Which is why I have a plan. Do you trust me, Shana?"

She smiled. "Do you trust me, little sister?"

"I'm bearing the marks to prove it."

"Fair enough." She rose to standing, tossing the coffee cup in the nearest garbage receptacle, then picking up the bag. "Lead on. It's your rodeo."

I TOOK HER TO BROOKS BROTHERS. Her first attempt at a disguise had given me the idea. Police might be suspicious if I returned to my condo with a female but not of a leading psychiatrist returning with a professionally attired gentleman. Maybe a colleague. A boyfriend. Or my own therapist. The possibilities were endless, and none of them included my recently escaped sister.

Shana was self-conscious in the store. And she couldn't stop touching. The shirts, the ties, the suits, at one point, the faux-painted wall. She had a wide-eyed quality about her, like a country hick recently arrived in the big city.

I picked out a classic dark-gray suit, while the salesman followed in our wake, eyeing Shana's wandering fingers anxiously, then my ravaged face and bandaged hand with growing concern. At last, I collected my sister, shoving her and the clothes into a dressing room.

"Holy shit," she exclaimed thirty seconds later.

"It doesn't fit?"

"Fit? Have you *seen* these prices?"

"Come, now, *darling*." I overemphasized the word, given the hovering sales clerk. "Quality costs, but you're worth it. Now, *try it on!*"

Shana emerged nearly ten minutes later. She was struggling with buttons, struggling with the tie. She looked like someone more at war with her wardrobe than at home in her clothes. But I buttoned her up, smoothed her out, then got her turned in front of the mirror.

Both of us stared. Was it the hair? Something about the lines of her face? Because God knows our father had never run around in a Brooks Brothers suit, and yet, for a second there . . . Shana might have been the one standing on the carpet, but it was Harry Day who stared back from the mirror.

I couldn't help myself. I shivered. Shana saw it. She thinned her lips, didn't say a word.

"We'll take it," I informed the salesman. "Clip the tags. He'll wear it out."

I added a long black wool coat to the stash, then handed my credit card to the attending salesman, who was still looking at everything but my face.

The credit card was my extra, the one I kept in my safe and not in my purse, in the event of theft. The police were most likely monitoring my other cards, given Shana had allegedly escaped with my purse. But this card should be clear. Even if the police tracked the purchase, a professional woman shopping at Brooks Brothers wasn't too suspect, was it?

From the clothing store, I took my sister down a few blocks to a walk-in hair salon. There, a bored kid tidied up her hack job, then, per my request, added blond highlights. A TV was on in the corner of the salon. Evening news covering the morning's prison escape, complete with flashing a photo of my sister's bored-looking mug shot. I glanced at the hairstylist. He didn't seem to notice the news or the photo. Or if he did, he didn't seem to connect a gaunt woman in prison orange with the nicely attired gentleman sitting in his salon chair.

I was still grateful to hustle us both out of there. Across the street to the drugstore for one last purchase: a pair of reading glasses with thick black frames. When I perched them on the end of her nose, Shana frowned, looking like she might sneeze.

But the end result was worth it.

Shana Day had disappeared completely. Now, a successful businessman stood in her place.

"Is this how your father looked?" Shana asked me. "You know, your *other* dad."

"No."

"Why not?"

"He was an academic; he preferred tweed."

My sister stared at me as if I was speaking another language. No doubt for her, I was.

"Roger," I announced briskly, straightening the glasses on her face. "We'll call you Roger. You're a doctor. In fact, you're my therapist. After this morning, no one would blame me for needing a shrink."

My sister touched one of the marks on my face.

"I am an expert in pain," she deadpanned.

Then she turned away, shifting restlessly under the weight of all the new clothes, fingers clenching and unclenching at her sides.

We continued down the street, me still looking over my shoulder, my sister with an expression that was once more impossible to read upon her face.

Chapter 35

SHANA'S FORMER FOSTER MOTHER, Mrs. Davies, was defiant.

"So she's escaped. What can she do to me? Ruin my sleep, damage my reputation, make me wish I was no longer alive? She's already done all that and more."

"Can we come inside?" Phil persisted. "Take a look around?"

The old woman finally complied, floral housecoat whirling around her ankles as she bustled down the narrow hall. She moved with more energy today than yesterday, D.D. noted. Rage had that effect on people.

D.D. walked through Mrs. Davies's home, while Phil conducted a quick sweep of the external perimeter. Outside there wasn't much land, given how tightly together the Boston houses were constructed. Inside, D.D. could say the same, given how much stuff Mrs. Davies had crammed into her family's home. Personally, D.D. thought there was barely enough room for Mrs. Davies inside the house, let alone an escaped killer.

They reconvened with Mrs. Davies in the rear of the house, finding her sitting on the sofa, stroking a black-and-gray tiger cat.

"Can you think of anyplace Shana would go?" Phil asked.

"Please. It's been thirty years. How many people have come and gone? Not even the city is the same, post–Big Dig and all."

D.D. and Phil exchanged glances. Fair enough.

"Mrs. Davies," D.D. spoke up. "Yesterday you mentioned a

foster girl, AnaRose Simmons, who was moved by the state after Shana's . . . incident."

"Oh." Mrs. Davies's expression softened immediately. "She was so beautiful. This pretty little thing, but so shy. Barely spoke two words, but sweet, very sweet."

D.D. had been thinking about it all night. She liked Samuel Hayes, and his posting of items on a murderabilia site definitely bore checking out. But if they were looking for a female . . . what about a little girl returned from a loving foster home to her crack addict mom's care due to Shana's transgression? Such a thing certainly would've pissed D.D. off.

"Have you heard from AnaRose at all?"

"Oh, no. I never followed up. I told you that."

"What about her, trying to get in contact with you, once she was of age?"

Mrs. Davies gazed at her sympathetically. "It doesn't work like that, dear. You think it might. But the number of kids I've seen. Most come and go, and when they go, they're gone. That's what the lifestyle does to them. They don't cling. They live only in the present, for they've learned the hard way, it's all they have."

D.D. frowned. "And AnaRose?"

"I don't know what became of her. If anyone would, it might be Samuel. He was like a big brother to her. They might have kept in touch."

"Speaking of Mr. Hayes—"

"Samuel?"

"We're worried about him as well," D.D. informed her. Across from her, Phil nodded, playing along. They hadn't been able to locate Samuel thus far. Why not recruit Mrs. Davies to their cause?

D.D. paused. "Do you maybe have a cell phone number? A better way for us to reach him?"

"Oh. Oh yes. Just one moment."

Mrs. Davies disappeared into the kitchen. D.D. tried hard not to think about that space, the piles of unwashed dishes, the rotting food, the cat hair covering the counters. A few minutes later, the older woman returned with a scrap of paper in her hands.

"I could call him if you'd like?" Mrs. Davies offered brightly.

"That would be great."

Mrs. Davies dialed the number. Nothing like a suspect receiving a call from a known number. Mrs. Davies was making D.D. and Phil's lives easier all the time.

Enough time had passed that D.D. was growing concerned, when:

"Samuel!" Mrs. Davies exclaimed. Her face split into a warm smile. All these years later, it was easy to see she still considered him to be like a son to her.

It almost made D.D. feel guilty.

"Have you heard the news, then?" Mrs. Davies continued. "Shana Day escaped. I have two fine detectives at my house now. They're worried about me, Sam. And they're worried about you, too."

A pause, Samuel saying something back. Whatever it was, it made Mrs. Davies frown.

"Well, I don't know. . . . I . . . Yes . . . No. Here. You talk to them. They'll want to hear from you directly anyway."

Without further prompting, Mrs. Davies thrust the phone into D.D.'s hand. She lifted it to her ear.

"Samuel Hayes? Detective D. D. Warren, BPD. We're working with the task force to locate Shana Day."

Phil nodded encouragingly. Emphasize Shana Day. They weren't suspicious of Samuel at all. No, he wasn't currently a lead suspect in the murder of three women, let alone under suspicion because he had possible ties to their other lead suspect, AnaRose Simmons. No, they weren't dying to interrogate him.

"In these situations," D.D. continued briskly, "it's a matter of protocol to visit an escaped inmate's known associates. In this case, that includes you. But I'll be honest, Mr. Hayes. Given Shana's track record, it's not so much that we believe you're involved with her escape, as much as we have reason to fear for your safety."

"What?" Samuel Hayes sounded startled.

"It would be best if we met in person," D.D. continued smoothly. "We can be at your residence ASAP. Address?"

"My safety? But, but, but . . ."

She had him right where they wanted him. Not defensive about a police visit but bewildered.

"Street address," she prompted.

He rattled it off, tone still uncertain.

"We'll be there just as soon as we're done securing Mrs. Davies's residence. Oh, and I wouldn't go out if I were you. Keep all doors and windows locked. Trust us on this one."

D.D. ended the call. She returned the phone to Mrs. Davies, who appeared suitably wide-eyed.

"Are you really so afraid . . . ?" the woman breathed.

"Better safe than sorry," D.D. assured her. "Same goes for you, Mrs. Davies. Best to stay inside, and keep the house shuttered tight. If you hear any sound out of place, dial us direct." Phil produced a card. "We'll have a patrol car sent here immediately. Okay?"

"Okay." But Mrs. Davies didn't appear frightened anymore. She had that belligerent look back on her face.

"Do you want to see her again?" D.D. asked curiously.

"There are some things I'd like to say."

"Such as?"

"I'm sorry."

"*Why?*"

"I am sorry," Mrs. Davies repeated evenly. "We were the parents. It was our job to do right by her. Then, when we realized we couldn't, we should've gotten her to a home or to a place where they could've helped her. But we didn't. We sat on our hands, waiting for something to magically change. For that, I'm sorry."

"Mrs. Davies . . . What Shana did, that wasn't your fault."

"I know that, too. That girl is the devil, and the devil will have her due. But she was still the child, and we were still the adults. That matters, Detective, don't you think? At least, it matters to me."

D.D. shook her head, unconvinced. Not all children were child-like. And she'd met enough youthful offenders to know that some were well beyond the reach of any well-meaning adult, let alone mental health expert or even dedicated parole officer.

Mrs. Davies assured them she would take all necessary precautions. Then Phil and D.D. conducted a slow drive around the block, eyes peeled, just in case they'd missed something, such as Shana blatantly peering around from behind a bush. Or a trail of blood leading to a neighbor's back door.

When the neighborhood remained quiet, they continued on.

Four P.M. The sun already beginning to fade, dusk approaching.

They went in search of Samuel Hayes.

THE ADDRESS LED THEM to an apartment building in Allston, one of the most densely packed neighborhoods in Boston. D.D. followed Phil up a very narrow flight of stairs, keeping her right shoulder against the wall, reminding herself to breathe deeply—then modified that request to include breathing through her mouth, when the stench of cooked cabbage and cat urine assaulted her senses.

Upon reaching the fourth-floor unit, Phil did the knocking. He indicated for D.D. to remain behind him and slightly to the side. He had his right hand floating around his waist, not far from his holster.

So many things they didn't know about Samuel Hayes.

Phil knocked a second time.

The door finally opened.

And they found themselves standing face-to-face with a man seated in a wheelchair.

. . .

"I HAVEN'T HAD THE HEART to tell Mrs. Davies," Samuel Hayes was explaining ten minutes later. They sat together in his one-bedroom unit, Hayes in his wheelchair, D.D. and Phil on the lone love seat in the modest space.

"I fell off a ladder a month ago, working on a roof. Apparently bruised my spine. First few days, when I still had problems moving my legs, the doctors told me it was due to the swelling; I just needed more time to recover. But four weeks of physical therapy and home exercises later, here I am."

"There's no elevator in this building," D.D. said. "How do you manage?"

"I get on the floor and belly crawl my way down four flights of stairs. The guy who drives the rehab shuttle then helps me load up. At the rehab center, they have a wheelchair waiting, which I can use while I'm there. Then, once I get home, I repeat the process of crawling up four flights of stairs. My legs may still be shit, but I'm finally getting those big guns I've always wanted."

Hayes flexed his right arm, his biceps bulging noticeably.

D.D. couldn't quite wrap her mind around it. Their top suspect was wheelchair-bound. Or at least claiming to be. He could be faking it, right? Then again, dragging yourself up and down four flights of stairs in full view of your neighbors seemed a pretty dramatic ruse.

Was this why the Rose Killer's victims had been ambushed while they slept? After all, then Hayes could've dragged himself onto the bed, done his thing, dragged himself off—

Ah hell, she was reaching for straws. Samuel Hayes was not their man. But then, who was he?

"Tell us about AnaRose Simmons," D.D. began.

Hayes blinked, clearly startled. "You mean the little girl in Mrs. Davies's house? Shit, I haven't thought of her in years."

"Keep in touch?"

"Nah." He shook his head.

"Tell us about her anyway," D.D. prodded.

Hayes blinked, seeming to have to search his memory banks. "Pretty girl," he said at last. "Like in that way where other people stopped and stared. Made me feel bad for her. Being a foster kid is hard enough. Being a *pretty* child . . ." He shook his head. "Not a good thing. But she was tough, too. You had to be, to survive being a kid in the system."

"Sounds like you were friends."

"We had a relationship of sorts. Including the first night she arrived, she walked into my room and announced that if I tried to touch any of her private parts, she was gonna scream. Then she walked out, like she thought I should know."

"She have reason to think that about you?" Phil asked.

"Hell no! I don't go around molesting little girls. Mostly . . . it made me feel sad. 'Cause clearly someone had, you know, to make her feel she had to say such a thing."

"You two were friends."

Hayes shrugged. "I liked her. She was a good kid. I tried to look out for her. Being a black kid in a white Irish neighborhood of Southie wasn't easy."

"Who picked on her?"

"Anyone, everyone. She was a fish out of water, and she knew it. But she kept her head up walking. She didn't socialize much, though. She came home, went to her room. Probably felt safest there."

"What did she think of Shana?"

Hayes shook his head. "Never saw them interact."

"Really? Only two girls in the house . . . ?"

"Shana led a fast life. She didn't even hang out much. AnaRose . . . She was a good girl. Quiet. Smart. I think she took one look at Shana and saw everything she wasn't going to do, in order to one day lead a better life."

"When did you last see her?"

"Ah hell . . . I dunno. Since she moved out thirty years ago."

"State moved her out," D.D. prodded. "Sent her back to her addict mom, after Shana cast doubt on Mr. and Mrs. Davies's ability to control their foster children."

Hayes squirmed uncomfortably.

"You've never talked to AnaRose since?"

"How? I don't know where she went. Not like foster kids run around with phone numbers attached to their chests or forwarding addresses. We're all temporary. We know that."

"Think she could be a killer?" Phil asked.

"What?"

"AnaRose. Had to be a tough life. From her perspective, Shana fucks up and she pays the price. Can't blame her for hating Shana after that."

"Hating Shana? Please, get in line."

"Really?" Phil switched gears. "Tell us about Shana."

"Come on, man. This was all thirty years ago. I barely even remember those days."

"You two were an item?"

"Says who?"

"For one, your foster mom."

Hayes flushed, ducking his head. "Oh yeah, I remember now."

"Nothing like guilt to make it all come rushing back," Phil assured him.

"Okay. So. Shana came on to me. Totally initiated things. We had sex a couple of times, say a half dozen. But then Mrs. Davies ordered us to cool it. Shana might not have cared, but I did. Mrs. Davies was—she still is—the closest thing to a mom I've ever had. She accused me of disrespecting her and Mr. Davies. And that hurt, you know? So I cooled it. Not like Shana cared. She just wanted sex. If I wasn't available, then she moved on."

"And how did that feel?" D.D. asked.

Hayes took a moment to compose his reply. "When you're

a seventeen-year-old boy, to find out just how easily you can be replaced . . . That's not the best feeling in the world. But it was classic Shana. She wasn't interested in your feelings. Only her own. I might have been a kid, but I wasn't totally stupid."

"Did she show up in your bedroom again?" Phil asked.

"Couple of times. I continued to tell her no. She finally got the message."

"Very noble of you."

Hayes shook his head. "It wasn't like that. Shana never claimed to have feelings for me or vice versa. I was merely convenient for her. That's all."

"Oh yeah?" Phil drawled. "At which point did she gift you with items from her father, Harry Day?"

Hayes stilled. Then, "Ah fuck."

"We saw the note listed on the Internet, Sam. Thanks to Harry's meteoric rise to fame in the past twenty-four hours, looks to us you're all set to score a major profit. Convenient, don't you think, that Shana's escape should bring her father back into the limelight, and here you are, holding items that once belonged to a notorious serial killer."

"Okay, okay." Hayes sounded a little desperate. "It's not what you think."

"What do we think?"

"I mean, I didn't get the items from Shana. I never even heard her talk about her father. All the kids in the neighborhood knew, of course, and we'd jaw about it, but only behind her back."

"How'd you get the letter, Sam?"

"I found it."

"You *found* it?" Phil's tone was dubious.

"Yeah. Right before my fall. I was on the job, working a long day. Came home to a large manila envelope sitting in front of my door. I opened it to discover some old documents, the letter, that kind of thing. At first, I didn't understand, but then, when I saw the name Harry Day . . . I did a little Internet research, confirmed the items probably belonged to him. As part of that, I also discovered some websites where you can sell this kind of crap—I mean, can you believe people *wanting* to collect anything once touched by a murderer? I didn't do anything right away, but then, last week . . . I'm not exactly working these days, you know. If someone wants to send me money for a stupid note I found on my doorstep, who am I to judge?"

"You *found* it?" Phil pressed again.

"Yeah."

"Show us the envelope, Sam."

Hayes pushed his wheelchair back with obvious effort. His small living space was not meant for a person maneuvering in a large chair. It took several attempts to get the chair turned and headed toward a side table piled high with miscellaneous clutter. Samuel dug around, both Phil and D.D. keeping their gazes fixed on his hands, prepared for any sudden movements, because wheelchair or not, something about Sam Hayes just didn't add up.

"Got it."

He returned, equally laboriously. D.D. had to fight the urge to rush over and shove his chair back into position herself.

Phil took a second to pull on a pair of latex gloves. First he inspected the eight-and-a-half-by-eleven manila envelope. No writing was on the outside, nor had the envelope been stamped or sealed. Just a plain envelope, looking like it'd come straight out of the box.

Next, Phil opened the flap, then slipped out half a dozen pieces of paper.

"Birth certificate," he read out loud, for D.D.'s benefit. "In the name of Harry Day."

She raised a brow.

"A personal letter to a customer, about some carpentry project he was working on. Three notes to his wife. And this."

The last item was a piece of faded yellow construction paper, folded in half to form a card. On the outside, it read in a small child's script, *Daddy*. Inside, a more mature handwriting had written out *Happy Father's Day*. The card was decorated with red and blue crayon forming various squiggles and what might have been a cluster of stars. Inside the card, in a large scrawl, the *S* turned backward, the card was signed: *SHANA*.

A Father's Day card. From a little girl to her daddy. From one killer to another.

"Do you have any idea what this might be worth?" D.D. exclaimed.

"Yesterday, not much," Hayes said. "But now . . ." His voice trailed off. He seemed to realize the increased value of his cache wasn't doing him any favors.

Ten thousand dollars was D.D.'s first guesstimate. Then again, an item this rare and personal . . . For the right collector, it could be priceless.

"You *found* this?" Phil pressed again.

"Swear to God."

"And you didn't question it? Ask your neighbors if they saw who dropped it off? Call the police to tell them you had just received items that once belonged to a murderer?"

"Talk to my neighbors? I don't even know who they are. Before this, I worked dawn to dusk. Now I'm a shut-in, except for my twice-weekly stair crawl. Either way, I'm not neighbor-of-the-year material. In this building, we do our own thing, and everyone is happy."

"But you must have wondered . . ."

"Sure. I wonder why I didn't better secure that fucking ladder. Or why I thought it was so important to work on the roof, even though it was drizzling out. I wonder about a lot of things, Detective. Doesn't mean I get the answers."

"You understand how this looks," Phil stated.

"You mean, like I had thousands of dollars' worth of reasons to help Shana escape and Harry Day become front-page news again?

Except I haven't even spoken to Shana in thirty years. Not to mention she scares the shit out of me. And, by the way, *I can't walk or drive*. Some great accomplice I'd make."

"There are hand-controlled vehicles for people in a wheelchair," D.D. said.

Hayes gave her a look. "Does this look like the apartment of a guy who can afford a custom rig? You know why I listed that stupid note? Because I could use the cash. And the first thing I'd like to do is get myself into a building with an elevator. I'm not dreaming big these days, Detective. I'm just happy I still dream."

"Tell us about Donnie Johnson," Phil said.

Hayes blinked. "Huh?"

"Donnie Johnson. Thirty years ago. What did you see that evening?"

"Nothing. I was in my room doing homework. I didn't come out until after all the commotion. Mrs. Davies yelling to Mr. Davies that something was wrong with Shana."

"Did you see Shana?"

"No. Her room was on the third floor. After the um . . . incident . . . Mr. and Mrs. Davies moved my room to the second floor, closest to them. I remember walking out into the hallway, then realizing there was blood smeared on the stairs. But by then, the front door was banging open, Donnie's father bursting into the house . . . It scared me. All these adults, looking so out of control. I retreated to my bedroom and stayed there."

D.D. decided to gamble. "That's not what Charlie Sgarzi says. He claims you were jealous of his relationship with Shana. And you turned on his cousin in revenge."

Hayes frowned. "Charlie? Charlie Sgarzi? What does he have to do with any of this?"

"We told you; we're looking into all of Shana's former associates. And given that she and Charlie were also once an item—"

"Whoa, whoa, whoa. What?"

Hayes's voice had picked up. Hostility? Jealousy? D.D. and Phil exchanged another glance, Phil's hand once more wavering near his holster.

"Charlie Sgarzi claims he and Shana had a relationship of sorts," D.D. said slowly. "He described them as being fuck buddies."

"Bullshit!"

The word cracked around the tiny space.

D.D. didn't speak again, merely waited.

Hayes ran his hand through his disheveled brown hair. Then again. "Hang on. I got something else to show you. It'll just take a sec."

Once more he worked his chair around, back to the paper-strewn table. But this time, he leaned down, reaching for a battered old box. He couldn't bend over far enough to reach it. Phil got up to assist, placing the box on Hayes's lap. Beneath Phil's close scrutiny, Hayes removed the lid.

More papers. Hayes riffled through them before finally exclaiming, "Got it!" He waved a faded Kodak in the air.

Phil returned the box to the floor, then helped Hayes back over. The man handed over the photo immediately, as if this should tell them something.

D.D. saw four teenagers. The colors of the instant photo had run over the years, making the features of each boy appear slightly melted. She could pick out Hayes. Shaggy brown hair, a once-dark-green Celtics shirt that had become lime green with age. The two other boys weren't familiar at all.

Then, at the far left. Gangly-looking, nearly slender, with long black hair cut short in front, long in back, Metallica T-shirt and a black biker's jacket covered in metal studs and silver chains.

"Charlie Sgarzi," she said.

"The Great Pretender himself," Sam assured her. "In one of his many disguises."

"What do you mean?"

"Charlie was the ultimate phony. I mean, these two boys, Tommy, Adam, they were into heavy metal. So when Charlie was around them, he was into heavy metal. Shana was Ms. Tough Shit, so around her, he jammed a pack of Marlboros into his back pocket. But you could also catch him in collared shirts, smiling sweetly up at his mom. Or with painted black nails and a long trench coat, hanging out with the Flock of Seagulls crowd. He adapted to his audience. Just as long as it got him a place with the in crowd."

Phil shrugged. "So he suffered from an identity crisis. He was a teenager; these things happen."

"But being a confused kid wasn't what he was trying to hide."

"Then what was it?"

"Charlie wasn't fucking Shana. Charlie's gay."

ACCORDING TO HAYES, he had a radar for these things.

"Trust me, you don't make it through the foster system without learning how to spot the boys who like other boys. Especially the ones who are pissed off about it."

"Charlie was afraid of his parents' reaction?" D.D. asked.

"Hell if I know. I mean, his parents were conservative, sure. A happy homemaker married to the local firefighter? But I don't think it was his parents. I think it was Charlie himself. He wanted to be just like everyone else. Except, he had this thing, you know. Nowadays, maybe not such a big deal. But thirty years ago, being a boy who liked boys in a place like Southie could get you killed. So he fought it. Spent all his time becoming someone else. He was good at it, too. A real actor. But, of course, I knew the truth."

"Because you possess the world's best gaydar?" D.D. arched a brow.

"Nah, because I caught him with Donnie."

"What?"

"He had his hands down his cousin's pants. I saw it, clear as day.

Then Charlie looked up, spotted me and made a big show of pushing his cousin away, like they were just roughhousing or something. But I knew what I saw, and he knew it, too."

"How did Donnie appear?" Phil asked.

"Upset. I don't think he was happy about Charlie's attention. But Charlie was bigger, stronger. What could Donnie do?"

"And you didn't tell this to the police thirty years ago?" D.D. demanded.

Hayes shrugged. "No one asked. Besides, Shana was the one pulling a bloody ear out of her pocket. Even knowing Charlie had assaulted his cousin, I still think Shana was the killer. Charlie had a mean streak, sure, but he was direct. When he wore his leather jacket, Mr. Tough Guy, you looked out. But in a button-down shirt, Mama's Boy, no problem. It was like he had a switch, flipping things on and off. Even violence was simply a matter of being in character."

D.D. felt as if her head was going to explode. "When did you last speak to Charlie?"

"Shit. Another lifetime ago. I mean, I left the neighborhood just six months after Shana's arrest. Haven't seen him since."

"Do you know he's working on a book on his cousin's murder?" Phil spoke up.

Hayes shook his head.

"He hasn't tried to contact you about it?"

A smirk. "Like he's really gonna ask me any questions about Donnie."

D.D. nodded. Which might lend some truth to Hayes's story, as it seemed suspicious, or just plain conspicuous, that Charlie had contacted or interviewed everyone *but* Shana's foster brother about the night of the murder.

"If Charlie wasn't sleeping with Shana, what was their relationship?"

"I dunno. Frenemies? I mean, they hung out from time to time. In a neighborhood that small, beggars can't be choosers. But Shana considered him to be a big phony. Threatened to slash his stupid coat on a number of occasions when he pissed her off. Charlie appeared to stay clear of her. Then again, I'd catch him watching her from afar. He seemed fascinated by her. You know, from a safe distance."

"You think he'd help her break out of jail?"

"Charlie? Shana? They've kept in touch?"

D.D. nearly said no, except that wasn't the truth. Charlie had written to Shana. Several times in the past three months. She'd never replied. That was the big deal, right? He'd written but she wouldn't answer his notes.

Unless that was somehow the code. No reply was a reply.

Because the truth of the matter was, there'd been a major change in Shana's life starting three months ago. And that had been Charlie Sgarzi, aka the Great Pretender, supposedly working on his book. What were the odds that Charlie's reappearance and Shana's disappearance weren't related?

"You think Charlie would help her?" D.D. repeated.

Hayes made a face. "The Shana I knew . . . She was crazy, and not in a good way. Whatever I might have thought about Charlie, he was never stupid. In fact, he was pretty fucking clever. So him, choosing to get involved with her . . . Nah, I don't see it. Then again, people change."

"Have you changed?"

Hayes nailed her with a look, gestured to the chair.

"I mean since that night, what did you learn?"

"Don't let your foster sister play with sharp objects."

"Mrs. Davies misses you."

Hayes squirmed, the guilty flush back on his face. "Are we done?"

"We're going to take your Harry Day gift package."

"Fuck!"

"But maybe, if we can corroborate your story, one day we'll give the items back."

"Nah." Hayes seemed to surprise even himself with his change of heart. "I don't want them. The money, sure. But the actual stuff . . . Harry Day hurt people, you know. Ruined lives. Destroyed families. And so did Shana. Mr. and Mrs. Davies, they were really good people. And after that . . . You're right; I should call Mrs. Davies more. I just . . . I never want to bother her, when, of course, the thing she likes best is to be bothered. Guess I didn't change. Thirty years later, I'm the same stupid shit."

D.D. didn't have anything to add to that.

She and Phil thanked Hayes for his time; then Phil collected the manila envelope and its enclosed documents. They gave Hayes the same spiel they'd given Mrs. Davies about keeping a low profile; then they were out the door.

"Charlie Sgarzi," Phil said, shaking his head as they quickly descended the stairs. "I don't get it. First he tells us he blames Shana for ruining his family. When in fact he was preying on his own cousin. Then he claims to be having a vigil at the MCI to hold Shana responsible for his mother's death, but a day later, returns to help break Shana out of prison? To what end . . . ? A better scene for his novel?"

"I don't understand Charlie's relationship with Shana any better than you do," D.D. assured him. "But as far as being the lead suspect for the Rose Killer murders . . . Forget some long-lost girl AnaRose Simmons or wheelchair-bound foster brother Samuel Hayes. Charlie Sgarzi's looking good to me."

"You understand that means he killed his own mom. The same son who slept on her sofa every night, brought her favorite soup, tended to her every need? This is our lead suspect?"

They had reached the bottom of the stairs, both of them panting lightly.

"It's because of his damn book," D.D. said. "This all started when Charlie decided to write an instant bestseller in order to support his mother. Except . . ." She touched her left shoulder gingerly, as a new idea suddenly occurred to her. "Holy shit, Phil, *we* are Charlie's novel! He's not writing about his cousin; that's yesterday's news, and what have the murderabilia websites taught us about old crimes? They don't pay nearly as well as nationally recognized murderers hot off the press. Hence, Charlie created the greatest New England predator since Harry Day: the Rose Killer. Guaranteed to terrify a population, capture major media attention and, one day soon, earn him that seven-figure advance for an insider's account of the murderer who slaughtered his own mom. Charlie isn't writing about Donnie and the old neighborhood anymore. He's writing about us."

Chapter 36

WE SHOULD'VE RETURNED to the safety of my condo, but we didn't. No one seemed to recognize Shana, and as darkness fell, we felt safer and safer with her new guise. On second thought, Shana wanted to try real pizza. I took her to the best dive I knew, where you could buy a slice the size of a football and the cheese hung down in gooey strings. At first, the kid behind the register was too shell-shocked by my mangled face to respond to our order. He stared at me, mouth slightly ajar.

Shana leaned in. She gave the kid a single hard look. He yelped slightly, rubbing his arms as if to ward off a chill, then jumped to it. He gave us both slices for free.

We ate them walking along the sidewalk, smearing pizza grease across our faces and feeling smug, as if we'd gotten away with something.

Shana declared it the best fucking pizza she'd ever had. She remembered other pies, from before. In prison, she often took out each memory of her life before incarceration, replaying each moment in her head like an old family video. Maybe that was why she forgot nothing. She had turned memory into an art form, serving as her own family album.

The hour passed five, daily commuters rushing to catch buses, subways, taxis, everyone bundled up against the bitter chill.

We steeled our shoulders against the evening's bite and soldiered on, not speaking, because that would make all of this too real and subject to doubts and anxiety and hesitation. Better to just be. Better, certainly, not to think of the hours ahead.

Can you pack a lifetime into a single afternoon? Remake a family, reforge old bonds?

I took Shana through Boston Common to the Public Garden, which was beautiful even this late in the fall. Like in the clothing store, she couldn't stop touching. The bark of a particularly majestic tree. The dangling fronds of a naked weeping willow. The prickly sticks on a border hedge. We stood on the bridge, watching tourists snap photos of the lake that in the spring would host the swan boats. Then we walked up Newbury Street, where Shana gawked at the store windows with their designer clothes and overpriced wares.

Her fingers were still flexing and unflexing at her sides, but she never slowed down, even as numerous pedestrians crashed against her, and at one point, she nearly became entangled in a dog leash. Her eyes remained fierce, drinking it all in. She reminded me of a hawk, not quite ready to take flight but already remembering the promise of open skies.

We roamed. Over to the Prudential Center, then, using the pedestrian bridge, into Copley Center. We went nowhere. We went everywhere.

And sometimes people stared at me, and sometimes people stared at her. But in the rush-hour frenzy no one looked too hard or for too long. My sister had been right in her instinct to get lost in the crowd. It was easier to hide in plain sight.

Shana told me stories of lousy prison food, guards who were actually nice, the joys of living with zero privacy and even less water pressure. But mostly she asked questions. About streetlights and fashion trends and what was with all the tiny cars that looked like you could fit them in a purse and who taught any of these people to drive anyway? She wanted to touch buildings. She wanted to stare at everything. She wanted to devour an entire city in thirty minutes or less.

My sister. The two of us, finally together again.

Six p.m. Air colder, sidewalks thinning slightly.

More pizza, my sister decided. This time, I ordered an entire pie, then a six-pack of beer. I carried the beer, Shana carted the pizza box, as I finally waved down a taxi, gave him the address for my building.

We didn't speak in the taxi. We didn't speak as we unloaded from the cab in front of my high-rise. Shana looked up, up, up, but she didn't say a word.

I saw a police cruiser parked on the corner, but no lights flashed on, no door popped open at the sight of me and a male colleague, clearly armed with dinner, heading into the building.

Maybe the cop thought I was smart to have a guy stay over for the night.

Who knows?

Mr. Daniels greeted us inside. He took one look at my red-scarred face, blanched and nearly stuttered.

I'd had a visitor, just an hour before.

"A Mr. Sgarzi. Charlie Sgarzi," Mr. Daniels provided anxiously.

Shana made a sound low in her throat. It might have been a growl.

Mr. Daniels shot her a nervous glance before continuing. "But I didn't let him up. I told him to leave his name and number, you would be in touch."

"But you told him I was out," I pointed out.

Mr. Daniels regarded me quizzically. "Well, I had to. He wanted to see you, and you weren't home."

I gave up on the matter, taking the note from Mr. Daniels and thanking him for his help.

In the elevator, Shana lurched awkwardly as the cable car began to move, then stood rooted in the middle, face pale as each floor rushed by. Upon reaching my floor, she was the first one out.

"Fast," she muttered. "Everything. So damn *fast*."

We reached the door of my unit. She stepped forward. I obediently fell back. Just like that. As if we'd been doing this for years.

Once inside, we set aside our dinner, then quickly searched the space. No sign of the Rose Killer. The surveillance equipment also remained intact, masking tape still in place.

"I'm going to need a knife," my sister said.

I led her into the kitchen, gestured to the butcher block.

She took her time selecting, not the largest blade, not the smallest, but the one that apparently felt exactly right. Then she pulled out the knife sharpener and set to work honing the edge of the blade.

This was it. Our moment was done. All the things we could've said. All the things we should've said. None of it mattered anymore. We were down to business.

Maybe my adoptive father had been right. I never should've opened that first letter so many years ago. I could've spent the rest of my life as Dr. Glen, never giving a thought to the Day family tree. Looking only forward, never back.

Shana shrugged out of her coat, opened the pizza box. Her blade of choice rested on the countertop beside her, within easy reach. I'd armed a serial killer, I dared myself to consider, but the thought remained vague, as if it applied to someone else. I'd broken the most notorious female murderer in the state out of prison. Then I'd brought her back to my apartment. A woman who could not bond and who was completely incapable of feeling empathy, love, remorse.

I touched my face with my bandaged left hand. Sensing the razor-thin lines I could not feel.

My sister. Who'd cut my face just so, staying true to her word. Who'd not bailed on me during those hours right after the breakout when she could've. Who, even now, ate pizza as if she hadn't a care in the world. She would take on another serial killer, she would protect her baby sister, because that's what she'd promised. To our father, forty years ago. To me, just this morning.

And I realized that all these years later, I still didn't know my sister at all, and yet, I knew her well enough. The nature of all families. The nature of each of us.

I reached across the counter. I squeezed Shana's hand.

And for one moment, my sister squeezed it back.

"Now what?" she asked, already helping herself to a second slice.

"Now," I said, "we wait."

Chapter 37

W<small>HAT DO WE KNOW</small> about Charlie Sgarzi?" D.D. thought out loud, as Phil drove them to the reporter's apartment. "He's a wannabe, the so-called Great Pretender. And what do we know about the Rose Killer? His murders feel less like crimes of the heart and more like staged productions. The deaths are almost too quick, while the post-mortem mutilation almost too shocking. Then there's the champagne and roses, which have never made any sense. More window dressing. Because all these years later, Charlie is still pretending. He's doing what he thinks a killer should do. Like a part he's researched for a play. Or a character in a novel."

Phil shot her a look. "He's become a serial killer to sell a book?"

"Sure. We know the murders are not motivated by obsession, compulsion or sexual sadist fantasies. Which pretty much leaves financial gain at the top of the list. How much you wanna bet, Charlie tried to shop around a book on his cousin's thirty-year-old murder, but no one was buying. Shana Day wasn't sexy enough. And Harry Day, her notorious father, was just plain forgotten."

Phil played along: "So Charlie concocts a killer operating in the style of Harry Day. Except, he can't manage the sexual-assault part, nor, apparently, stomach the kidnapping-and-torturing-for-days part. Leaves him with one signature element, removing human skin."

"Creepy enough to get the job done. And not being an experienced killer, he plays his odds. Ambushes sleeping women, chloroforms them to reduce any chance of struggle. Keeps it all straightforward. Because it's not about the killing. It's about the end game."

"His mom." Phil sighed heavily. "I mean, come on. Killing his own mom?"

"He had to."

"Why?"

"Because his mother's death removed him from being a suspect, while simultaneously giving him the insider's perspective for selling the novel. I was wrong about the inciting event for the Rose Killer. It wasn't Charlie investigating Donnie's murder. It was his mom getting terminal cancer. That brought him back to town, remember? Got him on this path of thinking about the past. Once he realized he couldn't sell novel A and started considering novel B . . . Well, by then his mother was pretty near the end, right? You saw her. And frankly, compared to what the cancer was doing to her, the days, even weeks, she had left, I bet Charlie convinced himself the Rose Killer's method was kinder. She'd never feel a thing. But doing the deed was still harder than he'd anticipated. The hesitation marks, remember? For all of his planning, some things were easier said than done."

Phil grimaced, clearly not loving the theory, but no longer arguing. "And you? You don't even know Charlie Sgarzi. Why shove you down the stairs?"

"Like we thought, I must've caught him off guard. He returned to what appeared to be a vacated crime scene and ended up coming face-to-face with a homicide detective. Split-second decision, he shoves me down a flight of stairs. Then probably ran the hell out of there, grateful to have gotten away with it. Except, like you and Alex said, I came back. Started hunting again, which I'd like to think scared him, but most likely got him thinking, too. What does every villain need? An archnemesis. And planned or not, the Rose Killer now had one. Scary for him as the killer, exciting for him as a future bestselling author.

Another reason to egg me on with a personal note left in my house; Charlie's earning a larger book advance by the minute."

Phil grunted. "And helping Shana escape?"

"That I don't understand."

"Finally, an honest answer." He rolled his eyes.

"It's Sam Hayes that seals the deal," D.D. informed him impatiently. "How else do you explain the materials from Harry Day appearing on his doorstep? Charlie placed them there in order to position Hayes as the red herring. Or maybe, if Hayes hadn't fallen off the ladder and injured his back, the lead suspect. But again, every great drama needs suspects. So Charlie created one: Samuel Hayes, who once upon a time had a relationship with Shana Day and now has her father's personal documents in his possession. Looks guiltier by the minute, right? Especially when all Samuel can say is that he *found* the items. Come on."

"But Hayes is crippled," Phil rebutted. "Makes him a piss-poor prime suspect."

"Ah, but his injury is recent, and according to Hayes, he received the materials *before* he fell off the ladder. In fact, the envelope would've arrived shortly after the Rose Killer's first victim."

Phil scowled. She was winning; she could feel it.

"And Dr. Adeline Glen?" Phil prompted. "The Rose Killer has been stalking her, too. We assumed as a fan, but under your theory . . . ?"

D.D. considered it. "The crescendo," she murmured. "Because this game can't go on forever, and the Rose Killer must end on a high note. By killing the daughter of his idol. The bloody finale."

"Then what? The Rose Killer simply disappears? Never to kill again?" Phil wrinkled his nose. "Pretty disappointing, if you ask me. In real life, and in a book."

"You're right: The case demands resolution. Otherwise, Charlie won't be able to get quotes from the detectives involved, let alone clearance for publication. For Charlie's plan to work, the Rose Killer must end up caught. But how . . ." D.D. rubbed her temple, starting to feel the beginning of a headache.

"Charlie plans on surrendering?" Phil asked. "Wait, that won't work, either. Killers can't profit from their crimes. We nail Charlie as the Rose Killer, Charlie's publishing career is over."

"Sacrificial lamb," D.D. deduced. "Only way it could work. Charlie frames someone else for the murder. Hell, maybe that was why he brought in Samuel Hayes. Charlie would kill Dr. Glen, then return to Hayes's apartment and ambush him with chloroform. Once Hayes was unconscious, Charlie could hide the murder kit in the apartment, maybe even forge a suicide note, then load Hayes into the tub."

"The tub? Why the tub?"

They were almost at Charlie's apartment now. D.D. talked faster.

"Because that's how Harry Day died, remember? Slit wrists in a bathtub. A fitting end to a fitting criminal career. Wraps up the case, launches Charlie's publishing empire. Five, six months from now, Charlie's signed a major publishing deal while making the talk-show-circuit rounds. Maybe he even goes on to score his own show, à la Nancy Grace or John Walsh. Fortune and fame. What more could a Great Pretender ask for?"

"Samuel Hayes to have not fallen off a ladder."

"Details, details."

Phil pulled up just down from Sgarzi's apartment building. D.D. immediately popped open her door. She wasn't feeling her shoulder or Melvin or her headache anymore. She was feeling anticipation and excitement and adrenaline. She was feeling everything she loved best about this job.

"Wait."

Phil's firm tone brought her up short. "Stay," he ordered. "No way you're going to confront a possible triple murderer, D.D. You're not even on the job. Let alone, if anything happened . . . Alex will kill me."

"Alex won't kill you," she argued reasonably. "He'll just process the scene of your death very sloppily."

"D.D."

"Phil."

"D.D."

"No. I'm not staying in the car like a helpless puppy. We're partners. You've always had my back; I've always had yours. Now, give me the thirty-eight I know you keep in your glove compartment. In case of emergency, that'll be enough for me to get the job done, one-handed or not. Besides, there's no reason for us to get ahead of ourselves."

"What do you mean?"

"We play Charlie like we did Hayes. We're not here to accuse him of being the Rose Killer; we're here to talk to him about Shana's escape. His safety and security is our primary concern. We're the good guys, his bestest buds. And hey, as long as we're here, let's walk around, check out the locks on the windows, take a peek at anything we can spy in plain sight."

She could tell Phil still didn't like it. But they had been together forever, mostly because Phil had never been good at telling her no.

He took the lead. She followed him up, obediently staying two steps behind.

They were both out of breath by the time they arrived at the door of the walk-up unit. Phil once more motioned for her to step to the side. She made a show of acquiescing. In the end, however, it was all for nothing. Phil knocked and knocked, but Charlie never came to the door.

Chapter 38

THE PIZZA DIDN'T SETTLE WELL. I'd consumed only one slice, accompanied by a single beer, but now I could feel it like a brick in the bottom of my stomach. I shifted restlessly in the kitchen, acutely aware of my growing nausea, as well as a slow, crushing level of fatigue.

The events of the day finally catching up. The inevitable crash that followed any adrenaline rush.

Across from me, I could tell Shana felt equally uneasy. She'd eaten most of the pizza, a choice I could tell from her expression she now regretted. She'd also opened a beer, but it remained only half-consumed. She was nursing it with greater self-restraint than I would've imagined. Fourteen-year-old Shana had probably downed entire kegs. Her forty-four-year-old counterpart had finally learned patience and discipline.

Either that, or she really was worried she was going to vomit.

Shana rubbed her temples. She stood abruptly, the sudden change in equilibrium making her sway on her feet.

"Come on," she said thickly. "Let's tend to your wounds."

She headed for the master bath. I followed in her wake, barely summoning the energy to walk. I should put on a pot of coffee. At this rate, we'd be hard-pressed to keep our eyes open long enough to confront a killer.

In the master bath, I got down my daily medical kit, while Shana roamed her hands over the marble countertop, the sleek stainless steel fixtures. The walk-in shower, with its four shiny nozzles, fascinated her. But what she returned to again and again was the sensuously shaped soaking tub. Her fingers, dancing along the polished edges, following the line that dipped down the middle, then back up at both ends.

"Not like Mom and Dad's," was all she said.

With my bandaged left hand, I couldn't open the antiseptic wipes. Shana did the honors. She carefully swabbed each cloth over the myriad of angry red lines marring my face. The doctors were concerned about my risk of infection, given that I wouldn't feel the accompanying pain. I hadn't had the heart to tell them it didn't matter, just as I hadn't the heart to stop my sister's ministrations.

"It doesn't hurt?"

"No."

"What's that like?"

"I don't really know. I have nothing to compare it to."

She unwrapped my left hand. Beneath the mitt of gauze, my index finger was encased in its own special plastic shield. Shana didn't bother removing the protective tip, tending to the other cuts on my hand instead.

When she was done, she picked up the gauze, but I shook my head. I didn't want to be rewrapped like an Egyptian mummy. I wanted to lie down, curl into a ball and sleep.

My head felt so heavy. My limbs as well.

I was going to make something, I thought. Do something in the kitchen, but now I couldn't remember. My thoughts kept floating away, harder and harder to corral.

Beside me, Shana swayed on her feet, her gaze once more locked longingly on the pedestal-mounted tub. . . .

My phone rang.

The noise shrieked through the condo, momentarily penetrating my stupor.

With effort, I retreated from the bathroom into the bedroom, where I picked up the cordless phone from the nightstand.

"Dr. Glen?" Charlie Sgarzi's voice came over the line.

I nodded before remembering he couldn't see me. "Yes," I murmured, licking my lips.

"Are you okay? You sound funny."

"Just . . . tired."

"Yeah. Well, it's been a rough day. I gotta say, Shana's escape has left me rattled. I don't feel like I can go home, but I don't have anywhere else to go, either. I wondered if, you know, maybe you'd meet with me. We could keep each other company, compare notes. Two heads being better than one, and all that."

"No . . . thank you."

"I could come to your building if you'd like. But not your apartment," he added hastily. "I mean, unless you preferred me to. But we could just sit in your lobby. There's gotta be cop cars outside, right? That'll be good. Extra guards."

I rubbed my temples. Not sure why. Maybe to ease the cotton that seemed to be filling my ears, stuffing my head. Say the word *no*, I tried to tell myself. But my lips wouldn't move. No word came out.

I stood there, holding the phone and swaying on my feet. And finally, deep down in the last vestiges of my consciousness, I felt the first prickle of fear. That this was more than greasy pizza and the aftereffects of a trying day.

What I was feeling, what my sister was feeling, was far, far worse. Especially given the Rose Killer's penchant for attacking unconscious women . . .

A noise from the bathroom. A clatter. Like my sister had suddenly fallen to the floor.

At the last moment, I got it. I looked up to the corner of my bedroom ceiling where the carbon monoxide alarm should've been. Except it wasn't there anymore. It had been removed by the Rose Killer, most likely right after he tampered with my heating units and began the process of poisoning me.

Window. If I could get to a window. Crack it open. Get my head out.

But my legs wouldn't respond. Slowly but surely, I crumpled to the floor.

"Dr. Glen?" Charlie's voice over the phone, which had landed next to my face.

I stared at it. Willed myself to whisper *help*. But all that came out was a sigh.

"Are you okay?"

My eyes drifting shut.

"Dr. Glen?"

Call the police, I tried to say. But the words didn't come out.

I became aware of a new sound.

The bolt lock on my front door sliding smoothly open, by a person who very clearly had a key. Then the knob turning. Door opening.

The police didn't matter anymore.

The Rose Killer was already here.

Chapter 39

I<small>T TOOK</small> D.D. <small>A BIT</small> to find the building superintendent for Charlie's apartment. The older man, hunch shouldered, heavyset, worked a long string of keys before selecting the magic implement.

"We're worried about Charlie's safety," D.D. made a big show of telling the man. "We have reason to believe he's in immediate danger. We just want to ensure he's okay."

Judging by the look on the building super's face, he couldn't have cared less why they were entering his tenant's rental and whether or not they had probable cause. But D.D. and Phil went through the motions of laying the groundwork for their case anyway. Just in case.

Once the door was open, the super backed off. Work to do, he informed them gruffly; shut the door behind themselves when they were done. Then he was off, and Phil and D.D. stood alone in the middle of Charlie's bachelor pad.

"Got a call while you were out," Phil told her, the moment the super was out of sight. "A guy came forward about thirty minutes ago, said he picked Shana up on the highway. It appeared to him that her car had broken down. Given the high-end vehicle, the fancy clothes, it never occurred to him she might be an escaped convict. Not to mention, at that point, there'd been nothing in the news."

"A guy? A random guy?"

"Salesman. On his way to a conference in Boston. Said he let her out at Fanueil Hall. She told him she could walk to her place from there."

D.D. frowned. It was full dark outside, casting shadows all around Charlie's empty unit. It was past dinnertime. Long after she should've been home from this morning's adventure. Her shoulder throbbed again, as well as her sense of foreboding. They were close. At that pivotal moment right before a case finally snapped together or irrevocably fell apart. So which was it? Because they didn't have much time left.

"The Rose Killer didn't help Shana escape?" she reiterated, still studying the apartment, willing it to show them what they needed to know.

"Apparently not."

"Then who set the firecrackers that created the initial diversion?"

"Investigative team is still working on it."

"I can't believe Shana's escape is not connected to the Rose Killer," D.D. said flatly. "Those two things have to be related."

"I'm not disagreeing." Phil swept his hand around the living room. "Meaning there's something here we're not seeing, and we'd better figure it out. Quick."

He snapped on the overhead light, and they got to it. D.D. started with the double row of bookshelves behind the sofa. Phil, being the computer guru, took a seat in front of the TV tray bearing Sgarzi's laptop. D.D. found four rows of true-crime novels, including nearly the entire Ann Rule library.

"He was definitely researching the genre," she commented, flipping through titles such as *The Stranger Beside Me* and *Green River, Running Red*. Next she came across half a dozen books on writing. Then, more disturbingly, three hardcover homicide textbooks, all of which promised genuine crime scene photos.

D.D. flipped open one of the textbooks to a yellow-flagged page. "Postmortem Mutilation," read the chapter head. All righty then.

"D.D."

She put the book down, crossed over to where Phil was currently glued to Sgarzi's computer screen.

"Video files," he informed her. "Looks like from some kind of low-rent surveillance cameras, over-the-counter crap. There's dozens of digital images, going back four to five months. All unlabeled."

"Open the most recent."

He shot her a look. "You think?"

She smiled at her computer-whiz partner, who was now working the mouse. She picked up the yellow legal pad sitting next to the computer.

Who am I? Charlie had scrawled across the top of the page. *Good neighbor, helpful journalist.*

What do I look like? Upscale professional, blends in on the elevator, nothing to look at here.

Primary motivation? Concern for her safety, just trying to help.

Purpose of operation: Saving the best for last; Harry Day's daughter, Shana Day's one weakness, now my final prey. Because I am not like you and you are not like me. I am better. Always have been.

Net gain: Resolution. Winner takes all.

"D.D." Phil's voice intruding, low and urgent.

D.D. glanced up. Phil had been forwarding through the black-and-white video file. A still shot of what appeared to be a clothes-filled closet. Except now the door was opening. The head and shoulders of a woman appeared.

Dr. Adeline Glen, walking toward the cameras.

Abruptly staring straight at them.

A white piece of tape appeared in her hands. Then the screen went blank.

"She found it," Phil murmured.

"She taped over the lens! What time? What time?"

"I don't know." Phil started scrolling around. "I found a date stamp, but no time. The date, however, was . . . yesterday."

D.D. stilled, feeling suddenly blindsided. "But Adeline was with us most of yesterday. Meaning it had to be after she returned home. Sometime last night. She searched her apartment, discovered a surveillance camera in her own bedroom and . . . *didn't* call us for help?"

Phil looked up at her. "That doesn't sound good."

It didn't, and then, in the next instant . . . D.D. closed her eyes. She got it. What they hadn't known, the missing piece of the puzzle, what they'd had to come here to find. "Adeline did it," she murmured. "Adeline is the one who created the diversion in the prison parking lot. She tossed the firecrackers under the vehicle right before walking in. The timing would fit."

"She broke her own sister out of prison?" Phil asked, voice incredulous. "Agreed to have her own face mutilated?"

"She can't feel pain, remember? But she can feel fear." D.D. tapped the monitor, the frozen video frame. "She must've known it was the Rose Killer who was watching her. Had even been watching her for months now. If she called us, what would we do?"

"Offer police protection," Phil said immediately.

"Which we'd already offered and she'd already declined. Whereas, if she negotiates some kind of deal with her sister . . ."

"I'll free you from prison in return for you taking on my serial-killer stalker," Phil provided.

"Shana won't just protect Adeline. She'll end this game once and for all. What did Adeline tell us that day? This is what Shana does best."

Phil pushed back his chair. Without another word, they headed straight for Adeline's condo.

Thirty minutes and counting.

Chapter 40

I WATCHED THE FRONT DOOR of my condo open. Sprawled on the bedroom floor, I couldn't move a muscle to respond. My eyelids were heavy, my skin clammy, while my stomach continued to roll queasily. Flu-like symptoms, except it wasn't the flu. It was carbon monoxide poisoning.

Charlie Sgarzi strode into my apartment. He no longer wore his oversize trench coat. Instead, he was clad in well-tailored tan slacks, a button-down pin-striped shirt. He looked both smaller and sleeker. Less a caricature, more a focused predator, finally moving in for the kill.

On his face he wore a mask that covered his mouth and nose. He also carried with him a dark-green duffel bag that contained items I knew too much about. Especially the surgical-grade scalpel and the mason jar already prepared with formaldehyde.

After closing and securing the front door behind him, Charlie slipped the copy of the key he'd obviously made for my condo back into his pants pocket.

Then he came to me.

"Paul Donabedian," he announced, his voice muffled through the mask. He stuck out his hand. "Pleased to meet you. I rented a unit in this building two months ago. Gives me plenty of reason to enter and exit without arousing suspicion. And once a person is past the doorman, well, no one's watching anymore, right? I've been taking the stairs up to your condo for weeks, scoping out the unit, making a master key, then, of course, installing my little cameras. But you found them, didn't you, Adeline? Had a little snit and taped my lenses. As if such a thing would really stop me."

He stepped over my body. I should move. Roll over, lash out at him. Or at least stumble for the door. My chest felt unbearably tight. A sense of building pressure as my lungs fought with increasing desperation for oxygen.

Charlie set down his duffel bag on the bed. Then he crossed to the electric heating unit next to the bed, reaching behind it to flip the kill switch. Next, he opened the two windows set on the far side of the room, airing out the space.

I willed my lungs to expand, to inhale the first tendrils of fresh air. But the windows were too far away. Or I was already too far gone.

"Don't want the carbon monoxide levels to be too high," Charlie stated. "Might affect me, too. Not sure, really, how good these masks are. Besides, removing the obvious carbon monoxide levels will make things more interesting for the investigating officers. A renowned doctor, intelligent, insightful, forewarned, a woman who really should've known better, still found murdered in her own bedroom. Think of the drama of such a scene. Readers will go nuts."

He returned to his duffel bag. Unzipped.

On my right hand, my fingers twitched. Signs of life. Or simply the beginnings of a seizure due to my oxygen-starved brain?

"You should feel privileged, Adeline. I saved the best for last. The first two women were specially selected, of course. But what I loved most about them was that they lived alone, they were attractive and they made for great victims. I mean, ugly women, unsympathetic characters no one cares about. But two pretty females with good jobs, caring friends and supportive families—that grabs headlines. That sells books.

"I think your father thought the same. You ever study the full photo gallery of his victims? Not a fugly among them. He had good taste. As the soon-to-be bestselling author of his biography, I've done my best to follow in his footsteps. Except I don't have the luxury of my own home with a private workshop or loose floorboards, of course. Apartment living in Boston has its downfalls."

He pulled on latex gloves. Then drew out a small, clear glass bottle. Chloroform. In case the carbon monoxide poisoning wore off. In case I attempted to put up a fight.

I strained for sounds from the adjoining master bath. Shana. He didn't seem to know she was here. If she regained consciousness, still had her knife . . .

"Now," Charlie said briskly. "I need you to do something for me, Adeline. This case needs to wrap up tonight. Things are getting too hot, what with the intense police investigation, not to mention your sister having flown the coop. Otherwise I might have played things out for maximum tension, but then again . . . No need to take unnecessary risks. I've brought a few pieces of hair with me, generously donated by Sam Hayes, whether he knows it or not.

"I need you to, um . . . place them down there. You know. Then later, when the ME examines your body, he will comb them out. DNA matching will lead them to Sam's apartment, where it turns out he lives all by his lonesome, with no one to provide a solid alibi. He also happens to be the proud owner of some priceless Harry Day memorabilia. If the police can't build a definitive case out of that, I don't know why I've even bothered."

Charlie withdrew a ziplock bag. With his gloved hands, he opened it, removing two short brown hairs. He bent over me, peering into my glassy eyes, my torn-up skin.

"Wow, look at you. Always knew Shana was a bitch. Still, to tear apart her own sister . . ." He clucked his tongue, then pressed the strands of hair into my open right hand, folding my fingers around them.

"She didn't . . . do it," I heard myself whisper.

"Your face?"

"Your cousin."

He froze. His expression changed, and with it, so did his demeanor. Professional, composed Paul Donabedian was gone. Like a chameleon morphing, Charlie Sgarzi took over his place, his eyes suddenly hooded, faintly menacing. All these years later, still most comfortable in his role of neighborhood thug.

"Don't talk to me about Donnie," he growled.

"You killed him."

He glared at me.

"Accident? He wanted . . . you to stop."

"We were wrestling. Just wrestling!"

"Shana found you. Bending over him. Knee on his chest? Hands around his throat?"

"Shut up!"

"You . . . killed him. But she . . . went crazy. Grabbed the switchblade. You ran. She fell on Donnie instead."

"She hacked off his ear!"

"She . . . covered . . . your crime."

"Girl was fucking nuts."

"Psychotic episode. You broke her. And no one . . ." My lungs finally expanded. A short tease of fresh air, wafting across my nose. I nearly sighed with pleasure. "No one was there . . . to put her . . . together again."

"What's done is done. I learned my lesson. Got out of Dodge. Went to New York and made something out of myself."

"Charlie," I murmured.

"Fuck off!"

"I used to study people . . . trying to understand how they experienced pain. But you must study them for . . . everything. Any kind of emotion. You . . . have none of your own."

"Well, let's hope I can fake success well enough, because by tomorrow morning, every news show is gonna want to interview me. How I survived my mother's murder at the hands of the recently discovered Rose Killer. How your family, for the record, basically cost me everything. But those who taketh can also giveth back. I'm the foremost expert on Harry Day, not to mention the Rose Killer. First thing tomorrow, I'm getting in front of those cameras and I'm owning this case. Book deals, TV appearance fees, film rights. Mine. All mine. No more pretending for me. I'll have it all, once and for all."

"Your mother . . ."

"She was dying!" Charlie roared. "Did you see what the cancer had done to her? Did you? Worst fucking killer there is. I drugged her tea. She went to sleep. Thank God for small mercies."

More air, creeping in, slowly but steadily. Could it reach down the short hallway into the master bath? Would it find my sister?

Charlie ripped off his mask, apparently confident in the air quality now, as well as impatient to get on with the main event. "Hair samples. Tuck 'em down your pants. Do it."

I kept my bleary gaze on his. "She loved you."

He frowned at me. "Course. I was a good son. I took care of her."

"After killing her nephew . . . destroying her sister."

"I didn't mean—"

"Long hair. Did you have long hair?"

"What?" He startled, blinking at me. I inhaled another deep breath.

"Did you . . . have long hair?"

"I had a mullet. It was the eighties. Why?"

I smiled. "You looked like a girl . . . from behind. That's what Shana saw. Our mother bending over our father. I knew it."

"You're as nuts as she is."

A new voice sounded. Quiet. Menacing. Pure Shana. "But not nearly so dangerous."

CHARLIE WENT FOR HIS DUFFEL BAG. The scalpel most likely. But then his hand found the small bottle of chloroform. Without a second thought, he smashed it into the waiting rag, then grabbed the whole pile and slammed his fist toward Shana's head.

He caught her in the side. The carbon monoxide still poisoning her system had dulled her reflexes. She staggered, went down on one knee. He seized the opportunity to grind the glass- and chloroform-drenched rag into her face.

His ferocity surprised me. I could tell from Shana's face, his sure-footed attack had caught her off guard as well. Maybe once upon a time Charlie had been an aspiring thug, but sometime in the past thirty years he'd transitioned to the real deal.

I worked on rolling to my knees. Time to get up, time to help out.

But I'd gone down in the bedroom, closer to the tampered-with electrical unit, where no doubt the density of carbon monoxide was higher. I couldn't seem to get my feet beneath me, to rise to standing.

I looked over in time to watch my sister grab Charlie's crotch with her right hand. She twisted. He howled, releasing the rag with one hand, as he instinctively cupped himself with his other. One knee down. Then he snarled and popped Shana in the nose. Her head snapped back. I heard a crunching sound, most likely her nose exploding. But she recovered quickly, going for his throat, her fingers squeezed together to form a human blade.

Up, up. Come on, Adeline, time to stand up.

Shana hit him. Three, four times. Her speed seemed to be returning, her system clearing. But she remained a bantamweight, a thin, wiry female taking on a larger, stronger male.

Charlie nailed her hard. Jab, jab, uppercut. She stumbled back; then he slugged her again in the eye, hard, fierce shots. A man who'd clearly spent some time in a boxing ring. A man who relished pain.

Scalpel. In the duffel bag. On my feet now. I found it. Hair strands fell to the floor. Smooth silver handle took their place.

One step forward, then another, the blade held tightly at my side.

Shana trapped in a corner, Charlie pounding on her mercilessly. She didn't appear desperate, however. In the spare moments when I could see her face, I saw nothing but pure determination. She'd come to kill this man. And apparently, she wasn't stopping till she died trying.

Charlie didn't notice me. Locked on my sister, grunting with the force behind each explosive blow, he existed in his own world. One where he was finally strong enough, smart enough, tough enough, to take down the legendary Shana Day.

Another step, then I stood directly behind him. Scalpel raised. One last breath:

I am my father. I am my mother.

I am the family conscience.

I drove the scalpel down between his shoulders, severing muscles, nerves, tendons. Calling upon four years of medical school to pick my mark with expert care, so that the blade slipped deep between the vertebrae, where I then twisted it for maximum damage.

Charlie's body sagged. His head turned slightly, and I could see his stunned expression. He opened his mouth as if to howl.

But no sound ever came out. Shana wrenched the scalpel from his back and, in one smooth move, sliced it across his exposed throat.

Charlie Sgarzi fell forward. My sister stepped out of the way.

Just as knocking came on the front door.

"POLICE!" PHIL CRIED OUT. "Dr. Glen, this is Detective Phil. Can you hear me?"

Shana and I looked at each other. Neither of us said a word.

"Adeline." A different voice. D. D. Warren's. "Are you okay? Your neighbors have reported sounds of a disturbance. Adeline, open the door if you can. We need to confirm you're all right."

My sister and I still looking at each other.

A fresh sound. Louder. Most likely Detective Phil, testing his shoulder against the door.

"They'll get the building manager," I informed Shana quietly. "He'll let them in."

"How long?"

"Five, ten minutes."

"Long enough," she said, and I knew what she meant. I had made a promise to her this morning in the prison interview room. Now it was time for me to deliver.

We didn't talk. We walked to the bathroom together, Shana already shedding clothes as she went. The aspirin was still out, part of the medical kit sitting on the counter. I handed her four tablets. She swallowed them as a single fistful.

Then her fingers, running so lovingly around the tub. As I turned on the first faucet, then the second.

She didn't wait for the water to achieve perfect temperature. Naked, her body a mess of long, roping scars and short, crisscrossed marks, she climbed in.

"I can't go back," she said.

I nodded. Because I'd known; I'd always known. What was the one thing my sister craved most after all these years? Freedom. Complete and total freedom. The kind that came only with death.

"You didn't kill Donnie," I told her, because I didn't know if she even knew.

She shrugged, leaning her head back against the smooth white porcelain. "Hardly seems to matter."

I could hear banging again. Phil trying to break down the door, no doubt while D.D. went in search of the building manager. I walked to the bathroom door. Shut it, locked it. Not the sturdiest door in the world, but at this stage, it was simply a matter of buying time.

"Were you in love with Charlie?" I asked my sister curiously. "Is that why you gave him some things from Dad? The items I guess he gave to Samuel Hayes."

"Didn't give him anything from Dad. But we talked about . . . from time to time. I knew he was different. He could fool others. But never me. A beast always recognizes another beast." She sighed heavily. "I had a box with Dad's stuff. Kept it under my bed. Maybe

Charlie took it afterward. I never thought to ask about my personal possessions after I was arrested. I never woulda been allowed to have 'em anyway."

"But did you love him?"

She looked at me, her nose smashed, her eyes already swelling shut, her face a pulpy mess.

"Adeline," she said seriously, "I don't feel things like love. I can hate. And I can hurt. All the rest is a mystery to me."

The water was up to her waist now. She reached down to the floor, picked up the knife she'd carefully selected and sharpened just hours ago.

"That's not true," I told her. "You love me."

"But you are my sister," she said, as if that should explain everything.

No more pounding. My condo, so quiet, as my sister handed the knife to me.

"I don't know how."

"Nothing to it."

"Please . . ."

But my sister simply stared at me. Her last request, my one promise, as she lifted her pale forearm and held it out to me. This close, I could see thin white lines from previous blades. Like a road map, showing the way.

"Remember what I told you," she said gruffly. "The instructions he gave to Mom. How to do it right."

I remembered.

I found a thin blue vein, once again, picking my spot with care. Then, slicing down, slow and steady, while my sister's arm trembled beneath me.

She sighed. Not even a gasp, but a genuine sigh, as if more than her blood was leaving her body. Maybe her rage. Maybe her pain. Maybe all those terrible appetites and horrible desires our father had beaten into her when she'd been too young to defend herself but still old enough to know better.

She raised her second arm. And I cut it, too. Then both arms slid down, into the bathtub, already turning pink as her life bled out into the water.

"I love you," I whispered.

"She didn't tell him that," Shana mumbled. "Mom. Dad. She never loved him. But I did. But I did. . . ."

Her eyes drifted shut. Her head lolled back.

More sounds now. Knocking, pounding, Detective Phil shouting a final warning.

I checked my sister's pulse. She was gone. No more prison cells for Shana Day. No more days left to dread. No more lives left to ruin.

One last task. I crossed to the bathroom door. Unlocked it. Least I could do given the state of D.D.'s shoulder.

Then, shedding my own clothes. Removing the silk bathrobe that hung on a hook near the tub.

I took up position next to my sister's body, studying first the blade, then my own smooth white forearm.

My fingers trembled. Funny for a woman who couldn't feel pain. Who would've thought?

And then . . .

Chapter 41

D.D. AND PHIL BURST INTO THE APARTMENT, guns drawn, Phil taking the lead, D.D. flanking him, her injured shoulder tucked protectively behind his form. The apartment manager was already fleeing down the hall. Hightailing it downstairs, where backup would quickly be arriving, as well as the SWAT team and any available officer in Boston.

First thing D.D. noticed was the stench of blood. Second thing she spotted was a green duffel bag on the edge of a king-size bed, in the room straight ahead.

"Bedroom," she mouthed to Phil.

He nodded shortly, easing his back against the wall, then making a rapid advance.

"Jesus."

Stepping around his shoulder, she spied Charlie Sgarzi facedown in a pool of blood. Whatever had happened in here, it certainly hadn't gone according to the Rose Killer's master plan.

Phil inspected the body more closely, then shook his head.

"Slit throat," he whispered.

D.D. arched a brow. "You tell me, but doesn't that strike you as Shana's handiwork?"

Phil grimaced, arriving at the same conclusion. Shana Day, one of the most notorious female murderers in the state, had to be somewhere in this apartment, along with her sister, Adeline.

Now Phil gestured to a short hallway with two closed doors. He took the first, D.D. doing her best to provide cover with her one good hand.

Phil kicked in the door, revealing the walk-in closet. He conducted a quick search, covering the corners; then they were on to door number two. Master bath, D.D. thought. From inside, she could hear the sound of running water.

Phil tested the knob.

He gave a short nod to indicate that it was unlocked.

She resumed her flanking position.

Phil twisted the knob. Shoved hard on the door.

D.D. sprang inside, leading with Phil's backup thirty-eight.

And there stood Adeline next to a bloody tub, a knife already arching over her bared wrist.

"No," Phil yelled.

D.D. didn't bother. Adrenaline. Danger. Determination. Everything she loved about her job.

D.D. pulled the trigger.

THE KNIFE WENT FLYING across the room. Not a bad shot, single-handed, D.D. thought, though in truth, her target had been only five feet away.

The knife hit the floor. Phil was already on the move, kicking it farther away from Adeline.

The doctor didn't move. She just stood there, surrounded by a sea of water and blood, and smiled at them.

"You didn't have to do that," she murmured.

"Don't be ridiculous," D.D. snapped, straightening. Looking behind Adeline, she could see a second female collapsed in the rosy tub. Shana.

"Slit her wrists," Adeline said, a statement, not a question. "The price for her help. She's already gone. I checked before unlocking the door."

"Taking up where your family left off?" D.D. asked harshly. She was pissed off. She wasn't sure why. The Rose Killer was dead, Shana Day clearly beyond help. The worst was over, and yet D.D.'s heart was still pounding, and she felt furious about the whole damn thing.

Standing before her, Adeline swayed slightly. The shock, adrenaline crash. The doctor placed a steadying hand on the edge of the tub. "Charlie killed those women," she whispered.

"We know."

"You'll find hair. In my bedroom. Samuel Hayes. But not his fault. Charlie brought the strands to incriminate him."

"We know that, too. Charlie targeted Hayes to be his fall guy. Except then Hayes literally fell. Off a ladder. Guy's wheelchair bound. No way he did this."

Adeline smiled wanly. "Good. In my closet, behind the bureau, in a cutout in the floor . . . Charlie left behind mason jars. Victims' skin. Trying to mess . . . with my head. It worked."

"For God's sake, sit down!" D.D.'s temper broke. "Seriously, Adeline. If you'd simply told us when you'd discovered the video cameras . . . Instead, you broke your sister out of prison, putting yourself, not to mention the whole fucking state, in danger. When, if you'd just given us twenty-four more hours . . . We figured it out. Everything that happened thirty years ago, let alone what Charlie has been doing now. The whos, the whats, the whys, the hows; we know it all. You didn't have to do this, Adeline. You didn't."

"But I did."

"Adeline." D.D.'s gaze narrowed. Beside her, she could sense Phil's growing concern. The doctor's face was very pale. Dangerously pale.

"Please tell Superintendent McKinnon I'm sorry."

"Self-defense," D.D. muttered. "Mitigating circumstances, your own psychotic break. Plenty of ways to justify what happened today." She took a step closer to Adeline. Then another, searching for marks on the doctor's exposed wrists. "What matters is that Charlie is dead, and your sister can't hurt anyone anymore. Adeline? Adeline?"

The woman went down. Sank, really, to her knees. D.D. shot forward, trying to grab Adeline's shoulder with her right hand, but the floor was too slippery. She didn't catch the doctor as much as help ease her down, half-propped against the tub. In a pool of blood. So much blood, especially considering Shana's slit wrists were inside the bathtub . . .

D.D. closed her eyes. "Oh, Adeline. What did you do?"

"What I had to. There isn't enough nurture to overcome this nature, D.D. Just ask my adoptive father. He tried so hard, and still . . . here I am."

Adeline had slashed her upper thighs. Going after her wrists had merely been act two. No, the main event had already happened before D.D. and Phil had burst through the door. Another move Adeline had stolen from her sister's playbook.

"Adeline—"

"Shhh. All is as it should be."

"You're not your sister, dammit! You're a good doctor. You help people. You helped me!"

Phil was on the radio now, requesting immediate medical assistance, but they wouldn't be in time. Just like the SWAT team and backup. Everyone pouring in the building, charging up the stairs, storming into the unit.

All of them, each and every one of them, too late. Just as D.D. and Phil had been. Too late.

Phil was yanking down towels. D.D. ignored Adeline's protest, ripping open the front of her robe to expose her gashed upper thighs. The femoral artery. Jesus. She couldn't believe the woman had lasted this long.

Phil handed over more towels and she piled them on the wounds, pressing hard, her face so close to Adeline's she could already feel the cool pallor of the woman's bloodless skin.

"Hang on," D.D. gasped. "Come on, Adeline. Fight for me, okay. You and me, taking on the Melvins of the world. It doesn't have to be like this. It never had to be like this."

Adeline's hand moved against her. To help, to hinder? Instead, her cold fingers brushed against the back of D.D.'s hand.

"Hold . . . my hand?"

D.D. didn't want to. She had to apply pressure. She had to fix this mess, heal these wounds. She had to save this woman because she was strong and intelligent and . . . and . . .

"Shit!"

She couldn't do this. Adeline was dying. Really, already gone, and D.D. wanted so badly . . .

Phil nudged her aside. He took over pressing against the towels. They weren't even that bloody because most had already drained out, onto the floor.

D.D. picked up Adeline's hand. She cradled it on her lap.

Behind her, the SWAT team finally burst through the door in a stampede of pounding footsteps.

Adeline smiled, as if at a joke only she understood. Her eyelids fluttered down.

"It's okay," she whispered. "Where I'm going . . ."

She squeezed D.D.'s hand one last time.

And then she was gone.

Epilogue

Dear Detective Warren:
If you're reading this, then the worst has come to pass.

The service was small, but that wasn't really a surprise. Dr. Adeline Glen had lived a very private life. Upon her passing, there was only a handful of colleagues, a prison superintendent and a couple of Boston cops to bid her good-bye.

Alex had come with D.D. Phil as well. They huddled off to one side, a somber trio, listening to a minister's highly impersonal service, before the casket was lowered and the first clod of earth followed.

I'm sorry I didn't tell you more. About the cameras,
the mason jars, the final twenty-four hours when I
realized what the Rose Killer was planning, but also what
I was capable of as well.
As we discussed, everyone has triggers. It turns out, a
smaller, defenseless victim triggers the good in my sister,
Shana, while a raging killer triggers the evil in me.

Shana Day had been buried the day before. A simple wooden casket, another hole in the ground. Apparently, Adeline had found the markers for her parents' graves years ago and made the arrangements to expand the family plot.

Mrs. Davies had attended. Her presence hadn't surprised D.D. The older woman had walked right up to the casket and whispered a few words. Nothing D.D. could hear, but she'd bet money the woman had finally delivered her apology, necessary or not.

> *I took a calculated risk breaking my sister out of prison. I gambled on her trigger being as strong as mine. But more, I gambled on our connection. That all these years later, we had forged a bond. We were sisters. And together, we would make our last stand.*

In the days since the bloody scene in Adeline's apartment, Phil and Neil had kept busy processing Charlie Sgarzi's apartment. In a locked file cabinet, they'd found copious notes, photos and other research material that had gone into the making of the Rose Killer. Surveillance videos of his victims. Website printouts on proper chloroform dosages. Handwritten logs tracking each victim's schedule as he performed his reconnaissance. They even found newspaper clippings on D.D., as well as a fuzzy photo of her at the second crime scene. Best Phil could tell, Charlie had stumbled upon her by accident at the home of the first victim. But being a true-crime aficionado, he'd immediately recognized her as the lead investigator from several high-profile local cases. In that instant, he'd made his decision. The Rose Killer would take on Boston's best detective. A duel of equals, a battle of wits. Apparently, according to Charlie's notes, the stuff great drama was made of.

D.D. would like the record to show that she'd won. Except, now no book would ever be written.

> *If you're reading this, I hope that the Rose Killer is now dead. Slain by Shana's hand, if not my own. I would like to think that would be the end of the violence, but of course, that's not to be.*

*I have a hobby. I've never told anyone about it. It
involves seducing men, then removing a small sliver
of skin from their backs while they sleep. And yes, I
preserve my souvenirs in formaldehyde, tucked beneath
my closet floor.*

*Doctor, heal thyself, you think. Trust me, over the
years I've sworn to stop, demanded of myself to be the
person my adoptive father wanted me to be. But the little
girl who spent the first year of her life sleeping on top of
the world's most gruesome collection of trophies simply
can't let go. She is the ultimate Exile, and all these years
later, she is still demanding to be heard.*

The service was wrapping up. Superintendent McKinnon walked
over, looking especially regal in a severely tailored black suit.

"Detectives," she said by way of greeting.

"Superintendent."

D.D. had personally met with the superintendent just the day before. Not at the MCI but over coffee. Two women, sharing memories
of an old friend.

The superintendent's feelings had been hurt by Adeline's actions.
It had taken until that moment for D.D. to realize that's how she'd
felt, too. Why hadn't Adeline trusted more, asked for help, ever told
either of them what was going on?

D.D. would've personally stayed over at Adeline's condo if it
would've made a difference. The superintendent muttered she might
have been able to clear Shana for a family-emergency furlough,
something. If they'd just known . . .

But Adeline had not confided in either of them. Instead, she'd
formed a plan on her own. Leaving D.D. and the superintendent to
sort through the wreckage of the aftermath.

"Things finally quieting down?" D.D. asked Superintendent
McKinnon now.

"I think the reporters almost believe I have nothing to say."

"What about the talk shows?"

McKinnon shrugged one elegant shoulder. "Initial demand has already passed. An escaped killer on the loose is exciting. One that's now dead and buried . . . not so much."

D.D. nodded. She understood what the superintendent wasn't saying. That a highly dysfunctional relationship was still a relationship. After spending ten years managing, worrying and stressing over Shana Day, to have her just be gone . . . It left a mark, whether you wanted it to or not.

"How's your shoulder?" McKinnon asked.

"Look." D.D. gingerly raised her left arm. Not pretty, but better.

"Great!"

"Yep, anytime now I'll be back to cracking heads and taking names. Or at least terrorizing my fellow detectives."

Beside her, Phil smiled. He'd missed her being on the job. Neil, too. She could tell.

The superintendent waved in farewell, then worked her way across the cemetery toward her car. Phil's cell phone was already vibrating at his waist. He unclipped it from his waistband, walking off.

D.D. and Alex stood alone.

I know, Detective Warren, that had I asked, you would've helped me, too. You would've summoned the cavalry, girded your loins and waded into battle on my behalf.

Thank you for your faith in me.

But in truth, I've been lucky to have lived this long. A woman with my condition, I should've succumbed to infection or some other injury long ago. The constant diligence preached by my adoptive father saved me, but maybe it doomed me, as well. I spend night after night inspecting my own skin, while diligently denying myself

even the simplest of life's pleasures, a walk on a beach, a
hike in the mountains, a crazy night out on the town.

And for what? The lover I've never taken? The kids
I've never had? The life I've never truly led?

I'm tired, D.D. I've been isolated too long by a
condition that sounds like a blessing but is ultimately a
curse. I've lost my connection to humanity. I've lost my
sense of self.

Alex remained patiently waiting. D.D. leaned against him, not quite ready to leave the graveside but not sure why.

"Adeline left her entire estate to a children's service agency," she commented now. "And we're talking a considerable sum of money. Apparently Adeline was pretty successful, not to mention what she'd inherited from her adoptive father."

"It stands to reason she'd want other children to have a better chance," Alex said.

"You mean, better than her and her sister."

"Adeline confused making a bad choice with being a bad person," Alex supplied reasonably. "Maybe because bad choices were her family legacy, so she only needed to mess up once to decide the exception proved the norm. But she'd been granted a huge opportunity when she was adopted, and she used it to build a real life. She was intelligent, empathetic, valued. Even when she went off the rails . . ." Alex shrugged.

D.D. understood what he was trying to say. "You had to like her style. I mean, the look that had to have been on Charlie Sgarzi's face when he saw Shana standing there . . . I hope it was worth it."

"She helped you," Alex said somberly. "For that, I'll always be grateful."

"You know, you get older, acquire more aches and pains, then of course, do something stupid to wind up injured like I did, and it's easy to be bitter. I didn't want to hurt. Or slow down. Or feel so . . .

weak. But Adeline was right: Melvin is looking out for me. And pain brings us together. A shared building block of the human experience. Adeline never got to feel that bond. In the end, it got to her."

"Do you think her sister loved her?" Alex asked. "It's what Adeline wanted, but after everything she did, is it what she got?"

"I don't know. Adeline herself stated enough times that Shana wasn't capable of such emotions. Then again . . . They knew each other, I think, understood each other in a way other people never could. Even if Adeline didn't magically feel sisterly love, I bet she felt less alone with Shana by her side. And for Adeline, I would think that would be enough."

Alex nodded. They remained standing there a moment longer, the backhoe now in play, summarily filling the grave with dirt. Ashes to ashes, dust to dust.

D.D. wanted to say something. Felt she should say something, but what? She hadn't known Adeline that long, or obviously, that well. And yet still, she mourned the woman's loss.

"Thank you," she whispered at last, head tucked against Alex's shoulder. "For what you had to teach and for what you helped me learn. And no, I still don't approve of what you did, Adeline, but I do understand. I hope it was worth it for you. I hope you and your sister did stand side by side, and for that moment, you finally felt as if you belonged. As if you had family. And now . . . Peace, Adeline. Peace."

D.D. straightened up, took a deep, cleansing breath. Her eyes were burning, but that was okay. Tears, like pain, were another great equalizer. And nothing the great D. D. Warren couldn't handle.

She kissed her husband on the cheek. "Thank you for coming with me."

Alex squeezed her hand. "Always."

D.D. smiled. She kept her hand in his, and together, they walked away.

If you're reading this letter, Detective Warren, then my story is done and I no longer have to be afraid of the dark.

My sister and I have finished our dance. Two lost souls, finally connecting when it mattered most.

Now, I picture us as little girls again. A four-year-old big sister, a nearly one-year-old baby. We are holding each other's hands and we are smiling.

We are about to do what we've waited forty years to do.

Shana will take the first step.

And I will follow. As we step out of the shadows of our parents' house. As we walk away from our father's legacy of horror.

As together, two sisters finally head into the light.

Acknowledgments

This book was an interesting and personal journey for me. As someone with a bad back, I've spent the past ten years learning much about various pain management theories, techniques and treatments. Like D.D., I was initially skeptical of the Internal Family Systems model and this whole naming-your-pain business. And yet, like D.D., I've learned that the strangest things can help, and talking to your pain is certainly more productive than cursing it. For that, I would like to thank Benita Silver, clinical psychologist, who provided Adeline with her expertise in Internal Family Systems therapy. Please understand that any mistakes in Adeline's explanation of the model and therapy are mine and mine alone.

Also, after years of helping rebuild my back, chiropractor Shawn Taylor seemed to take gleeful delight in maiming the legendary Detective D. D. Warren. With the help of his wife, Larissa, he devised her extremely rare and painful avulsion fracture. Physical therapist Gary Tilton then assisted with the proper recovery program. Again, all mistakes are mine and mine alone.

Next, my deepest appreciation to Wayne Rock, retired Boston detective and longtime friend, for helping me understand how the BPD would handle an injured detective, not to mention one who'd discharged her weapon. Thanks, Wayne, and yes, all mistakes are mine and mine alone. There've gotta be some perks to being the author!

Being one of those people who aren't terribly comfortable in funeral homes, I had a lot to learn about proper practices and licensing in Massachusetts. Thank you, Bob Scatamacchia, for patiently explaining the inner workings of a funeral home as well as basic embalming techniques. It's one of those businesses no one likes to talk about, and yet we'll all need in the end. Thank you, Bob!

Speaking of death, Tonya Creighton was selected this year's winner of the annual Kill a Friend, Maim a Buddy Sweepstakes at LisaGardner.com. She nominated Christi Willey for a star-making turn as a prison parolee.

Dawn Whiteside captured the honors for the global sweepstakes, Kill a Friend, Maim a Mate. She selected Christine Ryan to die, the first winner to appear on page one of a novel. Hope you both enjoy!

Finally, Kim Beals won the rights to name a character at the annual Rozzie May Animal Alliance charity auction. She chose to honor her father, Daniel Coakley, a true gentleman, beloved by his family. Congratulations, Daniel!

Once again my editors, Ben Sevier and Vicki Mellor, went out of their way to make this a better book. I'd like to say I got it all right the first time, but nope. On the other hand, thanks to a great editorial team, no one will ever be the wiser. I'm also deeply indebted to my agent, Meg Ruley, for her brilliant insights and practical guidance. In a business this crazy, it is good to have her by my side.

Last but not least, my love to my amazing family, creative forces in their own right, who keep me on my toes and ensure that life will never be boring. Perfect!

TURN THE PAGE FOR AN EXCERPT

From #1 *New York Times* bestselling author Lisa Gardner, a thrilling new novel that sends missing persons expert Frankie Elkin into a national forest looking for a young man who disappeared without a trace. But when the search team encounters immediate threats to their survival, Frankie realizes she's up against something very dark—and she's running out of time.

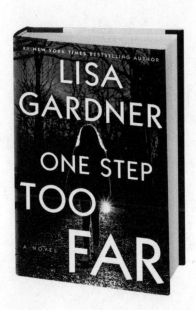

Chapter 1

THE FIRST THREE MEN came stumbling into town shortly after ten A.M., babbling of dark shapes and eerie screams and their missing buddy Scott and their other buddy Tim, who set out from their campsite before dawn to get help.

"Bear, bear, bear," first guy moaned.

"Mountain lion!" second guy insisted.

Third guy vomited.

Maybe, maybe not, Marge Santi thought, as she sidestepped the spew of liquid. Marge situated the young men in a corner booth of her diner then got on the phone and summoned Nemeth. To be polite, Marge also contacted Sheriff Jim Kelley, likable guy, respected by the locals, but an officer with a whole county to tend and the drive to prove it. For immediate action, Nemeth it was.

Nemeth, former Shoshone National Forest ranger, now local guide, knew what he was doing. First, he plied the three men with coffee. To judge by the rank odor of fear and booze emanating from their pores, they didn't need anything else. Two cups later, he had most of the story.

Five guys set out into the woods for a bachelor party weekend. All friends since college, all with some experience camping, though the trio agreed future groom, Tim, was The Man. Had been backcountry hiking with his father since he was six. He was the reason they were camping. The other four wouldn't have minded a golf weekend or quality time at a casino/resort. But for Tim, the woods were his happy place, so into the mountains they'd gone. Fully equipped, packs, tents, sleeping bags, two-burner propane camp stove, cans of beans and franks, and yeah, as much beer and Maker's Mark as five fit young men could carry. Which was to say, a lot. But they weren't total idiots. Again, Tim knew his shit and oversaw their packing himself.

They'd hiked seven miles yesterday, looking for the perfect camping spot in one of the deep canyons, near a broad river. Once they found it, they'd unloaded packs, pitched tents, and popped open the first six-pack, leaving the other four to chill in the ice-cold water.

Dusk came fast this time of year. But all was good. They built up a fire, roasted hot dogs, and ate baked beans straight out of the can. Many fart jokes ensued.

More beer, followed by whiskey chasers. How much booze can five young healthy men drink? Plenty. But no place to be, no cars to drive, no nagging cell phones to answer given the lack of reception.

Just them and the starlit sky. They killed off the first bottle of Maker's Mark, started in on the second. Tim sat next to the fire and scratched away on a piece of paper. Working on his wedding vows, writing a letter to his beloved? They teased, but he refused to fess up.

Hour grew late. How late, no one knew, and it hardly mattered. They finally turned in for the night, two men each in two tents; Tim, the future groom, in a single shell all by himself. One of his last nights on earth sleeping alone. Should enjoy it while he could, they joked.

Then . . .

A sharp keening wail. Crashing in the trees around them.

"Grizzly," Neil said now, sitting in the diner.

"Mountain lion," Josh insisted.

Miggy, short for Miguel, crawled out of the booth and vomited some more.

Maybe, maybe not, Nemeth thought. Marge got a mop.

At the camp, the men had burst from their tents, flashlights bob-

bing, nerves strung tight, trying to pinpoint the source of the disturbance. Build up the fire, Tim demanded. Make noise of their own.
Double check the food stash they'd strung up in the trees away from
their campsite.

Which is why it took a few minutes, maybe as long as five or ten,
before they realized their party of five had become four. Where the
hell was Scott?

Miggy had been sharing his tent and Miggy had no idea.

"No . . . fucking idea," Miggy clarified for Nemeth, in between
bouts of dry heaving.

Tim, future groom, got serious. Scott could've wandered off to
pee. Scott could've just plain wandered off, drunk and disoriented.
But given the cold temps, dangerous terrain, and carnivorous local
wildlife, they needed to find him.

Arranging their group into two pairs, Tim directed the first duo
to start searching north of the campfire while the other would cover
the woods to the south. Whoever found Scott first would blow their
emergency signal whistle.

Except they didn't find him. Up and down the water, bushwhack-
ing deeper and deeper into the forest. No Scott. But they did find
trampled brush. Broken tree limbs. Possibly blood.

"Grizzly bear," Neil moaned.

"Mountain lion," Josh ventured.

"Fuck me," Miggy whispered.

That, Nemeth agreed with.

Four A.M., the fall air brutally crisp, the clear night relentlessly
dark, Tim made the decision: They needed help, and given the total
lack of cell reception, hiking back out was the only way to get it.
As the most experienced—and sober—member of their party, he
grabbed his pack, clicked on his trusty head lamp, and set out for
civilization.

Neil, Josh, and Miggy huddled around the fire for another three
hours, pounding water and working themselves into a terrified frenzy.

First glimpse of daylight, they refilled their canteens and hit the trail. Left everything behind. Tents, sleeping bags, food. Young men, fit and now semi-sober, they were on a mission to get the hell out of there as fast as humanly possible.

Still tough going. They half ran, half stumbled their way up and down steep terrain, clambering over boulders, careening through brush, splashing across streams. Till they came to the trailhead and their rented ATVs. All five of them. Shouldn't there be only four?

Which is when they started to get worried about Tim.

ATVs to town. Town to diner. And now . . . help. Nemeth. Sheriff. Cavalry. Hunters with big guns. Any kind of assistance, all kinds of assistance. Help.

First thing first, Nemeth unfolded a topographical map. Had the men walk him through their journey. They knew their trail, could guess where along the river they'd camped. Nemeth ran his finger along various geological features, thinking, thinking, thinking. Marge worked the phone, brewed more coffee.

Being a mountain town, they had a local team of fifteen volunteer search and rescuers. Given the circumstances, however, this would be all-hands-on-deck. Neighbors contacted neighbors, people started pouring in, and Nemeth did what he did best: organized the efforts.

First up, hasty team. He wanted his best searchers dispersed along key perimeter areas circling the PLS—point last seen—of their two missing hikers. Fortunately, the same location applied to both missing men, their camp. Working some math, the average distance a person could travel an hour in that terrain, Nemeth drew a massive ring around the site. Hasty teams would hike, ATV, horseback into various points along this ring, then work in toward the epicenter, conducting a down-and-dirty search of the trail and surrounding areas as they went. Look for the men, but also look for signs of human passage, in case that provided additional data on where Tim the experienced hiker and Scott the drunk buddy could have gone.

Ramsey, a town of four thousand situated at the edge of the Popo Agie Wilderness, was filled with experienced outdoorspeople. The mountains were both a lifestyle and a professional calling. Nemeth was a veteran general working with expert foot soldiers.

Which made it very hard for the family to accept what happened next. The first eight hours of the search turned up Scott, wandering blindly along the rocky banks of the river. Still clad in his long underwear, face covered in scratches, fingernails caked with dirt. Clearly disoriented and shell-shocked.

"Grizzly," Neil whispered.

"Mountain lion," Josh repeated.

"Shit . . . ," Miggy moaned.

Even sobered up, Scott couldn't provide any details about where he'd been or what he'd done. He remembered drinking with his buddies around the campfire and teasing Tim for working on his wedding vows. Scott went to bed and . . . Daylight. Cold. So cold. Wandering in nothing but his stocking feet, till he found his way back to the river and followed it. Eventually, people appeared and a shrill whistle blew and now he was here and hey, where was Tim anyway?

Timothy O'Day. Thirty-three years old, first member of his family to go to college, graduating from Oregon State University with a degree in mechanical engineering. Described by his family and friends as a regular MacGyver. Engaged to be married to Latisha Gibbons, whom he'd met three years ago through his college buddy, Neil. Latisha hailed from Atlanta, worked in marketing, and spent her weekends in a state of perpetual motion, hiking, biking, skiing, every bit as crazy as her future husband.

Everyone said they looked beautiful together. The ultimate, modern-day L.L. Bean couple. They'd buy a house, adopt a Lab, and produce 2.2 gorgeous dark-haired children to chase along trails, down mountains, across streams.

Theirs was to be a wonderful, magnificent life lived out loud.

Until hours stretched into days stretched into weeks.

Tim's family arrived onsite. His father, Martin, driving from Oregon to Wyoming with his mountaineering equipment piled in the back. Martin was a lean, nut-brown professional carpenter and experienced outdoorsman ready to take up the charge. In contrast, Tim's mother, Patrice, appeared nearly translucent, a pale shadow of a woman. Cancer survivor, the locals learned. Fifteen years ago, multiple bouts, barely made it.

Marge made it her mission to serve the women coffee aboveboard and administer a little medicinal assistance on the down low.

Martin conferred with Nemeth, as well as Sheriff Kelley, who'd taken charge of the search efforts. In the beginning, Martin would nod, approve, express his gratitude. By day five, he questioned and stewed. Day seven he headed into the woods himself, snarling under his breath when both Nemeth and Sheriff Kelley tried to hold him back.

The hasty teams stopped being hasty. Search efforts slowed, grew more methodical, no longer hoping for an easy victory but now settling in to scour the wilderness foot by foot, trail by trail, grid by grid. Choppers scanned with infrared. Air-scenting dogs tracked areas of interest. Couple of psychics called in with hot tips, most involving flowing rivers or dark caves.

More volunteers showed up. The National Guard arrived to assist. Until twenty-three long, arduous, exhausting days later, as the temperatures plummeted and snow blanketed the upper elevations . . .

The searchers faded back to their real lives. The canine teams went home. The choppers were redirected to new missions. And only family and friends remained.

Martin O'Day fought the good fight the longest. He had a lifetime of experience and the advantage of being the one who'd trained his son. He headed back into the mountains, expedition after expedition, while Patrice held press conferences with her future daughter-in-law by her side. Twin advertisements for grief and desperation.

The college friends, Neil, Josh, Miggy, and Scott, did their best to assist, while having to accommodate the demands of jobs, family, obligations of their own.

Martin O'Day searched for his son. Then he searched for signs of his son. And then he searched for his son's body.

"Grizzly bear," Neil whispered.

"Mountain lion," Josh argued.

"God-dammit," Miggy said.

As for the real answer, the woods never said. Seasons turned into years and Timothy O'Day became one more missing hiker, vanished without a trace.

HERE ARE THINGS MOST FOLKS don't know: at least sixteen hundred people, if not many times that number, remain missing on national public lands. Hikers, day-trippers, children on family camping trips. One moment they were with us, the next they're gone.

There's no national database to track such cases. No centralized training for search and rescue—or, in many cases, even clear jurisdictional lines to identify who's in charge of such operations. There's also little in the way of designated funding. A large-scale search effort can cost upward of three hundred thousand dollars a day. For many county sheriffs, that's their annual budget.

Meaning, when the volunteers go away, so do rescue efforts. Leaving behind a family with little hope and no closure. Most will continue on their own for as long as they can. Some, such as Martin O'Day, continue the hunt every year, assisted by friends, funded by online campaigns, and advised by various experts.

According to the article I'm reading in a local paper, Martin's been at it for five years. This August will be his final attempt. His wife, Patrice, is now dying from the same cancer that tried to kill her before. She wants to see her son one last time. She wants her body to be buried next to his.

I sit in a diner not so dissimilar to the one Tim O'Day's hiking buddies must've rushed into the morning after. I've spent the past twelve hours on a bus and am now catching my breath somewhere west of Cheyenne and south of Jackson, Wyoming. I don't particularly know, and I'm enjoying a sense of freedom—life on the road—as I read the article again, then again. Something about the story has sunk into my skin, refusing to let go.

My name is Frankie Elkin, and finding missing people is what I do. When the police have given up, when the public no longer remembers, when the media has never bothered to care, I start looking. For no money, no recognition, and most of the time, with no help.

I have no professional training. I'm not a former detective or a registered PI or ex-anything special. I'm only me. An average, middle-aged white woman, short on belongings, long on regret. I tried real life once. There was a house, a job, even a man who loved me enough to hold my hand as I fought my way sober.

In the end, the walls closed in; the relentless sameness drowned me. And the man who loved me . . .

One day, a woman in my AA meeting talked about her daughter who'd disappeared and the police's total lack of interest in searching for a young woman with a troubled past. I became intrigued, started asking questions, and the next thing I knew, I'd found the daughter. Unfortunately, the daughter's fucked-up boyfriend chose to blow off her head and abandon her body in a crack house rather than let her go. But it got me going. And despite the fact the case didn't have a happy ending, or maybe because of that, one search became another, which became another.

Ten years later, this is now my life. I travel from place to place, armed with only my good intentions. Currently, I've been traveling by bus to Idaho to take up the case of Eugene Santiago, an eight-year-old boy now missing sixteen months. I read about Eugene's disappearance in one of the various online cold case forums I frequent. Something about his soulful dark eyes, his very serious smile. I don't always know why I choose the cases I do. There are so many of them out there. But I spot a headline, I read an article, and then I just know.

Kind of like now, I think, setting down the local paper. I haven't done a woodland search in forever. Mostly I work small rural communities or dense urban neighborhoods. I gravitate more toward kids than adults, minorities more than Caucasians. But my mission is to help the underserved, and as the families of those sixteen hundred people vanished in public parks will tell you, they are so underserved.

Mostly, I keep thinking of Timothy O'Day's mother, who just wants to be buried next to her son.

Eugene Santiago has been missing for nearly a year and half. A few more weeks won't make a difference. And while there may be no chance of finding Tim O'Day alive, I know from experience that finally bringing home a body can still make a difference.

I pick up the bus schedule and plot my new destination.

LISA GARDNER

"No one owns this corner of the genre the way Lisa Gardner does."
—#1 *New York Times* bestselling author Lee Child

For a complete list of titles, please visit
prh.com/LisaGardner